'Mee⸍⸍⸍⸍⸍⸍⸍⸍⸍⸍⸍⸍⸍⸍⸍⸍⸍⸍⸍⸍⸍he sinner". She is a killer seven times over, clad in a second-skin, black leather motorcycle suit. She is Austrian – but not the yodelling type. Rather, she's bent on a singular, sinister mission to force her ⸍⸍⸍⸍⸍ on upon the villa⸍⸍ ⸍⸍ she has kidnapped at gun point⸍

'Perched on her Puch mo⸍⸍⸍⸍⸍ ⸍⸍⸍⸍⸍ and burning with crusader's zeal, Magdalena is ⸍⸍⸍⸍⸍⸍⸍⸍ Quixote, astride a steel Rozinante . . . As she tears through the European Union in search of love, liberty and in pursuit of happiness, Magdalena charges at the windmills of bourgeois mores, Church hypocrisy, nationalist instincts, and our selfish failure to listen to or care for others . . . Unfettered by moral scruples or social constraints, our leather-clad heroine acts out every woman's most subversive wish – and every man's – as she roars through conventions on her Puch, crashes into propriety and leaves sacred cows dying in her wake . . .

'In the end, we, like the priest, are wholly in Magdalena's spell, and want this magical morality tale to go on and on and on . . .'       Cristina Odone, *Literary Review*

'Faschinger rings the changes with wit and ingenuity . . . Magdalena is a spellbinding raconteur'
                    Margaret Walters, *The Sunday Times*

'A Euro Star . . . extraordinary . . . A book as bizarre and readable as this deserves a boggle-eyed readership'
                    Philip Hensher, *Mail on Sunday*

Lilian Faschinger was born in Austria in 1950 and holds a PhD in English Literature from the University of Graz, where she worked for seventeen years. She has received literary prizes, both for her own writing and for her achievements as a translator of such authors as Janet Frame, Gertrude Stein and Paul Bowles. She is currently working on a translation of John Banville's *Athena*, and on her next novel. She lives in Vienna, though wrote *Magdalena the Sinner* in Paris.

# Magdalena the sinner

Translated from the German
by Shaun Whiteside

## Lilian Faschinger

review

First published in 1995
by Verlag Kiepenheuer & Witsch

First published in paperback in 1997
by HEADLINE BOOK PUBLISHING

A Review paperback

10 9 8 7 6 5 4 3 2 1

ISBN 0 7472 5459 1

Printed and bound in Great Britain by
Mackays of Chatham PLC, Chatham, Kent

HEADLINE BOOK PUBLISHING
A division of Hodder Headline PLC
338 Euston Road
London NW1 3BH

für meine Freunde

'It's vague, life and death'
Samuel Beckett, *Malone Dies*

'And now you will listen to me, Reverend Father. Now it's your turn to lend me your ear, your Catholic priest's ear, fine-tuned to every gradation of cardinal and venial sin, which has been sympathetically turned to so many people in the past. You won't be able to block your delicate Catholic ears, the dark blond hairs sprouting from the outer auditory canal. You can't shut ears when your hands are bound. And you will not be able to block out my words with prayer formulae and liturgical chants, nor will you be able to call to your organist to help you to drown out my words with his organ point. Your organist, along with his organ and his organ point, is far away. You can't call for help with a gag in your mouth, any more than you can pronounce prayer formulae or intone liturgical chants with a gag in your mouth. You are helpless, Reverend Father. My words, my sentences will rattle on your eardrum like apples thrown by unruly children at car windscreens; its membrane will start to vibrate in terror and the sound waves will carry from my mouth to the hammer, anvil and stirrup. Your stirrup will speed to convey them beyond the oval window to the inner ear. The impression of the sound will crash through your vibrating cochlea like a metal ball crashing through the spiral channels of a pinball machine, before continuing onwards to the scala tympani. The nerve impulses will dash, via the auditory nerve, to your cerebral cortex, which will finally ensure that you hear me. The little bulbs in your brain will light up, red, green, blue and yellow, like a colour organ, rhythmically connected to the music of my speech, and finally you will hear me.'

With these words the sinner began, after she had sat me beneath the robinia in the tall grass of early summer, resting my back against the trunk, whose warm, cracked bark my hands could feel, although, because of the faded hemp rope knotted round them, they were gradually growing numb. And while she tied the knot in a green nylon washing line a little tighter over my ankles, she continued.

'It's strange, Reverend Father,' she said, 'even now that you are in my power, every last hair on your head, your alb, your dalmatic and your stole, all in my power, even now I'm afraid that one of the saints whom you invoke so often and for such different reasons might come to your aid and, with a single gesture of his conically shaped hands – carved over and over by countless woodcarvers – might condemn me to immobility, the same immobility to which you are condemned at present, might, with a single glance from his martyr's eyes – carefully painted over and over by countless fresco painters – render me mute, as mute as you are. I need every spark of my alpine common sense, every last trace of my Austrian sense of reality, formerly so highly developed, to defend myself against my fear of such a miracle. The fear, for example, that Saint Sebastian might emerge from the undergrowth into this glade, gaunt and pierced with arrows, yet with a remarkable spring in his step, that he might draw one of the arrows and pierce my heart with it, my heart with its yearning for communication, before I have the chance to pour it out to you. The fear that Saint Catherine might slide down from the top of this robinia, astonishingly radiant and physically intact after her death on the wheel, that she might, with a single word from her saintly mouth, loosen the knots in the green nylon washing line that I have tied so carefully, the faded hemp rope, that she might take you in her arms and float away with you to the top of the robinia and beyond. The fear that Saint George, at your bidding, might burst in on a bay horse, lift you up on to his saddle and ride off with you, not before he had cut off my head with a powerful stroke of his sword. I must banish such images, they are unfounded phantasms, since it was I, after all, who abducted you from the little parish to which you devoted such conscientious care, from the church with the pretty wine-coloured onion tower where you were celebrating Whitsun Mass.'

With these words the sinner shook her long, strawberry-blonde hair, sat down in front of me in the grass, paused for a moment and squinted into the sun. At the memory of the event that had so suddenly changed my life, I felt the hairs on my forearms standing on end.

'It was much more difficult than I had imagined,' she said then, 'although I had been watching you for days and knew all about your day-to-day priestly routines. Maybe I should have chosen another situation, in which you would have been alone. I should have pressed the barrel of my Smith and Wesson into your back while you, quietly humming something about the Holy Ghost, arranged the white and red Whitsun roses in their vases, changed the wax candles on the altar, having spread it with the red Whitsun altar cloth. I should have surprised you in the sacristy, polishing the paten, the holy water fonts, the Communion chalice, the ciborium, I should have lain in wait for you in the evening, in the graveyard that surrounds your church, I should have covered your mouth with my hand, in its black motorcycle glove, while you were on your way from the church to the vicarage. Perhaps that's what I should have done, it would have been much easier. What led me to choose the Whitsun service as the stage for my action was my liking for spectacle, my penchant for attention-seeking devices, my love of an audience.

I need an audience, Reverend Father, a need that you, as

a priest, will surely understand. The audience is the witness; without an audience any action is void from the start, the watching audience is proof of the active life. You must admit that my action was a remarkable public event, that it must have prompted a strong feeling of community, a sense of the original brotherhood between fellow human beings. While the two of us sit here beneath the robinia, in this remote place, the effect of my Whitsuntide action, my successful church happening, is reverberating far and wide. People from your parish, after centuries of mutual hostility over foundation stones that moved in the night, are going up to one another and asking, "Have you heard any news of our priest? Has the cathedral chapter offered a ransom?"

So the two of us, Reverend Father, have complemented each other nicely by allowing a process to unfold, allowing the collective finally and most beautifully to rediscover its sense of cohesion. You joined in instinctively, you demonstrated your sense of dramatic tension. You deserve to be congratulated. Your face when you turned round during the consecration, when you heard the heavy step of my motorcycle boots, was highly expressive, and will have impressed itself indelibly upon your congregation. The wide-open eyes, the posture, as if frozen, the hand that dropped the chalice when I walked up to you wearing my black biker's helmet, the dark visor lowered: you have a natural talent, Reverend Father, you are a born actor. A measured quality, an economy of gesture combined with an intensity of expression – it seems you have a gift. Sadly your server did not demonstrate the same actorly qualities, although we might attribute this to his youth. The fact that he began to swing the censer in childish panic, uttering shrill little cries, when he saw you being threatened by me considerably spoiled the transparency of the theatrical action; while on the other hand the resultant billows of incense made it easier for me to disappear with you, the victim of the abduction. Though

4

perhaps the spontaneity of the server's acting technique made up for lack of any sense of fine gestural nuance.

The congregation of the faithful behaved impeccably: they rose from their seats and, excited, astonished and respectfully silent, followed the individual phases of my staged event, a performance that any director can only dream of. The faces of the faithful suggested that they would soon experience a catharsis, that fear and pity would grip them the moment I had left the nave with you. And it is this catharsis that gives my admittedly drastic action its human justification, and it should also fill you, Reverend Father, with pride, to have made your own contribution to this purification of the human heart. There was something sublime, even something of the wedding, about the way the two of us walked down the aisle, flanked by the faithful, standing in respectful silence, up to the Romanesque portal. With your instinctive talent for theatre you immediately grasped the opportunities presented by this little scene, you kept your eyes fixed straight in front of you, in spite or because of the pressure of my Smith and Wesson in your back, you raised your priestly head, and refused to be irritated in the slightest when the organist in his loft, having long since interrupted his organ point at the cries of the server, called down to you in horror, "Reverend Father, stay! Your congregation needs you!" Yes, truly, there was something of the wedding about it: I was the groom, leading you from the church after the reading of the vows towards a new life, you the bride, humbly and respectfully following the one who has chosen her. A success, I thought, having led you to my Puch motorcycle, made you sit in the sidecar and driven off with you. The unity of time, place and action preserved in exemplary form – the theatrical ideal.'

The sinner fell silent and plucked grass stalks from the ground, then a clover leaf.

'Not a four-leaf clover,' she said. 'All my life I have kept an eye out for four-leaf clovers. Not once have I found a four-leaf clover. It has not been my lot to do so. Other people walk through the countryside and have only to lower their eyes to spot a four-leaf clover. They go home with a little bunch of four-leaf crimson clover, hare's-foot clover, sulphur clover or knotted clover. They give them to their friends and relations who put the clover leaves in books and stack other fat books on top of them. Piles of books stand around in their apartments, piles of dictionaries, stacks of volumes of *Encyclopaedia Britannica*, and in the bottom book in each pile, a pocket edition of Burton's *Anatomy of Melancholy*, for example, the letters of Maria Theresa to her daughter Marie Antoinette, or a well-thumbed copy of Thomas Bernhard's *Frost*, in the bottom book of each pile is a four-leaf clover, slowly drying. By now the friends and relations can barely cope with the well-intentioned gifts of the one chosen to find four-leaf clovers, they have one four-leaf clover after another forced upon them, and it restricts their freedom of movement since they are obliged to make their way round their artistically furnished apartments in period blocks, negotiating piles of books on the floor, each one containing a barely, half, or fully pressed four-leaf clover.

But I never find anything,' she said, turning the stem of her little three-leaf crimson clover in her fingers. 'Not a thing. Unattached as I am I have plenty of opportunity to roam around, park my Puch motorbike and sidecar next to a hazel bush, walk along a meadow path and immerse my eyes in the grass, run through with countless clover leaves. I pounce on the clover leaves. This time it'll be a four-leaf clover, I think. But it isn't a four-leaf clover, it's a normal trifolium hybridum, an ordinary trifolium incarnatum, a common-or-garden trifolium pratense. You are looking at me thoughtfully, Reverend Father. Maybe you're wondering whether I'm short-sighted, whether it might all be down to some innate or acquired myopia that I have never found a four-leaf clover. I assure you, it's not that. I have unusually keen eyes. Keen eyes are an inherited trait on my father's side, my father's side of the family has unusually keen eyes. And anyway, spotting four-leaf clovers has nothing to do with having keen eyes, as I have discovered over time. It has to do with intuition, Reverend Father, nothing but intuition. Someone with this gift will go into a field of clover, a field of white clover, for example, or clustered clover, containing no more than two four-leaf clovers. He will stand there for a moment and sniff the air in a four-leaf-clover-sniffing sort of way, and then, without hesitation, he will go to a particular spot in the meadow, he will bend down, stand up again holding one of the two four-leaf clovers in his right hand, turn round, walk out of the meadow and give this four-leaf clover to his companion.

I think I remember reading in an American scientific journal about an experiment that was carried out in Yale, or rather in the environs of Yale, with a representative cross-section of such sensitive and non-sensitive people; sensitive and non-sensitive people of different ages, different skin colour, different social origin and different sex as well as different religious creed were sent into the majority of Connecticut's clover fields. Apparently the results were astonishing. The least gifted of the sensitive subjects still found twenty-five point eight times more four-leaf clovers than the most gifted of the non-sensitive subjects. The difficulty in establishing quasi-ideal preconditions for this research did not lie so much in finding a representative number of sensitive and non-sensitive subjects as in the exhaustive recording, prior to the experiment, of all the four-leaf clovers in the clover fields of Connecticut which, with the agreement of their farmer owners, were used in the experiment.

The fact that I do not belong to this exclusive class of four-leaf clover finders is something that I shall have to come to terms with. It is a talent that life has withheld from me, however much I should like to bestow it upon myself. And it is not an ability that can be arrived at with practice. You can spend hours standing in fields full of clover; if you are not one of the gifted ones, you will find catchflies, buttercups and yarrow, perhaps even meadow knotgrass and annual meadow grass, but no four-leaf clover. You have to come to terms with this, just as you must come to terms with all the other adversities, disappointments, outrages and disillusions that life tends to throw one's way. And you must also see the positive aspect of such a non-talent. It prevents even more piles of books piling up in artistically furnished apartments in period blocks, taking up even more room and being an even greater hindrance to the freedom of movement of the artistic people in their artistically furnished apartments in period blocks. This thought has always been a comfort to me.'

The sinner smiled at me. A flawless brow, so high that it rather frightened me, and slightly rounded towards the front, fine, transparent little veins at the temples with a thicker vein running vertically through the middle of the forehead, more or less prominent, apparently, in direct proportion to the urgency of her speech. A self-reliant chin, cool blue eyes which, likewise in direct proportion to the passion of her speech, could darken to an unsettling dark blue, a little round mole about an inch above the right-hand corner of her mouth. The whole set in the Baroque frame of her strawberry-blonde curls which fell low over her shoulders. Her smile deepened.

'Why are you looking at me like that, Reverend Father? No, don't lower your eyes, have a look. Just have a look. Take in everything that your eyes can grasp, let them sweep over me gently and attentively, let your eyes, so accustomed to deprivation, graze upon me.'

She continued in this fashion, stretching her torso in its tight black leather jump suit, sitting in the grass like a wicked mermaid washed up on the beach. Then she reached to her throat and opened the long, gleaming silvery zip a few inches, revealing a shimmering triangular patch of skin which gently rose and fell, producing a play of light and shade on her torso. The sight of it suddenly made me so ill at ease that I looked upwards and began to study the foliage above me, made in such opulence by our Creator, although not before I had inadvertently watched the sinner raising her arms and running her long white fingers through her strawberry-blonde curls, producing a firework display of red and yellow lights. While I held my eyes pointing towards the sky and, prompted by the early summer foliage, tried to devote myself to a lengthy contemplation of the endless diversity of God's creation, she continued with her dark voice which I was forced to listen to, unable to move because of my bonds, nipping this meditative intention in the bud.

'Priests never look you in the eye except in emergencies,' she said. 'Either they lower their eyes in accordance, I assume, with the demands of Catholic humility, or else they raise them to Heaven, for the purpose, I presume, of praising God. These eye movements, avoiding, as they do, the average person, have always irritated me. Eyes that move only in these directions will inevitably come to rest only on the extremes of human life, on those who crawl on their bellies or those who take to the skies, neither of whom particularly attract me. But sometimes they give a quick dart sideways, rapid as a chameleon's tongue, weighing up an average person in a split second before returning swiftly to Heaven or the earth. Why do you not look me in the eye, Reverend Father? What are you hiding? What are you afraid of? I realize that these questions, and those that will follow, are entirely rhetorical on my part. I hope you will forgive my insistence on the rhetorical figure. In reality, of course, your answers are of no interest to me, as is obvious from the black gag that I've put in your mouth – a screwed-up black body stocking by Kashiyama, as it happens. Its elasticity makes it ideal for the purpose. Before my abduction, my action, I did a bit of practice with gags and fetters, so as to leave nothing to chance. I'm not a person who likes to leave things to chance. The knot round your wrists is a clove hitch, the one round your ankles a double fisherman. Whether I have to tie a hangman's noose will depend entirely on your behaviour. You will surely know that properly tied knots grow tighter the greater the load they have to bear, which is why I would advise against any sudden movements.

My point is that you should listen to me in silence, that you should not interrupt me – I have been perpetually interrupted – and that you should not cut me short – I have been perpetually cut short. If you were to cut me short, if you were to interrupt me, you would place yourself in great danger, a danger even greater than the one in which you are currently suspended. For because I have been interrupted so often, because I have been so often cut short, I have grown over-sensitive, extremely susceptible to any disturbance of the flow of my ideas, of my speech. If you are forever being interrupted you get no further than the trickle stage, a frustrating state of mind that produces irritation and unpredictability in the thinker or speaker. There are people who specialize in the sabotage of evenly flowing thoughts, distracters, interrupters, signal-jammers, whisperers, know-alls, interveners, spoke-in-the-wheelers, insinuators and other such shady characters, including, of course, parents and other blood relations first of all, then whole professions, chief among them primary school teachers, secondary school teachers, technical college teachers, grammar school and university teachers and all manner of psychologists, psychiatrists, psychoanalysts, psychotherapists and others supposedly in charge of the welfare of people's souls. As you belong to the last-mentioned group, I have taken my precautions so as to enjoy our conversation uninterrupted, and at the end of it I shall, in all likelihood, take the black Kashiyama body stocking out of your mouth, put it back on under my leather jump suit and demand one single sentence from you: *ego te absolvo*.'

At these words, with some surprise, I let my eyes slip from

the top of the robinia and focused them on the face of the sinner who was thoughtfully running her right index finger over her dark brown mole, without interrupting her discourse.

'I want to make a confession, Reverend Father, that's all. For decades I have been trying to establish the right conditions for a confession, but only now have I succeeded in doing so. It started with my parents. Every attempt to confide in my mother or father came to nothing. My mother interrupted me in the middle of my second sentence, usually with the words, "Don't talk nonsense," and went into the kitchen to make some tea. My father mumbled something about a complicated child and closed the door of his study in my face, while I waited on the threshold to unburden myself. The teachers listened to me with a disconcerted expression up to about the beginning of the fourth sentence, usually at break time, in the corridor that echoed with the noise of the pupils. Sensing their impatience I faltered, and the fourth sentence expired in a meek fade-out, whereupon the teachers clamped their books, their marked and unmarked exercise books, under their elbows and said, "We will have an opportunity to go into this in depth at some point. But I'm in a hurry right now, I have a test to do with the fourth form." Reverend Father, you will be able to imagine the effect that such shattering dismissals must have had on a little girl's innocent willingness to confess. You, devoted as you are to Christian Agape, will be able to empathize with the little girl with the high forehead, standing at the kitchen door, the study door, the staff-room door, powerless before all these apparently enormous wooden doors, forced to stack up all the unvoiced thoughts, the unheld conversations, like boxes of explosives in a hidden subterranean ammunition store. You will be able to imagine the little girl with the strawberry-blonde hair walking back and forth between the disappointing parental home and disappointing school, that journey growing more and more of an effort, the boxes growing more and more numerous, heavier and heavier. After the passionate and committed delivery of the seminar paper on Erasmus of Rotterdam and European humanism by the young lecturer in the loden coat, the girl with the dark-brown mole above the right-hand corner of her mouth, who had by now grown bigger, hopefully approached him and began to open one of the boxes of explosives. With a shudder, the young lecturer drew his loden coat round his narrow chest and took two steps back. "Come and see me during my consulting hours," he said in the middle of her third brief sentence, having cleared his throat and held to his mouth a hand with a signet ring on its little finger. As the next three consulting hours were cancelled, the girl, who had now grown bigger, whose hair now hung low over her shoulders, sought out a psychologist who interrupted her in the middle of her first sentence and asked her to fill out a multiple-choice test and to remain silent while she did so. Half an hour later he pulled the test out from underneath her nose and, with the words, "You are not alone!" pushed her out of the door. I ask you, Reverend Father, who can be surprised that after these experiences I hit upon the dangerous idea of lighting the fuse to the explosives in my subterranean ammunition store and blowing it up, suddenly being free of it? If I had thought of forcing someone to listen to me earlier then maybe I wouldn't have had to become a murderer, a man-killer seven times over.'

The sinner looked at me.

'You're looking at me as though you want to say, "So why didn't you go to one of the Catholic confessionals so richly abundant in this country and its neighbours?" Isn't that what you're trying to tell me with your questioning gaze, your wide hazel eyes? I shall not leave you waiting for the answer to your mute question. Reverend Father, despite my distaste for those cramped three-part cabinets, I was entirely willing to step inside one and send my confessions through the lozenged grid to a priest who would listen to me with understanding and benevolence. Despite the fact that the wooden benches in the confessionals are hard, and that the barred little windows remind me of prisons, of high-security installations, I was ready to sit down and open myself up to a kindly Catholic priest's face, round and healthy. Having – for reasons that I shall come to shortly – abandoned my settled life for the life of a nomad, my paths have often taken me past the most varied types of Catholic churches, past cathedrals, monasteries, chapels, oratories, past parish churches, pilgrimage churches, convents and baptistries. As soon as I had sold up my movable and immovable possessions, I bought a Puch bike with sidecar which I always parked outside Catholic churches.

Despite my revulsion for the smell of incense that permeates churches as the smell of fish does fishmongers' shops, as the smell of medicines does chemists' shops, I have taken heart, I have walked through Romanesque, early Gothic, late Gothic and High Baroque portals, and stopped by the elaborately carved confessional. I have sat down in front of Burgundian, Austrian, Bavarian, Sicilian and Tyrolean priests, I have introduced my confessions with German, French, Italian and English phrases, I have tried to tell my story comprehensibly, coherently and excitingly. My experiences were diverse and surprising, but not in a single case did I manage to deliver a complete confession and attain forgiveness.

Once, in a little church in an idyllic setting in Oxfordshire, the cleric even fell asleep. At least I noticed after about half an hour of strenuous confession that he was fast and sound asleep. I was at a loss because I didn't know exactly when he had drifted off and how much of my self-justification he had listened to while fully conscious. I had just given him a detailed description of a murder and was afraid that it might all have been in vain. I stretched my hand through the grid and prodded my index finger into his breastbone to wake him up, whereupon he sat up with a shout, stared at me, crossed himself and stammered something in Latin. Then he jumped up and dragged me from the confessional and over to the holy water font where he sprinkled me liberally with that curious fluid. Then he pushed me through the portal into the open air, and I heard the door falling closed behind me with a dull thud. I tried to explain his behaviour to myself, and reached the conclusion that he must have had a terrible Catholic nightmare in the confessional. I reluctantly mounted my Puch sidecar bike and went on driving through the autumnal English woodland towards Ascot-under-Wychwood.

Alarming as this incident was, something yet more unedifying was yet to come. Driving through the Upper Valais, after the exhausting journey through the Furka Pass, I decided to have another go at making a confession. The unusual ugliness of the Swiss clergyman struck me very forcefully, the thin, long, dirty hair with the skull visible beneath it, the constantly smiling, thin-lipped mouth with the dilapidated yellow teeth, the receding chin and the wart in the middle of the forehead. Just as I was about to embark upon a truthful depiction of my third murder, deliberately ignoring the chronology of events, his smile grew even wider and he stretched his bony hands through the lozenged grid and reached single-mindedly for my breasts, covered by the black leather of my leather jump suit and my Kashiyama body stocking, and clutched them with his long fingers. I tried to remove his fingers, and had to summon all my strength because the priest proved to have a degree of tenacity and physical strength in stark contrast to his physiognomy. His priestly fingers stuck to the leather like magnets. Only when I dug my long nails into the backs of his liver-spotted hands did he loosen his grip, allowing me to bite him hard in his thin thumb. He gave a shriek, instantly pulled his fingers back through the grid, rushed from the confessional and disappeared down a flight of stone stairs into the crypt. I left the church quickly, after glancing at the remarkably well-preserved frescoes in the vestibule. On the way to my bike and sidecar I thought how differently I would have reacted if the father confessor had been a good-looking young man, and began to recall another unsuccessful confession in one of the many Baroque churches of Syracuse. These memories were so delightful that I was still dwelling upon them as I drove on into the Lower Valais.

I had sat down patiently on the hard wooden bench of the Baroque confessional, and waited for a priest. When the little door was pushed aside, I looked up into the middle of the large black pupils, surrounded by an amber-coloured iris, of a Sicilian who must have been a recent recruit to the priesthood. He smiled at me and invited me to speak. I noticed how the young face, surrounded by light-brown curls, on a powerful neck with a prominent Adam's apple, was beginning to stimulate my fantasy. I had never told my story so vibrantly, so colourfully, so zestfully and with such brio, while keeping it convincing and consistent. The young priest listened attentively, from time to time nodding most charmingly and understandingly, and at various points in my exposition he slightly lowered his long-lashed lids. His cheeks began to redden, his delicate, brownish nostrils began almost imperceptibly to quiver. First of all I had chosen an event from my early youth as the object of my confession, a fairly venial sin for which I nonetheless sometimes felt deep shame, and which I really believed I regretted. Curiously, in the course of my truthful and detailed account of the embarrassing incident I found myself growing increasingly warm, a physiological change that seemed to transfer itself to the young priest, as he began to fan himself with his missal, without ever flagging in the attention that he so kindly devoted to me. The delicate and, at the same time, masculine gesture with which he moved the missal back and forth in his powerful fingers fired my imagination most beautifully, which in turn intensified his willingness to concentrate as a listener, as the ardent gaze he turned on me bore out.

The heat in my part of the confessional increased, mingling at the grid with the Sicilian fire that emanated from his amber eyes. Suddenly I noticed that I couldn't keep up the intensity of the narrative, that the tautness of the excitement and the narrative pace was easing, that a curious weakness was beginning to creep from the soles of my motorcycle boots into my calves and thighs and higher. On the other side of the grid the young Catholic cleric briefly licked his lips, retracted his tongue in terror and hoarsely cleared his throat. Because of my sudden attack of weakness I lost the thread and no longer knew what I was telling him, and broke helplessly off. Clearly gripped by a similar fatigue, the priest briefly leaned his Botticelli head against the grid. Likewise, I lowered my hot forehead towards the cool bars, and suddenly his yellow-brown curls and my strawberry-blonde curls were twining themselves together and round the grid like lovely little snakes. You will forgive me, Reverend Father, but here my memory, clear as day up to this point, dims a little. Before my inner eye there appears a picture of interwoven hair and fingers, intersected. What happened then? Reverend Father, what happened then? Did we stand up and walk from the confessional? Did each of us push aside our velvet curtain? Did we walk wordlessly through the empty church to the steps leading to the organ loft? Was I walking behind him, footstep for footstep? Reverend Father, the pictures grow blurred. And in the organ loft, what happened in the organ loft? The organ pipes we leaned against, the powerful labial and lingual pipes, were also cool. I remember a roaring in my ears, an organ point unlike anything you have heard from your organist. But there was no organist in the loft in the Baroque church in Syracuse, the church was empty apart from the young priest and me. Did the currents and whirls from the heat between us set the pipes resounding, did we ourselves produce the organ wind that reached the pipes from the wind trunk and there produced those notes, those incredible notes that surrounded us with such force that we slid down against the organ pipes?'

Here the sinner broke off, closed her eyes and sank down in the high grass so that I could no longer see her face, which had been turned towards me only a moment ago. I had been so involuntarily enthralled by the account of her Sicilian confession that I had forgotten my uncomfortable situation, which now appeared before my eyes all the more clearly. On the one hand her beauty and vitality attracted me, while on the other I felt repelled by her, and thought her entirely unpredictable. A woman with the gall to abduct a Catholic priest from a packed service must certainly have turned away from God. And almost in passing she had mentioned several murders that she had committed, and I wondered whether she had been speaking the truth or whether she had only invented these crimes to frighten and torment me. It was barely imaginable that this charming woman should have killed men. Her way of life was, of course, very unusual, and some of her views were in striking contradiction to the run of her sex. I thought of my dear sister Maria who did my housekeeping and who would doubtless be pacing up and down in the rectory, restless with concern for me. I hoped that a search had been called for me, that the glade where we were would soon be surrounded by police, that heavily armed members of an anti-terrorist unit would soon step out of the shadows of the wood, that a voice amplified by a megaphone would order my abductor to give herself up, assuring her that we were surrounded and that resistance was pointless, and telling her to put her hands over her head. I thought about the many things I had to do. The parish letter had to be prepared, the next sermon written and the string quartet invited for the planned church concert. Who would baptize the children, deliver the marriage and funeral sermons? I knew that my sister Maria would not be an adequate substitute for me in my absence.

Unlike the sinner, she had chosen the right way, my sister, who was five years older than I was. I would never forget that at a crucial point in her life she had resolved to put herself at my service and thus at the service of the congregation and of God. As a young girl she had been very beautiful and, on a

17

purely superficial level, had perhaps borne a certain similarity to the sinner, although her beauty, unlike the sinner's, was of course a reflection of the flawlessness of her soul. I remember her combing her long hair every evening in the bedroom we shared in our youth. She sat by the mirror in her high-necked white cambric nightdress, and the light of the lamp on the chest of drawers beside her gently stressed the contours of her body. From my bed I watched her unweaving her long braids and then running the brush repeatedly through her wavy chestnut hair, from top to bottom, in a movement that never ceased to delight me. Even now, when she takes the black hairpins from her bun and combs her long grey hair, with a motion that is a little more weary but still very charming, I still sometimes think of the time when we were half-grown, of that gold-framed mirror above the chest of drawers, reflecting the picture of her innocent face. My absence would be painful to her, I knew, for over the course of the years we had grown very used to one another.

The idea of my sister worrying also began to worry me, and in order to distract myself, in my mind I allowed the beads of the rosary that she had given me on a trip we had made together to the Holy Land to slip through my hands, the hands that the sinner had tied to my back with hempen rope. One imaginary Hail Mary bead after the other, one invisible Our Father bead after the other ran through my fingers like this, many small pearls and a few larger ones, a painful rosary. One Our Father after another, one Hail Mary after another I prayed beneath the robinia, my mouth sealed shut with the blasphemous piece of clothing. At the thirty-fourth Hail Mary the sinner's strawberry-blonde hair rose from the grass.

'You won't believe this,' she said, 'but telling stories makes you hungry, particularly if they are memories connected with intense emotions.'

She stood up, went to her motorcycle, which she had moved a few yards away into the shadow of a spruce tree, and began rummaging around in the panniers. She returned with a large tomato and a slice of apple pie, sat down in the grass in front of me again and bit into the pie. Watching her eating, seeing her good manners, watching the way she guided the apple pie to her mouth with an elegant motion of her slender right hand, just far enough, the way she daintily bit into it without opening her eyes, the way she slowly chewed, her lips closed, without pulling a face, swallowed without stretching her neck, it was hard to imagine that she had yielded to carnal sins with a consecrated priest in a Sicilian organ loft. For although her story had become less precise towards the end, although she had been unable to fill some of the gaps in her memory, there was hardly any doubt in my mind that the story had been about such a woman. I had always had the idea that women, with the exception of my sister Maria, are mysterious and inexplicable, even demonic creatures, and with the exception of my sister Maria I had avoided them whenever I could; now my early intuitive judgment was being most emphatically borne out. Even better than before, I now understood the treatises, at first apparently hostile, that medieval theologians had written against this sex; I now understood their claim that women are sweet to look at from the front, while their rear is devoured by snakes, spiders and scorpions. I understood the insistent warnings of pious monks against these vessels of sin, with whom one should have nothing to do unless one wishes to be hurled into corruption and forfeit eternal life. Women, with the exception of my sister Maria, dragged you sinking with them into a stinking morass, they forced you into unnatural acts which, when remembered, sent the blood to your cheeks, they confused your mind with their deceitful talk, their underhand insinuations, they sucked you out like an enormous tarantula, leaving nothing behind but a light and empty shell. The woman sitting eating in front of me was a typical example: beautiful form, diabolical content.

'*Gedeckter Apfelkuchen*,' the woman said suddenly and

pushed the rest of the apple pie into her mouth. '*Gedeckter Apfelkuchen* with cinnamon. Basically I only came to Austria for the baking. For the baking and for you. Apart from its baking, there's nothing in Austria worth coming back for, nothing you feel homesick for when you've finally left its borders behind you. But you miss the baking. The lack of Austrian baking has soured the most beautiful foreign places for me. I have sat looking over the Gulf of Salerno, a razor-sharp sickle moon above me, a San Pellegrino bitter in front of me, I've looked down on the dark sea and almost wept because I hadn't had a *Rosinenpotize* for six months. I had just had breakfast with an affectionate lover in the fifth arrondissement in Paris, in a little kitchen with sloping walls and a view of the Pantheon, and the idea of having *Spritzstrauben* sent me into such a deep melancholy that my affectionate lover got up and left. Simple *Spritzstrauben*, squeezed into hot fat and baked golden on both sides. Laurent couldn't see it.

The worst was in England. It was in Devon. Exeter. It was in a bakery in Exeter. I started an argument with the lady behind the counter because there was nothing in the shop window that remotely resembled *Dukatenbuchteln, Ribiselschaumschnitten* or *Germgugelhupf*. Even in Exeter you should have been able to expect a variant on the *Germgugelhupf*, a variation on *Ribiselschaumschnitte*. One might have accepted that there was no grated lemon peel in the *Germgugelhupf*, one would have put up with the fact that the blackcurrants used in the *Ribiselschaumschnitte* had not been de-stalked with proper care. But nothing at all? I left Devon and caught the ferry for Calais. Austrian baking either keeps you in the country or draws you back. I could quote countless examples. Austrian baking has put an abrupt end to highly successful careers abroad because the Austrian careerists couldn't stand being abroad without Austrian baking. It has made people come back to Austria even though they knew that the police there were after them. Which do you like best, Reverend

Father, *Hausfreunde, Schlosserbuben, Damenkaprizen*? I can't claim that there's anything for me in this country; on the contrary, whenever I come back for the baking I think it's an unpleasant country, and that one should treat the majority of its inhabitants with extreme caution, with great reserve, unless one wishes to suffer irreparable damage. Were it not for the baking I would not have set foot on Austrian soil for years. Those who prefer an independent way of life, changeable people like myself, are always in danger in Austria. They don't like people like that in Austria, particularly if they're women. They are happy when they leave, unsettled when they come back. The nomadic life arouses suspicion in Austria, in Austria the settled life is the desirable one. Settled people are trustworthy. Every time you move you arouse suspicion, every time you travel you arouse scepticism. No one with a penchant for the non-settled way of life will have lost anything by leaving Austria. A non-settled woman like myself should take to her heels as soon as possible. It's only for the baking, only for you, that I'm here.'

Now she bit daintily into the firm tomato, and the red juice didn't spurt in a high arc through the little gap in the middle of her upper incisors, and it didn't drip from the corners of her mouth and down her chin and on to the smooth black leather.

'I've chosen an Austrian priest to hear my confession because it's clear to me that only an Austrian priest will be able to empathize completely with this confession. Only an Austrian priest will be able to put himself unrestrictedly into the winding passages of an Austrian brain, whose cerebral volutes are, of course, different from the convolutions of the inhabitants of other countries. He alone will be able to penetrate really deeply into the grey and white substance of an Austrian person. Only an Austrian priest will advance straight to the left and right cardiac vestibules of an Austrian person, only he will not be thrown by what he sees in that person's ventricle. His blood won't freeze in his veins if he catches a glimpse of the monsters, the dreadful creatures that dwell in Austrian ventricles, because in all probability he will not be unfamiliar with the conditions under which such monsters creep into Austrian ventricles. If I were really consistent, I would have abducted a priest from Carinthia, a priest from the northern shore of Lake Ossiach, a priest from the village where I was born. He would be familiar with the historical, social, cultural and linguistic preconditions of these pericardial ghouls. But as I am not really consistent, I am confessing to you, an East Tyrolian and not a Carinthian, you who will doubtless have a sense, because of the geographical proximity of East Tyrol to Carinthia, of the execrations, the horrors and terrors that lurk in the average Carinthian ventricle. The confessions of Magdalena Leitner will not shock you excessively.'

The sinner stood up, stretched her arms out and twirled in a circle for a while, so that her long hair flew like a whirling merry-go-round with empty seats. Then she stood straight, legs together, and touched the ground in front of her feet with the palms of her hands, her hair flowing down on them like a bright orange waterfall. She repeated this about twenty times, then she went to her motorcycle with its sidecar, bent her right leg and leaned one elbow on the black leather saddle.

'I should have decided to buy this machine long ago,' she said. 'Just as I should have decided long ago to abduct you. Then a lot of things would have happened differently, a lot of things that took such a complicated course would have been cut short. Since I disposed of my movable and immovable possessions, since I adopted the nomadic life, I feel very relieved. There wasn't much. My entire immovable possessions consisted of a four-hundred-square-metre boggy meadow adjoining my parents' land. My parents had given me this meadow, with a little stream running through it and soft cotton grass and high, sharp-edged reeds, with the insane suggestion that I should build a little house for myself there, next to them. Reverend Father, do you understand? Complete nonsense, on a bog like that. Perhaps one could have erected a sort of pile dwelling, an unorthodox little pile dwelling from the Hallstatt period, that's one possibility, but you must bear in mind that the land was diagonally bisected by the little stream. And it's life-threatening to live so close to a stream, on or over a stream, so to speak.

Any moderately talented water diviner will be able to tell you what it means to live on or over a stream. It would be suicide, physical, if not spiritual suicide. Apart from the various incurable physical illnesses that such a watercourse can cause, the immediate proximity of water drives you mad. If you live by, on or above such a watercourse, within the shortest time you succumb to profound mental derangement from which death alone will save you. Water drives you mad, Reverend Father, that is a scientifically established fact. I would have moved into the little pile dwelling next to my parents, and within a few months I would have gone completely mad, after a few months my insanity would have been beyond recovery. Out of maternal and paternal love my parents would not have sent me to a psychiatric clinic even if everyone had advised them to do so. So I would have gone on living in the pile dwelling, my hair would have become more dishevelled by the day, my eyes and cheeks more hollow, my skin more grey. Over time I would have grown unpredictable, so that my parents would have become frightened of me and stopped daring to bring me my food in person, pushing it instead through a purpose-built flap in the door of the pile dwelling. Soon, apart from my parents no one would have dared to come near me. That's where the madwoman lives, the schoolchildren would have whispered on the way to school, pointing to the pile dwelling. When her mother wanted to bring her her food, she bit off her little finger, they would have said. Now her mother has a plastic prosthetic finger. And it would have been the truth.

At night I would have looked out of the window of the pile dwelling and spoken to the full moon above the silver lake in a language of my own. Sometimes I would have left the house in a blood-red kimono adorned with black flowers, I would have stroked the white cotton-grass blossoms and read the future in them, a bad future for the region. I would have dipped my hands into the water of the stream and seen many things in the eddies. In the meantime my parents would have had to fence in the property with barbed wire. My madness would have become more and more pronounced, along with the clairvoyance that it caused and encouraged. Whenever my mother or my father brought me my food, I would have said astonishing things to them. Word would have got around, and the day would have come when my parents would have brought the first people to me to have their fortunes told. Then more and more would have come, my parents would have been able to remove the barbed wire, my fame would have spread far beyond the national boundaries, and people with interpreters would have come from as far afield as Slovenia, Friuli and the Veneto. Thanks to this fulfilling work as a clairvoyant I would have grown more placid, and I would have stopped biting people. My parents would have kept the fees earned by my predictions, which would almost always have come true. After all, I wouldn't have had any use for the money myself. That's how it would have been if I hadn't sold the little plot of meadow for a pittance to a bank clerk from Mödling, who put a fish pool in it. It was a possible future that was rendered impossible by the sale of the meadow.

Sometimes, Reverend Father, sometimes I think that madness is not the worst of all possible futures, madness coupled with clairvoyance, a combination that occurs with great frequency. Maybe as a madwoman I would have been able to make my fortune. The opportunities for making one's fortune in this world are limited, Reverend Father, you have to employ every last one of your talents in your attempts to attain this goal. And a talent for madness is a gift that should not be underestimated, as numerous examples from history testify. The mad are the wise, that much is clear, Reverend Father. When I tell you that, I'm not telling you anything new, the history of the Catholic Church and its saints is a story of madness that has, not always, but sometimes, been wisdom. The history of the Catholic saints is the history of a long series of people who were obviously but not always creatively mad. I have always had a great deal of respect for mad people, an attitude that I recommend to you. But you will hardly need such a recommendation, as a man of the Church I am sure that you will already have respect for the mad.

In a life like mine you often come into contact with mad people, in my nomadic life frequent encounters with mad people are inevitable. Even if you wanted to, you could not avoid the mad, they stand on every street corner. I like seeing them, with a practised eye they are easy to recognize. Has it struck you that there are more and more of them? They are not official saints any more, but our age has its secret saints. The Church could never keep up with the beatifications, the mad are multiplying at such a rate, but there's no need to beatify today's mad people, it's enough that they should be acknowledged and respected. In a sense the mad guarantee the functioning of our world; because of their clairvoyance, their prophetic abilities, you will always find them in places where danger lies. Their sixth sense leads them into dangerous and ever more dangerous situations and relaxes them. That is the inestimable merit of the mad. Who knows how many fires, explosions, serial killings, acts of terrorism and plane crashes have been avoided because a lunatic was at the site of the potential danger at the right time. Their intuition leads mad people to ominous places over which disaster looms like a huge black storm cloud, places where the time fuse of fate is ticking louder and louder by the minute. I smile at them, thanking them with my smile for having in all probability protected me from misfortune. Contrary to public opinion, mad people bring good luck, just like black cats.

Madness as a calling, a talent placed at the service of humanity, is an interesting topic. These assertions almost make me regret that I didn't stay with my parents and become a mad clairvoyant. By selling up my goods and chattels I robbed myself of that eventuality. Standing at a crossroads, I rejected that possibility and opted for a non-settled lifestyle, a decision with serious consequences, which ruled out madness as a way of life and ushered in the beginning of my career as a sevenfold man-killer. Those were the two possible paths that fate had placed before me. Other people stand at the crossroads presented with the possibility, for example, of having a solid marriage and becoming the mother of four children or remaining unmarried and hurling themselves into a long series of love affairs, thrilling or otherwise. They will be able to choose between a life selling hardware and software for Apple Macintosh, and a career as second violinist in a radio orchestra. Madwoman or murderess, those were my alternatives. No others were placed before me.

Fundamentally, I'm not unhappy with the path I have beaten for myself by disposing of my immovables and movables, because there are a number of points in favour of the man-killing alternative, particularly the fact that a life as a murderess can be considerably more active than the life of a madwoman. As a murderess you respond much more directly to the outside world, you are active, whereas the life of a mad person is an internalized, an introverted existence. Murderesses are active people of sanguine or choleric temperament, resolutely intervening in the world around them and changing it vigorously as they see fit. Madwomen are brooding types, their bodily humours tending to be melancholic or phlegmatic. We may assume that the majority of murderesses are daytime people who like getting up early and get tired at nine o'clock, while mad people are night owls who pace up and down in their rooms at three a.m. and are still in bed at ten o'clock in the morning. It's all a question of temperament. The sanguine-choleric aspect must have predominated in me; no one with a predominantly melancholic-phlegmatic structure would have been able to rid themselves of their immovables with so little hesitation.

Where my movables were concerned, I sat amidst my furniture, my pots and pans, my curtains, carpets and paintings, my books and clothes, and tried to imagine what it would be like to live without all these things. I sat on my sofa, which I had moved into the middle of the big room, I sat there despondently, my elbows on my knees, my chin in the palm of my hands, surrounded by piles of books, open and closed cardboard boxes and crates, rolled-up carpets. I had taken the paintings off the walls and was now looking at the rectangular patches, a little lighter than the rest of the walls, where they had hung. How could I go on living without the sofa where I had lain, kneeled, sat and stood, on which I had eaten, drunk, read, written, thought, which I had pulled out into a bed every evening, in which I had slept alone or not alone, and, alone or not alone, had my breakfast? This broad, heavy sofa with its comfortable arms and its light grey cover represented the innermost sphere of my life, my immediate habitat; it had absorbed my aura like a massive sponge. To leave it behind, to abandon it, to sell it, meant homelessness in the highest degree. At the same time this item of furniture hampered my freedom of movement, it was like a cumbersome ship, so big that people had been a long time noticing that it was about to sink and they would drown if they didn't leave it in time.

Reverend Father, I didn't know it was so difficult to leave a sinking ship, that you feel guilty afterwards, as if you are the captain, obliged to go down with the ship. But you are not the captain, just an ordinary seaman who has signed up for nine months' service. Once I realized this, I called a junk dealer who said he was prepared to take the sofa off my hands, and to collect it straight away. While I was waiting for the van to arrive I had a look at the rest of my furniture. I ran my hand over the veneer of the shelves, pulled out the empty drawers of the desk, pushed them back in again and, with my index finger, drew a spiral on the dusty glass of the round table top. Then I unscrewed the bulbs from the lamps and sat down on each of my four chairs in turn. When the doorbell rang I got up, and when I reached the threshold of the room I glanced back. If I tell you that the room was flooded with water, that the lighter furniture and the books were rocking on the surface of the water, and that only one corner of the sofa was left protruding, it will hardly surprise you, Reverend Father. As a man of the Church you are doubtless familiar with the phenomenon of visions, many Catholic saints spent their whole lives having such visions. Of course this vision of mine was a quite insignificant, completely irrelevant vision. Of course this vision of mine, of the flooded living room, should not be compared with the visions of the Catholic saints, which transcended time and space; it is barely worth mentioning. When I came back with the two young furniture packers the water had vanished and the furniture stood there as though it had never been submerged, there was not a sign that only a corner of the sofa had protruded from the surface a second before.

While the two young furniture packers in their white vests were agreeing on the handholds they should use to carry the unwieldy piece of furniture down the steps, I had the opportunity to consider the muscles that moved beneath their smooth skin. For a while my senses devoted themselves entirely to this play of muscles, to the sinews that stood out on the insides of their underarms, on their throats and the backs of their necks, and to the sharp smell that had permeated the living room since they walked in, and in order to abandon myself to these impressions for a little longer, I offered them a beer once they had stowed the sofa in the van. The young men took the opened bottles, coated with tiny drops of water, in their big fists and put them to their lips. The movement of their Adam's apples while they drank was another sight that captivated me, which is why I promptly offered them a second bottle, which they did not refuse.'

After this sentence the sinner's eyes, which had for some time been concentrated on a point an indeterminate distance away, turned to my face, rested there for a while and then slowly moved over my neck and further down.

'I wonder,' she said quietly, 'I wonder what kind of muscles, what kind of sinews lurk beneath your alb. Are you wearing a vest, Reverend Father? What kind of underwear are you wearing? Are you wearing any underwear at all? And if so, where do you buy it? Are there underwear regulations for Catholic priests? Do the colours, the material change as the colours and the material of your priestly vestments do, according to the sabbaths and holidays of the Church year? Is that how it is, Reverend Father, is that how it is?'

Magdalena, who had strayed far from the path of God, smiled at me.

'I'm tempted to take the Kashiyama body stocking out of your mouth even before I have really begun my full confession, just to have an answer to that question. But I shall not yield to the temptation. There are other ways of finding out about these things.'

And with these words she edged closer, took the seam of my dalmatic, then the seam of my alb, and lifted them both a little.

'Dark grey socks,' she said. 'Worsted. I didn't notice them when I was binding your ankles with the washing line.'

The sinner's touch was very disagreeable to me, and to distract myself from it I tried to imagine my sister Maria, still wearing her nightdress, putting those socks and everything else in my room early the previous morning, on the clothes horse, as she did every day. But try as I might, the contours of my dear sister remained strangely vague, I couldn't even imagine her long grey hair that I was so fond of. When I felt the sinner's cool hands on my bare skin above the tops of my socks, the familiar figure in the pastel-coloured nightdress vanished, dissolving into nothing. In its place I saw my abductor's face very close in front of me, the mole, the full upper lip, the bluish veins running vertically through her brow. Her eyes were half closed, probably to examine the questionable patch of skin more carefully with what was without a doubt a highly developed sense of touch.

'Relax,' she said, 'just relax. Pleasantly dry, your skin. The hairs are softer than I expected. Asthenic type, weak muscles, thin bones. Interesting. A little scar on your shin. Slim ankle, as I imagined. Ankle joint, calf bone, Achilles tendon. But you're trembling,' she said, and finally drew back her hand. 'Obviously I've touched a slightly vulnerable place. Forgive my thirst for knowledge, Reverend Father, I shall give you a chance to know me a little better before I satisfy my curiosity further. I have absolutely no wish to violate your priestly feeling of modesty. Although you are in my hands, that is not to say that I have no understanding of the reticence towards women that accords with your position. An attitude very different, for example, from that of the average furniture packer. While my two furniture packers were drinking their third beer, it suddenly became clear to me that I couldn't keep any of my movables, that I had to free myself of all my goods and chattels, my books, my clothes. It was a kind of epiphany, a phenomenon with which you, as a Catholic priest, will doubtless be familiar, a lightning-flash of inspiration which, in my case, was curiously linked with the rising and falling Adam's apples of the furniture packers.

I discussed this epiphany with them, and they understood immediately and suggested that they take the rest of my furniture off my hands in return for an appropriate sum. The smaller furniture packer said he could use the desk, while the other thought he would be able to use the shelves, the round table and the chairs that went with it. They had potential buyers for the lamps, and likewise for the carpets and paintings. Hearing this I unrolled my carpets, and the furniture packers proved highly knowledgeable about their date and provenance, and the weaving technique with which they were manufactured. The smaller furniture packer recognized straightaway that the largest of the four carpets was a piece made of little Senne knots, from near Kerman in the Iranian salt desert, and that the most beautiful was an example of the Gördes technique from near Tashkent. The larger furniture packer also demonstrated a remarkable body of knowledge which was not restricted to the history of the Turkish kilim but extended to the celebrated Bayeux tapestry, the Gobelins showing the mysterious lady with the unicorn in the Musée de Cluny in Paris, as well as Spanish carpet manufacture as practised from the thirteenth century in Alcarez, south-west of Albacete. After the viewing of the carpets I offered them a fourth beer, which they did not refuse, and turned the paintings away from the walls. They proved to be knowledgeable about painting as well. The larger of the furniture packers dated my little English hunting scene very accurately, and there followed a brief and stimulating discussion about nineteenth-century English landscape painting in general and William Turner in particular, especially about his way of depicting light, as further developed by the French Impressionists. After the smaller furniture packer had correctly estimated the value of a Japanese wash drawing, we talked a little about the sinboku technique which had developed in fifth-century Japan under the influence of Zen, as well as the Japanese colour woodcut, discovering a shared love of Utamaro. Before I began searching through the stacks of books standing around the room for a volume of Hokusai woodcuts, to show the smaller furniture packer a painting of which I was very fond, entitled "Women in Love", I opened two more bottles of beer.

Basically I was not very surprised by the extent of the two furniture packers' knowledge, having often noticed that so-called simple people generally reveal a greater artistic understanding and an extreme sensibility, whereas the so-called cultured classes are almost always the stupidest. I have never experienced deadlier boredom than in the society of the so-called cultured classes, I have never had to listen to more simple-minded conversations than as a guest of so-called art lovers in their artily decorated apartments. I have suffered torture sitting at their tables, with their artily arranged meals in front of me. I have desperately sought excuses to leave those rooms, filled to the rafters with their recherché arty music.

There is hardly anything more tedious than the conversation of the so-called cultured classes, hardly anything more stultifying than the environments they have made for themselves. You see one artily decorated apartment, you've seen them all. If you've choked down one artily prepared meal, you've choked them all down. The conversations of arty people consist of prepared, standardized components, the interposition of an original word throws them out of kilter, profoundly disturbing their equilibrium. The worst of these, of course, are the academics. Liberal-minded academics have taken the art of deadening the spirit further than anyone else, the Francophile, Italophile, Anglophile academics with all their cultural holidays, from which they return laden with spices and cookery books. If you commit the indiscretion of sitting down at one of their tables, you are forced to eat dishes which, according to them, are eaten exclusively in the north-east of Madagascar, and even there only by a minority of Christians of Indian origin, meals only eaten in the vicinity of Bogotá, and even in that region consumption is restricted to the holidays of the Jewish-Indian minority.

I owe a great debt of gratitude to the two furniture packers because, by helping me to rid myself of my movable property, they also helped me to opt for a nomadic way of life and thus to say farewell to the so-called cultured classes. Not that the so-called cultured classes, the so-called cultivated classes, let me leave unhindered. They had grown accustomed to seeing me sitting on their sofas, with their Sumatran batik throws; they liked me talking to their dull-witted children whose dull wits thrived in various painting, ballet and flute classes run by dull-witted arty people in the company of larger, dull-witted, arty children. Because of an innate good-naturedness, an acquired submissiveness and compliance, for a long time I was unable to free myself from these dangerous associations. I had fallen into bad company, from which only resolute action could free me. It was high time, because the leaden triviality, the paralysing boredom of cosmopolitan academics had already encroached upon me and threatened to render me completely incapable of motion.

You must try this recipe that we found in southern Burundi, the cosmopolitan academics cried; you must listen to these songs performed only in a little mountain village in the interior of Sardinia during Easter week by three ninety-year-old women, which have thankfully been made accessible to us by the tireless efforts of a Viennese ethno-musicologist; you must try on this mask carved from the wood of a two-hundred-year-old sequoia by a Shawnee tribesman directly descended from Chief Tecumseh. Those masks: if you accepted an invitation from cultured academics you always found yourself sitting under or next to terrifying statues and masks from all parts of the world, which these academically cultured people had brought back from their cultural holidays and hung in their own homes on the edge of town, on walls whitewashed by illegal workers from Eastern Europe, or put on the parquet floors, polished until they shone by cleaning ladies from south-east Asia. For you must know, Reverend Father, that cultured people love everything primitive. The more cultured the cultured person, the more primitive the primitive things that he loves. I had nightmares every time I visited cultured people, their masks and statues pursued me into my sleep.

Once I had clearly recognized the growing psychological threat to me from liberal-minded cultured people, particularly from the many psychologists, psychoanalysts, psychiatrists and psychotherapists of various schools, I considered how I might best escape them. In my innate good-naturedness and my acquired submissiveness and compliance I had allowed these psychotherapists, psychologists, psychiatrists and psychoanalysts to get close enough to force upon me their frightening masks, their terrifying images. You should guard against psychologists, psychotherapists, psychiatrists and psychoanalysts as a good Catholic guards against the temptations of the flesh. They convince you of the absolute unviability of your own soul until you believe them and allow them to help you, you let them work like mechanics of the human soul with their oil-stained fingers, a step that many people have lived to regret. Because by allowing them to help you, you are not helping yourself, of course, you are just helping the psychiatrists, psychologists, psychoanalysts and psychotherapists of various schools. Anyone who has observed them for any length of time will be aware that these psychiatrists, psychoanalysts, psychologists and psychotherapists are urgently in need of help. Reverend Father, never have I, as someone who has inherited unusually keen eyesight on my father's side, come across such a concentration of serious, extremely serious behavioural dysfunctions, such glaringly obvious oddities of facial expression and gesture along with other human curiosities and oddities as I have among psychotherapists, psychiatrists, psychologists and psychoanalysts; nowhere else have I had the infallibly sure sense of dealing with creatures who were absolutely unable to cope with life. So cunning is this species, unfortunately, that it only becomes apparent when you have fallen into the trap of one of its members. And once a harmless person has fallen into their trap, they demonstrate an astonishingly resilient hold on their prey, the harmless person, conduct that becomes comprehensible once one realizes that each harmless person who falls into their trap is a means towards their own cure. Once he has slipped into the net, once they have lured him into their practice and he lies helplessly on their couch, in their power at last, they wish, understandably enough, to keep him and use him to begin their own healing process.

Once the unsuspecting person has recognized the methods of the psychologists, psychotherapists, psychoanalysts and psychiatrists, it is often too late, because the psychiatrist, psychologist, psychotherapist or psychoanalyst is already sitting opposite him in his practice, looking at him with satisfaction as a spider looks at a fat bluebottle. It is what you might call a vicious circle, Reverend Father, because even if the harmless person, having been left almost without funds because of the average fee of these psychoanalysts, psychotherapists, psychiatrists and psychologists, should manage to escape one of them, the next one is lying in wait for him and his remaining cash.

The group of psychiatrists, psychotherapists, psychologists and psychoanalysts played a central part in my strategy of flight from the cultivated, cultured classes, because I knew that they were the ones who would most violently resist my breaking away. I had first to render the whole of the cultured, cultivated classes harmless. I decided to attack them with their own weapons. An acquaintance who dabbled in sculpture had once made a crude wooden bust of me and given it to me as a present. I couldn't bring myself to throw the crudely sculpted head away, so it lay in my bathroom cupboard for years. Receiving an invitation from the cosmopolitan academics, I took it out, pulled a number of rusty nails out of an old board, knocked them into the wooden head and presented it as the nail-studded fetish of a Malinese shaman. I used the keen interest, the general excitement that this provoked to make my getaway.

I left the house, but I noticed that two members of the group of psychoanalysts, psychiatrists, psychotherapists and psychologists were coming after me. Having banked on something like this, I stopped at the next street corner and let them catch up with me. Then I gave both of them, a forty-year-old psychoanalyst of the Lacanian school and an elderly orthodox Freudian, a few buzz words to launch into a specialist discussion. While the two of them were at loggerheads I got into the next Number 7 tram. I sat in a window seat, and before the tram turned off towards the station, I cast a glance at the two of them, standing gesticulating at the side of the street. I recently learned that they have married and are on honeymoon in Heidelberg where they are studying the Prinzhorn collection of art by the mentally ill. You see, Reverend Father, although I slipped through their fingers they have found new ways of continuing their healing process energetically, and at the expense of people who are unable to escape them because they are either dead or in clinics.'

After these remarks which, persuasive as they sounded, seemed incompatible with traditional Western logic, Magdalena paused for a moment. I was somewhat dazed, and assumed that my drowsiness had been caused by her intonation, the hypnotic rise and fall of her melodious voice.

'You see,' she said then, 'you see how difficult the enterprise of leaving one's home may become. Only when a person wants to leave his home does he realize how many people have benefited from his presence, and for this reason don't want to let him go. After I had quickly put two more beers in their hands, the two pleasant young furniture packers drove off with my furniture, and only then did I decide to leave the rest of my household goods, my books and my clothes to various charitable institutions, and made a few phone calls to this end, whereupon several charity workers appeared, happy to take my possessions and to be able to send my Alessi lemon-squeezer, my edition of Schwitters and the sequin-strewn little black number that I had bought cheaply from a young Viennese designer to various parts of the world suffering the effects of tidal waves, wars, famines, earthquakes, volcanoes and revolutions.

As a Catholic devoted to the principle of Agape, you will also doubtless have given some of your possessions to the disadvantaged of this world. Do you never think about their new owners? I often wonder who is now wearing my sequined little black number for what occasion in Rwanda, and I hope she's a beautiful woman. I wonder who in Somalia will have the chance to wear my fur-lined Bruno Magli boots, and I imagine a Bosnian, machine-gun fire whistling around her, going out to get the lemons that she will put in my Alessi lemon-squeezer. And the edtion of Schwitters? I see it impaled on the bayonet of a Latin American guerrilla who has happened upon it during the counter-revolutionary plunder of a poverty-stricken farmhouse.

Have you wondered which evacuated flood victim is now wearing your worn-out alb? And whether the worsted socks that you have so carefully darned have vanished into a southern Californian fault after an unexpected aftershock? As one familiar with the more metaphysical dimensions of life by virtue of your Catholic religion, you will doubtless have wondered what mysterious bond connects you with the Icelandic fisherman sitting in a hastily thrown-together barracks after the last devastating eruption of the volcano Hekla, wearing one of your rather threadbare cassocks. Such questions lead into dizzying areas of speculation, comparable to the scholastic problems of the high Middle Ages, don't you think? Without further ado, you can imagine the beautiful Rwandan woman being shot while wearing my sequin-strewn little black number, the little black number being ruined, run through with bullets from Russian, French, American machine guns, the edition of Schwitters being burned along with the poor Latin American farmhouse razed by the counter-revolutionaries, the Alessi lemon-squeezer still working but buried beneath the corpses buried beneath the ruins of a Bosnian house. And it is entirely imaginable that the Bangladeshi flood victim gave your alb to his cousin who used it as a nightshirt and appeared some three months later, at two o'clock in the morning, at a police station with a knife in his hand saying he had stabbed his wife in their bed, and that the daughter of the Icelandic fisherman, sitting at her Singer sewing machine, later redesigned your cassock into a short, if high-necked, little black number, whose attractive brevity led a motorist, who picked up the Icelandic fisherman's daughter on the road between Borgarnes and Stykkisholmur one evening, to rape her, bringing the high-quality material of your Austrian cassock into contact with Icelandic sperm. It's all within the realms of possibility, don't you think? Mysterious are the concatenations of human destinies or, as you would say, the ways of God are unfathomable. You have slumped a little, Reverend Father. Wait and I'll set you upright again.'

Magdalena rose to her feet, grabbed me by the shoulders, drew me up and pressed me to the tree trunk. It was true, her reflections on the clothing of my profession had depressed me somewhat, and as my mood had declined, I had slipped some way down the trunk of the robinia.

'Such thoughts can be thought,' she continued, 'such ideas can be nurtured, even if they are not particularly pleasant thoughts, not particularly cheering ideas. The indirect consequences of charitable acts are sometimes astonishing. After the charity workers had snowed themselves under with my household goods, my books and my clothes, as I stood on the parquet floor of my empty rented apartment, for which I had already given notice, I counted the money left to me from the sale of my movable and immovable possessions. It wasn't a great deal but it would be enough to buy a Puch motorcycle and sidecar.'

The sinner cast a loving eye towards the vehicle in the shadow of the spruce tree.

'You know, when I bought the bike and sidecar I fulfilled a childhood dream. When I was a little girl my Great-Uncle Karl, who owned a bike like that, would sometimes put me in the sidecar and drive around with me. I sat in the open Felber sidecar, the wind blowing though my hair. The memory of those outings in the Felber sidecar is the loveliest memory of my life.'

So saying she took a serrated-edged photograph from the breast pocket of her leather one-piece and held it to my eyes. It showed a man of about sixty with a bushy moustache, in a leather coat with wide lapels and a wide belt sitting on the saddle of just such a motorcycle, wearing leather helmet and motorcycle goggles.

'That's my Great-Uncle Karl,' said Magdalena. 'Once he nearly drowned when he drove into Lake Ossiach in an alcoholic state. He had three serious accidents, one a fractured skull, one an impacted kidney, one a *contusio cerebri*. The fourth time he didn't survive. Broken neck.'

She put the photograph back in her breast pocket.

'The Puch 800 with Felber sidecar hasn't been made for decades, as I'm sure you know. It was only manufactured for a few years. The Puch with the highest cubic capacity. A four-cylinder engine with opposed cylinder power action. The special thing about it – apart from the extremely large cubic capacity, eight hundred cubic centimetres, and the four-cylinder four-stroke engine – was that the opposed cylinder engine had a degree of aperture not of one hundred and eighty degrees but only one hundred and seventy. Unbeatably soft suspension, galvanized steel shafts with manually adjustable shock absorbers. Very economical fuel consumption. You hardly ever see these bikes today.

39

Just when I was thinking about leaving home, there was a man of about seventy in the town where my parents lived, who had in his shed a Puch 800 with sidecar which he hadn't used for years, and even then only very rarely, and which was thus as good as new. I had spoken to him a few times over the garden fence when he was mounting metal leg guards that he had seen advertised in a specialist motorcycling magazine. At first he was suspicious about a woman taking an interest in his motorcycle, but when he realized that I knew the model and talked about it as passionately as he did, he relaxed, opened the garden gate and showed me his bike in greater detail. Finally he let me get into the sidecar as my Great-Uncle Karl had done, and drove me around the village. You can guess how elated I felt. Imagine that you were allowed to touch an ankle bone of Saint Faustina, set in ivory and covered with rubies and sapphires. Or a diamond-studded Baroque monstrance. Or a page of the first edition of the 1486 incunabula *La Danse macabre* published by Guy Marchant in Paris. Or imagine the Pope inviting you to tea to pay tribute to your services to the Catholic Church of East Tyrol. Such images as these will give you an idea of my elation. After this I visited the man more often, we discussed technical matters, the advantages of the Veigel tachometer over the old tachometer, the most economical use of the shock absorbers and the overhead cams, the proper carburettor settings. The man came to trust me, and after a while I had the feeling that he would sell me the bike if I asked him to. I voiced my wish, and while he let his eyes slide over my body, he said that a machine like that basically wasn't for sale. But I held out. After two more visits we struck a deal and he named a price that was acceptable to me.

After I had sold the twenty-by-twenty-metre patch of land to the bank clerk from Mödling and given my furniture, my clothes and my books to the two pleasant furniture packers and the charity workers, after I had broken away from the cultivated, cultured classes, particularly the psychoanalysts, psychologists, psychiatrists and psychotherapists among them, and become the owner of the Puch bike and sidecar, I packed some necessities into the metal panniers embossed with the Puch insignia, including an edition of the *Divina Commedia* by Dante Alighieri published by G.C. Sansoni in Florence in 1905, a German paperback of Artemidor of Ephesus's interpretation of dreams, Lingen's *Big Illustrated World Atlas*, my Swiss Army knife, my pink Sony Walkman, two cassettes of *The Well-Tempered Clavier* by Johann Sebastian Bach and a habit of the Order of the Barefoot Carmelites given to me by the younger of my two elder sisters when she left the contemplative order after a year's novitiate without taking a vow. I did not imagine that my escape would meet with any further obstacles, particularly not from my parents who had turned away from me in disappointment after I had sold the twenty-by-twenty-metre patch of land that they had given me, but not before they had held up my elder sisters, both of whom had settled in their immediate vicinity, as a glowing example.

By turning away from me in disappointment, my parents made it easier for me to leave. Had my mother not turned away from me in embarrassment, she would, without hesitation, have used the arsenal at her disposal to keep me back, the arsenal of her cookery. Come to lunch before you go, she would have said in passing. You shouldn't set off on a journey with an empty stomach. And in my naivety, underestimating my mother as always, I would have delightedly agreed. Reverend Father, I could – and will, in all probability – tell you of human tragedies, of grave dramas based on people rashly underestimating their mothers. Underestimating mothers is one of the most culpably negligent acts, one of the most unpardonable acts of thoughtlessness that anyone can commit.

In my unbounded thoughtlessness and negligence I would have turned up on time at my parents' house, and my mother would cheerfully have led me to the round dinner table laid with the white cambric tablecloth that she had embroidered with brightly coloured flowers, and the matching napkins in the old silver napkin rings, with the Bohemian crystal glass goblets, and the porcelain service left by my grandmother, and she would have served up a *Milzschnittensuppe* as a first course. She would have sat next to me, rested her forearms on the tablecloth and watched with satisfaction as I emptied my plate. Then she would have ladled my soup plate full again, and continued to watch as I ate the slices of bread cooked in hot fat, spread with delicious shavings of spleen, rubbed onions, breadcrumbs, salt, pepper, nutmeg and finely chopped parsley. While I leaned back with a pleasant feeling in my stomach, she would, humming, have served up *Fogosch à la hongroise*. Warmed up somewhat by my double portion of *Milzschnittensuppe*, I would have begun to eat the pike perch from the end that would have been the head end of the fish had she not cut off its head. I would have worked my way through to the end that would have been the tail end had she not cut off its tail, and helped myself generously to the sauce poured over the fish, made of fish stock, slices of mushroom, onions, sweet paprika and sour cream, and parsleyed potatoes. Slightly befuddled by the Swiss Riesling that she had poured me, I would have had difficulty in preventing her from filling up the empty plate again. With a smile she would have taken the fish plate away from under my nose and returned two minutes later with the loin roast *nach Wiener Art*. She would have placed the roast, smelling wonderfully of greens, bacon and garlic, in front of me and, somewhat exhausted by devouring the headless and tailless pike perch, I would have gone on eating. The well-hung roast, larded along the grain, would almost have melted on my tongue, and, full though I would soon have been, I wouldn't have been able to stop until the plate was completely empty. Too exhausted to resist, I would have allowed my mother to put two slices of meat on my plate, and I would have eaten up those two slices along with the rest of the caper sauce, while my mother cooed encouragement.

As I would barely have been capable of moving, my mother would have put the Bohemian crystal glass with the heavy red Spätburgunder to my lips and made me drink till the wine ran from both corners of my mouth. As soon as my mother had disappeared into the kitchen with the meat plate, my head would have dropped to the cambric tablecloth she had embroidered, and she would have gently pulled it back up by the hair only after she had put the dessert down in front of me. As if through a veil I would have seen that it was rice Trauttmansdorff. My mother would have supported the back of my neck with one hand, and with the other she would have wielded the silver fork full of rice with whipped cream and cherries. Incapable of protesting with my mouth full, I would have spewed some of the rice and cherries on the flowery embroidered tablecloth, whereupon my mother would nimbly have grabbed my arms beneath my armpits and dragged me to the living-room sofa, where I would have slumped in deathly pallor.

Quietly whistling, my mother would have rushed back into the kitchen and returned with a crystal bowl full of *Linzer Augen*, which she would have placed beside me on a low table. As soon as she had held my nose shut, with a view to making me open my closed mouth, putting one *Linzer Auge* after the other into my mouth and pouring coffee in afterwards, I would have lost consciousness. And during this loss of consciousness I dreamed.

I dreamed I got up from the sofa, swept the *Linzer Augen* and Grandmother's coffee pot off the low table with my hand and ran out of the front door, pursued by my mother. With my last bit of strength I managed to shove aside the heavy side of bacon with which the door was barricaded. I ran over the lawn, slipping several times on the *Pischinger, Sacher* and *Doboschtorten* hidden in the grass. Just before my mother caught me, I fell into the moat surrounding the property, filled with various different sauces. I looked back and saw my mother wringing her hands at the edge of the sauce moat. After I had swum with some difficulty through the sauce rings, the bordelaise sauce ring, the béchamel sauce ring, the Cumberland sauce ring and finally the vinaigrette ring, and pulled myself up on land on the other side, I found myself facing my final obstacle, a mountain of curried rice. I slowly ate my way through the mountain, always at risk of being suffocated by the great mass of rice. But finally I reached the other side. I was free. And then, Reverend Father, I woke up.'

Magdalena was breathing audibly, clearly somewhat exhausted by the effort of telling the story. I opened my eyes, which I had kept closed throughout her story, and was curiously pleased to see her sitting in front of me.

'But this is speculation, Reverend Father,' she continued, 'idle speculation and dubious daydreaming, on the inaccurate premise that I hadn't sold the marshy property which had originally belonged to my parents, and that they had not turned away from me in disappointment.

In reality, one Friday in April I started my Puch 800 and headed southwards, towards the range of mountains that separates Austria from Italy. The sky was cloudless, it was unusually warm for the time of year. I was wearing the headphones of my Sony Walkman, listening to *The Well-Tempered Clavier* by Johann Sebastian Bach and humming along. I was so carefree, so immersed in the music and the sight of the daffodil-filled spring landscape around me, that it was only when I reached the beginning of the road winding up to the pass which forms the border with Italy that I noticed my sisters were following me in the elder one's Audi. I should have expected it, Reverend Father. I should have expected my sisters to object to my leaving the family. In the rear-view mirror which the previous owner had fitted on the handlebars, I saw the Audi coming closer. In terms of speed, of course, a Puch 800 is not a match for the newest and most expensive Audi. On certain occasions the bike and sidecar have reached a speed of one hundred and ten kilometres per hour, but these are exceptions. On the zigzagging road leading steeply into the mountains, I couldn't get it up to more than eighty kilometres per hour. In the mirror I saw the younger of my two elder sisters in the passenger seat stretching her right arm out of the open side window and trying to signal me to stop.

My situation grew more and more precarious. There was only one bend separating my sisters and me, and I knew they wouldn't hesitate to overtake me and cut me off. In the excitement my pink headphones had slipped to the back of my neck, and I heard the cries of the elder of my two sisters who was stretching her head out of the side window as she drove. "Unreliable woman!" she cried. "Have you forgotten you're an aunt, that you have four nieces and three nephews, two of whom are your godchildren as well, four nieces and three nephews to whom you owe your auntly goodwill, your auntly interest, your auntly favour? One aunt isn't enough for seven nephews and nieces! How will your sister bear all her auntly responsibility all by herself, take four nieces and three nephews to the fair, think about the birthdays of three nephews and four nieces, praise the essays, drawings and handiwork of a total of seven nephews and nieces? Irresponsible woman! Leaves her sister in the lurch with a total of seven nieces and nephews! The most devoted aunt in the world would not be up to such a task. Come back! Face up to the duties that nature has placed upon you and don't shirk them! Your four nieces and three nephews, two of them godchildren, are waiting for you! Don't disappoint them as you have disappointed our parents, and declare your aunthood!"

While she was exclaiming these things she must have kept on accelerating because the Audi was so close that I could clearly hear the voice of the younger of my two elder sisters, who is naturally quieter than the elder of my two elder sisters. "And another thing!" she cried. "And another thing! Who will now wear the habit of the Barefoot Carmelites? It fitted you as though it had been poured on, you looked wonderful when I gave it to you at the end of my novitiate. I placed such hope in you, not just as an aunt but also as a future Barefoot Carmelite. Aunt and Carmelite, you would have been so ideal at both. How can you abandon a fulfilled life as an aunt, a happy life as a Barefoot Carmelite in favour of a vagabond lifestyle, an inconstant life without a fixed abode, an unsheltered gypsy existence? You are a defenceless woman. Who will protect you from thieves, robbers, murderers, rapists, against wind and weather? Who will preserve you from hunger and thirst? We, your two elder sisters, don't understand you, any more than do our seven nephews and nieces. Turn round, before it's too late, opt for a happy, perfect, carefree life as a sevenfold aunt and member of the greatest contemplative order of the Catholic Church. Don't expose yourself willy-nilly to a life of danger on the road. Stop now! Your and my nieces and nephews and your future fellow Carmelites are waiting for you!"

My sisters had by now come within thirty feet of me, for their imploring pleas had hit their target and made me take my foot off the accelerator. I was about to drive to the edge of the road, stop the bike and remorsefully clasp my two sisters in my arms when the Mediterranean suddenly appeared before my inner eye. Reverend Father, as my compatriot you will know what the sea means to an inlander. That detail of the Mediterranean that appeared unexpectedly before my inner eye – a piece of ochre-coloured cliff, a pine looming into the pale blue sky, silvery, glittering waves, a shimmering, pink, sandy beach – made me cast aside the doubts that my sisters' entreaties had awoken in me, and with a jump that would have done justice to a motocross rider I leapt over the untreated wooden fence bordering the narrow mountain road and began a slalom between the tall trunks of the spruce forest. Before I plunged into the darkness of the forest I saw my sisters getting out of the Audi and trying to climb over the wooden fence in their narrow skirts. There was not the slightest prospect of their ever catching up with me.'

Magdalena wrapped her arms round her knees, looked into the sky and sighed.

'Oh, my sisters,' she said. 'If you had a sister you would know what I'm talking about, you would know how ambivalent feelings towards sisters can be.'

I thought of Maria, who would by now be close to despair, but the idea of her despair left me strangely unmoved. Maybe the sinner's claim was accurate, maybe feelings towards sisters really were ambivalent. Recently her concern, however well meant, actually had grown a little tiresome, and when she pulled the curtains in the morning I no longer found her hair in the morning light as attractive as I had, and her features seemed a little careworn, by no means as lively as, for example, the face framed in strawberry-blonde hair that the sinner turned towards me.

'On the one hand I'm fond of my two elder sisters,' Magdalena continued, 'on the other I felt a profound feeling of happiness when I leapt over the fence and left them behind. Not for nothing had the military and the police force bought this particular Puch model in its day, and used it in the most remote and mountainous parts of Austria. Thanks to the manually adjustable shock absorbers and the particularly soft differential suspension in the front fork, the Puch 800 can cope with extremes of terrain, and this was to my advantage when I was escaping my sisters. So I drove between the spruce trees, which were fortunately spaced quite far apart, over the soft needle-covered ground further into the forest, and had a brief rest there. Three hours later the Po Valley lay before me, and next day the Mediterranean. I was finally abroad.

Austria remained behind the high mountain chain, the homeland where I had never felt at home. Do you feel at home in your homeland, Reverend Father? Even if you didn't feel at home in our homeland of Austria, it can't be a problem to you, because for you a country, for you Austria can only be a substitute home, a stand-in home, a surrogate home, for the simple reason that your true home is of course the community of the faithful, the Catholic Church. A Catholic's home is in the womb of the Church, a Catholic is never homeless. I'm not a Catholic; I am, you might say, a paradoxical woman. Whenever I'm in my homeland of Austria, I sometimes feel strange, I sometimes feel as though I'm not there. Nowhere do people look at me in the street, if people look at me in the street, with more amazement than they do in Austria. They generally look through me. But if they do look at me there's such astonishment, such alarm in their eyes that I hurry home and stand in front of the mirror to see whether I've grown a second head, whether a big eye has sprouted in my forehead, whether a fiery birthmark has appeared on my left cheek. I check my limbs to see if I've grown a hunchback or hooves, and it is a great comfort to me to see that I haven't changed. Sometimes when my compatriots have looked through me I look in the mirror and expect to see nothing at all. It's always cheering when I see my reflection in it, a reflection that I find pleasing.

It's much the same when I address my compatriots in the street in our national language. Hardly have I uttered my first sentence than my compatriots stare at me in speechless bafflement. When that happens, too, I try to reassure myself, I go home and speak a few sentences into the little microphone attached to my pink Sony Walkman. What if my vocal apparatus, rather than generating expressive sounds with a view to communication, rather than producing comprehensible words and sentences, had merely grunted? What if my glottis has ceased to function, what if my vocal cords are too long or too short and have therefore produced nothing but a babble? I press Play and sigh with relief every time I hear my pleasant-sounding voice coming out with something clear and coherent, sometimes even something sharp and witty. An accumulation of such mysterious events meant that it wasn't long before I didn't feel at home in my homeland. On the other hand, I had only to cross the border of Austria and walk on foreign soil and I felt immediately at home. Even if all I could do was stammer broken sentences in a language largely unknown to me, people nodded and understood. Even if I remained silent because I was unfamiliar with the foreign language, if I tried to make myself understood with the help of facial expressions and gestures, there were no communication problems whatsoever. When I was abroad I never needed a mirror because no one cast doubt on my existence by looking through me, because no one tried to suggest, with a stunned and thunderstruck expression, that I was abnormal, a curiosity, a monstrosity. To me, foreign people were a friendly mirror.'

Here Magdalena fell into a brief silence and absently stroked a tuft of grass to her left. While I considered her relaxed features, her slightly open mouth, the little gap between her top front teeth, the curl that hid her right eye, her lowered left eyelid, its rim of lashes casting a gentle shadow over her cheek, I tried to imagine someone looking through her, not being aware of her. How could this woman be nothing to a passer-by? How could the visual stimuli radiating from her form not penetrate his cornea, how could they fail to pass through the lens and the vitreous humour, how could they not be received by the retina and carried on to the brain via the visual nerve? It was unthinkable that Magdalena's image, cast by the dioptric apparatus, should not be transformed by the retina into nerve impulses, that the colour-sensitive cones would not reproduce the light orange of her curls, the blue of her eyes, the white of her straight teeth, that the rods, sensitive to light and dark, would not reproduce the curves of her torso embraced by the black motorcycle jump suit, the charming line of her neck. What else could be the point of the passer-by's yellow patch, his hundred and fifty-two million or so optic cells?

'So I drove along the coast of the Gulf of Genoa,' Magdalena interrupted my reflections on the clearly often insensitive optical apparatus of the average Austrian passer-by. 'Just beyond Lerici, in the distance I saw a cliff jutting far above the sea, crowned by a church. Although at this point in time, a point in time that was still before I committed my first man-murder, I was not filled with any need to confess, I decided, attracted by the beauty of the view, to drive up the winding road to the church. The view of the sea was breathtaking. I parked the Puch 800 in the forecourt of the church, dotted around with little headstones, and went to the portal which bore the legend: Abbazia di San Michele Arcangelo.

Do you like fairy tales, Reverend Father?' Magdalena asked suddenly and looked at me. 'But of course you like fairy tales. Through your reading of the Old and New Testament, as a priest you'll be familiar with all kinds of fairy tales and their tellers. The prophets of the Old and New Testament must be among the most talented story-tellers, just as the Old and the New Testament are among the most beautiful collections of fairy stories, bringing together the most exciting and moving tales of magic, miracles, farce, fate and formulae in all their great diversity. And since you like fairy tales, since you must like them as a Catholic priest, you are practically obliged to like them, you will, indeed you must, like what I am about to tell you.

Abbazia di San Michele Arcangelo, it said over the portal, which was locked. When I turned round, a toothless little manikin with a large jangling bunch of keys emerged from a side door and said I must have come to see the coffins. Before I could answer, he took me by the hand and pulled me behind him inside the old abbey, through the nave, past a gleaming silver Archangel Michael swinging his sword, and down a flight of stone steps. With a rusty iron key the manikin opened a beautiful wrought-iron door and entered a huge room with shelves filled with old books running along the walls and up to the ceiling. The manikin tapped the yellowed leather spines with their faded gold letters.

Secrets, he giggled, many secrets. No one reads the books, no one learns the secrets.

The manikin pulled me onward, down a second flight of stone stairs into the depths of the church and past a statue of Christ bleeding from countless wounds beneath a transparent nylon tarpaulin.

Our Christ, explained the manikin. For the processions. Our processions are the longest. People come from far away to see our processions.

The manikin walked with me to one of the little round window openings.

Look, he said. Look at the sea. There's the sea.

The abbey was on a cliff straight above the sea, and one looked through the windows as through the portholes of a vast ship. Down below lay the sea, an endless area of grey corrugated cardboard. In the distance the vague outlines of an island were discernible.

My pretty, giggled the little manikin and looked up at me. My beauty. And he raised his right hand, stroked my shoulder and pinched my cheek. Ah, my little one, what you will have to put up with. There, he said, taking his hand from my hip to which it had slipped and pointing into the semi-darkness of the corridor. Go. There's another flight of steps.

And with these words the manikin turned round and left with his rattling bunch of keys. I slowly walked on, along the winding corridor and down a short spiral staircase, until I was standing by another iron door. I pressed on the big cold handle and the door yielded. I found myself in a kind of chapel, a lower church, a room dimly lit by candles, with two rows of dilapidated pews. I walked through the rows to the altar, covered with a crimson cloth, with two little gilded coffins in front of it to the right and the left, like children's coffins.

The lids of the coffins, also covered with crimson cloths, were pushed aside and the coffins were empty. On the altar, side by side, stood four skulls, in an arrangement which suggested an absent fifth. I stopped in front of the altar and looked at the red and gold glittering coffins, the white gleam of the skulls and the faded fresco of a pelican feeding its young with its blood on the dirty altar wall. When I noticed a long black shadow behind the altar, I took a few steps towards it. The outline of a larger coffin emerged. In this coffin lay a man with the fifth skull on his chest. I bent over him, and he opened his eyes, looked at me, took the skull in both hands and sat up.

An extraordinary abbey, he said. Have you met that curious curator?

I stared at the death's head in his hands.

Ah yes, he said. You see, I wanted to make use of the opportunity. You don't often have the opportunity to lie down in a coffin during your lifetime. A peculiar sensation. New sensations are always interesting, don't you think?

The man stood up and stepped out of the coffin. He was over six feet tall and extraordinarily thin.

Hold this, he said, pressing the death's head into my hand. Then he brushed down his black diesel jeans and his black denim shirt.

That, Reverend Father, is how I met the man from the Frisian islands.'

Magdalena stood up, walked the few paces to the little stream which, partially hidden beneath tufts of grass and pillows of moss, flowed at the edge of the glade, folded her arms behind her back and gazed into the water. I felt hot, the sun was shining straight into my eyes and blinding me.

'That's how it started. Beginnings are nicest, don't you find, Reverend Father? Beginnings like the one with the Frisian. After the beginning, which is also the high point, begins the decline: a downward slide along a gentle slope, a fall from a cliff, a downward swing in the air like that of a feather or a plane leaf in the autumn, white-water rafting with or without a helmet, a vertical drop in a lift, a tumble down a spiral staircase. It's always a decline.'

She bent over. Something in the grass beside the stream seemed to have attracted her attention.

'I have always loved beginnings,' she said. 'I seriously wonder whether one of the motives that led me to become a sevenfold man-killer was my need to cut short the decline and thus usher in a new beginning all the more quickly. I seriously wonder about that. Declines must be cut short. If one cannot completely eliminate declines, one can still reduce them, with various interventions, with various manipulations, to their shortest possible duration.

A curious creature,' she said, bending even lower. 'Most curious. As I said, it is a matter of cutting declines as short as possible. You can never fully rid the world of declines, you can never fully eliminate them, because of the laws of Western logic. If a beginning is isolated as a beginning, if nothing follows on from a beginning, then it ceases to be a beginning. And beginnings must under all circumstances be preserved.

A kind of grasshopper,' she murmured, pushing a tuft of grass gently aside, 'a praying mantis. Extremely rare. And while all beginnings are breathtaking, eruptive, intoxicating, fabulous, no beginning is like any other. You start to go into a skid one foggy November day on the motorway, you roll over twice, you lose consciousness, wake up in the ambulance, gaze into the green eyes of the orderly and you're lost, and so is the orderly. You fall down the escalator in a supermarket taking a thirty-year-old painter and decorator with you, and even as the two of you are falling you feel that the physical attraction is enormous. In an attack of rage you smash up your apartment and hospitalize your wife and children, and they put you in a straitjacket and take you to the nearest psychiatric clinic, and in the ambulance there's a pale student with her wrists bound who sets your heart racing just to look at her. You announce the bankruptcy of your small business, and while the rather stout official is explaining everything you need to know about the minimum wage you'll be living on from now on, you realize that you've suddenly found your animus in him. You are burying your father and fall in love at first sight with the lady in the flower shop, past the first flush of youth, when you're ordering the wreath. In the launderette you open the security lock on the front-loader and take out your spin-dried washing, to discover that everything has been dyed pale blue because the customer before left a dark blue sock in the machine. You're bawling out the customer who is just getting his washing out of the drier and folding it up, and while you're shouting at him you notice all the physiological symptoms of an incipient passion.

The sleeping cars of destiny derail at such beginnings, the Pullmans of fortune jump the tracks, the brake vans of fate head for the embankment, the narrow-gauge light railway of life slips from the line. After such beginnings you cease to be who you were before. Beginnings are the best.

It really is a *mantis religiosa*,' Magdalena said and rocked her curly head from side to side. She carefully reached into the grass, stood up, came up to me softly and held out her hollow hand. In it was a curious creature that I had never seen before, a delicate, light-green insect about three inches long with a narrow body, extended front legs, folded wings and a triangular head.

'*Mantis religiosa*, the praying mantis,' explained the sinner. 'So-called because it lies in wait for its prey with its arms raised as though it was praying. This is the second praying mantis I've ever seen in my life. I found the first on the Kaiserstuhl in Baden. Judging by its size, this one must be a female. And the females devour the males once copulation is completed.'

The sinner put the insect on my left knee and took a step backwards.

'Stay still, Reverend Father,' she said. 'I'll be back in a second.' She ran to the Puch bike and sidecar and fetched an empty jam jar from one of the panniers. She held it up. 'One of my mother's jam jars. Raspberry 1990. Eaten long ago. I love raspberry jam.' She came carefully closer. 'An unusual catch,' she said, while the jar enveloped the mantis on my left knee, and then she turned it round and screwed on the lid. 'We can't just let it fly away, Reverend Father, don't you think? Such a rare insect.' She held the jam jar in front of her. 'Let's observe it. Let's study it. Such an interesting insect. Eats the male. Insect cannibalism. Keep your eyes open, Reverend Father. Keep your eyes open for a male. In all likelihood that there's a male in the vicinity.' She put the jam jar beside me on the ground. Then she resumed her story.

'When I saw the Frisian I immediately realized that this was one of those beginnings,' she said. 'I recognized in him a male archetype that I had often encountered in dreams, in the form of a skeleton over six feet tall, which was pursuing me while I tried to escape it. In the lower church of the Abbazia di San Michele the skeleton had finally caught me. The Frisian's expression when he looked at me suggested that I embodied one of his dream figures as well. If we hadn't heard the manikin's shuffling steps and rattling bunch of keys we would have lain down together in the coffin, surprised and delighted at this unexpected encounter. But as it was we put the fifth skull in the gap between the others on the altar and gave the manikin a tip. He took the note and bowed before us a number of times.

*Cari, carissimi*, he said. Ah, the lovers. What you will have to put up with. Ah, you lovers.

He stood between us, took my right hand and the left hand of the Frisian, placed one on the other and giggled.

Go, he said. Go, and enjoy.

We left the abbey, and it was quite natural for the Frisian to sit in the Felber sidecar and drive on with me. He left his bicycle to the fat daughter of the curator, who was hanging up the washing on a little terrace over the sea next to the abbey.

We decided to take the ferry in the next port and travel to the island that was visible from the Abbazia. During the crossing I stole a number of sidelong glances at the Frisian who was staring silently at the sea and chain smoking. He was an ugly man, of an ugliness that I found very attractive. His legs and arms were thin and lanky, just like his fingers. He was slightly hunchbacked, his head was fairly small, his eyes were deep-set, the skin of his face was covered with old and badly healed acne scars, his teeth were rotten and, like the ends of his fingers, yellowish-brown with nicotine. His mouth was big, his lips wide and pouting, turned down at the corners like the mouth of a fish and enclosed on both sides by deep-etched lines like parentheses. He held the cigarette in his right hand, and with his left he pulled at the flaps of skin on his lower jaw. He laughed a lot; his laugh was shrill and spasmodic and made me start. The unlovely exterior of my companion was underlined by his burning, fixed stare. Overall, however, these repellent physical characteristics had an irresistible effect on me. His ugliness was so concentrated that it finally transcended itself, becoming a new, darkly glimmering beauty which was all the more fascinating for carrying within it all the sensuality of ugliness.

Beauty is always concealed within ugliness, and ugliness within beauty. I have always been interested in surface ugliness, because beneath the surface of ugliness lies beauty, passion, sensuality. It is a good idea to consider surface beauty with scepticism, because beneath the layer of surface beauty in all likelihood there lies real, not surface, ugliness, ugliness, coldness and boredom. Are you, like everyone else, a devotee of goodness, truth and beauty? Of course you are, like everyone else, a devotee of goodness, truth and beauty. Think again, Reverend Father. Become, as I have, a fan of surface evil, untruth and ugliness, and begin your own transformation and that of the world around you.

It was the sensuality that I perceived beneath the ugliness of the Frisian, the passion that I saw in this man, who resembled on the one hand a daddy-longlegs and on the other a carp or a perch, that made me expect something of my stay on the island whose details grew more distinct as we, leaning our arms on the railing, stood on deck.

An island is a place of longing, Reverend Father, it is paradise regained after years of aimless wandering. The knowledge that your stay in a place of longing is limited, that you will sooner or later be expelled not only from the original paradise but from every subsequent paradise regained should not diminish your joy at arriving in this paradise, but it does.

Our island was an illusion of bluish outlines in a glittering sea, a utopia of bays and jutting cliffs, bathed in the scent of lemon and orange blossom, an acoustic mirage of gently lapping waves and the drawn-out notes of passing ships.

We rented a little house standing alone in the middle of a lemon grove above a cliff that fell to the sea. I would rather have taken an apartment near the little fishing harbour in the south of the island, but the Frisian said people were not to be trusted, we should keep well away from them, put as much distance as possible between ourselves and them. This should have given me pause, as should the fact that I had first met him lying in a coffin, with a skull on his chest. But at this point thinking was not my main concern, thinking was by no means my main concern. I wasn't thinking at this point, and limited myself to longing for the nights with the Frisian in the little blue house and, when those nights had fallen, to enjoying them. My assumptions about the sensuality and passion concealed beneath the ugliness of the Frisian had not deceived me.

These were long nights, in which the body of the Frisian,

consisting of little more than skin and bone, revealed an astonishing tenderness, sensitivity and devotion. We often spent these nights in a hidden place outside. Behind the house a narrow path twisted steeply down to the sea between spiky, yellow-blossomed gorse bushes. Once darkness had fallen the Frisian looked at me, took me by the hand and nodded towards the door. He gave me just enough time to grab my sleeping bag and a bottle of wine, then he pulled me out of the house and down the little moonlit path to the rocky plateau of the shore. There we stretched out the sleeping bag on a boulder smoothed by the water and lay down. The waves crashed against the rocks, white fountains rose up around us and a gentle shower of pulverized drops of water fell on our bodies, which were pale green in the light of the moon. We couldn't hear our stammering, the crashing waves drowned everything out. The shadows of the bats that lived in the grottoes dotted along the shore cut through the air, darker even than the darkness. Sometimes a brightly lit ship would drift slowly by.

During the day we went walking on the island, often disturbed by the hunting dogs fetching the dead birds that the islanders had shot for pleasure, and enjoyed the yellow of the lemons and the blue of the scented artichoke flowers. We fed the two cats that roamed around our blue house and cautiously put their paws across the threshold. One cat was thin and wild and blind in one eye, the other was gentle and elegant, with the grey fur and blue eyes of a Siamese cat. We didn't know whether they belonged to anyone. The one-eyed cat ran to the Frisian, the other liked to sit on my lap and touched my face protectively with claws retracted. The Frisian told me nothing about himself and the life he had left behind, and I didn't ask him. He talked very little generally, but our nights compensated for his laconic nature. For hours he sat on the stone bench behind the house staring into the open sea. When I tried to stroke his high forehead he brushed my hand away. After a while I would increasingly find him in murmured conversation with himself. I couldn't understand what he was saying because he spoke quickly and quietly to himself, in a hissing tone that frightened me. He accompanied his words with extravagant gestures of his arms, and during these monologues his eyes stayed wide open. I tried to get him to come with me to the harbour and the little market more often, to be with people, but having been closed off from the very beginning he only became more afraid of them, edged along the walls of the houses and avoided them, so that we were soon viewed with sympathy or suspicion, which disturbed him all the more and sent him back to our blue house all the quicker. When I went to the centre of town on my own, people asked me if my husband was ill.

I tried to ignore the Frisian's curious condition but I did notice that his melancholy was slowly gripping me, depressing me and making me more monosyllabic as well. I had financial worries too. So far I had paid the rent and paid for daily groceries, as the Frisian had no money to speak of. I racked my brains for ways of getting hold of money. Once, after I had put on the brown Carmelite habit with the white cloak and walked up and down in the lemon grove in front of the Frisian, I had an idea: I would take the ferry to the port on the mainland, put on the habit of the Barefoot Carmelites when I got there, and try to get some money by petty theft. I was convinced that the nun's garb would make stealing considerably easier. Hardly anyone would suspect a nun of being a thief, certainly not in Italy. Would you suspect a Carmelite of being a thief?

I didn't breathe a word to the Frisian, who knew nothing of my finances, allowing him to believe I had access to unlimited funds. The fact that I was supporting him didn't seem to trouble him in the slightest; we never discussed money, just as we never discussed any other personal things, our past, our family relations, our education. He seemed happy enough to live with me and eat what I put in front of him. And as long as he gazed at me in the evening, took me by the hand and drew me from the house and down to the seashore, I would not ask him any questions, and would ensure that he slept enough and ate enough to stay in good enough shape to keep our nights as satisfying as they were.

Incidentally, he found me so exciting and desirable in my Carmelite habit that he undressed me, regardless of any possible disturbance by one of the roaming bird-hunters or one of their dogs, in the middle of the lemon grove, first taking off the white scapulary, then the gown, spreading the clothes out on the grass beneath the lemon trees, smoothing them flat and laying me gently upon them.'

As if acting out the story in her memory, the sinner ran her beautiful, slender hand delicately over the grass and sighed. I must confess, I was horrified by the sacrilege of which she talked so lightly, this profanation of a consecrated item of clothing, its blasphemous misuse, the abuse of a profession dedicated to a life pleasing in the sight of God. But for all my rage, it required an intense effort to erase the image that the sinner's words had aroused in me of the two young people lying on the white Carmelite cloak.

'Quite honestly,' the sinner continued with her blasphemous tale, 'I find your blossom-white alb very appealing as well, such a pure, immaculate white.' She slid her beautiful, slender hand beneath my dalmatic and felt around the white material above my knee, at which my patellar reflexes reacted and my legs, bound together with green nylon washing line at the ankles, shot into the air.

'A pretty knee,' she whispered, 'round and smooth.' Then she slid her hand to the back of my knee, at which I twitched a number of times, as I am very sensitive there. 'Ah, and the back of your knee, so soft,' she murmured, drawing her hand slowly back, letting her fingernails slide gently down my calf. 'To be very honest, I find men in women's clothes highly seductive. Unfortunately, one seldom has the opportunity to see such a thing, only at church services and in dubious establishments are my desires assuaged.

Anyway, the Frisian pulled my Carmelite habit with its white cloak over my head, just as I could pull your dalmatic and stole over your head if I wanted, your alb and your pluvial, if you were wearing a pluvial. But I could only pull your priestly vestments over your head if I first took off the hempen rope with which your hands are tied. And as I would probably not be prepared to do that, I would simply pull up the alb, the dalmatic and the stole and throw them over your head, and you would be sitting there with your vestments over your head, not only incapable of moving, but blind as well. The idea appeals, I must admit. A priest with his vestments over his head, an ascetic priest's body without a visible head attached, a body doubtless hardened over the course of time by strict religious exercises, by sexual abstinence, by fasting, perhaps even by self-flagellation, a bound priest's body entirely in my power, perhaps scarred by scourging, that is an idea which, I must admit, rather excites me. Gently running the tips of my fingers over those scars, which no one has ever touched, is an enticing idea.'

When she said that the sinner's eyes glittered, and for the first time I became seriously aware of the situation that I was in. This woman, sitting in front of me and talking without interruption, was mentally ill, an unpredictable lunatic who would not hesitate to act upon spontaneous, crazy impulses, to lay hands on a man of God, a body on which no woman had ever laid hands, apart from the occasional gestures of harmless tenderness of my sister Maria. In my mind's eye I saw myself sitting in extreme indignity, the uniform of my vocation over my head, abandoned to the groping fingers of this fearless woman, to those slender fingers narrowing like candles to their tips, which had already begun their explorations, their shameless reconnaissance. I was in extreme danger.

'But Reverend Father, there are already drops of sweat on

your brow,' the sinner interrupted my desperate thoughts. 'Wait.' She came closer, and with a cambric handkerchief that she drew from one of the many zip pockets concealed in the depths of her motorcycle jump suit, she wiped the drops from my forehead with her delicate fingers.

'Stay still,' she said, 'don't twitch. It's only the beginning of June, and it's so hot already. But your face is turned straight into the sun. Wait.' She took a few steps back, unzipped more of the little pockets in her motorcycle jump suit and finally found what she was looking for: a classically designed pair of black sunglasses with very dark lenses. Holding the earpieces with both hands she approached me again and put the sunglasses on my nose.

'There,' she said, 'so that you don't damage your eyes, Reverend Father. Nothing would be further from my mind than to treat you disrespectfully. They don't look too bad on you, the Ray-Bans, a souvenir of Jonathan Alistair, of whom more shortly. I took them when it was all over.

When our financial situation was becoming more and more hopeless, I packed the habit of the Barefoot Carmelites into a big plastic bag and took the ferry to the port on the mainland. There I went into the ladies' toilet in the main railway station and changed. I left the plastic bag with my jeans and the T-shirt in left luggage. Then I got into a bus on the most heavily used line.

Come, Sister, come, said a well-dressed lady, helping me up the two steps into the crowded bus. A young man immediately stood up and offered me his seat, an offer that I refused with a word of thanks because, if I was to carry out my plan, I had to stand between the closely packed passengers. What can I say, Reverend Father? It was easier than I had imagined. First I took a fine calf-leather purse out of the elegant handbag of the well-dressed woman who had helped me on to the bus, which was child's play. After I had let the calf-leather purse disappear into the folds of my habit, she smiled at me and said: A terrible crush, isn't it, Sister? But around this time of day you can't get a taxi, and the bus is your only option.

The bus stopped, and when the young man who had offered me his seat was pushing his way past me to the door, I carefully pulled his little wallet out of his back pocket. As the bus was setting off, I saw him standing at the bus stop, reaching for his back pocket and throwing his arms in the air. I was constantly being pushed backwards by new passengers, and found myself standing next to a harmless-looking little elderly man with a bald head and a black briefcase. It was not difficult to steal his flat wallet, visible beneath the material of his trouser pocket, while he looked out of the window. I got out at the next stop. I strolled through the town, turned into a side alley and examined the contents of the three wallets. Surprisingly, the young man had had the most cash on him, while the well-dressed lady's calf-leather purse held only a few coins, a pocket diary and a photograph of a little girl. I took the money out of the two men's wallets, threw them away and kept the calf-leather purse with the pocket diary, the coins and the photograph. I walked on and sat down on a bench in a park, next to a young woman whose little child was playing in the sandpit.

Such heat, the woman said. But the child insists on going to the playground. Aren't you hot in your nun's habit?

We chatted for a while, until she jumped up and ran after her child which had climbed out of the sandpit and was heading on all fours, at astonishing speed, towards the exit of the little park. I took the opportunity to open the zip of a little side pocket in the young mother's plastic rucksack on the bench, remove a turquoise fabric wallet and pull the zip closed again. My curiosity was so great that I took a quick look into the wallet which contained a credit card. When the mother came back, with her child on her arm, I joked a little with the ugly small child and then said I would have to go, my fellow sisters were waiting for me for communal prayer. I took my leave with the words: God's blessing be with you and your child!

Then I went into a big store nearby, used the credit card to buy clothes and food for myself and the Frisian, and a big bag in which I put everything. I was treated with the greatest courtesy, people let me past, and believed me when I said my Mother Superior had sent me to buy the clothes and the food for a family whose house had burned to the ground, and which was therefore without funds.

Ah, what good people you are, you and the other sisters, the salesgirl said. You never think about yourselves, only ever about other people. You'll be sure of a place in Heaven.

Towards evening I took the plastic bag out of left luggage, changed in the ladies' toilet at the main railway station and took the speedboat back to the island. The Frisian was sitting on the bench in front of the house, deep in conversation with himself, and barely noticed my return. Even when I unpacked the bag and showed him the things I had bought, he displayed no sign of delight or surprise. Still, in the evening he drew me from the house and down to the sea, as he had not done for two weeks. For the inexorable decline had begun, Reverend Father. The Frisian's behaviour was growing stranger by the day. I was suffering from his change, and his ever more apparent depression weighed leadenly on my emotions. Even his body, at first infinitely light, to my great joy, seemed to have become much heavier, almost crushing me during those increasingly rare nights on the seashore.

One day when I came home from the market he was standing on a chair in the middle of the room with a rope round his neck attached to a hook in the ceiling. When he saw my shocked expression he smiled sadly, slipped the rope over his head and got down off the chair. When I asked what he was up to, he said he was always in search of new sensations, as he had been when he had lain with the skull in the coffin. He was addicted to new sensations, it was in his nature, and if new sensations didn't appear of their own accord over a certain period of time, he was seized by a compulsive need to provoke them through various actions of his own. In his life he had experimented a great deal with sensations, had produced and savoured almost every possible sensation. When he took me by the hand in the evening and pulled me down the steep path to the sea, it was quite obvious that he had been concerned only with new sensations. And the sensations that he had felt during the many nights that he had spent with me on the sea-smoothed rock on the beach had been, in a sense, entirely new to him. But unfortunately it had struck him lately that sensations which had at first been new were being repeated, and thus ceased to be new. This was the reason for his depression, his melancholia. He was forever forcing himself to have new sensations, and forever these new sensations wore off. Did I not understand how dispiriting his experience of sensations was? Did I not understand that he was a Sisyphus of sensation, for all eternity rolling his rock of sensation up a steep mountain, only to see it roll back into the valley, and having to start his sensation-work all over again. He no longer knew, he said, what to do. All that was left to him was the sensation of death, the only one still unknown to him.

Reverend Father, after this confession I tried everything to awaken new sensations in the Frisian, an attempt condemned to failure from the start because he was interested only in the idea of the sensation of death. No other sensations were intensive enough. I cooked meals for him that I had never cooked before, I put on music I had never put on before, I played love games with him that I had never played with him before, I put the one-eyed cat on his lap – he didn't react to anything. He seemed to have withdrawn to a universe to which I had no access, and I noticed that he was becoming more and more of a burden to me. His thoughts, revolving exclusively around death, hung like heavy black velvet curtains in the house, which I had constantly to lift, constantly to shove aside. When I left the house I was afraid of my return, of the state in which I would find him.

For a while I put up with this situation, unbearable as it was, but when he hardly ever bothered to take me by the hand in the evening and draw me from the house, I began to loathe him, to wish that he would finally, once and for all, savour the unbounded sensation of death. But he wasn't consistent enough. If he tried to savour to the full the sensation of gassing himself, by blocking all the cracks in the doors and windows and turning on all the gas taps, a quarter of an hour after he had put his head in the oven the gas company began a strike that it had announced some time previously, and when I returned from shopping I found him lying in front of the oven, not suffocated in the slightest. If he thought it was time to abandon himself to the utterly new sensation of a long free fall leading to impact on a solid surface, and if, to this end, he jumped from the cliff behind the house which dropped vertically to the sea, ten feet into his free fall he would be caught by the trunk of a pine tree and have to be rescued by the local fire brigade, which cost me a considerable sum of money and forced me to set off for the mainland once more in my Carmelite habit. If he decided to immerse himself completely in the sensation of opened veins, he did it so clumsily that he merely fainted, and I was the one who had to stump up the cost for the cleaning of the bathroom carpet. If he wanted to sample the sensation of a fatal overdose, he underestimated the dose and had to be brought to the port on the mainland in the speedboat, where his stomach was pumped, another act of Samaritanism that was not without its cost. Once, when he had turned his attention to the sensation of a bullet in the brain, the one-eyed cat jumped up on him just as he was firing the pistol he had found in the tool shed, with the result that he singed his hair and a bit of skin on the top of his head, which at least incurred only the expense of an Elastoplast.

Reverend Father, you will understand that after these and similar events the Frisian began to repel me as much as he had originally attracted me. You will also agree with me when I say that inconsistency, although not one of the seven deadly sins, is not a positive character trait, and that it is entirely understandable if a woman whose lover, over a long period of time, shows the indecision, tepidity and irresolution shown by the Frisian, soon loses all human respect for him and finally turns away from him. If the Frisian had at least been consistent in regularly continuing our nocturnal trips to the sea, I would patiently have put up with all the other sensational escapades, and I would have paid all the resulting costs without demur. These nocturnal trips would have been perfectly adequate compensation for his sensational eccentricities. But unfortunately the trips became increasingly rare, and in the end they stopped entirely.

As the frequency of our trips diminished, so my desire increased that the Frisian should finally be led to the goal of his desires, that final unknown sensation. After three weeks, when he had made no move to take me by the hand and lead me from the house, my resolve was firm: I would supply him with the sensation of drowning. Of all the sensations of death, the sensation of drowning would be the most interesting, the most unusual for him, for the element of water was the strangest to him.

Whenever our nights at the seashore had left me overheated, I had swum far out, into the black sea beneath a new moon, into the silver sea beneath a full moon, and enjoyed the silence, the quiet splashing produced by my swimming strokes, the cool water. At first the Frisian had called to me, anxious that my strength might desert me before I returned to the shore. When he realized how well I could swim, he admired me for it. He himself was a non-swimmer, a reason for me to pity him. It is quite natural for someone who has grown up on an Austrian lake, who has been familiar with water from childhood, to pity all those people who have never known that close connection with water. Someone who, from the outset, loves contact with water so much that her mother has to chase her from the water of the lake because she won't leave it of her own accord naturally despises people who are afraid of water. She can't understand why everyone doesn't, as she does, immediately jump into every sizeable body of water, she can't understand that there are people who dip their big toe into the liquid for a second, immediately pull it back out again and make for the hills, who don't twist and turn in the water like a fish, who haven't mastered all the strokes, the breast stroke, freestyle, backstroke and butterfly, who don't enjoy jumping off the thirty-foot board and diving to the bottom of the lake.

After I had realized how wary the Frisian was of water, but that he was also attracted by it at the same time, I tried to lead him carefully to it. First I got him to sit on the edge of the rock and dip his feet in the water. The next step consisted in slowly walking into the water with him so that it covered his calves, his knees, his belly and finally reached up to his neck. Then I made him dip his head under the waves. Once he had acquired something of a taste for water I began to teach him the strokes, to help him coordinate the movements of his arms and legs. He learned slowly but within a few weeks he was swimming cautiously, his head raised high, a few yards into the sea. But his movements were still somewhat uncertain.

Believe me, Reverend Father, it wasn't easy to take the decision to drown the Frisian. I'm not a born murderer, I'm not a natural murderer. No one could accuse me of standing on street corners on foggy Saturday evenings in November with a thin nylon rope or a knife under my trenchcoat, in wait for innocent men coming back from the late show at the cinema, their approach betrayed by the sound of their heels echoing through the silence of the night. I would never roam the woods looking out for lonely male mushroom-collectors with slender necks. It would never occur to me to follow an adolescent boy, the last passenger off the last train at the terminus, down the long, tiled corridors of the subway with murderous intent. It is not in my nature to entice men to my apartment on threadbare pretexts, to carve them up and put them in the freezer until further notice. On the contrary, Reverend Father, look at me: my body exists to be embraced by a man's body, my skin exists to be caressed by him, my mouth to be kissed by his mouth, my hair to be tousled by his hands. Even from the Frisian all I wanted was – at the seashore, in the moonlight – to be embraced, caressed and kissed. I became a murderer against my will; the inexorable negative transformation that occurred in the Frisian turned me into one. I acted in self-defence, Reverend Father. I resorted to that serious measure because otherwise I was the one who would have died.

The symptoms of grave melancholy from which the Frisian suffered soon manifested themselves in me as well. I had nightmares, I talked to myself, fell from a state of overbrimming cheerfulness into deep sadness, started stammering when I talked to the inhabitants of the island, and soon I was edging myself along the walls of the houses with the same fear of people that afflicted him. My pulse grew slower, my eyes grew hollower, and whenever I left the house I was afraid an aeroplane might fall on my head. I began to believe that the two cats were bewitched, that they were really my two elder sisters whose narrow skirts might have meant that they couldn't climb over the fence that I leapt over on my Puch 800 but who could still pursue me, in this new transformation, far beyond the Austrian borders. When I looked into the tall Venetian mirror in the hall of our blue house, I saw a slightly hunched woman with thin, elongated arms and legs and a rigid, burning gaze, a woman with a fairly small head, a large mouth and wide pouting lips, pulled down at the corners like a fish's mouth, and enclosed on both sides by deep-etched lines like parentheses.

Reverend Father, I had started to look weirdly similar to the Frisian, a phenomenon that frightened me and first set in motion the idea of a violent elimination. This idea, at first nothing but a vague notion, assumed more concrete form after I had caught myself standing on the high cliff and staring down at the sea, dreamily weighing a rope in my hands in the tool shed and absent-mindedly giving myself tiny cuts to the wrist with the razor. But it only became a firm resolution when three weeks had gone by without the Frisian taking me by the hand and down to the seashore at night.

To the right of the place at the seashore which we no longer frequented there was a small but deep grotto, reached by swimming through a little entrance, with bats which hung from the roof and flew out in the evening through a crack in the rock which let in a little light from above. Sometimes I swam in, turned round and watched the clear water of the rolling waves practically filling the entrance. I touched the wet cliff walls that formed the grotto, with little crabs running over them and coral-red marine plants growing round about. I loved being surrounded by the semi-darkness of the shimmering cliff walls and looking down into the blue-green deep below me. I wanted to lure the Frisian into this grotto, where he had never followed me. It wasn't going to be easy. I waited for a moment when he was in a good mood. Lately that had only happened when he had had a great deal to drink over dinner. I bought expensive, heavy south Italian wines and prepared delicious meals.

One evening, when the full moon had risen like a golden disc above the horizon, when he was tranquilly leaning back after dinner on the little terrace behind the house and had begun slurred renditions of Frisian sea shanties, I walked over to him, took his hand and pulled him to his feet. Now it was I who guided him to the path that led down to the sea, and the Frisian, brought by the wine to a state between apathy and erotic attraction, allowed himself to be guided. Once we had reached the shore I wrapped my arms round his neck, described the beauty of the little grotto and suggested that we swim the short distance to it. He was easily persuaded, and swam slowly behind me, through the high, narrow entrance to the grotto. It was dark in there, apart from a moonbeam which fell through the narrow crack in the rock. I turned to the Frisian, and could see only the black outline of his head and shoulders against the cave entrance. The alcohol and the unfamiliar surroundings seemed to put him in a sensual mood, and for the first time in weeks he came over to me and began to touch me under the water. But it was too late. I grabbed him by his gaunt shoulders and, with all the strength at my disposal, pushed him beneath the surface of the water. He immediately understood that it was a matter of life and death and began to defend himself. But I would never have let myself in for such a struggle if I hadn't known that the Frisian was physically weaker than I was, a fact that had been clearly proven during our long nights at the seashore. His delicate, fragile body was just as weak as it looked.

But now the Frisian was fighting for his life, and the survival instinct gave him powers that he had never developed before. Time and again I pushed him beneath the surface, time and again he slipped from my grasp and shot out of the water, his mouth gaping wide. He tried to grip the wet cliff walls of the grotto with his spidery fingers but slipped away each time. He struck around him and grabbed me by the hair but quickly tired as I had only just taught him how to swim and he wasn't yet used to staying above the water for a long time. He reappeared above the surface less and less often, his resistance grew ever weaker. I am a strong woman, my ancestors were all peasants and craftsmen from the Austrian provinces. I didn't stint in my efforts; on the contrary, I wrapped the Frisian's legs in my own so that he was unable to move. Half unconscious, he abandoned his resistance. At that moment I was tempted to leave him be, to bring him to the shore and lay him gently on our sea-smoothed boulder. But that wouldn't change anything, he would go on slipping into his melancholy and dragging me with him until we finally crouched side by side like indistinguishable twins on the edge of the black hole. Realizing the hopelessness of the situation, I summoned all my forces and pushed the Frisian's body beneath the surface for as long as I could. He reared up once more beneath the water, and then he stopped moving. I carefully loosened my grip, but didn't quite let go of the body. When he still showed no sign of life I grabbed him under the arms and pulled him to the shore. There I laid him on his back on our boulder. Waiting for him to open his eyes was pointless.'

The sinner fell silent. Clearly overwhelmed by the memory of the dead Frisian lying on the beach, she twisted her face into a painful grimace, closed her eyes and ran her hand over her forehead. I stared at her. Had this woman been speaking the truth? Had she really lured a man into an ambush and murdered him in cold blood? I felt the hairs on my forearms standing on end, and even had the feeling that the hair on my head was doing the same.

'It was no problem presenting the Frisian's death to the police as a swimming accident. Policemen are generally of unparalleled stupidity, and in Italy they seem to be stupider than anywhere else, just as the inhabitants of pronouncedly Catholic countries are generally a fair bit stupider than the inhabitants of other countries. This judgment is by no means aimed at you personally, Reverend Father, the dignitaries of the Catholic Church are naturally excluded from this judgment. The dignitaries of the Catholic Church are, of course, anything but stupid. To keep such a large number of people as the Catholics stupid for thousands of years, the dignitaries of the Catholic Church, that is, those who define the guidelines of the Catholic Church, must themselves naturally be very clever, particularly the higher-ranking dignitaries. This is not, however, to imply that the lowlier dignitaries are altogether stupid. But it would not be accurate to describe them as clever, more appropriate terms would be cunning, sly, crafty, as lowly dignitaries in general need to be cunning, sly and crafty to be able to sail in the wake of the higher dignitaries, just as everyone who wants to sail in someone else's wake needs to be cunning, sly and crafty. The Catholic faithful, those whom their shepherd, Christ, so accurately described as sheep, are not, like people who live under dictatorships, like psychologists, psychiatrists, psychotherapists and psychoanalysts, free to think what they want. They may be convinced that they are thinking what they want, that their freedom of thought is limitless, but a large part of the material from which their thought is constructed is prefabricated for them, and thus they are naturally unable to build bold thought-buildings, just rather modest Catholic prefabs, not architectural masterpieces but standardized thought-prefabs. This prefabricated building style on the part of Catholics is also generally discernible in their external appearance, for which the aforementioned metaphor coined by the shepherd is not inappropriate.

A few days later the Frisian's mother, like most Frisians a non-Catholic and thus not given to thinking in prefabricated blocks, arrived from Uithuizermeeden in north-east Holland. Unlike the Catholic police on the island she was not convinced by the notion of a swimming accident. She gave me a sidelong, scrutinizing look and asked me a lot of questions about the relationship between myself and her son. Even after I had given exhaustive answers to all these questions, she remained sceptical. I really wanted to say to her, what do you expect? Be happy that I've spared your son a long, melancholy life of pain! Be happy that I've cut it short, that you won't have to devote the rest of your own life in Uithuizermeeden in north-east Holland to taking care of your son who would never have found his way out of the labyrinth of his melancholy but would have penetrated deeper and deeper inside it, that you won't have to spend your life comforting him after his nightmares, talking him out of his hallucinations. Be happy that you won't be forced to walk with him into the marshes, standing up to the salty sea wind with him, accompanying him on his ever more morbid expeditions into the world of sensations! Thank me, I wanted to call to her, thank me for bringing forward his death, for hastening his departure! I refrained from doing so, for in all likelihood the mother who had arrived from Uithuizermeeden would have held little sympathy with my argument. This wouldn't necessarily have undermined its plausibility but it would still have contradicted the Frisian mother's notions of death which, although not Catholic, were well-worn nonetheless. The mother set off with the simple coffin in which her son now finally lay, but not before she had thrown me one last sceptical glance from the deck of the ferry. I went on living in the blue house for a while, feeding the cats and spending the occasional night alone on the seashore.'

The sinner glanced at her watch. 'And now, Reverend Father, let us listen to the news,' she said, walked to the Puch bike and sidecar, fetched the Walkman from a pannier, swung on to the saddle and put on the headphones. 'Another five minutes,' she said. 'Another five minutes until the news. I'd be very surprised if they were on our trail. That would really surprise me. Why would they be on our trail when I haven't even demanded a ransom for you? I'm not interested in money, as you know; I'm not, like other kidnappers, interested in promoting an ideology, I'm not interested in obtaining the release of like-minded comrades. That can't be an issue for me because I have no like-minded comrades, a fact that occasionally saddens me, but only occasionally. Once you have like-minded comrades you're dangerously close to those sheep mentioned by Jesus the shepherd. And like-minded comrades prove loyal only in the rarest cases, they generally betray you sooner or later, such behaviour is rooted in the nature of the like-minded comrade.

As I'm a woman, the obvious thing would be to seek out like-minded women comrades for me, an enterprise even more likely to end in failure. If like-minded comrades are unreliable,

like-minded women comrades are even more so. My experience
of so-called like-minded women comrades could not be more
shattering. In the past so-called like-minded women comrades
have always turned against me after short periods of supposed
solidarity, after short periods of fake conspiracy they have
always most perfidiously betrayed me, dropped me, denounced
me, suspected me, defamed me, blamed me, since which time
I have kept my distance not only from like-minded comrades
but more particularly from like-minded women comrades, I
have avoided them like the plague. Reverend Father, the
greatest disappointment in my life has been the betrayal of my
like-minded women comrades, the acts of underhandedness,
malice, spitefulness, the resentment, ill will, envy and contempt
on the part of my own sex. It all started with my mother, with
my sisters. Nothing gave my mother and my sisters more
mischievous pleasure than exploiting my innocence, abusing
my openness. If no one was looking, one sister would take
delight in kicking my shin, the other would revel in hitting
me on the head with my doll, my mother would rejoice in
pulling my hair. The hidden sadism of so-called like-minded
women comrades towards the members of their own sex went
significantly further than the open sadism of their like-minded
male comrades.

The Austrian like-minded women comrades are the worst
because the most unhappy. If any fellow woman succeeds
in breaking out of the vicious circle of Austrian women's
unhappiness, then for decades they will pursue her with
their hatred beyond the national boundaries. If an Austrian
woman dares not to accept Austrian women's unhappiness,
if an Austrian woman thinks it natural that she should most
violently reject the women's unhappiness imposed upon her
by Catholic Austria and go in search of a woman's happiness
that seems only natural, she brings upon herself not only the
opprobrium of the Austrian men who have been profiting
from the unhappiness of Austrian women for centuries, but

more particularly the irreconcilable hostility, the embittered vengefulness of all the unhappy Austrian women, whose numbers are more or less identical with those of Austrian women as a whole. They hate it if an Austrian woman does not willingly suffer with them. If it occurs to an Austrian woman to raise her voice in song, not only countless Austrian men's hands but also countless Austrian women's hands will grab her by the throat and throttle her breath from her, countless Austrian women's voices will try to drown her rising song with a shriek of woe. If an Austrian woman takes a few hesitant dance steps, not only countless ungainly Austrian men's feet but also countless ungainly Austrian women's feet will immediately get in her way to trip her up. If an Austrian woman begins a liberating laugh, not only numerous massive Austrian men's fingers but numerous Austrian women's fingers will land on her mouth to stop that laughter in its tracks. There is nothing that the majority of Austrians, male and female, hate more than singing and dancing women. The majority of Catholic Austrians, male and female, hold the view that woman should take a masochistic pleasure in the suffering imposed on her by nature, that she should wallow with masochistic delight in the unhappiness that is her lot. If women who want to sing and dance remain in Catholic Austria, then in all likelihood they will end up in the madhouse, in prison or committing suicide. For women who want to sing and dance, Catholic Austria is the most unsuitable country on earth.

The news, Reverend Father, here is the news,' the sinner's melodious voice interrupted its flow, and she listened for a while, her head tilted to one side and her hands on the earpieces of her pink headphones. 'They're looking for us everywhere,' she said, 'but they have no idea where we are. They won't find us; after all, they can't comb all the woods of the East Tyrol, let alone all the woods of Austria, they can't scour the whole of the Austrian forest, since it covers about half the surface of Austria. Apart from that, when it comes to intellectual limitation, the Austrian police give the Italians a good run for their money. We have nothing to worry about, Reverend Father.'

She went on listening. 'The cardinal is talking,' she said. 'The cardinal is talking about a shameless sin, he is describing me as a monster, as a ghoul, as a lamentable excrescence of the human race. He's talking about tradition and morality, of limits which must not be transgressed but which have been transgressed. They're holding a special service, Reverend Father, a special service in St Stephen's Cathedral, a national special service in your honour, a special service, broadcast on radio and television, with a minute's silence.' She listened again for a while. 'The community of the faithful is with you in spirit, says the cardinal. The community of the faithful appeals to you not to be weak in the hour of your affliction, to find strength in thoughts of the martyrdom of the saints of the Catholic Church, to remain steadfast in the face of the temptations of the godforsaken madman who has dared to abduct a man of God.'

She giggled. 'Of course they think the abductor's a man. Obviously the Pope has been made aware of this monstrous occurrence, says the cardinal. The Pope will appear in a special broadcast on television this evening, to address the Austrian people, and the people of East Tyrol in particular.'

After continuing to listen attentively, the sinner removed her headphones, switched off the Walkman and shook the flood of her hair.

'The end of paradise,' she said quietly after a little pause. 'The end of the island paradise. First peace, tranquillity and happiness, then, inevitably, entanglement in sin and guilt. Entanglement in sin and guilt is not to be avoided. Maybe for you, Reverend Father, a priest becomes less easily entangled in sin and guilt than do we non-priests, a priest is doubtless better at avoiding the snares of sin and guilt than are we non-priests. A priest in his alb jumps nimbly over the snares in his way.

For us non-priests this avoidance is impossible, we non-priests entangle ourselves in sin and guilt until we can no longer find our way out.'

The sinner was right there, I thought, and suddenly felt sorry for her. With the help of my sister Maria I had so far managed to keep myself far from sin and guilt; my sister Maria had always given me a timely warning if I risked incurring sin and guilt. Before my ordination, such lapses would have been entirely possible. One is most likely to fall from the path in one's youth, in one's youth one is susceptible to all manner of temptations, particularly, of course, to temptations of the flesh. Before my ordination, female creatures similar to the sinner had occasionally approached me, with the intention of enticing me into the abyss of guilt and sin, an intention which, because I was concentrating so hard on my theological studies, I did not generally recognize as such. Had it not been for the unstinting vigilance of my sister Maria, my elder by five years, had it not been for the fact that she immediately saw through attempts at enticement, I might never have achieved ordination, I would have remained a non-priest and remained entangled in the snares of one of those female creatures.

'You look as if my ropes are a bit tight,' the sinner said and slid from the saddle of the motorcycle. 'Are my ropes cutting into your flesh? Wait, and I'll loosen them a bit. We don't want you to have blood congestion. A toxic hyperaemia wouldn't be any help to anyone at the moment.'

She skilfully began to loosen the knots in my bonds, without giving me even the tiniest opportunity to escape.

'Practical, a clove hitch,' she said. 'Very practical.' She stepped back. 'Better?' she asked. 'You're feeling better, I can see. And you should feel better in my company. If you aren't feeling well you can't listen properly.'

She sat down in front of me again and picked a daisy.

'Loves me, loves me not,' she murmured, as she plucked its petals. 'Or, as Igor used to say in his bad French, *je t'aime / un peu / beaucoup / passionnément / à la folie / pas du tout*. That was in Paris. We were sitting in the Bois de Vincennes, and Igor was plucking a daisy. I was slowly getting used to his Ukrainian or Ruthenian accent. Igor refused to shake off his Ruthenian, or Ukrainian, accent, although his accent made his French difficult to understand, and although we were, as a result, exposed to countless greater and lesser hostilities on the part of the Parisian population. The Ukrainian, or Ruthenian, language had always been exposed to hostilities, said Igor, even in the Russian Empire it had been disparaged as a lesser dialect of Russian, and sometimes it had been prohibited to print and publish books in the Ukrainian, or Ruthenian, language. If one criticized his accent, one was also criticizing his mother tongue, Ukrainian, or Ruthenian, which after all the years of oppression really needed no further criticism. In learning the French language he had made an enormous concession, he said. He understood the need to be understood in the national language but he was neither willing nor able to deny his accent.

Igor plucked the last petal of the daisy. *Pas du tout!* he cried, so that all the other Parisians sitting and lying in the grass in the warm weather looked up with a start, and jumped to his feet. *Pas du tout!* I knew you didn't love me! I knew it from the start! He took my hand, pulled me to my feet and pushed me in front of him to the nearest Métro station. A young Parisian was about to intervene but I waved him away. I was used to such performances, in all the arrondissements of Paris and sometimes in the Banlieue as well, Igor had attracted the attention of the population with performances such as these. For weeks I had been cursing the day I met Igor.

After my secluded life on the island I was drawn to the city. I travelled to Paris. Paris, another place of longing, not an island paradise but a place of longing nonetheless. You have a flood of images in your head, images of a city of love, of couples kissing on the banks of the Seine, in cafés, in front of the Hôtel de Ville, of fragile women doing smoky-voiced battle with *chansons* in bars and needing to be protected by lovers much younger than themselves because of their fragility. On every street corner you see painters, writers, sculptors, they're running around all over the place and they're talented and they're forever painting, writing and sculpting, they're forever being creative and they drink too much and die an early death and undergo the transfiguration that automatically attends it. Just as the concept of paradise includes within itself the expulsion from paradise, the word longing implies the non-fulfilment of longing. The most important thing about Paris is not the loving couples, the fragile singers, the painters, writers and sculptors, the most important thing in Paris is a parking space. Once you've arrived in Paris, the place of longing, your sole longing will be to find a parking space.

On the advice of a passing Parisian I parked my Puch bike and sidecar near the Glacière Métro station, beneath the elevated tracks. The passing Parisian said there were very few free parking spaces in the centre of Paris, and if I was lucky I would find a free parking space under the elevated tracks near the Glacière Métro station, the parking spaces there were the best. So that I could intervene in the event of an attempted theft or whatever, I immediately booked in to a cheap hotel room near the psychiatric centre of Sainte Anne, or more precisely in the Rue de la Santé, with a view of my Puch 800. The hotel was called the Hôtel d'Avenir. I took my luggage up to my room, had a shower, lay down briefly on the sagging bed and then decided to have a bite to eat in a little bistro nearby, called the Odessa, because I hadn't stopped between Dijon and Paris and was therefore hungry. As there were no tables free, the friendly waiter sat me at the same table as a man whose face I couldn't see, since he was reading a broadsheet newspaper in Cyrillic script. A candle was burning on the table, and every time the man turned a page I stopped chewing my blinis because a corner of the newspaper was edging dangerously towards the candle flame. I was too shy to warn the man. To distract myself I looked out of the open window above the table, out on to the street, and when I turned my head back to my companion hidden behind the Cyrillic script, the newspaper was blazing away. The man looked in astonishment at the burning newspaper and didn't move. I picked up my half-full glass of beer and poured it on the flames. Then the man sprang to life, and he too tried to put it out with water from the jug on the table. But the newspaper went on burning. Making a quick decision I tore it from his hand and threw it out of the window on to the pavement. Having burned the tip of the middle finger of my right hand, I put it into my mouth, and in the window there appeared a heavily made-up elderly lady with a white poodle on her arm.

What are you thinking of? the lady said furiously. What are you thinking of, throwing burning paper into the street? You could have hurt my dog! The woman stomped around on the burning bits of paper until the last little flame had gone out. Incredible, she said, cast another glance through the window and left. The man and I looked at one another and began to laugh. A beer and a vodka, yelled Igor from Odessa, and when my beer arrived I dipped my smarting middle finger into it.

A little later I drove Igor home in my sidecar. He made some tea in the pretty samovar given him by his Yalta-born grandmother, which he had brought to Paris and which he still heated with charcoal. He lived in a tiny house consisting of one big room, at the back of a tenement, right next to the Montparnasse Cemetery in the Rue d'Odessa. When he had first come to Paris he had been very homesick for Odessa, Igor said, and when he had chanced to see the street sign, he had decided to seek a residence in this street. And here he was also very close to the grave of the chess world master of many years' standing, Alexander Alekhin, who was buried in Montparnasse Cemetery. He himself had been a reasonably good chess player, as a child and an adolescent he had occasionally taken part in tournaments, and had been a great admirer of Alexander Alekhin. If his passions became too much for him, he went to the grave, adorned with a marble chessboard and a half-relief of the master, which the International Chess Association had donated ten years after his death in 1964.

I didn't quite understand what Igor meant when he spoke of these passions which were too much for him, and asked him, but he said only that the game of chess was a gift from God, it cooled the hot-bloodedness so typical of Ukrainians. When the *Kiev Evening News* had burst into flames, he added, rather apropos of nothing, he had been about to read a report of a tragedy that had taken place some days previously in Dniepropetrovsk, in which a 43-year-old bulldozer driver had buried his 46-year-old wife and her 28-year-old lover under a pile of stones, the contents of the shovel of a high-shovel bulldozer. Whether the two of them had survived he couldn't say, because the end of the article had burned away under his fingers. Do you play chess? he asked. I said my ex-fiancé from Upper Austria had taught me but I played very badly. He fetched his chessboard, with the beautiful chessmen carved in walnut by a cousin of his grandmother from Yalta, and we played for a while. But he didn't seem to be concentrating very hard and kept asking me questions about my ex-fiancé from years ago in Upper Austria.

All of a sudden he knocked over the chessmen, cried that he would wipe my Upper Austrian ex-fiancé from my memory once and for all, lifted me from the worn-out but cosy armchair, carried me in his arms up the five steps to the big brass bed which stood on a kind of pedestal, and laid me on the mattress which was stuffed with Ukrainian goose feathers. Where the Frisian had been tender, sensitive and devoted, the Ruthenian was passionate, impetuous and hot-blooded. In the big nineteenth-century brass bed with the goose-feather mattress, from the flea

82

market at the Porte de Vanves, we made love until it was light.

Igor was not only as satisfying a lover as the Frisian, he was also almost equally impoverished. He earned a few sous tearing tickets in a little cinema near the Jardin du Luxembourg, not enough to enable us to live without money worries. So I donned my Carmelite habit, bought myself a monthly ticket for the whole of the Métro network, and set off for the carriages in the rush hour. Regrettably, because of their secular tradition, the Parisians did not show the same deference to a Barefoot Carmelite, they did not show the same respect as the dyed-in-the-wool Catholic passengers on the bus in the Italian port, which meant that I had to improve my dexterity if I was not to be caught very soon.

For this reason Igor, who knew of my activities and at first had no objections to them, introduced me to one of his friends, a White Russian from Minsk, a skilful pickpocket called Sergei, who put himself at my disposal to teach me something of his art. Sergei was not only very talented at his profession, he also drew on a rich supply of experience, and I considered myself lucky to be his pupil. I made rapid progress. Unfortunately, my lessons with Sergei, who lived with his Senegalese girlfriend and her five children in the nineteenth arrondissement, came to an abrupt end when Igor surprised us in the middle of one of our practice sessions, which we usually, so as not to be disturbed by his Senegalese girlfriend and her five children, held in my room at the Hôtel d'Avenir, which I had kept on because of the free parking space which could be seen from the window.

Sergei, who was about to show me how to open the clasp of a woman's pearl necklace in the middle of a crowd without her noticing, was standing behind me for this purpose and brushing my hair aside because it was in the way. At that moment Igor walked through the door, and what he saw led him to the wrong conclusion. He first accused Sergei of being a traitor, a vulgar seducer and adulterer, and moved on from there to the tragic history of the Ukraine which had endured centuries of oppression by the Russians, and thus by him, Sergei. He need only mention the partition of 1667, the Northern War and Masepa, 1796 and the annexation of the regions on the right bank of the Dniepr and Volhynia in the wake of the Second and Third Polish Partitions, not to speak of the suppression of the Saporov Cossacks in 1775. Then he pulled him to the door by his coat lapels, threw him down the stairs and called after him that he was sorry the hotel stairs didn't have a hundred and ninety-two steps like the Potemkin steps built between 1837 and 1841 on the Nikolai Promenade in his home town of Odessa on the Black Sea.

When the Spanish dancing master in the next room, disturbed by the noise, opened his door and demanded an explanation, Igor called him a pomaded gigolo, accused him of having had his eye on me as well, and forbade him ever to talk to me again. Then he closed the door to my room, called me a whore, slapped me a couple of times and threw me down on the narrow bed. What can I say, Reverend Father? It was a night that I have never forgotten.

Igor's jealousy, as intense as it was unfounded, which I had suspected since the first evening when he had asked me all those peculiar questions about my Upper Austrian ex-fiancé, had erupted for the first time. Although the attacks came ever more frequently from now on, I couldn't bring myself to leave him as long as our nights remained what they were, a glittering firework of love. Unlike the Frisian, whose sexual interest had been in inverse proportion to his increasing melancholy, Igor's capacity for love was certainly not hampered by his jealousy; on the contrary, the more insane his rage was, the more impressive, at least initially, were his subsequent demonstrations as a lover. I fell deeper and deeper into a dilemma which was finally to prove insoluble.

To my erotic dilemma was added a financial one, after Igor

watched me stealing in a Métro train on line four between the Porte d'Orléans and the Porte de Clignancourt. I had suggested that he get an idea of my professional activity in this way. When he saw me pulling a wallet out of the back pocket of a lanky young black man, he leapt to his feet and began to make a scene in the middle of my work, which of course required the utmost concentration. Had the Métro not pulled in to St Sulpice at that moment, we wouldn't have had a chance to make our getaway. The passengers on the Métro, enraged at me and my disguise, would doubtless have grabbed me and handed me over to the police. Even when we were running through the corridors of the Métro, Igor did not stop hurling his accusations at me. What kind of job was that? he cried breathlessly. What kind of occupation was that for a woman, constantly coming into the closest contact with male buttocks? The money he made by tearing tickets was enough for us both after all.

While we were running across the square in front of the Church of St Sulpice, he cried imploringly that the only possible way of keeping me from returning to this repellent occupation lay in marrying me. As long as I would agree to a marriage in the Russian Orthodox rite, he would be happy to do this, and it was time for me to move in with him in the Rue d'Odessa and keep house for him. When I voiced my objections to this suggestion for reasons of principle, he became so furious that he dragged me to the fountain in the middle of the square in front of the church and ducked my head in the water-filled basin, a kind of behaviour which attracted the attention of the inhabitants of the *quartier*, who had never before been confronted with the sight of a Barefoot Carmelite having her head ducked in the basin of the fountain in front of the Church of St Sulpice. A Ukrainian in exile who chanced to be passing, and in whose restaurant Igor had briefly worked, brought Igor to his senses by reminding him of his duties as a Ukrainian patriot. My wimple drenched, I followed Igor to his little house behind the tenement on the Rue d'Odessa, and into the big brass bed.

Igor's veto on the practice of my occupation as a thief on the Métro led to such a decline in our finances that I was constantly forced to think of new ways of acquiring money, and finally approached Igor with a suggestion. What would he think if I transferred my activity to the cinema where he worked? I asked. The darkness during the screenings would favourably influence the practice of my craft, and at the same time I would be under his control, which would certainly diminish his jealousy.

Igor thought about my suggestion for a while and finally agreed, on condition that I restrict myself to women, to which I had no objections since it would be impossible to take wallets out of the back trouser pockets of men who were sitting down in the cinema, as opposed to standing up in the Métro. He had no difficulty in getting free tickets for me. The first film which gave me an opportunity to prove my skill was *Rear Window*, with James Stewart and Grace Kelly. I left my nun's habit in the hotel, as the darkness imposed by my new surroundings rendered disguise unnecessary. Before going into the cinema I closely inspected the women waiting in the queue, hoping that the keen eyesight I had inherited from my father's side of the family would help me to recognize the more affluent among them. Walking into the auditorium I noticed where the ladies sat down, so as to relieve them, in the course of the screening, of their jewellery, of their handbags, which were sometimes hung casually over the back of the seat or placed on the seat next to them, or of the wallets inside them.

The shift in my field of activity proved definitely advantageous, and within a short time we had recovered from our financial straits. Because Igor kept his eye on me at all times his jealousy also improved, although I occasionally had to deny the insinuation that I was using the darkness to push more closely past the knees and thighs of the male cinema-goers than was absolutely necessary, or, by politely asking them to let me past, making them stand up, which gave me the opportunity to come into contact not only with their knees and thighs but with the whole length of their bodies.

I generally managed to distract him from his concerns, but sometimes I couldn't keep him from brooding gloomily, getting drunk on vodka and finally insulting me most brutally, partly in French, partly in Ukrainian or Ruthenian. The next day he always regretted what he had said or done, begged me for forgiveness and immediately set off for the grave of the former chess world master Alexander Alekhin, to hold mute conversations with the spirit of the late lamented and have a game of mental chess with him. He returned from the cemetery as if transformed, saying that nothing assuaged the Ukrainian passions better than a game of chess.

My life with Igor could have continued to run on reasonably satisfactory lines, we could have gone on being useful to one another in the same workplace, had I not been gripped by the passion of cinephilia. While I was plying my trade in the dark, I started silently speaking the dialogue with my lips – since the Hitchcock festival had been running for a long time I already knew much of it by heart. Increasingly often I would cast a sidelong glance at the screen and what was happening there. If Igor's cinema near the Jardin du Luxembourg had not been showing the films of Hitchcock but French love stories, Czech animations or Oscar-nominated American wide-screen epics, my concentration would never have lapsed, I would never have succumbed to the temptation of taking my attention from the act of stealing and turning it towards the screen. But Hitchcock's films began to draw me into their spell. It was not only the excitement of the plot, the believable depiction of the psychological abysses of the characters that enticed me into casting these sidelong glances; more particularly it was Cary Grant and James Stewart whose attractive appearance enchanted me and magnetically attracted my gaze.

Reverend Father, I gladly accept the bulk of the guilt for the spectacular failure of my career as a cinema thief. But Igor's morbid jealousy, which excluded me from contact of any kind with other males, also contributed to it. Igor's morbid jealousy forbade even the most innocuous contemplation of males in his presence, which was why, in the darkness of the cinema auditorium where no one could check the direction of my gaze, I satisfied that blameless need, a need which, in all innocence, became ever more uncontrollable, until in the end the owner of the cinema threw me out. Fortunately he didn't hand me over to the arm of the law.

Because of my frequent glances at the screen, I had begun to fumble occasionally, to miss the moment to pounce, and it wasn't long before a lady furiously tore her bag out of my hand when I failed to take it quickly enough. I mumbled something about making a mistake, an apology that the lady eventually accepted. But the next lapse of concentration came when a robust American woman in her mid-fifties grabbed my hand as it slipped gently into her handbag, held on to it with an iron grip and dragged me past the horrified Igor, out of the auditorium and in front of the cinema owner, who did not hand me over to the police out of consideration for my relationship with Igor but told him the next day to start looking for a new job.

Because we were both unemployed, Igor grew more and more irritable, and his control over me grew more rigid. In my despair I confided in my neighbour, the Spanish dancing master, who gave me the sympathy that I longed for. During a hasty, muttered conversation on our landing it struck me that he had an interesting profile and a sympathetic smile. The fact that Igor's unpredictability rendered any contact, however superficial, with the dancing master extremely dangerous made that contact seem more and more desirable, and in my dreams the profile of Cary Grant was soon superimposed with the profile of the Spaniard from Santiago de Compostela, who had lived in Paris for five years.

Reverend Father, I had not been aware that the inexorable decline had already begun. Igor was drinking more and more, and when the waiter in the Odessa bistro wished me *bon appétit* one evening and gave me a friendly smile as he placed a plate of borscht in front of me, Igor lashed out and knocked the plate from his hand, an unconsidered reaction that had us barred from the restaurant. This made Igor so furious that he punched me in the ribs on the way home, whereupon I fell over and broke my middle finger. I went to the outpatients department of the Hôpital de la Pitié, where they knew me and put my finger in a splint. The next day Igor appeared contrite and meek with a bunch of daisies in the Hôtel d'Avenir, leading me to conclude that he had had a conversation and a game of chess with Alexander Alekhin. We spent passionate hours on the narrow hotel bed, hours only made slightly less unforgettable by the fact that the Spanish dancing master was practising some new flamenco steps at the same time, which rather diminished my capacity for self-abandon since the staccato tap of the high heels of his dancing shoes was clearly audible in our room.

Towards evening I accompanied Igor to the door of the hotel, and when we were walking past the hotel porter in a close embrace, the porter addressed me and handed me a registered letter from the mother of the Frisian, from Uithuizermeeden in north-east Holland, asking if I knew what had happened to her son's silver cigarette case. The silver cigarette case that her son had inherited from his father, her husband, who had died eight years, nine months and thirteen days before, from a tick bite on a trip to Austria, should have been in her son's estate, but it was not in his estate. Igor did not know the sender of the letter, whose Christian name was abbreviated, or the language it was written in, which was unfamiliar to him, and this led to a repeated attack of jealousy in the little hotel foyer, which held, apart from us and the hotel porter, three wealthy hotel guests from Guernsey who always stayed at the Hôtel d'Avenir when they came to Paris on business. When these three guests protested at Igor's performance, serious consequences ensued. The following day, when I entered the hotel after another brief visit to the outpatients department of the Hôpital de la Pitié with my right arm in a sling – Igor had dislocated it in the street after the unpleasant scene – the hotel porter waved me over and quietly informed me that Paris was full of hotels in the same price range as the Hôtel d'Avenir, and I would certainly have no difficulty finding a new room.

There I was, unemployed and homeless, and I had no option but to move in with Igor in the Rue d'Odessa. He interpreted my expressed refusal to marry him, on grounds of principle, as meaning that I wanted to keep certain erotic freedoms for myself, and his suspicion grew boundless. At first he allowed me to put on my Carmelite habit again and go in search of new sources of money in the library of Ste Geneviève near the Panthéon, in the British Council library and the huge reference library in the Centre Beaubourg. Readers often left their places to take a book down from the shelf, to put another one back, or to put a question to the staff, which gave me the opportunity to have a quick look through the bags they had left at their seats.

This new occupation did not bring in a great deal as the readers were generally underfunded students, but at least I had the feeling that I wasn't completely dependent on Igor. I had left my Puch 800 under the elevated tracks near the Station Glacière, and when, some two weeks after leaving the Hôtel d'Avenir, I went to collect it and park it in front of Igor's tiny house behind the tenement block, I found a half-wilted bunch of carnations and a letter from the Spanish dancing master in the sidecar, asking me to contact him. He had grown used to my presence in the Hôtel d'Avenir and missed me a great deal, he wrote. The idea that I was at the mercy of my violent boyfriend gave him sleepless nights, and since I had left, my face, my cool blue eyes, my high forehead and the little round mole an inch above the corner of my mouth had been constantly in his mind.

Reverend Father, I read this letter with trembling hands, because in my mind I often ran my fingertips gently along his profile. I drove my Puch 800 to the Rue d'Odessa and parked it in front of the tiny house. Incapable of throwing away the half-wilted bunch of carnations, I took it out of the sidecar and put it in a vase, whereupon Igor, sitting in the room with a half-empty bottle of vodka, immediately became suspicious and tormented me with questions about where it had come from. He assumed that a student researching in one of the three libraries I frequented had had his eye on me and had given me the flowers as a present. In a rage he smashed the full vodka glass on the wall above the big brass bed, pushed me to the bed and threw me on the vodka-drenched goose-feather mattress. It was not an unforgettable night. Because of his excessive alcohol consumption, Igor's qualities as a lover had been in decline for some time; more and more often he would fall asleep in the middle of our love-play.'

Magdalena broke off and rapidly sliced the air. 'A fly,' she said. 'I've caught a fly. We must feed the praying mantis. If we don't feed it, it will die on us.' She took the jam jar, unscrewed the lid, threw in the captured fly and immediately put the lid back on. Then she watched as the fly was devoured by the praying mantis. It was slowly growing dark, and I had some difficulty clearly seeing my immediate surroundings through the heavily tinted lenses of the sunglasses.

'It was less and less a case of sparkling fireworks,' the sinner continued. 'If brightly coloured rockets, wonderful orange palms, purple stars, glittering green bursts of fire had still soared into the sky during our nights together, I would never have decided, after a not very lucrative afternoon in the library of Ste Geneviève, to drive to the Hôtel d'Avenir on my Puch

800 wearing my Carmelite habit and seek out the Spanish dancing master. I briefly nodded to the hotel porter, who didn't recognize me and, out of a certain respect for a nun, didn't ask who I was going to visit. As I stood at Pablo's door, my heart was beating wildly. I knocked, he opened, and without a word, without asking any questions about my unusual attire, he wrapped his arms round me and then slowly removed my habit, one item after another. First he stripped off my white scapulary, then he loosened my belt, then he gently pulled my tunic over my head, and finally he led me to the bed, beneath a still from Carlos Saura's film *Carmen*. The hours that followed consoled me for Igor's increasing inadequacy as a lover.

It's growing dark,' Magdalena said. 'I'll take off your sunglasses. You don't need them any more. Sorry I didn't think of it before.' She stood up, walked over to me and took the sunglasses off my nose. Then she stretched and yawned. 'Twilight is tiring,' she said. 'What I'd really like to do is lie down and sleep, but I'm sure you want to know how things with Igor developed, don't you?'

I opened my eyes wider and nodded to assure her of my interest in the ending of this episode. In the meantime I had recovered from the little shock her story about the death of the Frisian had given me. Of course there was no excuse for her behaviour but no one could seriously claim that her acquaintance with the Frisian had brought her a great deal of happiness. Divine providence did not seem terribly well-disposed towards her, because clearly the relationship with Igor was heading towards an unedifying conclusion. My fear of the woman, my horror at her actions, was mingled with a hint of sympathy.

'Although Pablo implored me not to go back to Igor, since he had a sense that something terrible was going to happen, as darkness fell I donned my nun's habit once again and drove my Puch 800 to the Rue d'Odessa where Igor, already completely drunk, was waiting for me. Reverend Father, it would have been better had I taken Pablo's advice, but despite all the scenes, despite all Igor's maltreatment of me, I still felt a degree of loyalty towards him. I had not completely abandoned hope that our nights might once again become what they had been, a sparkling firework of love, but this was an illusion, as I finally realized when I saw Igor sitting dead drunk at the table. When he saw me he slowly rose to his feet, supporting himself with both hands on the table. He mumblingly took me to task, accused me once again of being a whore and reproached me with betraying him with the student who gave me the bunch of carnations. His attempt to hit me in the face with his fist was unsuccessful, because in his drunkenness he missed and only brushed my left ear. One final spark of hope glimmered within me when he pushed me to the bed and threw himself upon me, but within a minute he lay on top of me, heavy and snoring.

Reverend Father, when I was lying there like that, the motionless body on top of me, the vodka-bloated face beside me, something happened deep inside me, something utterly detached from my conscious will. It was a sort of duplication. One part of me stayed lying underneath Igor, apathetic, hopeless and completely broken, while another freed itself from Igor's embrace, unnoticed by him, and went to the table, on which one empty and one nearly full vodka bottle stood next to a burning candle. The candle was one of many consecrated candles that Igor's grandmother from Yalta sent to Paris from time to time, and which came from the little Russian Orthodox chapel in which she used to pray for the spiritual salvation of her grandson, far from the Ukraine. They were long white wax candles which were supposed to protect Igor from jinxes and lightning, and from death by fire or water.

The vodka came from his grandmother's cousin, the same cousin who had carved the chessmen. Each month a box of carefully packed vodka bottles would arrive. The alcohol content of this vodka, illegally distilled by Igor's cousin who

owned a farm on the great bend of the Dniepr, was almost
eighty per cent, and I had sometimes used it to *flamber* the rice
Trauttmansdorff with which I occasionally spoiled Igor. The
part of myself that had freed itself from Igor's heavy body took
the almost full vodka bottle and the burning candle from the
table and walked back to Igor with the stilted, automatic steps
of a robot. Then the human-machine part poured the vodka
over the bed and over Igor, who opened his mouth even in
his sleep to catch some of the drink, and brought the candle
flame into contact with the fringes of the one hundred per
cent acrylic bedcover on which we had so often made love.

Before my Frankenstein half turned mechanically round and
walked from the little house behind the tenement, it saw flames
catching the bedcover on which Igor and its second, apathetic,
despairing half lay. The Frankenstein half took the key from
the lock, closed the door behind it and locked up. It sat
on the saddle of the bike and sidecar, looked over to the
window, a square glowing red in the darkness, started the
engine and drove off towards the Hôtel d'Avenir. At the end
of the boulevard, round, big and orange, was the full moon.'

Magdalena fell silent. She sat in front of me in the darkness,
I could only see her outline, which reminded me of a squatting
Indian. The end of her story had shaken me, and made
me frightened once again of this woman, of her alarming
divisions. Examples of this kind of loss of consciousness
were not unknown to me, it seemed not unlike the ecstatic
states of the saints, the trance states of some nuns of the
late Middle Ages, but I couldn't remember an instance that
had had such terrible consequences, apart from rare cases of
self-immolation for religious reasons, in which perpetrator and
victim were one and the same. When I thought of Igor and his
behaviour, I wondered for a moment whether he had really
been an innocent victim, but then brushed the thought aside
and mentally crossed myself.

'Pablo was very happy to see me. Although I hadn't been

aware of it, I had brought with me the vodka bottle containing the remainder of the vodka, and the half-burned consecrated candle, and we drank to our new happiness by candlelight.'

It was now so dark that I could only hear Magdalena's voice, and could hardly see her outline.

'I'm not trying to justify myself,' the voice said after a long pause. 'I'm not trying to justify myself, Reverend Father, but I've never wanted anything but love. If you look for love and get something which you at first think is love and which at first really is love, but which turns inexorably into something that no longer has the least to do with love, the consequence is disappointment. If the face of someone you took to be your saviour, your ideal, turns increasingly into a caricature, so great is the disappointment that you begin to hate the face. If you expect understanding and meet with incomprehension, the disappointment becomes a desire for vengeance. At the beginning you have the wish for love, at the end the desire to annihilate the former object of love, who is now the object of hate. There is nothing more dangerous than a woman whose longing for love has been unremittingly disappointed. Such a woman is more to be feared than any brainwashed terrorist, any religious fanatic, if you understand what I mean. I could say a lot more on this subject, Reverend Father, we could talk about this topic for hours. But now I'm tired, and we're going to sleep.'

I watched the shadow move towards the Puch bike and sidecar and come back with a large object. It was very quiet, the gurgling of the water in the little stream, the chirping of a cricket the only sounds. Occasionally the little greenish light of a glow-worm swayed through the air. Something that felt like a blanket was spread over my legs. I heard a rustling sound and saw the shadow stretching out on the ground beside me. When a bird suddenly flew squawking from the tip of the robinia, a head pressed close to my hip. I wished I could put my hand on the strawberry-blonde curls.

I woke in the middle of the night, startled by a terrible nightmare. I was sitting in the sidecar looking up at Magdalena who was sitting at the handlebars in the habit of the Barefoot Carmelites. We were in a bare mountain landscape, on a steep uphill road. To the left, rocks covered with fine nets against falling boulders soared skywards, to the right was a deep abyss, with no protecting rail along the road. Magdalena had her pink Walkman on her head and was singing *The Well-Tempered Clavier* loudly and tunelessly. She was driving very fast, her nun's veil flapping in the wind, and when she took corners I felt dizzy. From time to time she interrupted her discordant singing and laughed a laugh that echoed through the rocky landscape, giving me a start in the sidecar every time. Her features changed from one minute to the next, became more and more distorted, more and more ugly, reflecting more and more intensely the insanity, the rage for destruction within her. I was very frightened, and cried out that she was going far too fast for me, begging her to ease off on the speed if she didn't want to risk an accident. But she couldn't hear me, her pink headphones seemed to be getting bigger and bigger, and now even I could hear the music of Bach's *Well-Tempered Clavier* roaring through the barren mountain landscape. All of a sudden I saw that Magdalena was doing something with her right hand to the link between the motorbike and the sidecar. No! I cried when I saw the sidecar coming away from the motorbike and hurtling towards the abyss. Then I woke up, with the terrible laughter and Bach's roaring music still ringing in my ears.

I took a deep breath and slowly calmed down in the quiet, starry, early summer night. Beside me I heard the sinner's even breathing. I didn't know what time it was exactly, perhaps about three or four in the morning. It was cool, but the blanket over my legs protected me against the cold of the night. I tried to move my hands, still bound against my back. Since Magdalena had loosened the knots in the faded hemp rope a little, some of the feeling had come back to them; but my whole body hurt because of my uncomfortable position. I tried to pray, appealing to God to show me a way out of my hopeless situation. But God, hitherto fairly reliable when it came to listening to my prayers, stayed as mute as a fish. I noticed that my respect for him was declining, that his silence was beginning to irritate me. Be so good as to help me, I heard myself saying to him despite my gag, it's your duty, after all. As a priest I'm under your direct protection, I'm closer to you than other people are, so I also enjoy certain privileges, preferential treatment on your part. What about the lightning you use to punish your enemies? Brew up an early summer storm and hurl a stroke of lightning at this sinner who is holding your servant against his will. Just after I had uttered this wish I retracted it, because if you considered the thing rationally the lightning wouldn't just kill Magdalena but me as well, since she was right next to me, since she had pressed her head to my hip.

I gave God further suggestions about rescuing me, but he didn't act on them and maintained an embarrassed if not a helpless silence. I sat in the darkness, looked at the glittering stars above me, and felt the cracked bark of the robinia behind me. The cracked bark! Maybe that was a possibility. I began moving my fettered hands up and down against the bark a little, in the hope that this might roughen the faded hemp rope and finally tear it. I had to be careful, because the sinner's curly head was at my hip. I rubbed and rubbed the rope against the robinia bark, a very tiring exercise. I couldn't give up or go to sleep, chafing through the hemp rope was my last chance. A narrow red strip was appearing at the horizon, a bird was beginning to sing. The world was reappearing slowly from the darkness and assuming solid outlines. I saw that there was a plaid blanket over my knees, and that Magdalena was sleeping next to me in a sleeping bag. She sighed quietly, shifted even closer to me, laid her head on my groin and wrapped an arm round my thigh. This closeness, the weight of her head, the warmth of her hand, which I could feel through the dalmatic, through the alb, disconcerted me somewhat, provoked in me impulses of a sensual kind inappropriate in a priest. Unsettled by this sign of reprehensible animality I began to chafe violently against the trunk of the robinia with my fettered hands, so violently that the sinner sat up from her sleep, rubbed her eyes and immediately understood what I was on the point of doing.

'Well, look at this,' she said. 'Reverend Father is making an escape attempt. That isn't nice of Reverend Father. That isn't nice at all. Trying to make off like this before confession's over. I'm nowhere near the end of my confession. I would have thought my confession would be of interest to you, all your facial expressions seemed to point to your profound involvement. In the end it doesn't matter whether you are interested in my confession or not, whether you are profoundly involved or not, interest and profound involvement don't come into it. As a Catholic priest it is your task, your duty and obligation to listen. The father confessor from Oxfordshire that I mentioned at the beginning tried to get away from my story by going to sleep, and you're thinking of escape. That isn't nice at all. Let's see how far you got with your escape attempt.'

The sinner stood up and had a look at the faded hemp rope. 'In fact, if you hadn't woken me up you'd have done it before long. Most regrettable, all this, most regrettable for you. You'll understand that I have to tighten the conditions under which you're held here. After a failed escape attempt any prisoner is subjected to tighter conditions of imprisonment. Because of the attention and sympathy indicated by your facial expressions, the obvious excitement with which you have been following my confession, I had already decided to remove your gag very soon, and thus give you the opportunity to comment on my exposition. But as the circumstances have changed in such a distressing manner, this gag removal will not take place. On the contrary' – and with these words she pulled the black Kashiyama body stocking even tighter, with a jolt that tore my head back – 'on the contrary, the gag will not be removed as planned, the gag will be tightened. And the knot will not be loosened, as I planned yesterday, the knot will be reinforced.'

Having said these words Magdalena went to the Puch bike and sidecar, and from one of the panniers she took a tangle of green, with which she walked back to me. 'I've got another few yards of nylon washing line. Nylon washing line is considerably more reliable as a fetter than hemp rope.' She unrolled the tangle, wrapped the line round me and round the robinia trunk at the same time, and circled the trunk and me a number of times with the line in her hand, so that I finally sat bound tight to the trunk. She tied the rope and cut off the excess with a little pair of pliers which she took from one of the many pockets in her jump suit. She walked up to me with the excess rope, laid it playfully round my neck and pulled it tight until I could hardly breathe. Then she loosened her grip, took the rope from my neck and rolled it up.

'I may have to tie another hangman's noose,' she said, as if to herself. Then she turned back to me. 'It will depend entirely on you and your future behaviour whether I have to resort to radical measures or not. Another escape attempt could force me to use this little tangle, which I shall put back in the pannier for the time being, for the purpose that I have just demonstrated. I would prefer not to have to take such a step, but if it came to it I would not baulk at it.'

She stowed the tangle in the pannier and came back with a pear and another piece of apple pie. She took a large bite out of the pear.

'*Gute Luise*,' she said, 'an old variety, one of the best varieties of pear. My grandmother had a *Gute Luise* tree in her orchard. You don't often find this variety these days. When I was driving through the Lesach Valley towards East Tyrol a few days ago, I bought a bag of *Gute Luise* from a farmer's boy at the side of the road, out of sentimentality, so to speak, in memory of my grandmother and her orchard.'

She ate the pear down to the core, threw the stem away and held the slice of apple pie under my nose. I was very hungry, and the smell of cinnamon made my mouth water.

'I would probably have shared the apple pie with you,' she said. 'For breakfast I would very probably have allowed you to have half of the piece of apple pie. As things stand now, obviously I won't do that, anyone could understand it would be idiotic in the circumstances to share the apple pie with you. A poem, an apple pie like this,' she said, and quickly devoured it.

'By the way, I've noticed that you look like Pablo from the side, your profile is not dissimilar to Pablo's. I don't suppose you have a bit of Spanish blood in your veins? Don't look so surprised, it's not impossible. For example, one of your forefathers could have undertaken a pilgrimage to Santiago de Compostela. The whole of Europe, the whole Catholic world used to make the journey to Santiago de Compostela, as you doubtless know. Why could this pious East Tyrolean forefather on this pilgrimage, somewhere near Santander, perhaps, or around Oviedo, not have met a pretty Spanish girl and set up a family with her in St Jakob in Defereggental? That, or something like it, might explain why it is that your profile is like Pablo's.

Anyway, Pablo also told me a lot about Santiago de Compostela and the bones of Saint James the Elder, which are supposed to have been found there in the year AD 830 or thereabouts. His favourite meal was Coquille Saint Jacques, a shellfish recipe served in a scallop shell, the emblem of pilgrims on their way to Santiago de Compostela. On the second day of our new happiness I bought two of these shellfish at the market that takes place three times a week in the Place Monge, and cooked them on the hotplate that Pablo had smuggled into the hotel room in the Hôtel d'Avenir. For want of a tablecloth

I spread my white Carmelite cloak on the little round table to give the meal a festive touch, put on it the candle stump left over from Igor's consecrated candle, his vodka bottle with about three inches of vodka left in it, as well as the two plates of shellfish. Pablo, who came home tired from his flamenco course, was delighted by the surprise. We ate and drank and then lay down on the narrow hotel bed where we had to stay for several days as we very soon realized I had been sold bad shellfish.

Have you ever had food poisoning from shellfish, Reverend Father? Food poisoning from shellfish is extremely unpleasant, it involves vomiting, diarrhoea, cold sweats, shivering and a weak pulse. Our new happiness was considerably restricted by this attack of food poisoning from shellfish, and made rather suspicious by my previous negative erotic experiences I wondered with trepidation what curious incidents fate held in store for me this time. But when I saw Pablo's haggard green face I felt great tenderness and affection for him, and perked up again. He had been more seriously affected than I had, he was very sensitive where the quality of shellfish was concerned. We called a doctor who forbade Pablo to eat mussels, cockles, oysters and scallops until further notice. After three days we left the hotel, still very weak and clutching the banisters, to go shopping, and when we passed the hotel porter he recognized me and banned me from the establishment again. Pablo showed solidarity and stoutly informed the hotel porter that he would not stay in a hotel that put unprotected young women out on the street for a mere trifle. The hotel porter said that it would not be a great loss if he left the hotel because for over five years the other hotel guests had had their peace disturbed by the clattering of his high heels and the loud music coming out of his room at all hours of the day and night.

We dragged ourselves exhaustedly through the streets. A kind of nostalgia sometimes drew Pablo to the Rue St Jacques, one of the oldest streets in Paris, which had in former times been the starting point for the pilgrimages to Santiago de Compostela. There we saw a sign with the inscription "Concierge wanted" pinned to the doorway of a building. We walked through the doorway into the little cobbled courtyard of the building, asked for the owner of the building and knocked on her door. She was a woman of about sixty from Montpellier with a pug, who gave us an extravagant welcome, with a glass of lemon liqueur from the south of France, and immediately offered us the concierge's job. She had already seen a number of applicants, she said, but their faces hadn't appealed to her. But when she had seen the two of us standing on her doorstep she had known straight away that we had suitable faces for a concierge. Pablo in particular had a suitable face for a concierge, she said, and smiled at him. Then she asked him whether he could carry out minor repairs to the building. Pablo said he could, his father, a plumber from Santiago de Compostela, had been a very practical man and had taught him a few things in this field, although he had sadly died in a sanatorium for alcoholics. Madame Martel from Montpellier took her pug on her arm, stroked him, expressed her sorrow at the death of Pablo's father and delight at Pablo's skills as a craftsman, and said we could move into the concierge apartment straight away; because of the high standards she set on faces the apartment had been empty for some time.

So the very same day we moved into the little concierge apartment, and the Puch sidecar bike served us well as a means of transport. Madame Martel allowed me to park it in the courtyard of the building. Pablo, who was often tormented by homesickness for Santiago de Compostela, just as Igor was often overwhelmed by homesickness for Odessa, was happy to live in the Rue St Jacques as it gave him the feeling that he could set off homewards at any time, as the pilgrims had set off for his home town in former times. As a woman from Austria, this homesickness was incomprehensible to me. I wasn't homesick for Austria, if one overlooked the quite specific homesickness for Austrian baking, which was not homesickness in the true sense of the word. Just as Igor had chosen to surround himself with other expatriate Ukrainians, Pablo surrounded himself predominantly with expatriate Galicians; just as Igor had always sought out Ukrainian restaurants, Pablo was constantly in search of Galician restaurants; just as Igor had been drawn to all the places where Ukrainian music could be heard, Pablo was drawn to the places where Galician music could be heard; just as Igor had inquired about Ukrainian newspapers at every kiosk, at every newsstand Pablo inquired about Galician newspapers.

In my case it was quite different. If I chanced to hear an Austrian dialect in the street, I instantly fell into a bad mood and cast a furious glance at the person who had used this dialect, as I was irritated by the clumsiness, the vulgarity of the tone of most Austrian dialects. I avoided expatriate Austrians and Austrian institutions abroad like the plague, as both the average expatriate Austrian and the average Austrian consulate or cultural institute, the average Austrian embassy or trade delegation are generally distinguished by a spectacular ignorance and blasé attitude, a striking indifference and lack of interest. It didn't occur to me to ask for an Austrian newspaper at a kiosk; I was glad not to have to see the pitiful or, rather, worthless figures that dominate the Austrian public arena, or to have to learn anything about the lamentable or, rather, sinister events in Austrian political life. In a way I envied people like Igor and Pablo the love, the pride that they felt for their country. I had never felt pride or love for Austria, Austria had never managed to fill me with love or pride, rather it had often filled me with rage, disappointment, contempt, grief or at least with shame. So I found Pablo's homesickness for Galicia partly incomprehensible, partly touching and enviable. Basically I wished I was homesick for Austria, but I wasn't homesick for Austria.

The following months with Pablo in the little concierge's apartment were a period of initially unspoilt, gradually slightly spoilt and finally very seriously spoilt happiness. At first I was glad to be able to hang my Carmelite habit in the cupboard, because our income as concierges and the regular income from Pablo's lessons meant that we had no money worries. My chief responsibilities consisted in cleaning the staircases of the two entrances and the cobbled courtyard, and in the morning distributing post in the building, pushing it through a gap under the doors or ringing the doorbell if it was bulky. I also had to ensure that no suspicious characters entered the building, and to be available to answer inquiries. This kind of work appealed to me, and it also gave me the opportunity to improve my knowledge of the French language with many little conversations with the residents of the building on the various landings. Pablo gave his dancing lessons and practised at home, which gave no one cause to complain, as the old Parisian building had thick walls and the concierge apartment was on the ground floor where the stamping of the flamenco shoes would only have disturbed one of the *clochards* who repeatedly took up lodging in the cellar until I flushed them out and chased them from the building.

Also living in the building was an elderly widower who had fled from Budapest in 1956 and for decades had been a cemetery attendant at Montparnasse Cemetery. I liked chatting to him, he was a very cheerful man for his age. He told me about his day in the cemetery, about all the cats in the cemetery grounds, which he couldn't bear. Everyone wanted to see Baudelaire's grave, he said, they all wanted to know the way to the tall gravestone with the bas-relief. And it wasn't his grave, it was just a memorial; Baudelaire was in a family plot on the other side of the cemetery. But recently people were increasingly asking for Sartre, Sartre was in fashion with visitors to cemeteries. As far as he was concerned, he found Baudelaire repellent if a genius, while Sartre he found merely repellent, even more repellent than the cemetery cats. I could not imagine the kind of oddballs who visited the cemetery, said Monsieur Szabó, in cemeteries you met the most peculiar people, cemeteries were a collecting tank for the most diverse kinds of weirdos.

Among others, one young man had often visited the grave of a former Russian chess world master, sometimes even set out chessmen on the chessboard that adorned the grave, and played chess with himself, or with the dead man. Alekhin always wins, Bela, the young man with the strong Slavic accent, with whom he had after a period of time had a paternal relationship, almost one of friendship, had said in resignation, I never win against Alekhin. He had not stood in the way of the eccentric young man, who lived right next to the cemetery, although his conduct fundamentally offended against the order of the cemetery, said Monsieur Szabó, and today he was glad of this, because a few days ago he had read in a newspaper that the young man had come to a terrible end. He had burned to death in his bed, and had only been identified with difficulty. Ah well, he added, he had drunk a lot, and that would have been the indirect or direct cause of death. Recently he had often come to the grave of the chess world master with a vodka bottle, his conversations with him had grown increasingly loud, and sometimes he had poured the vodka over the grave and begun to sing or cry. To Monsieur Szabó's questions he had not given precise answers, only saying that women were not to be trusted, they constantly had other men in mind, and if you gave them the opportunity they would have no hesitation in getting involved in the crudest way with those men. Ah well, Monsieur Szabó said, a sad story. But now I must give fresh water to my goldfinch.

If I ever gave a thought to Igor's death I did so only very rarely and for a few moments, because I had started a new life with Pablo. If the Frisian had been distinguished by tenderness, Igor by hot-bloodedness, it was his sense of rhythm that made

Pablo a good lover. If you were familiar with the sexual act, which of course you cannot be, you would agree with my claim that rhythmic harmony is of central importance for it. As a dancer, what's more a specialist in Spanish and Latin American dances, Pablo had a strongly developed sense of rhythm, and as his lover I was able to enjoy this natural talent of his. Dance and the sexual act are closely related to one another, as will be clear to you even if you can demonstrate no practical experience in one sphere or the other. Just as a couple only enjoy dancing if they manage to achieve rhythmical agreement, a couple can only enjoy the sexual act if rhythmical harmony exists. At first I was admittedly rather clumsy, my sense of rhythm both in dancing and during the sexual act was somewhat underdeveloped. But after Pablo had put the metronome beside the bed, my sense of rhythm improved at a stroke. The regular ticking of the metronome accompanied our nights of love and helped us to reach unsuspected heights of ecstasy within a few weeks. Normally Pablo introduced our nights by putting on a CD with Spanish or Latin American dance music and, with a little bow, invited me to dance. Dancing with him was wonderful, you couldn't feel your own weight, you floated, you melted away. Once Pablo felt that this prelude had lasted long enough to put us in the mood, he danced closer and closer to our French double bed and bent my body so far back that it was almost lying on the bed. It was joy to yield, and slowly sink back on the bed.

During this fulfilling initial period I thought nothing of the fact that Pablo often received calls from women who visited his dance courses. Pablo worked in a dance school in the Marais where he taught the Latin American dances rumba, samba, paso doble and cha-cha-cha, as laid down in the world sport programme of the International Dance Sport Council in 1963, in contrast to the standard dances, but sometimes he also gave private tango, bolero, fandango and flamenco lessons. It was only natural that a lady who had been practising at home after the lesson and didn't know where to take it from there should call him up to ask him for advice. Even when one of these callers asked me, in a curiously brusque tone, who I was anyway, to which I replied that I was Pablo's longtime companion, even when she laughed loudly at this and put the receiver down I was not worried in the slightest.

Pablo was also very busy, because when he wasn't dancing he was carrying out repairs on various parts of the building, which made us very popular in the building. What a skilful young man I had, said the young fashion designer, always dressed in black and with matchstick-short hair, who lived in a little studio on the third storey; the Art Deco lamp she'd found in this delightful little boutique near the Place Vendôme, he'd fitted it to the ceiling in no time. Enviable, she added with a mysterious, almost sad look from her big dark eyes, it must be enviable to have a man like that. In her job she practically only ever met men who didn't know how to hammer a nail into the wall, apart from the fact that half of them were gay and the rest bisexual. Perhaps I could tell my husband there was something wrong with her hot water tank, the water was so hot that she had scalded her hand two days before. She showed me her left hand, bandaged with gauze. She was sure he could sort out the minor fault in a matter of minutes. It would be wonderful if he had a moment in the evening, it could even be late, it could even be midnight, she didn't mind. She glanced at her hand. How she would finish her work on the burgundy evening dress in time for the big fashion show she really didn't know, she said. Such a chance, this fashion show, such a chance for her career. Then, with the words, "A wonderful man!" she went down the stairs. I informed Pablo of the fashion designer's wishes, whereupon he murmured something about impertinent residents who just exploit you, but at about eleven o'clock at night he went to her studio. A little later I looked out of the window to see if

107

there was a full moon. As I did so, my eyes fell by chance on the lighted window of the fashion designer, and the silhouette of a couple dancing in a close embrace. I turned away abruptly from this phantasm of betrayal.

When I left the flat two days later to go shopping I saw Pablo, who was just returning from his lessons, bending the fashion designer's graceful torso over the banisters. As soon as he saw me, he immediately drew the torso upright and I acted as if I hadn't noticed anything. I assumed he had told her a little about his job and, in reply to her question, shown her one of the basic tango steps. Nevertheless I felt my jealousy awakening. But I told myself it was ridiculous, I knew from personal experience how one could be tormented by unfounded jealousy, unfounded jealousy was the beginning of the end. All suspicion fled when Pablo put on a CD of Argentinian tangos in the evening, danced with me through the living room and gave me the feeling of being as light as a feather. Our dancing pleasure was briefly disturbed by two telephone calls which Pablo took and, after a few sentences that I didn't understand because they were whispered, ended, but that hardly mattered.

A few days later the wife of the travelling salesman from the attic apartment on the sixth floor, a rather ample but attractive forty-year-old, asked whether my husband could fix her tap, her tap was dripping, and the constant noise of dripping was really disturbing her. I communicated her request to Pablo, who muttered a few Galician curses between his teeth but still went up the steps to the attic apartment with his blue painted iron toolbox. Shortly after this I began to clean the stairs as I did every Thursday, and so, armed with a broom and a dustpan, I went up the stairs to the sixth storey. When I lifted the doormat by the door of the travelling salesman's apartment to sweep away the dust beneath it, I heard music. I knew this kind of music, it was a slow bolero, to which I had often danced with Pablo to our wide French double bed.

The Brazilian woman probably had a similar musical taste to Pablo's, they came from countries with similar cultural influences. She had chosen this bolero to make the repairing of the tap less tiresome. I put the doormat back down and stood up, when my eye caught the keyhole.

Reverend Father, I don't know exactly why I put my left eye to the keyhole and peered into the apartment, it was a reflex action. In the oval detail that presented itself to my eye, I saw the naked legs of the Brazilian woman from her toes to about a foot above her knees. These far from slim, rather stocky legs were dancing. I put my ear to the keyhole, and as well as bolero music I heard the clattering of castanets. Before I went to the next door to sweep the dust from under the mat, I looked through the keyhole again, with my right eye this time. Next to the naked dancing legs of the Brazilian woman from Belo Horizonte, this time I saw a second pair of legs, legs in blue working trousers, feet in Pablo's shoes and socks. The two pairs of legs, the naked one and the clothed one, were moving slowly to the rhythm of the bolero. The clattering of the castanets had stopped. I stood up and walked to the next apartment door where I mechanically went on with my work.

The image of the two pairs of legs stayed in my head while I removed the dust from under all the doormats, while I swept one step after the other until I had reached the ground floor. The doubtlessly unfounded jealousy that had awoken in me when I had chanced to see Pablo bending the fashion designer's torso over the banisters reawakened. Reverend Father, if it were the case that marriage was not forbidden to Catholic priests but permitted, if it were the case that you had a wife, what would you think if you peered through a keyhole and saw your wife's legs, naked to about a foot above the knee, keeping time with the clothed legs of a man? Would such a sight not arouse jealousy in you as well?'

Magdalena paused as if to give me time to consider the

question. I made an effort to put myself in her position, but with the best will in the world I couldn't imagine being married to a woman. The only woman I could picture in this context was my sister Maria, and although I had always found my sister Maria's legs attractive, and still find them attractive today, even though their skin is run through with a good few varicose veins, and her feet have been slightly disfigured by ganglions, this image curiously provoked no jealousy in me whatsoever. At that moment Magdalena crossed her long, slim legs in their tight-fitting leather jump suit and sat on the ground, and suddenly I was able to empathize more successfully with the situation she had just described, and with the related feeling of jealousy. If I had a wife – I could see that wife's legs in just such tight black leather trousers, dancing in time with two men's legs – it was not beyond the realms of the imagination that I might be gripped by this feeling of jealousy, coming dangerously close to a mortal sin.

'Your expression betrays your efforts to empathize with my former situation,' Magdalena continued. 'I value that effort, Reverend Father, I value such empathy, even if such empathy is among the everyday duties of a Catholic priest. When I reached the ground floor after sweeping the stairs, my attack of jealousy fled, not least because I remembered Igor, and the unhappy consequences that his passion had for our relationship. I would not repeat his fatal errors but learn from the difficulties that an adverse destiny had placed before me. Reaching the bottom step I clearly realized that my concerns were unfounded. Even the naked legs of the Brazilian woman were no proof of any kind of misdemeanour. She probably went barefoot at home for reasons of comfort, and wasn't wearing any stockings either, and in all likelihood her knees were exposed because she was wearing a loose-fitting short housecoat. The Brazilian and Pablo were guilty of nothing, it was my own unrealistic imaginings that were leading me to make such assumptions. No, Pablo was beyond any suspicion of that kind. Had he not stood by me in my conflicts with Igor? Did he not accompany me each evening in rumba time, in samba time, in tango time to our wide double bed? I really had no cause to complain.

While I was sweeping the cellar steps I reproached myself for my suspicion. Utterly immersed in these thoughts I gave a frightened start when my broom touched something soft in the semi-darkness. It was the thigh of a *clochard* who lay sleeping on the bottom step of the cellar stairs. Roused by this ungentle touch, he rose from his sleep and let loose a flood of words and sentences which were largely incomprehensible to me. I had already had to make this *clochard* leave the cellar twice before, a demand with which he had always complied, albeit reluctantly. The second time I had threatened to tell my husband who would not be satisfied with merely throwing him out but would give him a thrashing as well. Now the *clochard* was back in the building, and it was up to me to make my threat reality if I was not to be considered unreliable. I was not keen, however, to fetch my husband from the Brazilian woman's attic apartment, not because I was afraid of coming upon the two of them but because it would have meant going up one hundred and thirty-nine steps which I had just been up and down. Somewhat undecided, I switched on the cellar light, leaned on my broomstick and for the first time I looked at the *clochard* a little more closely, while he went on yelling at me in a language which was unfamiliar to me but which sounded rather like English.

I hadn't noticed before that the *clochard* was young, younger than myself, because on the first two occasions he had been wearing his long straight black hair loose and the unkempt strands had fallen over his face and partly concealed it. But this time it was tied up at the back of his neck, and I saw his narrow, oval, pallid face very clearly in the harsh light of the cellar lamp. It was a beautiful, regular face, entirely dominated by his big dark eyes. His cheekbones were pronounced, and his thin but finely formed lips were so red that they looked as if he was wearing make-up. It was hard to say what his body looked like because it was hidden by several layers of big, worn-out clothing. Suddenly the *clochard* stopped cursing.

Why are you staring at me like that? he said in easily comprehensible English. Why are you staring at me like that, as if you'd never seen me before?

Then he started to complain that his peace was often disturbed in this cellar, about which he had no other complaints, by a noise on the ceiling above him, which sounded like the rhythmical stamping of somebody dancing, or two people dancing. Paris in general was an intolerably loud place for his sensitive ears; accustomed to silence from birth, the noise of Paris was one uninterrupted insult. He had often had cause to regret leaving the Outer Hebrides, the Outer Hebrides had been paradise, a paradise that he had sadly only recognized as such after he had left it. If you are born in paradise, if for years you know nothing but that paradise, then of course you don't see it as paradise, you think paradise is elsewhere. This mistaken belief had led him to leave the place of his birth, the Butt of Lewis, the northernmost point of the Isle of Lewis, the northernmost island of the Outer Hebrides, and go to Canada.

Once he had embarked upon the subject of paradise I began to listen, as the subject of paradise has always interested me, just as you, Reverend Father, are doubtless interested in the subject of paradise, in fact as a Catholic priest you have to be interested in it even if you aren't. The handsome *clochard* was clearly speaking about an island paradise from which he had exiled himself. When I quietly remarked that I understood what he was talking about very well, he reached out his right hand in a purple wool glove.

With your permission, Jonathan Alistair Abercrombie, he said and smiled, and I was struck by the fact that his upper canines were unusually long and pointed. I felt the *clochard* beginning to awaken my interest, and in order to prevent this interest taking root any more deeply I ordered him to vanish on the spot. At this he resumed his original attitude, gasping out a menacing torrent of words which I now thought I could identify as the argot of the Outer Hebrides, rolled up the thin straw mat on which he had been lying, put on a tight, brightly coloured woollen cap and a pair of very dark sunglasses, gathered up all his plastic bags and climbed the cellar steps. He opened the cellar door, turned round and said: You won't get rid of me as quickly as that, Madame. Then he closed the door behind him.

You won't get rid of me as quickly as that, said Jonathan Alistair Abercrombie. Isn't it strange the way some sentences assume a significant meaning in retrospect? You won't get rid of me as quickly as that, Madame.

When I came back to our apartment with my broom and dustpan, Pablo was sitting at the kitchen table reading a letter. When I walked in he put the letter aside, put on a compact disc of Brazilian sambas, drew me to him and danced with me towards the double bed in which we very soon managed to establish a rhythmic harmony. After a little while we fell asleep, and when I awoke it was already dark. Pablo was snoring quietly beside me, and I went into the kitchen to drink a glass of water. My eye chanced upon the pale lilac letter that was still lying on the kitchen table. Reverend Father, it is not my way to read letters meant for other people, but you must admit that the temptation to commit this doubtless venial sin was very great.

I cast a fleeting glance at the handwriting, which sloped strongly to the right, and against my will I read a sentence: Pablo, my dearest, *mon chou*, when shall we dance again? I bent over the writing and read another sentence, then a paragraph, then the whole letter, which referred, amongst other things, to a pug which still limped on its left back paw where Pablo had trodden on it in the whirl of the dance, and to strings from which no one else had ever drawn a sound, but from which he, Pablo, had drawn music. The letter was signed with the words "Your Spanish hibiscus blossom. P.S. Don't forget the castanets." Agitated by reading this letter, I walked to the window. Outside, Madame Martel, the widow from Montpellier, was just crossing the courtyard, and behind her came the pug, its left back paw in a white bandage.

Reverend Father, the ugly feeling of jealousy, conquered only a few hours earlier, stirred again. Again I told myself there was not the slightest cause for suspicious assumptions. Pablo, out of a kind of sympathy for the lonely sixty-year-old lady, who naturally knew that he was a dancing master, and under the influence of her lemon liqueur from the south of France, had simply allowed himself to be persuaded into giving a little demonstration after connecting her television to the building's common aerial. The widow, living in seclusion, had probably seen more in this gesture of neighbourly kindness than was really intended; the ill-defined widowly longings of the lady – who was not without charms despite her advanced years – would have won out over her common sense. Under the influence of unseasonably high temperatures, she had found herself succumbing to sultry fantasies which obviously had no basis in reality, and Pablo had become the focus of her otherwise repressed widowly desires which could no longer be kept in check because of those unseasonably high temperatures, unsuspecting Pablo, who had entered Madame Martel's apartment with the sole purpose of connecting her television to the building's shared aerial.

At that moment Madame Martel looked in my direction and we smiled at each other through the windowpane.

During the weeks that followed my reading of the easily misunderstood, doubtless completely harmless letter, I saw Pablo more rarely than usual, as he had assumed additional professional duties. During his absence he kept getting calls from his dancing pupils, which I would take for him. When

I explained to one of these dancing pupils that Pablo was often out of the building because he was extending his field of activity, she said my naivety was touching but hardly healthy, and didn't I know what kind of reputation my lifelong companion enjoyed, and why he was in such demand as a dancing teacher. I said he enjoyed the reputation of unusual dancing talents, and was in such demand because no other teacher of Latin American dances was endowed by nature with such a sophisticated sense of rhythm. To this, the dance pupil cryptically replied that I was beyond help, and put down the receiver. I was not thrown by such dark suggestions, and went conscientiously about my work as a concierge.

Late one afternoon, when I was shopping in the Marais and by chance walked past the dancing school where Pablo was employed, I saw him coming out of the entrance to the building, his arm round a young woman with short blonde hair. Reverend Father, it is certainly not in my nature to spy, to pursue, to lie in wait, to trail, to shadow. It was not I who took the initiative, it was my feet. When Pablo rounded the corner with the young woman, my feet declared their independence and began to follow the couple. They followed them from the Rue des Mauvais Garçons, where Pablo's dance school was located, along the Rue du Roi de Sicile and the Rue des Ecouffes to the Rue des Rosiers, where the two of them disappeared into the entrance of a building. My feet stopped there. They stood on the asphalt for an hour and a half, in my new leather Salamander shoes. They stood on the side of the street opposite the portal. And while they were standing there on the dirty pavement, my eyes glanced up to an open window on the first floor of the building. Framed by this window were the heads and shoulders of Pablo and the young blonde woman. These heads and shoulders were twirling in a dancing motion, staring abruptly in one, then in the opposite direction.

No doubt about it, the two of them were dancing to a tango.

Astor Piazzola's accordion music drifted quietly from the open window. For an hour and a half I saw the two sets of heads and shoulders, both entirely devoted to the dance, and could imagine the bodies beneath, their legs skilfully carrying out the complicated dips and cross-steps of the tango. After their two heads had inclined towards one another at the end of these one and a half long hours, after their profiles had fused in a long kiss in the window frame, my feet slowly set themselves in motion. Without my exerting the slightest deliberate influence on them, they walked down the Rue Pavé, crossed the Rue de Rivoli, walked further towards the Pont Marie, crossed the bridge and the Ile St Louis, walked over the Pont de la Tournelle to the Quai of the same name, and then found their way through the Rue des Bernardins and across the Place Maubert into the Rue St Jacques. While my feet were walking, my head was dealing with what my eyes had seen during the last one and a half hours in the window frame in the Rue des Rosiers. And by the time my feet had walked into the concierge apartment in the Rue St Jacques, a peripeteia in the sense of Aristotle's *Poetics* had been completed.

What I had recently classified as a delusion, the silhouette of Pablo and the black-clad fashion designer on the curtain, had not been a delusion, any more than the dancing couple in the window frame in the Rue des Rosiers had been a delusion. The curtain had been abruptly torn aside and had revealed what for a long time I had stubbornly refused to believe. I sat on the sofa in the living room of the concierge apartment and looked at my feet, which had led from the Rue des Rosiers to here without my intervention. Then I took off my new shoes, stretched out on the sofa and mused that this peripeteia was not a pleasant condition for me at the moment, but that, nonetheless, it doubtless represented an inevitable necessity for the progression of the tragedy. And the tragedy had begun a long time before. The exposition had occurred when I confided in Pablo about my unhappy relationship with Igor, or even earlier, when Pablo had opened his door in the Hôtel d'Avenir and complained of the noise caused by the scene between Igor and the pickpocket.

We fall from one tragedy into the next, Reverend Father. We think the tragedy is over, we think we're finally at the beginning of a comedy, we're convinced that what has just begun is a romantic comedy, but of course it's a new tragedy that is under way. We constantly delude ourselves, forever we see ourselves at the start of romantic comedies or at least at the start of farces, pantomimes, cheery musicals, light-hearted operettas, and of course what's beginning is really a new tragedy. We deceive ourselves, thinking that life is giving us tickets for romantic comedies. Life gives us only free tickets for tragedies, only tragedies play on the stage of life, even if some of them are romantic tragedies. Lying on the sofa in the living room of the concierge apartment, I welcomed the event that had opened my eyes, that peripeteia which guarantees that the tragedy will take its natural course and can be concluded according to its laws. If no peripeteia occurs in the tragedy, then one may perhaps be thoroughly unaware that one is in a tragedy. And not knowing that one is in a tragedy is a tragedy greater than any other, and leads to absolute chaos. If one is already in a tragedy – and one is always in a tragedy – one must be sure that this tragedy can unfold according to the rules, that it can play out according to the rules, and that it can conclude in the usual tragedy ending according to the rules. There must be an order to everything, Reverend Father, everything must take its course in accordance with certain laws, on this point you will surely agree with me. Just as my tragic view of the world is subject to certain laws, your Catholic view of the world is subject to certain laws; just as I talk about the Aristotelian tragic plan, you speak, from your pulpit, about the divine plan of salvation. While the radical Aristotelian reversal consists in the tragic villain's knowledge of his absolute vileness, your divine peripeteia consists in the knowledge of the absolute love and goodness of God and Jesus Christ.

On the way from the Rue des Rosiers to the Rue St Jacques, it was as if scales had fallen from my eyes: Pablo didn't dance only with me, he danced with every woman who was prepared to dance with him. The black-clad fashion designer wasn't the only one he twirled in the lively two-four or three-four time of the paso doble, a Latin American ballroom dance with simple steps which evolved from a Spanish folk dance. The Brazilian woman from Belo Horizonte wasn't the only one with whom he enjoyed a bolero accompanied by castanets, or a regularly paced, medium-tempo cha-cha-cha over various rattling instruments like maracas, cabazas and guiros. Madame Martel wasn't the only one with whom he abandoned himself in one of the three styles of flamenco – the Arabic-Indian, the Jewish-synagogue and the Gypsy-influenced – with its fast-switching rhythms, its hand-clapping and foot-stamping. And the blonde dancing pupil wasn't the only one with whom he enjoyed the tango, promenades in two-four time, performed in terse walking steps, interrupted by abrupt halts, which developed from elements of the habanera in the area around Buenos Aires. There were others, there were many with whom he almost glided along the floor in little steps in a fast-tempo samba with a regular beat and a strongly syncopated rhythm, with whom he abandoned himself to a rumba accentuated by pronounced hip movements, or danced through the room to the music of Manuel de Falla's fandango *El sombrero de tres picos*, always towards a bedstead somewhere nearby.

Reverend Father, you, being committed to Christian brotherly love, if you could say anything, would probably say that one of the most praiseworthy qualities of a person, particularly a woman, lies in letting other people, particularly women, share in what you yourself enjoy, not wanting to snatch everything selfishly to yourself. You would say that it is one of the noblest duties of a woman not only to tolerate a man's many activities, his intense engagement with the world around him, but to encourage him to engage in such outward-looking activities, to challenge him to do so and after his expeditions, his advances into neighbouring and distant territories, so exciting but so stressful, gladly to welcome him back, to care for him and lovingly to prepare him for the next expedition of the same kind. In holding such altruistic views, which you would doubtless express if you were able to, and which are designed to help women to achieve their noblest Catholic destiny, you are certainly right.

When I was lying on the sofa, my new Salamander shoes on the floor beside it, immediately after the beginning of the dramatic peripeteia, acknowledging Pablo's frequent changes of partner, a struggle began within me. Should I support this passion for dancing which, even if it was, to my chagrin, connected with an indiscriminate switching of partners, amounted to an art form, an art form which, like all art forms, is fundamentally to be encouraged? Should I see it as a useful training, keeping Pablo in shape for our bedroom performances? Or should I, selfishly, insist on being the only partner with whom Pablo danced towards beds?

To express it in your Catholic vocabulary, it was a struggle of the heavenly host against the powers of darkness, fought out on the arena of my frail human soul. You will be able to imagine, Reverend Father, that egomania, greed, petty self-interest emerged victorious over selflessness and magnanimity, over womanly devotion and considerateness. I did not pass the test that had been imposed upon me. When Pablo came home and asked me to give up my seat on the sofa on the grounds that he was dog-tired, his professional obligations were slowly exceeding his powers, I took him to task. At first he stubbornly denied any relationship beyond the purely platonic dancing relationship, and accused me of pathological possessiveness, doubtless going back to my disturbed relationship with my parents; he accused me of deviant suspicion, of unnatural envy for his success as a dancing teacher. After I had revealed to him what my eyes had seen and what my ears had heard, he talked about hallucinations provoked by the unseasonably high temperatures, about the delusions of a rich but under-occupied imagination, of *Fata Morganas* shaped by negative erotic experiences, thus confirming me in my original attitude towards the distressing events. Becoming somewhat uncertain, I mentioned the letter that I had found on the kitchen table and cast my eyes over. He reacted with unexpectedly violent rage.

How dare I spy on him, keep him under surveillance, violate the privacy of the post, he cried, incensed. I hesitantly observed that it had not been a violation of the privacy of the post as such, the letter had been lying open on the kitchen table, so prominently that it practically cried out to be read. At this, Pablo grew even more furious and yelled that I had destroyed his trust in me, how could he go on living under the same roof in such circumstances, how could he continue to put his faith in a woman who did not stop at such an abuse of human freedom? Without going into the content of the letter he stormed out of the apartment and did not come home until four in the morning, a habit that he maintained during the period that followed. We went on living together, but as good as never did we dance to our French double bed, as I had already been lying there for hours by the time he came home.'

Magdalena picked up the jam jar with the praying mantis, turned it mechanically in her hand and studied the insect keenly as she went on talking.

'What a delicate green, what a charming creature – Reverend Father, after this I came to a better understanding of Igor's jealousy. It had been without foundation, while there were good grounds for my jealousy, but the feeling itself was probably very similar. Almost every night I lay sleeplessly in the big double bed, alone with my imaginings. Everywhere I saw Pablo dancing with beautiful women, in the streets and squares, in the parks of Paris, under a starry night sky. In the deserted Place Vendôme he glided past the glittering precious stones in the windows of the jewellery shops with an elegant woman in a black evening dress, in the empty Place de Catalogne he danced around the oval of the overflowing fountain with a barefoot girl in a white dress, in the silent Jardin du Luxembourg he twirled around the raised stone floor of the pavilion with an exotic beauty with long, black, shining hair, dressed in a sari that glittered with all the colours of the rainbow. Such imaginings tormented me more than the considerably more realistic and tangible pictures of Pablo and Madame Martel, Pablo and the black-clad fashion designer and Pablo and the somewhat plump Brazilian woman from Belo Horizonte, none of whom, incidentally, ceased to remind him of his duties as a concierge, forever asking him to perform little services and favours, tasks with which he always complied, however grumpily. If he had continued to let me share in his talents as a dancer, if he had not neglected me on those long moonless nights, I might have grown used to not being his only dancing partner. But as it was, in his absence the night-time hours filled with tormenting fantasies, and I began to loathe him as I had loathed the Frisian.

Not that I thought of his removal at first, not that I deliberately considered his extermination. But my thoughts kept returning to the shellfish poisoning that had so fatefully marked the beginning of our happiness. And I was surprised, from time to time, to find myself taking a book on toxicology down from the shelf in one of the many bookshops in the *quartier*, and, for example, taking a look at the tables featuring the names, the active ingredients and effects of the most important native toadstools, as well as the possibilities of confusing them with edible mushrooms, or leafing through a book on botany and lingering over the colour plates showing plants such as meadow saffron, monkshood, hemlock, henbane, thorn apple, arum or belladonna. And when I asked the salesman in the chemist's shop next to our house for vitamin C in fizzy tablet form, I also asked, to his – and my own – astonishment, whether he knew which poisons were most effective, to which he gave me the somewhat hesitant reply that to his knowledge aconite, usually prescribed as a pain-reliever in cases of neuralgia, coniine, colchicine, a remedy for gout, and the rat poison strychnine were the most poisonous. I thanked him for his information, and when he called after me asking why I wanted to know, I pretended not to have heard and quickly closed the glass door behind me.

Reverend Father, I assure you, Pablo would still be dancing today, in spite of everything, if I had not got wise to the Brazilian woman from Belo Horizonte. I don't mean the comparatively harmless discovery that I made when I peered through her keyhole, I mean an outrage on her part aimed at me personally, with a view to my destruction.

One day a pleasant young man knocked on the door of the concierge apartment and said he was from Leconte and Co., Madame Martel had asked him to install a satellite dish on the roof, would I be so kind as to show him the way to the roof. I went up the stairs with him to the sixth storey, and showed him the ladder used for getting through the skylight and up on to the roof. He leaned the ladder against the skylight, climbed up, pushed up the pane of glass and emerged on to the roof. Growing curious, I followed him. I had seen a number of films in which criminals, pursued by the police, had run over the roofs of Paris, and had been fascinated by the wide zigzagging rooftop landscapes that opened up there, and which provided a wonderful view over Paris. The metal roof of our building sloped in places, but elsewhere it was flat and easy to walk upon. While the pleasant man from Leconte and Co. was fixing the satellite dish, I strolled up and down on the roof, let the wind blow through my hair and enjoyed the view of the Seine, the Panthéon, the Sorbonne, Notre Dame, the Institut du Monde Arabe and all the grey roofs with the rust-red chimneys that looked like the clay pipes that you fired at in the shooting ranges of my childhood to win a red crepe paper rose or a white plastic skeleton.

By chance my eye fell upon the skylight of the Brazilian woman, whose husband was often away on business. Drawn by a vague impulse, I risked taking a few quite dangerous steps across the slope of the roof, prompting a quiet exclamation of horror from the man from Leconte and Co., and stood beside the skylight. I looked in. The Brazilian woman was crouching right below me on the floor of her living room. At first I couldn't see exactly what she was doing, but when I bent further down I saw that she was holding a severed chicken foot in one hand and a chicken head in the other, and was making sweeping gestures with them. In front of her on the floor was a big blank sheet of paper. She moved the chicken foot and the chicken head towards the paper and began smearing it with the blood from the chicken neck. I put my head still closer to the opening to get a better view of what she was doing. It was my name, Magdalena Leitner, that she was writing with chicken blood.

I nearly fell through the window in my terror. At the last second I regained my balance and stumbled up the slope of the roof, where the man from Leconte and Co. caught me. I closed my eyes and mumbled that I had had an attack of vertigo. He carefully sat me down beside the newly installed satellite dish on a little flat area of the tin roof, sat down beside me and put his arm round my shoulder. We sat there like that for a while. In the distance the domes of the Sacré Coeur glowed pink in the light of the setting sun.

There was no doubt about it, the Brazilian woman from Belo Horizonte was practising voodoo to destroy me and win Pablo as a long-term dancing partner for the times when her husband, the travelling salesman, was away.'

Magdalena fell silent, shaken by the unparalleled under-handedness of her former rival. I must admit that I was also horrified by the story of this heathen's insidious behaviour, although I was not surprised, having been alerted long ago, by various writings of pious and well-intentioned men, to the fundamental perfidy of the female sex. At the same time I was touched by Magdalena's innocence. I saw her sitting slumped on the Paris tin roof, profoundly disappointed by the lack of solidarity in the actions of her fellow female, and I was flooded with sympathy. If only I could have loosened my bonds, sat down with her in the grass and put my arm round her shoulders like the young man from Leconte and Co., at least to assure her of the support of men after this betrayal by her own sex. Was it possible that someone could resort to such diabolical practices, could defy God's commandments in that way?

'Of course the cult of voodoo is a concept with which you will be familiar, Reverend Father,' Magdalena continued, 'containing elements of Catholicism as it does. At first a secret cult, in the nineteenth century it spread from Haiti to other parts of the Caribbean, to the United States, and to Brazil.'

At this point I should have liked to add a few words, because I didn't like the way Magdalena mentioned such dangerous manipulations in the same breath as Christianity, even trying to establish common features between them. What did this primitive heathen cult of sacrifice have in common with the Catholic religion, towering above such magical machinations on an incomparably higher ethical and moral level? Magdalena was definitely going too far now.

'You look as if you'd like to say something, Reverend Father. Before your escape attempt I might perhaps have allowed you to express your opinion; after your escape attempt we will regrettably have to refrain from any expression of opinion on your part, as you will certainly understand.

After this event my general state deteriorated considerably. Thrown by what I had seen, I constantly imagined I could recognize the physical signs of being bewitched. I suffered alternately from migraines, stitches and attacks of dizziness, which I attributed to the malicious actions of the Brazilian woman towards me. My suspicions began to extend to the widow Martel and the black-clad fashion designer. When Madame Martel met me on the stairs, her gaze seemed more penetrating than before, and I did not consider it impossible that she knew about the Evil Eye, because of the proximity of Montpellier to Spain. And I considered it thoroughly possible that the permanently black-clad fashion designer, whom I sometimes saw standing motionless at her window on the third floor staring down at me, was one of those young people who, as Monsieur Szabó had revealed to me, met for Satanic Masses in the catacombs of Denfert-Rochereau. A woman with a man on her mind is capable of anything, even of a bond with the Devil himself, don't you think, Reverend Father?

Life in the building on the Rue St Jacques became ever more fruitless. My physical complaints were accumulating and Pablo was hardly ever at home. Apart from Monsieur Szabó I met no one in the building without suspicion. It was during this time that I met Jonathan Alistair Abercrombie in the cellar again. Weakened by all my difficulties, I didn't have the heart to chase him away; on the contrary, I was even pleased to see the handsome young man sitting on the steps surrounded by his plastic bags. From now on he appeared more often, and from time to time I leaned my broom on the cellar wall, sat down beside him and talked to him for a while. As he talked he often ate a sausage, popular in France, made of fresh pig's blood, which he cut into fine slices with an unusually large, gleaming knife that he took from a leather sheath on his belt.

After leaving the Outer Hebrides for Canada in a spirit of adventure at the age of seventeen, he told me, he had worked in Quebec on the building of an ice palace. Subsequently, working on the building of ice and snow palaces had become his passion, his vocation. I could not imagine what wonderful buildings could be constructed from ice and snow, keeps and towers, oriels, battlements and embrasures, palaces with arched portals, vaults and elegantly turned columns. There were various methods of erecting such buildings, all of which derived finally from the architectural principle of the igloo. The architectural principle of the igloo stood at the beginning of ice palace construction. Just as the Eskimos cut wind-pressed snow into blocks with big knives or wooden saws, big blocks had originally been sawn from the ice sheets of rivers and lakes with special long pieces of metal. These blocks had been lifted on to the ice walls with horse-drawn block and tackles, put in the right place with enormous pincers and carefully inserted by so-called ice bricklayers.

When Jonathan Alistair Abercrombie talked about his ice palaces, a little colour came to his pale face, and his otherwise rather rigid features grew mobile.

He had taken part in the winter carnival in Quebec a number of times, he said. The ice and snow palaces were built for this winter carnival, which was an extraordinary event. Since 1980 they had sadly stopped building ice palaces because of the expense, and now made only snow palaces, which were also impressive enough but naturally lacked the wonderfully transparent effect of the true ice palaces. Instead of sawing out ice blocks, they now poured tons of snow into big moulds, much the way one pours concrete, and in the end the moulds were removed, and there stood the snow building.

While the early heatwave continued, then, I sat with Jonathan Alistair Abercrombie who talked about ice and snow palaces and underlined his descriptions by making explanatory gestures with his hands in their purple woollen gloves. When I asked him why he dressed so warmly, he told me that it had often been very cold in the Outer Hebrides and later in Canada, and one had had to protect oneself well against the wind and the cold. It was a habit that he had kept up, and over time warm clothing had become something quite natural to him, and he got cold if he dressed like an average central or western European when the weather was warm.

I couldn't get enough of Jonathan Alistair Abercrombie's descriptions of the northern winter, the buildings of ice and snow. He seemed to address a landscape of ice and snow within me, a zone of wide, glittering patches of snow, an area of transparent, frozen waterfalls that I had never come across before.

As my psychosomatic complaints, which derived, I was quite convinced, from the black magic with which the Brazilian woman, and perhaps Madame Martel and the fashion designer as well, were trying to harm me, as these complaints grew worse, my aversion towards Pablo, to whom I owed all this, also increased. As I thought Monsieur Szabó absolutely trustworthy, and also suspected that because of his work as a cemetery attendant he would have some understanding of my metaphysical problem, I spoke to him when I brought him the quarterly *Amateur Ornithologists' Journal* to which he subscribed. Did he consider it possible, in his capacity as a cemetery attendant, that one could be negatively influenced by black magic emanating from malicious people, I asked him bluntly when he came to the door with his goldfinch, Charles, on his index finger. He looked at me for a long time and invited me into his living room, where he showed me to a chair beneath the portrait of the Hungarian freedom fighter Lajos Kossuth.

Without a doubt, he said, pointing his index finger, the goldfinch still perched upon it, away from himself, without a doubt one could transfer one's will to other people by using various practices. His late mother, a farmer's daughter born near Székesfehérvár and strictly brought up in the Catholic faith, had known about such things. I asked him if he knew how one could free oneself from such a spell, such a curse. He shook his head thoughtfully back and forth and said that his mother had sometimes carried out exorcisms, quite in keeping with the Catholic Church's exorcism regulations, and had had considerable success with them. Strictly speaking she had not had the right to do this, strictly speaking the *exorcismus solemnis* could, of course, only be carried out by a priest with permission of the bishop, but as a profoundly religious person she had considered it her duty to help her fellow man, when he was assailed by various demons, with the talent that God had given her. As a little boy he had sometimes attended these rituals and still had a good memory of the formulae, partly in Hungarian, partly in Latin, that his mother had uttered in the course of them.

With the goldfinch Charles on his index finger, Monsieur Szabó leaned forward a little and whispered that if I wished he could perform an exorcism on me, immediately, here in his living room; he would just have to put Charles back in his cage and get a fresh egg from the fridge. Hen's eggs had played an important part in the exorcisms carried out by his mother, the person being exorcized had had to hold a fresh hen's egg in both hands throughout the ritual. It was not ideal that it was not the egg of a free-range Hungarian hen but one from the supermarket on the corner, but in view of the complete change in political and economic relations in the meantime, we could accept this minor disadvantage. I thanked Monsieur Szabó for being so willing. He placed Charles in his spacious cage, woven from willow canes, covered it with a cloth, fetched the hen's egg, pulled the heavy dark-blue velvet curtains shut and lit a black candle. Then he told me to turn my chair round and look the freedom fighter and national hero Kossuth firmly in the eye. I did as I was bidden, and Monsieur Szabó pressed the hen's egg into my hand, stood behind me, placed his hands on my shoulders and murmured prayers and incantations to me. I looked Lajos Kossuth steadily in his fearless eyes, and the hen's egg in my hands grew warmer and warmer.

After what seemed to me to be a very long period of time, Monsieur Szabó ended his ritualistic action, and said he had acted in the best knowledge and conscience and in memory of his late mother, née Rákosi, and although the occasional brief peep from Charles, issuing forth from beneath the cloth, had distracted him somewhat, the demon that had possessed me must have been driven out. He took the hen's egg from my hands and tested its temperature. He said that the evil was now in the egg, even if it was not the egg of a powerful free-range Hungarian hen but the tiny, thin-shelled white egg dropped by a skinny little battery hen, it had had the strength, to judge by its relatively high level of heat, to draw pretty much all the evil into itself. He would keep the egg for two months and then burn it, as the ritual required. I could arise and go, I was healed. I wanted to thank him, ask him whether I could express my gratitude in any way, but he said no, and said my thanks were due not to him but to his dear departed mother, who had lain for decades in a plain family plot in an idyllic little cemetery set on a hill near Székesfehérvár where he would much rather have been cemetery attendant than in the vast necropolis of Montparnasse.'

I was rather alarmed that Magdalena had allowed herself to be exorcized by someone who was not a priest. Although the profession of cemetery attendant might have laid claim to a distant similarity to the priestly vocation, this vague affinity was by no means enough to permit him to undertake such a delicate procedure. As far as I could judge, he had gone to work in an extremely amateurish way, and had no means of testing whether Magdalena had actually been possessed by one or a number of demons. And it was certainly possible that he had not reproduced the precisely established incantatory vocabulary word for word. As a result of his thoughtless and superficial method, the demon or demons might not have fled but just clawed their way all the deeper into Magdalena's soul.

'Reverend Father, strange as it may sound, after this exorcism carried out by Monsieur Szabó, I suddenly felt better,' said Magdalena. 'I ran nimbly up and down the stairs and no longer needed to consult any of the many doctors who had never found organic causes for my complaints. If I saw the Brazilian woman, Madame Martel or the black-clad fashion designer, I merely glared at them, not deigning to speak to them. At the same time as this miraculous physical and spiritual healing, and because of my alienation from Pablo, my new amity with Jonathan Alistair Abercrombie deepened. He was now less irritable than before, as Pablo's constant absence meant that he was no longer disturbed by the stamping of dancing shoes above him. Sometimes I brought him a plate of rice Trauttmansdorff, and he was pleased when he saw me coming down the stairs with the flambéd dish glowing bluish in the semi-darkness. He told me more about his ice and snow buildings.

When he had stopped finding work building ice and snow palaces, he said, he had taken part in the international snow sculpture competition, to be able to work with his favourite material, frozen water, albeit on a small scale. Once, from an illustration in an art book, he had carved a copy of the Laocoon group, in the Vatican collection, by the Rhodes sculptors Hagesander, Polydoros and Athanadoros. While Jonathan Alistair talked, I considered his profile silhouetted against the bluish light of the flambéd rice Trauttmansdorff, with the high forehead, the noble, straight nose and the firm but not wilful chin. Without a doubt, I was dealing with an artist, an artist disguised as a *clochard*. I admired him for his sculptural creations which included not only the Laocoon group but also snow copies of Rodin's John the Baptist and Michelangelo's David, which he had glazed with water to give them a patina of ice. It saddened me to think that these wonderful sculptures had melted long ago, that I would never have the chance to see them.

When Jonathan had shared his past life with me, I too opened my heart completely to him, and told him how badly fate had used me, and how unhappy I was because of Pablo's untamable passion for dancing. He was clearly affected by my worries, and said that such male behaviour would be unthinkable in the Outer Hebrides; in the Outer Hebrides, particularly on the Isle of Lewis, and there most specifically on the Butt of Lewis, men were brought up to be faithful and steadfast. Pablo's behaviour was the typical behaviour of the inhabitant of a hot country; the inhabitants of cold countries were quite different people.

One day I steered our conversation to poisons, carefully beginning with the recipe for rice Trauttmansdorff, then moving on to all kinds of herbs and spices and the plants that produced them, finally turning to the general topic of medicinal and poisonous plants and the astonishing affinity between cookery and chemistry. Jonathan Alistair said that poisons could sometimes be beneficial, when they helped one to end a completely unsuccessful life. So saying, he rummaged at the neck of his torn pullover, drawing from it a little chain with a capsule. This, for example, was a capsule of potassium cyanide, a highly toxic, highly soluble powder, whose toxicity derived from its obstruction of iron for the breathing enzymes. His English uncle had taken this capsule from the corpse of a Nazi officer in the Second World War and given it to him, his favourite nephew, years later, when he was lying on his deathbed, and with his dying breath had told him to keep the capsule carefully, life could confront one with extremely unpleasant situations, with such a capsule one was prepared for the worst. He hoped that Jonathan Alistair would never have to make use of it, but if it came to the crunch he was armed, an idea which calmed him as he stood on the threshold of death, as he, Jonathan Alistair, was his favourite nephew. He had, Jonathan said, accepted the capsule and five minutes later the English uncle, whose favourite nephew he had been, but who had not, conversely, been his favourite uncle, had closed his eyes for ever.

I let the chain and the capsule slip through my fingers, and finally put it back round Jonathan's neck. Reverend Father, in that moment something happened that neither of us had foreseen: we slowly bent our faces towards one another and kissed, sitting on the last but one cellar step, in the glimmering bluish light of the rice Trauttmansdorff. From this kiss I sank against his shoulders, strangely enfeebled.

Later I often wondered what the impulse for that first kiss might have been. Perhaps it was the intuitive recognition of an inherent similarity, perhaps for Jonathan it was his last chance to give a new turn to his life and not to have to bite the cyanide capsule, perhaps for me it was an opportunity to put an end to my unsatisfactory life with Pablo. If we have reached the end, Reverend Father, and if we still have a spark of strength, we choose life. What are for you and your lambs the qualities of faith, hope and charity that the Apostle Paul pressed so warmly to the hearts of the Corinthians are for me and my kind scepticism, rage and vengeance. A good Catholic does not know vengefulness, isn't that so, Reverend Father? The need for retaliation is alien to a good Catholic. To a sinner such as myself, I fear, the emotion of vengefulness is not at all unknown; a sinner such as myself, I fear, is even capable of revelling in the feeling of vengefulness, just as you doubtless revel without interruption in the emotions of faith, charity and hope.

I had hoped that I would melt with Pablo in an eternally whirling dance. I had not expected that it would be a kind of round dance, in the wake of which you are forever letting go of the arm of one partner and flying into the outstretched arm of the next. Pablo had destroyed the most beautiful of my dreams, the dream of the perpetual paso doble, the unfading fandango, the timeless tango. And he would pay for the destruction of that dream with his life.

After Jonathan had shown me the potassium cyanide capsule, my plan was decided. It would not be henbane juice, not a decoction of hemlock or a brew of bittersweet nightshade that I would use to poison Pablo. I would not add thin slices of amanita to the mushroom goulash he loved so much, nor would I substitute bishop's mitre mushrooms for morels in the Chinese rice dish that I sometimes prepared. No, it was with easily soluble potassium cyanide powder that I would satisfy my need for revenge.

One night, when Pablo wasn't at home and I knew that Jonathan was spending the night on the cellar stairs, I crept to the cellar and took the capsule and chain from round the neck of the deeply sleeping figure, which was not difficult for me, after my intensive if abruptly interrupted training with the White Russian Sergei and all the subsequent practice in the Métro, the cinema and libraries. I threw the chain away and hid the capsule in a place where Pablo would not find it because of the interruption of any kind of sexual relations between us. Then I slipped back into the double bed and soon fell asleep. When Pablo came home at about four in the morning I briefly woke up and saw his familiar silhouette, standing out black against the cold light of the full moon falling into the room. In the morning I got up before him, went into the kitchen and, humming quietly, made coffee. I took the capsule from its hiding place, poured the powder into one of the two cups of sweetened café au lait that I had put on the tray, went back into the bedroom with the tray, still humming, put it on the bed where Pablo sat, having now woken up, took the cup meant for me, took a sip and, with a smile, wished Pablo good morning. Pablo looked at me with some suspicion, took the second cup and drank. The poison took effect very quickly. The suspicious expression remained even after his eyes had glazed over.

I turned round, left the apartment and went into the cellar where Jonathan was shaving himself with the help of a broken mirror. I took the mirror from his hand and looked into it. The face of a three-time murderer looked back. I kissed Jonathan's unusually red lips and ran my finger over his handsome straight nose. He asked me if I had found his little chain when sweeping the cellar steps. He had lost the little chain given him by his English uncle, a fact that worried him. I said no, I hadn't come across the chain. Then he said he was very sorry, but he had to leave me because he had decided to return to the Outer Hebrides, or more precisely to the Isle of Lewis, even more precisely to the Butt of Lewis, in an attempt to regain his lost paradise. He wanted to begin a new life and launch an annual festival of snow sculptures on the model of the one in Quebec. I asked him how he planned to travel, and he said he would hitch-hike, that was the only possibility open to him. Taken with the idea of a paradise regained, I had a quick think before offering to take him there in my sidecar. At first he looked at me in surprise, but after brief reflection he said it wasn't a bad idea. I rose to my feet and told him to wait for me, I would be ready in an hour. Then I went back into the concierge apartment, took the letter of farewell that I had prepared and placed it beside Pablo.

Reverend Father, at the risk of incurring your disapproval over my actions, as violations of the ten commandments, I must admit to you that for some time I had practised copying Pablo's signature with a view to writing the farewell letter of a suicide who had taken poison to escape his insurmountable psychological difficulties. I did suspect that the intellectual level of the French police was higher than that of the Italian police, but did not imagine that this minute advantage would enable them to see through my deception, particularly since my handwriting could not be distinguished from Pablo's, even by an experienced graphologist. When I had placed the letter on the bed next to the dead Pablo, and glanced once more at his suspicious expression, I quickly packed a few important things, left the house, and walked with Jonathan to my Puch sidecar bike, which was parked in the courtyard of the building.'

Magdalena fell silent, lay on her side on the grass and, eyes half closed, looked into the sun like a cat. Considering everything that this woman had been through, it was almost miraculous that she had kept her beauty, her youthful freshness. In contrast, I thought, my sister had aged fairly quickly, bearing in mind that she had led a peaceful life in the vicarage and, unlike Magdalena, had not been exposed to a series of masculine monsters.

Magdalena stood up and looked about in the grass for a while. 'Sadly there isn't a male praying mantis in sight,' she said. 'We'll have to wait. Telling stories makes you thirsty,' she added, and ran a pink tongue tip over her lips. She walked to the Puch 800 and began looking through the panniers. Finally she took out a clear unlabelled glass bottle.

'Austrian cider from the Lesachtal. When I bought the half kilo of *Gute Luise* apples from the farmer's boy, I got a litre of cider at the same time. Unfortunately there's hardly any left.'

She came closer, put the bottle to her lips, drank and gave a shudder.

'Very sour. And much too warm, of course. A barren region, the Lesachtal. A barren region with sour apples.'

She looked at the empty bottle, and at me. I was very thirsty.

'Your lips look dry. I hope you didn't think I would leave you any of the sour cider after your failed escape attempt.'

She returned to the panniers.

'Nothing left to drink, nothing to eat but two pears from the Lesachtal. We'll have to get in some supplies, Reverend Father.'

She took a map out of one of the panniers and unfolded it.

'The nearest village is no distance away,' she said after a while. 'About a mile and a half, I would say. That makes three miles on foot in a hot nun's habit. Torture, Reverend Father, but we've been through worse things than that, haven't we?'

She put the map back, and from one of the panniers she

took a plastic bag containing the separate parts of the nun's habit, which she spread out in the grass. Then she stepped out of her motorcycle boots, opened the long zip of her leathers, quickly removed them, and stood naked amid the daisies that grew on the patch of grass, against a background of light green hazel bushes covered with catkin.

Although I knew what a naked female body looked like, from my sister Maria and the various depictions of the Fall and some other paintings showing diverse scenes from the Old Testament, it still took my breath away, and the signs of menacing sexuality, which my body had revealed to me when Magdalena's head had lain in the area of my groin, made themselves felt once more. When I grew dizzy at the sudden and involuntary sight of those curving contours, those full convex and shyly retiring concave lines, those perfect and suggested hyperbolas, parabolas, ellipses and circles, those delicate cones, slender cylinders and regular spheres, my eyes sought refuge in the sight of a tiny ladybird, a seven-spot, I thought, that was creeping across my dalmatic. I concentrated on counting its black dots, and although there were only six of them, I mentally thanked our maker for creating the sensory world around us in all its diversity.

'Why do you cast your eyes down, Reverend Father? Why do you blush?' I heard the sinner's voice as if from a long way away. 'Do look at me.'

Slowly, very slowly I raised my gaze from the microcosmic miracle of the six-spot and let it slide across the patch of meadow separating myself from Magdalena, and up the length of Magdalena herself. She stood there, dazzlingly beautiful in the white cloak of the Barefoot Carmelites, and I thought involuntarily of the enchanting face of her unhappy namesake, Mary Magdalen, in the painting showing the sinner retreating into a grotto to do her penance, wrapped in a splendid red cloak and showing one bare shoulder. No, Magdalena Leitner was yet more beautiful, more beautiful even than that wonderful wooden statue of Mary Magdalen with her hands folded, her head bowed, and dressed only in her hair, more beautiful than the Mary Magdalen painted by an Italian, her left breast barely covered by her hair and her right hand, more beautiful than the picture of Jesus's woman friend sitting with her little pot of salve in the midst of an imaginary mountain landscape, much more beautiful than the Mary Magdalen, very conscious of her beauty, wearing an opulent dress and precious jewellery in a medieval painting that I saw in a German museum with my dear sister Maria, and even more beautiful than the painting showing her, her hair long and loose, looking up towards the risen Christ accompanied by two angels. I couldn't avert my eyes from her, I had to touch each fold of her habit with my eyes, I had to devour the entire shadow-play of lines and surfaces in the white nun's outfit. Plainly framed by the wimple, her face looked quite different, it had lost all its coarse sensuality and had an innocence, a spiritual, almost transfigured gravity that brought tears to my eyes.

'What's wrong with you, Reverend Father?' said Magdalena, wresting me from my contemplation of her. 'Are your eyes inflamed? No wonder, the light is so harsh. I'll put the Ray-Bans on you, even if you don't deserve such a favour after trying to escape.'

She came towards me on floating feet, picked the sunglasses from the ground and put them on my nose. I wanted to protest, because the heavily tinted lenses didn't do much for the miraculous whiteness, but sadly in my current situation my objection had to go unuttered. Magdalena walked up and down in front of me, swinging the lengths of fabric of the Carmelite habit like a beautiful woman presenting an elegant evening dress at a fashion show.

'Rather suits me, don't you think? White, black and red, those are my colours. Right, I'm going now,' she said. 'But I'll be back.' Then she added, with a wicked smile, 'But I can't tell you exactly when. It might be a long time, longer than expected, anyway. You never know who or what you're going to meet, do you? Who or what will cross our path on the pilgrimage of life, as you would no doubt put it.'

And with these words the beautiful Carmelite disappeared behind the dense foliage of an elder bush. The last thing I saw of her was the wafting white tail of her wimple.

I sat there in the direct light of the painfully hot early summer sun, glad that Magdalena had at least put the sunglasses on me. Although she had chosen to keep me prisoner in a lovely place in the countryside, a glade grown round and about with trees clad in fresh leaves, some of them still in blossom, a little stream running at the edge of it, my position was fairly uncomfortable. I was hungry and thirsty, the ropes were cutting into my flesh and there was little prospect of my freeing myself from this disagreeable situation in the foreseeable future. I wondered why God, in his infinite love and goodness, had put me to this test. Had I neglected my pastoral duties? I was unaware of any guilt. I sank into a bottomless pit of dejection, so deep that I was neither able nor willing to pray. Would I die of thirst here, tied to this robinia trunk? Would I starve before Magdalena came back? The sidecar bike stood in the shade of the spruce tree; Magdalena would hardly leave it behind, although she did run the risk of being recognized. It was a conspicuous vehicle, and the members of the Whitsun congregation who had run to the portal of the church to stare after us had definitely seen us driving off in it.

What if Magdalena planned not to come back, but to battle on with her Carmelite habit as she had done before? Although the idea implied that I would perish miserably here, of hunger and thirst, of the loss of circulation to my limbs, if no one found me, which was entirely possible as the glade was hidden and I couldn't attract attention by calling out, although I saw myself facing a probable martyrdom, like the martyrdoms of our saints, and although of course this was all down to

Magdalena and her dangerous, not to say crazy, ideas, I was already beginning to miss her, and I would have given a great deal to see her reappearing from the bushes, sitting down in front of me and opening her beautiful mouth with its straight teeth to go on with her story, because her confession was far from over. Of course, unpredictable as she was, at any point she could look for a new father confessor, a new listener.

So I sat there dangling over the deep gulf between hope and despair, contradictory emotions battling it out in my heart. To distract myself somewhat I tried to concentrate on God's wonderful creation, on the virgin landscape around me, and to find consolation in it. A big butterfly with beautiful markings settled on my right knee, gently spreading and folding its wings. They bore a black and white pattern mixed with a little blue and orange at the back. I studied the insect until it flew away. On the hazel bush in front of which Magdalena had recently stood, first naked and, immediately afterwards, in her Carmelite habit, a round bird with a short and powerful beak, black wings, a black tail and a red breast sat trilling a song. I remembered that my sister Maria had pointed out a bird like that on the elder bush in the vicarage garden, telling me it was a bullfinch. Big wood ants crawled over my alb in a long column. A bumblebee buzzed around my head, settling on a white dead-nettle next to me, which dipped beneath the weight of the fat, furry black and gold insect. A breeze arose and swept faintly through the trees and grass. The catkins swung gently, dropping golden-yellow pollen.

Suddenly I heard voices some distance away. Perhaps they were foresters, perhaps hikers. They could be my salvation. In spite of the gag I tried to utter some sounds, but the best I could manage was a quiet groan. I tried to raise my bound feet and let them fall back on the forest floor again, but the dull sound that this produced was not enough to attract anyone's attention. Gracious, almighty God, I prayed – for all of a sudden I was able to pray again – who led the children of Israel unharmed through the Red Sea, lead these people, whoever they may be, to me. And the voices came closer, I heard a laugh, an exclamation, a rustle of leaves, crackling undergrowth. A young couple appeared between the spruce trees, about twenty yards away. I continued my desperate attempts to make them notice me, but in vain. They stopped, kissed and walked on. Neither of them looked in my direction. They disappeared behind the tall tree trunks, and soon I couldn't hear their voices. Exhausted by my exertions I closed my eyes, and after a flood of drowsy images had passed through my head I went to sleep. It was an unsettled sleep, interrupted by fragments of dreams, periods of semi-wakefulness, a sleep from which I was finally torn by Magdalena's now so familiar voice.

'Look, Reverend Father, look at all the things I've brought.'

I groggily opened my eyes and saw Magdalena standing in front of me in her leather jump suit, and it was as if it had been merely in one of those dream fragments that had chased like wisps through my sleep that I had seen her first naked and then in her nun's habit. She put a big brown paper bag in the grass, took out her shopping item by item and placed it in front of me. I was very glad that she hadn't abandoned me, and would have wrapped her in my arms if I could. Her face was hot from her long walk, a few little drops of moisture stood out on her immaculate, slightly rounded forehead, and the veins that ran vertically across that forehead were clearly visible.

'Of course there was hardly anything to be had in the village, there was just one small shop attached to the filling station.'

She held a large piece of smoked bacon in front of my nose.

'East Tyrolean *Schinkenspeck*, slightly streaky.'

Then she put a rugged loaf of bread in front of me on the grass.

'Peasant bread from Upper Carinthia.'

Next she took two big bottles from the bag.

'Mineral water.'

And finally she took out a little basket and put it on the ground.

'And cherries. The first of the year. If you behave in a trustworthy fashion, Reverend Father, I may soon be feeding you some bacon and bread, giving you a drink of mineral water and finally shoving some lovely red cherries into your mouth. The filling station attendant, who also serves in the shop, was very friendly, by the way. Very forthcoming. There was a television on in the filling station, and guess who I saw on the screen?' Magdalena looked at me expectantly. 'You'll never guess. Your sister, Reverend Father. I didn't know you had a sister. When I was looking at you before the abduction I saw that woman in the vicarage, but I thought she was the cook. At any rate, your sister didn't look well at all. She's very worried about you. Maybe it was the colour setting on the television, but her face was very pale, with a slight greenish hue. She was constantly wiping tears out of the corners of her sunken, dark-rimmed eyes. And her voice trembled when, on the screen, she asked the man who had abducted her brother to treat him well, he was the dearest thing that she possessed in the world.'

While my sister's solidarity heartened and bolstered me, the rather sentimental tone with which she was apparently trying to gain my freedom embarrassed me somewhat. When Maria wept, as she did often and for the least cause, she certainly didn't look her best, and I considered it a lack of self-discipline, letting herself go like that in front of the Austrian television audience.

Magdalena giggled. 'The *man*! It still hasn't dawned on them that I might be a woman. Your sister is going through a hard time at the moment, Reverend Father. She said, in a cracked voice, she didn't have much money, being a vicarage housekeeper didn't bring in a great deal of money, but she was ready to give the esteemed abductor everything that she and her brother had saved, along with the silver casket that held the family jewellery. And with this she put a prettily chased casket on the table in front of her, an action that was clearly unanticipated judging by the surprised expression of the newsreader sitting next to your sister. Your sister opened the casket, took from it one piece of jewellery after another and held them up in front the camera so that they could be clearly seen. Among other things, she took out a diamond brooch, a present, she said, that had been given to her mother (and yours, of course), originally from the Zillertal, on the occasion of your birth by her father (and yours, of course), the eldest son of a respected notary's family from Lienz. Speaking of a monogrammed oval gold medallion, she remarked that it contained a photograph, along with a lock of hair, from her former fiancé, a respected clerk from Ausservillgraten, who had tragically lost his life in a rockfall during a hike in the mountains.

At this sad revelation she broke down in tears, but before the horrified newsreader could introduce the next item she had regained her composure and produced a white-gold tiepin adorned with a very expensive, she claimed, pea-sized, not quite round, pink shimmering pearl fished from the Mariana Trench, which her paternal grandfather, an ethically and morally upstanding man who had spent decades as a notary in Lienz, had worn to church every Sunday. When the newsreader, by now as white as a sheet, tried to interrupt your sister, she grew more resolute, loudly explaining that the platinum ring with aquamarine faceted with the rectangular step grinding technique had been inherited from her maternal great-aunt, one of seven sisters from Mayrhofen in the Zillertal.

While the newsreader, having by now lost all composure, tried with a series of grimaces to tell an invisible cameraman to pull the plug immediately, your sister, with a melancholy smile, held out the centrepiece of the family jewels, as she put it, to dangle in front of the camera, a long chain of garnets of unusually intense colour, found on the Grossglockner mountain, with an old silver clasp in the form of an edelweiss. The finder of these garnets, she told us, a mountain guide from Matrei, a pleasant and God-fearing man, had later emigrated to New Zealand where he had succumbed to an insidious bacillus of unknown identity. To round off the picture that the esteemed abductor might make of the family jewels on offer, your sister concluded, holding up a simple large cross of massive gold, she was showing this gem made at the beginning of the nineteenth century by a goldsmith near Udine, which a second cousin of her father (and yours, of course) had purchased on a journey to Friuli. Before she could go into further detail about the character of her father's second cousin who had later worked in Venice as a housemaid, the lunchtime news was abruptly interrupted.'

So my dear sister Maria, while I was fundamentally very grateful for her intervention, had given all of Austria's television viewers a taste of her typically extravagant rhetorical style, forever going off at tangents.

Magdalena took two particularly large pairs of cherries out of the little basket, walked up to me and hung them on my ears. Then she picked up the jam jar next to me and took a look at the praying mantis.

'She's looking a bit weary. Not enough oxygen. We'll have to change that.' From one of the pockets in her jump suit she drew a fat red knife and bored holes in the lid with a little steel gouge. 'Very useful, a Swiss Army knife, very useful indeed. There, now she's getting some air again. We'll have to be sure, after all, that when she receives the male, which will doubtless turn up soon, she'll be in good physical condition.'

I thought how ridiculous I must look, a priest tied to a robinia trunk in his Whitsun garb, with a pair of black sunglasses and two pairs of cherries on his ears, and I was glad my congregation couldn't see me in this humiliating situation.

'Time for me to go on with my confession,' said Magdalena. 'I have a feeling we'll have to hurry, although I can't explain why. And I'm no longer so sure whether an absolution from you will be required. The longer I go on talking, the less necessary an absolution from you seems to be, although I can't quite explain why I feel like this. You remember Jonathan telling me I wouldn't get rid of him so quickly. Reverend Father, how often we utter a truth relating to the future, unaware of its real significance. Had I understood the significance of Jonathan's sentence, uttered on the threshold of the cellar door, I would have nipped our relationship in the bud. We fall out of the frying pan into the fire, Reverend Father; hardly are you out of the frying pan than you land in the fire. At considerable personal risk I had got rid of the unreliable native of one of the world's hot countries, Pablo, and hoped to have drawn a happier lot with the reliable native of a cold country, Jonathan, a hope which, like all hopes, proved to be unfounded. However bad things get, there is no guarantee that worse isn't to come. And worse generally comes, much worse.

So Jonathan got into my sidecar and we drove towards Calais, after laying in a few of his favourite blood sausages from a *charcutier* he knew near Bastille. He said it was possible that these sausages were available in northern France as well, but since he wasn't quite sure of this, he preferred to cover his options with some supplies from the *charcutier*, in the quality of whose meat he had complete confidence.

From Beauvais the weather changed, it grew cool and windy, which put Jonathan – who felt at his best in bad weather because of his origins in the Hebrides and his years in Canada – in a good mood and set him off singing old songs in the sidecar, songs which, he told me, dealt with northern passions mingled with heather and peat moors, fishing and sheep rearing. I was surprised that Jonathan wore his very dark-tinted sunglasses even when the sky was cloudy, and when I asked him why he said his eyes were extremely sensitive to light, probably because the sun had shone so seldom during his childhood in the Outer Hebrides. We sped onwards, and after travelling for a few hours we decided to spend the night in a guesthouse near Longpré-les-Corps-Saints, on the Somme.

After taking a meal in our room, consisting of some slices of cold blood sausage, white bread and a bottle of heavy St Emilion, I took a shower. What can I say, Reverend Father? Hardly had I begun to soap myself from top to bottom with the perfumed soap I had brought with me from Paris when Jonathan, having removed his warm clothes, including his purple woollen gloves and his little cap, came into the tiny bedroom, slowly moved aside the plastic curtain patterned with blue fleurs-de-lys, joined me under the shower, took the lavender soap from my hand and continued the work that I had begun.

The half-hour that followed has etched itself ineradicably into my memory. We didn't notice when the water trickling down on us from the shower fitting began to overflow. Only when there was a loud knocking at the door of our room did we awaken from our oblivion to see that the tiled floor of the bathroom was flooded, and the generously flowered carpet of the room was completely drenched with water. The staff had been alerted by the water flooding out from under the door and over the ugly grey-green linoleum in the corridor, and glugging down the stairs and into the dining room, and when Jonathan and I came out of the shower hand in hand, wet and naked, and walked into our unlocked room, we found the thunderstruck guesthouse owner standing in front of us. We immediately covered ourselves with the two white terry towels supplied by the guesthouse, assured the plump blonde in her mid-fifties that of course we would pay for the damage, and were allowed to change rooms. I was hardly capable of carrying my luggage, which wasn't heavy, into the new room, so weakened was I by our half-hour under the shower. We slept extremely well.

The next morning we continued our journey after roughly estimating and accordingly paying for the water damage. Of course I was the one who paid the bill, because, like the Frisian, Jonathan had no money. Fortunately, before we left Paris I had had the presence of mind to withdraw all the money that Pablo and I had saved from his work as a dancing teacher and from our work as concierges, in the Banque Nationale de Paris, Maubert-Mutualité branch, and put it in one of the many pockets of my leather jump suit.

We drove northwards in a light drizzle, via Abbéville in the Somme Département where we paid a quick visit to the late Gothic church of St Wulfram, and on to Calais. Near Namport-Saint-Martin we had taken a short rest in a little poplar wood, and eaten more slices of blood sausage, and Jonathan had taken the opportunity to remind me, with a smile, of the previous evening, bent over me and pressed me gently into the moist grass beneath the poplars. Reverend Father, at the risk of embarrassing you, as one who will certainly have kept your distance from the more profane sides of earthly life, I must, since this is an integral part of my confession, describe the sensations that Jonathan's attentions aroused in me from the very first. Just as it had been the Frisian's tenderness, Igor's fire and Pablo's sense of rhythm that had attracted me, in Jonathan's case it was the attention that he devoted to my neck, particularly my throat, in the course of our erotic play.

You're looking at me in incomprehension, Reverend Father – no wonder, since your neck is always covered by your priest's dog collar. A priestly throat like yours, of course, can't tremble to the many nuances of the range of emotions with which Jonathan set my throat atremble, quite apart from the fact that such trembling is not, of course, what a priestly throat is destined for. A priestly throat is destined to be a protective casing, a kind of pipeline for the conveyance of priestly words through the elaborate interplay of the various organs of articulation, expressing pious exhortations and eternal truths. A priestly throat is not destined to be kissed by the made-up-looking lips of a handsome young man, to blush beneath the little bites of his white teeth. Have you ever heard of priestly throats to which such things have happened? An absurd idea. Precisely, as I just said, because of its dog collar, a priestly throat is never exposed to the light of day, except in the seclusion of his bedroom. But as my throat is not subject to such constraints, and is accordingly easier to get at, it was possible for Jonathan's lips and teeth, particularly his well-developed upper canines, not only to make it blush but even to make it swell a little.

Just as I had temporarily fallen for the Frisian, the Ukrainian and the Spaniard because of their individual talents, so I fell for Jonathan because of the virtuosity he displayed in his treatment of my throat. Just as a talented flautist puts his pursed lips to the flute's mouthpiece, sets the column of air within it vibrating by blowing, and coaxes from it the sweetest sounds, so Jonathan coaxed all manner of notes from my throat by the skilful use of his lips and teeth. So I looked up into the silvery, shimmering poplar leaves, and I yielded to Jonathan's skill. After those caresses I was always curiously enfeebled, but I didn't set too much importance on it.

Arriving in Calais we sought out a small hotel for the last night before our crossing to England. The next morning Jonathan got up, fresh and rested, although it was quite some time before I was fully awake. After eating a generous breakfast, knowing that it would be our last Continental one, we drove the sidecar bike to the Dover ferry. The weather had improved, and on the other side of the Channel we saw the white cliffs of the English south coast. We stood on deck, our elbows leaning on the railing, and as I looked at Jonathan from the side I thought of the Frisian, with whom, not so long ago, I had also stood on the deck of a ferry bound for an island, although in that case the island had been much smaller. I wondered whether Great Britain might also be considered among the places of yearning, the island paradises, or whether its size disqualified it, but I reached no firm conclusion. Jonathan was in a good mood and full of energy, although he was also slightly nervous, as one could tell from his right foot which tapped out a rapid rhythm on the iron deck. When I asked him why he was so ill at ease, he said that the Parisian climate had kept him from his work as an ice sculptor for so long that he was beginning to miss it. If an artist is unable to practise his art for a fairly long time, he becomes first ill at ease, then irritable and finally insane. It was time to continue his work, but he didn't know how. I comforted him and said he would find a way.

After our arrival in Dover, Jonathan said that we should begin by going to London for a few weeks, he had spent several months there after his years in Canada and before his years in Paris. The tramps of London were, almost to a man, very pleasant and civilized people, considerably more pleasant than the *clochards* of Paris, although this was not apparent at first glance. The Parisian *clochards* presented themselves as intellectuals, as philosophers, as poets, but once one began to scratch away a little at this intellectual philosophical, this poetical façade, it became clear that hardly a line of Rimbaud, hardly a sentence of Montaigne, hardly a phrase from Pascal's *Pensées* lay beneath it, that they basically thought about nothing but how they might come by, if not a superb red wine, then one that was at least passable, a cheese, if not outstanding, then at least acceptable. In fact, the largely extrovert Parisian *clochards* took not the slightest interest in the mental, let alone the spiritual life; they spent their time complaining that life had deprived them of the opportunity to drink the very best red wine and eat the very best cheese. *Clochard* intellectualism was superficial intellectualism, just as *clochard* poetry was superficial poetry, the Parisian *clochards* were hedonists, epicureans, materialists and positivists of the worst hue, who spent hours standing outside the windows of the elegant fashion shops in the Rue du Faubourg Saint-Honoré, the elegant jewellers' shops on the Place Vendôme, lamenting the fate that had denied them the wearing of suits by Versace, ties by Cardin and clocks by Cartier. A hedonistic, epicurean, materialistic, positivist rabble, Jonathan said contemptuously. On the other hand, under the Thames bridges he had often come across tramps who could declaim not one but several of the great Shakespearian monologues, quote whole pages from Bertrand Russell's *Religion and Science* and deliver long passages from Byron's *Childe Harold's Pilgrimage* by heart.

He would even go so far as to claim that the London tramps were among the most cultivated, sensitive tramps in the world, miles away from the crude pleasure-seeking, the insatiable gluttony and vain superficiality of the Parisian *clochards*. Their very faces frequently revealed a trait of spirituality, even of asceticism, which was very agreeable. He wanted to meet up again with some of the intellectually and spiritually highly developed tramps that he still remembered. The years in Paris had not been among his happiest, he had never felt at home among the Parisian *clochards*, the shallowness and insubstantiality of the Parisian *clochards* had repelled him from the start, he said. The only ones with whom he had been able to establish a certain, if not a hearty contact, had been the female Parisian *clochards*, perhaps because superficiality and insubstantiality are more easily borne in women than in men.

Jonathan said all this while we pushed the sidecar bike from the ferry and set off for London. We stopped for a while in Canterbury and looked at the cathedral, built in the Perpendicular style. In a niche in the wall there was a little statue of Mary that I liked very much. Her features showed not a trace of humility but expressed alertness and confidence, and she didn't look with a loving tilt of the head at her son held in her arms, as she usually did, nor at the viewer. Her head was averted both from her son and from a potential viewer, and her eyes were turned sideways towards something which was peripheral but which was clearly very interesting to her.

So we drove to London. In our sidecar bike, which attracted not the slightest attention of the average passer-by, we crossed the City towards Hampstead Heath. Here, in an abandoned garage, lived one of the cultivated tramps whom Jonathan knew from his months in London. This friend, a former milling cutter from Kingston-upon-Hull, with flame-red curls and a flame-red beard, was engrossed in a copy of Freud's *Totem und Tabu* when we arrived. He said that since he had visited the Freud Museum, not far from his garage, and cast his eye over the couch preserved there, Freud the man and his work had been constantly in his mind. He had read all his books in English translation, and decided to take German lessons from a tramp he knew from Braunschweig, who lived on the grating of a warm air shaft near the Royal Academy of Arts, so that he could read the books in the original as well. He offered us biscuits and tea which he prepared on a little spirit stove, and at Jonathan's request he said that of course we could park our sidecar bike in his garage, he had plenty of room. In principle he would be delighted to take us in, there was no shortage of places to sleep – he pointed to a pile of dirty mattresses in a corner – but he thought it better for us to look for a temporary dwelling in the centre of the city, since I – and here he smiled politely at me – would doubtless want to use my limited time to visit the most important London sights. He knew a former professional boxer with an interest in the theatre who lived in a small, architecturally remarkable, abandoned nineteenth-century textile factory near the Aldwych. If we liked, he could give us a letter of recommendation, he was sure that the man, a native of Liverpool, would be willing to put us up.

When he had written a few sentences on a piece of paper

scribbled all over with commentaries on *Totem und Tabu*, we set off for the textile factory he had told us about, climbed the dilapidated and banister-free stairs to the first floor, where we found the former professional boxer and three other tramps in the middle of a little colloquium on the theatrical work of Peter Brook. When four pairs of surprised eyes turned to us as we entered, we apologized for intruding and presented the letter of recommendation, whereupon we were given a hearty welcome and encouraged to join in the discusson of Brook's epoch-making 1963 staging of *King Lear* in the Aldwych Theatre just round the corner.

We spent the next few days visiting old friends of Jonathan's in various parts of London, discussing aesthetic, ethical and moral questions. I have very pleasant memories of this time, and Jonathan had not been exaggerating in his description of the London tramps. So we spent stimulating hours in the society of a former computer programmer from Worcestershire, who lived in a disused hangar in Docklands and turned out to be an expert in the field of English portrait painting. I shall never forget his critical assessment of the portrait of Lady Jane Grey in the National Portrait Gallery in St Martin's Place, or the interpretation, penetrating as well as sympathetic, of Milton's *Paradise Regained*, with which a Welsh former clerk at the Ministry of Defence held us enthralled one rainy Sunday afternoon in a corner of Hammersmith Underground station. We always spent the night on a threadbare dark red chaise longue in the abandoned textile factory not far from the Aldwych Theatre, the home of our friend, the former professional boxer from Liverpool, who often indulged in gin, and after excessive consumption of that particular liquid would sometimes deliver monologues from the blood-and-revenge tragedies of the English Renaissance, especially those of John Webster, but apart from this was an absolute sweetheart. We lay on the chaise longue in a big empty hall, with the wind blowing in through the broken windowpanes, along with large numbers of pigeons, and Jonathan eagerly devoted himself to my throat.

One morning, looking in the half-clouded mirror that I had fixed to the brick wall to comb my hair, I noticed two curious little holes on my throat. At first I grew frightened, then calmed down, telling myself that the hall and the chaise longue were doubtless infested with all manner of creatures, and that I had probably been bitten by some large insect while I slept. At the same time I noticed that my face was very pale, which I attributed to the unhealthy London climate. I decided to run half a mile in St James's Park once a day.

Jonathan clearly felt very good in London with his old friends; he seemed powerful and healthy and was full of enterprise and energy. I decided that this was due to the protein-rich food that he ate after we had finished the Parisian blood sausages. From his months in London he knew a little butcher's shop in Soho run by a fat Cockney and his red-cheeked daughter, and once a week he went shopping there, with his own money, incidentally, as he had started doing a few hours' work in the cold-storage depot next to the hangar where the former computer programmer from Worcestershire lived, and his work seemed to put him at ease.

He always returned from the butcher's shop in Soho with a rich selection of raw meat, big chunks of loin roast, rissoles, scrag end, tripe, sweetbreads and marrowbones, juicy chops and bloody steaks. I must admit that the first time I saw him biting into a raw piece of porterhouse I did feel sick. At first I also found it repellent when he noisily sucked the marrow from a bone, or devoured a steak so greedily that the blood ran from the corners of his mouth. During the eating process a gleam, or perhaps more of a glimmer, came to his dark eyes and frightened me a little. When I asked whether it was the custom on the Outer Hebrides to eat raw meat, he said this preference had nothing to do with his origins, it was an entirely personal need, a necessity, because if he didn't eat raw meat his strength abandoned him and he soon felt tired and exhausted.

Reverend Father, when he sat there on the threadbare chaise longue in the empty hall of the textile factory, lips and chin bloody from the consumption of a raw shank of cow, a dripping red pork chop in his hand, my passion plummeted. Because it was certainly a passion that had bound me to him and to his beautiful mouth, with which he excited the region of my throat so irresistibly. Suddenly I found it repulsive that the same white teeth that tore into a rump steak before my eyes would gently work the white flesh of my throat a few hours later. I grew dizzy, and fell into the armchair, covered with a ragged plaid, that stood next to the chaise longue.

Ah, passion,' Magdalena sighed. 'Isn't it funny the way a passion like that can vanish from one day to the next? A purely rhetorical question, because as a man of God passion will mean nothing to you, of course, apart from the Passion of Christ, which is considerably different from the passion that I mean, the ecstasy produced solely by the stimulation of the senses, condemned by you and your kind as the deadly sin of *luxuria*. You know what I mean?'

And so saying she stood up, walked over to me, brought her full lips close to my right ear and began nibbling at the pair of cherries dangling from it. This inevitably involved contact with my outer ear and earlobe, and even the extremely sensitive area of skin behind the ear, contact which was, strangely, extremely unpleasant and at the same time extremely pleasurable, and aroused in me a conflict of sensations, a revolt of the emotions the like of which I had never experienced before. But this time there was no use even trying to look into the foliage of the robinia and distracting myself with the colours and shapes of divine nature. I felt as though the blood in my veins was flowing more quickly than usual, as if it was crashing through my pulmonary arteries like a rushing torrent, swirling like a dangerous whirlpool in my clavicle veins, smashing against my cardiac walls like a tidal wave, thundering through my aorta like a raging flood.

And when, after she had eaten the first pair of cherries, she leaned down towards the second pair, and thus towards my left ear, my body's thermal regulation went completely out of control. The enormous increase in the supply of blood to the skin produced an unusually strong emission of heat, and I felt the hairs standing up on the back of my neck, and drops of sweat standing out on my forehead. When Magdalena had spent a long time on my ear, I gave up any effort at maintaining my physiological equilibrium, closed my eyes and succumbed to her labial attentions. But when I abandoned all resistance and decided to go with the wave that was carrying me, Magdalena suddenly stopped her mechanical manipulations of my left ear and went on talking.

'Once again the inevitable decline had begun. It was not only Jonathan's eating habits that began to revolt me, I was also annoyed that he took my bike from his friend's garage and, in the cold-storage depot where he worked, loaded the sidecar with blocks of ice which he brought to our hall, full of flapping pigeons, in the textile factory. There he worked on them with his big, gleaming knife and a metal saw, an enterprise which, because of the moderate English climate, was condemned to failure from the outset. He asked me to model for him, a desire with which I complied reluctantly, since the oceanic climate of Great Britain was on the one hand too warm for the production and more particularly the preservation of ice sculptures, while on the other hand it was too cold for a woman with a weakened constitution to stand naked for hours in the draught from the broken windowpanes. And it really did take hours each time, because when he had finally carved my torso out of ice and started on my thighs, the head began first to drip and then to lose its shape, until all that remained was an irregular ball of ice. When he had completed the left arm and set about carving the right one, the left one slowly began to melt until there was nothing left of it but a dripping stump.

Soon the floor was permanently covered with big puddles of water, which the pigeons would use to refresh themselves. I stood shivering in the middle of the big empty room, one arm outstretched or bent, my head turned upwards or sideways, and sometimes wondered whether I had been right to put a sudden end to Pablo's life, or whether it might not have been more sensible to put up patiently with his mania for dancing.

I began to think of escape, particularly since the progressive decline in my physical strength, and the constant increase, apparently related to it in some mysterious way, of Jonathan's dynamic activity, gradually began to strike me as suspicious. Every morning I lay more feebly on the chaise longue, every morning he leapt more vigorously from the couch. I thought I might have become anaemic from a lack of iron, and bought myself some iron tablets, but my condition didn't change, any more than it did when I took various vitamin preparations and minerals. It couldn't be anything to do with a lack of fresh air, as the wind blew through all the cracks and through the broken windowpanes. One morning, looking at my pale face in the mirror, I was struck by faint traces of dried blood on my throat, and my suspicions deepened. I thought briefly, and then went to the library of the British Museum in Great Russell Street, a journey that seemed very long because I was so weakened that I had to stop and rest for a moment at every street corner. In the library I ordered up a copy of Bram Stoker's novel *Dracula*, published in 1897, and sat down near the seat that Karl Marx had always used, to read the book.

Reverend Father, after reading for less than half an hour I was certain: I was in the power of a vampire, a revenant, a ghoul, who was feeding on my blood. The reason for the attention that Jonathan devoted to my throat lay not in erotic passion but in a desire for nourishment. The two little holes in my throat weren't insect bites but the traces of

Jonathan's well-developed canines – they granted him access to the fluid he needed. Now, too, I understood his excessive meat consumption: as I grew more bloodless, he had to get a supplementary supply of the precious liquid, and in the absence of fresh human blood he made do with the flesh of pigs, cattle and oxen. I had to act immediately, or end up lying in our big room bled dry, an empty shell.

I closed the book and dragged myself back to the textile factory. As you can imagine, I had been shaken to discover that I was acting as the chief source of nourishment for a vampire. I climbed the stairs, resting briefly on each step. The building was empty, the former professional boxer and his friends were off to a theatre festival in Scotland where they would meet up with tramps from Glasgow and talk about whether the politically committed theatre of the sixties could be revived, and Jonathan was still working in the cold-storage unit. I hastily packed my few belongings in two plastic bags, went back down the stairs and opened the front door. Outside the door stood Jonathan, a little earlier than expected. Clearly the late-afternoon traffic hadn't been as slow-moving as usual. He saw immediately that my suspicions had been roused, but didn't let it show, smiled at me, embraced me, devoted himself tenderly to my throat, forcing me slowly back into the hall and closing the door behind him. He gently pushed me up the stairs and back into our room, and by the time we were standing by the chaise longue, in my exhaustion I could not stop him taking the plastic bags from my hand, putting them on the floor, pushing me down on the chaise longue and gently digging his teeth into my neck.

Next morning, when he had washed, whistling, in the shower cabinet installed by the former professional boxer from Liverpool, breakfasted on a little steak tartare and set off for the cold-storage unit, I rose with difficulty from the chaise longue. From the mirror a deathly pale, sunken, hollow-eyed face stared back at me. I took my plastic bags and went back down the stairs with them, only to discover that the front door was locked. Jonathan had realized I had discovered who he was, and as my escape would make life very unpleasant for him, he was trying to prevent it. What was I to do? Of course there was no telephone in the house, and the only possibility lay in climbing out of the window, but I felt too weak for that.

Reverend Father, I had reached the end. I went back into the room, collapsed on the chaise longue and feverishly sought a way out. I sat there for hours, my hands folded in my lap, without reaching a solution. In the end I rose to my feet, paced back and forth for a while and, as I did so, bumped into the shabby old wooden table; on it, on some greaseproof paper, lay the steak tartare from the Soho butcher's shop that Jonathan had been eating for breakfast. I tried a little purely out of curiosity. It was raw, but minced and mixed with other ingredients so that it was nothing like the blood-dripping clumps of meat that he usually devoured. I thought this well-known and highly esteemed dish didn't taste bad at all, and ate a little, realizing that I was hungry. Recently my appetite had declined a great deal, probably because of my increasing exhaustion. I pushed a rickety chair to the table, sat down and ate ravenously. While I was eating I felt my strength returning, and when about half of the steak tartare was gone I felt as if reborn. A glance in the mirror showed me a pretty woman with a fresh complexion, gleaming eyes, red cheeks and full lips.

I walked to the high window to see the best way of getting down. In the same moment I heard footsteps on the stairs and just managed to hide what was left of the steak tartare behind the chaise longue before Jonathan walked into the room. He gave me a friendly greeting, then his eye drifted to the empty table and his face grew suspicious. When he asked the whereabouts of the steak tartare that he had bought the previous day, I said casually that I had wanted some meat and had eaten it, it had been delicious, the butcher in Soho was really excellent. And I hadn't left the house all day but had read the book *Ice Palaces*. I had found this book informative and instructive, particularly the chapter about a new method employed in ice architecture, namely the use of the shell structure. Jonathan was delighted by my interest in this innovative building technique and gladly answered all my questions about the wafer-thin domes and arches that could be built with this method. You sprayed the surface of an enormous balloon with water, he said, you froze the water and then removed the balloon, leaving behind a beautiful, transparent, thin dome of ice. In this way you could build domes with a diameter of twenty-five to thirty metres. On a mountain in Vermont there was a shell structure ice palace modelled on the church of Hagia Sophia in Istanbul, whose central dome opened up to the sky.

We spent a long time talking about this new building technique, so long that by evening Jonathan was too tired to devote himself as intensely to my throat as he usually did, and went to sleep before he had managed to leave me completely paralysed. After he had fallen into a deep sleep beside me, I reached carefully behind the chaise longue and quickly devoured what was left of the steak tartare, to get my strength back. Then I slid softly from our bed, took the sidecar bike's ignition key from the table where Jonathan had left it, and, with a plastic bag in which I'd carefully packed the belongings that were most important to me, namely the pink Sony Walkman with the two Bach cassettes, the Swiss Army knife, the habit of the Barefoot Carmelites, the G.C. Sansoni edition of the *Divina Commedia* and Artemidoros's *Interpretation of Dreams*, tiptoed to the window furthest from the chaise longue. I was sorry to leave the Lingen atlas behind but it was too heavy. When I had climbed on to the windowsill, Jonathan stirred with a sigh on the chaise longue, and I froze in terror. But when he stopped moving I forced the plastic bag, held with a string, over my shoulder, grabbed the drainpipe with both hands and slowly lowered myself down, gashing my right hand open in the process.

Landing on the asphalt of the pavement, I ran round the corner to the sidecar bike parked in front of the house. Reverend Father, you won't believe it, but the moment I tried to start the bike, Jonathan appeared from the sidecar and grinned at me with his flashing canines. Above him, between the television aerials, was a big, pale full moon. I was so startled that it was easy for him to tear the ignition key out of my hand and give me a shove, whereupon I stumbled into the middle of the street and fell over. Before he could run over me I recovered, grabbed the plastic bag and began to run for my life. He drove behind me and would have overtaken me very soon if I hadn't turned a corner at the last minute and run up a high flight of narrow steps between two houses. Jonathan stopped the bike and ran after me. The steps stopped at the top, and I turned round and saw him coming closer, long canines flashing. I thought I was lost when I saw a little wooden door in a wall beside me. I rattled the handle, and the door opened up into a dark room. I stumbled over the threshold, closed the door behind me, reached for the lock, noticed there was a key in it and turned it. At the same instant a naked lightbulb came on and I found myself in a shabby, sparsely furnished room. On a mattress on the floor a middle-aged man was sitting bolt upright, staring at me aghast. Outside, Jonathan began to break down the far from solid wooden door with his fists.

Help me, I begged the petrified man. Someone's after me, help me! We have to barricade the door!

I began to push the furniture to the door, a little table, a shelf, two armchairs, and finally the man, who was wearing a knee-length white nightshirt, threw aside the blanket covering him, rose from the mattress and began to join in. When wood started to splinter from the door under Jonathan's furious assault, the man in the nightshirt set about taking packages tied up with string, which were stacked along one wall of the room, and piling them up against the door. I helped him, and finally the whole door was behind the packages, which appeared to hold some kind of pamphlet. We heard Jonathan hammering at the door and stood by it with bated breath, our arms dangling at our sides. The thin hair of the slim, rather short man was tousled from sleep, and his dark moustache was also a bit dishevelled. After a time the noise stopped. Apparently Jonathan had abandoned his attempts to force his way in. Relieved, we sat down on the mattress in the middle of the room, covered with a white sheet.

Only now did I have the chance to apologize for my unauthorized night-time disturbance, to introduce myself and thank him for the shelter he had given me. He said that went without saying, and anyway the Battle of Armageddon, in which all the forces of Satan would be destroyed, was at hand. When I looked at him blankly, he added that Jehovah was great, pressed a book entitled *The Finished Mystery* into my hand, and said that this book by the pastor had already sold millions of copies. When I still didn't understand, he explained that the packages stacked up first along the wall and now against the door were copies of the magazine *The Watch Tower*, whose purpose it was to herald the kingdom of Jehovah, and which he therefore had to distribute among the people.

Reverend Father, the man who had offered me shelter was the Jehovah's Witness Michael Minulescu, whose father came from Puini in Transylvania and whose mother came from Reading. After he had offered me a glass of milk and a cheddar cheese sandwich, cleaned and bound my bleeding right hand and told me a little about himself, I began to trust him, and as I desperately needed to tell him about the incredible thing that had happened to me through my involvement with Jonathan Alistair Abercrombie, since his father, as chance would have it, came from Transylvania, the home of the famous Wallachian prince and vampire Vlad Tepes, known as Dracula, I began

160

to pour my heart out to him, a fatal error on my part as it later turned out. I talked until the sun rose over the roofs of London, visible through the little barred window of the room, drank four more glasses of English full-cream milk and ate two more cheddar cheese sandwiches. Then I fell exhausted on the mattress, dimly aware that Michael was gently covering me with a blanket of Highland sheep's wool and putting a pillow under my head, and fell asleep.'

Magdalena stopped for a moment and stared thoughtfully in front of her. A fine early summer rain had started to fall, making her strawberry-blonde curls a little curlier. For myself, I was protected against this precipitation by the dense foliage at the top of the robinia. She seemed not to notice the drizzle in the slightest, so caught up was she in the memory of the events, both exciting and painful, of her past. My respect for this woman, who had clearly got into the most difficult situations through no fault of her own, was rising by the hour, and I very much hoped that Michael Minulescu, whom she had met under such dramatic circumstances, would introduce a little peace into her unstable life. He seemed to possess positive characteristics such as helpfulness, solicitousness, moderation, and in view of the critical situation the fact that he was a Jehovah's Witness, one of those sadly misguided folk, was something best simply ignored.

'When I awoke the following morning,' Magdalena continued, interrupting my reflections about her future, 'Michael had already returned the furniture and the packages of magazines to their places, and brought me a cup of tea in bed. He sat down beside me and said he had been thinking about my situation for much of the night. Then he looked at me seriously, and said that I, having eluded the undead by a thread, had a duty to free the world from this monster. He found the phenomenon of vampirism particularly repellent, since both the consumption of blood and blood transfusion were strictly forbidden to Jehovah's Witnesses. Thanks to his

Transylvanian relations, whom he visited from time to time, he knew a little about vampires. I must surely know that if they are not rendered harmless they continue to spread their evil for ever. With these words he took, from a big black brass-handled trunk in a corner of the room, a stake carved by an uncle on his father's side of the family, from the wood of a Transylvanian alder that had stood by a pond in which a child had drowned, and solemnly handed it to me.

Go, and kill the monster! he said. You will be doing mankind an inestimable service.

Reverend Father, I must admit to you that I had not the slightest desire to comply with Michael's heated appeal. As soon as anyone reminds me of my supposed duties to the so-called general public, the so-called community, so-called humanity, as soon as anyone demands so-called altruism, so-called self-sacrifice, so-called common humanity from me, I get stubborn. I know that you will condemn me savagely for such a demonstration of apparently absolute autism, particularly disturbing in a woman, but all too often I have found that the very people who are forever talking about the common good, and who seem on the surface to fulfil the demands of that common good about which they are forever talking, are generally among the greatest hypocrites you will ever come across. And of course it is above all the good Christians, the good Catholics who talk about so-called brotherly love. Believe me, Reverend Father, a nomadic, unsettled way of life like my own provides ample opportunity to come into contact with a great diversity of people, and to gain both a broad overview and a deep insight. The overview, the insight that I had thus acquired showed quite clearly that you should keep away from people who constantly have the words common good, brotherly love, selflessness on their lips, and who appear to be engaged in translating those abstract qualities into practice.

It is not my intention, Reverend Father, to attack you personally. It can happen that practising Christians are good people, although it happens rarely; it is largely but not entirely unlikely that one will encounter good people among practising Catholics, although for myself, nowhere have I come across such treachery, such perfidy, such guile as I have among good Christians, good Catholics. The good people are the bad ones, the bad the good, that is how it is, Reverend Father, that is exactly how it is. It would not be enough to speak simply of a *coincidentia oppositorum*, a coincidence of opposites, as identified by the great German mystic Nikolaus von Kues, with whom you will doubtless be familiar, it is a matter of discovering that the truth is not that which is at hand, the side of the coin that is visible to everyone, but the reverse, the opposite. The only possible conclusion to be drawn from this is that one should mistrust apparently good people and turn towards apparently bad ones. Since I began acting according to this revelation, which I attribute to bitter experience, I am betrayed considerably less often, I am hardly ever disappointed.

If your face, Reverend Father, has assumed a disbelieving and rather wounded expression in the course of my digression on my reluctance to carry out the task imposed upon me by Michael Minulescu when he handed me the wooden stake, this digression was, nonetheless, an unavoidable necessity, and was interpolated so that you, as a member of the opposition, might share in the knowledge I acquired over some difficult years in my life, and perhaps to prompt you to a radical reversal, a radical change of position.

So I looked at the wooden stake that Michael Minulescu had pressed into my hand and felt no particular need to hammer it into Jonathan Alistair Abercrombie's bloodthirsty heart, at least not for the reason proposed by Michael, that it would be a service to humanity. It was just the fear of having to go on fleeing him, being pursued by him, living in mortal danger. You, as a representative of Christian *caritas*, will doubtless characterize this as an extremely egocentric motive, but, after thinking for a long time on the mattress with the white sheet, it made the idea of eliminating the monster as quickly as possible appear entirely valid.

What I didn't like was the instrument of his elimination, the alder stake. I asked Michael whether it was absolutely necessary for Jonathan to be killed with this stake, to which he replied that he believed this tool to be the only really appropriate one. While he was explaining this to me, another idea came to me, an idea which I wisely kept to myself, as I suspected that he would reject it forthwith. I rose to my feet and declared that I would carry out the task assigned to me.

As I went down the high, narrow steps with the alder stake in my bandaged right hand, Michael called after me, saying that as a sign that the monster had been successfully despatched I must bring back an object inseparably connected with him, one which might be said to embody his sinister power. In the event, he thought one of the vampire's canines might do the trick. I called back that I would try to fulfil this condition as well, and set off for the textile factory.

It was a bright Saturday morning, people were rushing busily through the streets, couples were kissing in the sun, sparrows were twittering in the gutter. Jonathan would be at home, he usually slept for a long time at the weekend. My steps quickened, I had nothing in mind but the idea of removing him quickly, so that I could return to a normal life. And the instrument of despatch would not be the wooden stake but Jonathan's big, gleaming knife. For one thing, the blade was razor-sharp, and for another I was handier with it than I was with the pointed piece of wood, as I had often used the knife to carve food, to cut a thread when doing little bits of embroidery, to carve a toothpick, in short for all kinds of everyday tasks, and for yet another, in my life so far it had always proved an advantage to kill an enemy with his own weapons. And even if Jonathan Alistair Abercrombie had at first been anything but an enemy, even if he had helped me rid myself of my faithless dancer and his magic-practising lovers, it remained an indisputable fact that he had become an enemy, and one who was after my blood.

The sidecar bike was standing in front of the house. I opened the door and entered the building. I slipped quietly up the stairs, put my ear to the door of our room and heard the quiet sound of running water. As I had expected, Jonathan was under the shower. On Saturdays and Sundays he would shower himself thoroughly in the cabinet installed by the former professional boxer, which stood in a corner near the door. Things were looking good, and I had to act immediately. I gently pushed the door open, pulled the knife from the leather sheath in the belt in the loops of a ragged pair of trousers tossed carelessly on the armchair, put the wooden stake on the chair and crept, grasping the handle of the knife with my injured right hand, past a dripping, only vaguely recognizable ice copy of Rodin's *Thinker* to the shower cabinet. Jonathan couldn't hear me because the noise of the splashing water masked my quiet footsteps, he couldn't see me because the wall of the shower cabinet was covered with condensation. I stopped for a moment, then jerked the sliding partition aside.

Jonathan stood there, wet and handsome, and for a fraction of a second I hesitated as the memory of our first night in the guesthouse near Longpré-les-Corps-Saints by the Somme shot through my head. But I immediately regained control of myself, raised my arm a long way back and plunged in the knife with all my strength. Jonathan looked at me wide-eyed, bared his canines in a strange smile, and sank to the floor of the shower cabinet. He lay still with his face on the tiles. He died instantly, my aim had been accurate. With the bloody knife in my hand I stood and watched the blood and water mingling into curious shapes around him. I thought of the proof of the killing that Michael Minulescu had demanded, but baulked at the idea of breaking off one of his upper canines. I cut off a strand of his long black hair, cleaned the knife and put it back on the table. Next to the dried, brownish bloodstain on the white muslin bandage with which Michael had bound my right hand there was now a big new dark-red stain. I took the alder stake, drenched it with Jonathan's blood, turned the tap off and closed the sliding door. I reached into the pockets of the ragged trousers and found the ignition key of the sidecar bike. Then, following an inexplicable impulse, I picked up the Ray-Bans on the table, looked for a small plastic bag, stuffed the stake, hair, key and sunglasses into it and left the room and the former textile factory.'

Magdalena fell silent. She was sitting in front of me in the light drizzle, her hair growing damper and damper. I wanted to tell her that I admired her for her courage, for her intelligence and for the resolution with which she had rendered the monster harmless. Her deed made me think of Saint George slaying the dragon. I felt that Michael Minulescu, although he possessed the positive qualities of helpfulness, solicitousness and moderation, had not exactly distinguished himself by his bravery in this business. He, who, as a man, should have assumed that difficult task, had simply delegated it to Magdalena by passing on the wooden stake. And Magdalena had risen to the challenge. What a woman!

'Oh no, it's raining,' said Magdalena, and looked up to the sky. 'I hadn't thought of that. I'm going to come and sit next to you under the crown of the tree, Reverend Father, under the crown of the tree we will be protected from the rain.'

She stood up and sat down beside me, after taking my sunglasses off. Although this woman was holding me by force, although I was completely in her power, although it was quite possible that she would shortly kill me, just as she had killed the melancholic Frisian, the jealous Ukrainian, the faithless Galician and blood-sucking Jonathan, I liked having her right beside me. I no longer understood myself. I had to try to distance myself from this dangerous person, who had not only wrapped the green washing line round me but was weaving the threads of her yarn tighter and tighter about me as well.

Magdalena put her head on my shoulder.

'It's nice, this rain,' she said. 'We're sitting under the tree looking out into the warm rain. Let's sit in silence for a while and concentrate on the sound of the falling rain.'

I felt the sinner's head gradually growing heavier. Perhaps she had gone to sleep, I couldn't see her eyes. It poured quietly with rain, and the blades of grass gleamed. The monotonous sound put me in a state between waking and sleeping, and I had a feeling of sliding out of myself and jumping on to a projecting branch of the robinia, like the bullfinch I had seen before. From the robinia branch I looked down on the unusual couple sitting so peacefully against the trunk.

I don't know how long I spent in that strange intermediate state. Suddenly, from above, I saw the sinner twist her beautiful mouth into a cruel smile, reach her slender left hand into the high grass of early summer, pull out the big gleaming knife and point the blade at the chest of the priest, whose eyes were closed. At this sight I must have given a start, because the next thing I heard was Magdalena's calming voice.

'What's wrong, Reverend Father? Why are you staring at me horrified like that? Have you had a bad dream?'

I saw Magdalena's face close in front of me, the astonished blue eyes, the long lashes, the round mole, some freckles scattered over her light complexion. The Magdalena I had just seen with the gleaming knife must have been a dream.

'Since you have woken me now, since I'm now awake, I might as well continue with my story,' she said. 'Although I would have liked to sleep on your priestly shoulder a little longer,' she said, rubbing her head on my shoulder like a cat, a movement that electrified me. I was sure there was a crackle at the point where hair and shoulders touched, even if I couldn't see it, that sparks were flying, even if I couldn't see them.

'So I drove the bike back to Michael Minulescu who was

preparing to perform one of his tasks as a Jehovah's Witness, distributing *The Watchtower* in the Underground. Now he was wearing not the knee-length white nightshirt but a dark brown suit which was worn and threadbare, but which gave him a trustworthy appearance nonetheless. He was also wearing polished black shoes, a plain, slightly yellowing white shirt, and a dark brown tie. He noticed my surprised expression. If one pursued an occupation such as his own, he explained, an occupation which sought to convince the unenlightened, to lead them to the right path, it was of the utmost importance to make an impression of honesty and respectability, or rather to give expression through one's outward appearance to the honesty and respectability that dwelt naturally within every Jehovah's Witness. Uprightness, reliability and moral maturity were indispensable preconditions for membership of the chosen who were called to spread the word of Jehovah's kingdom.

Before he could go into greater detail about the tasks of the Jehovah's Witnesses, I interrupted him and pulled the bloody wooden stake and the black strand of hair from the plastic bag as proof that I had carried out his instructions. When I had to reply to Michael's question about the canine by saying that I hadn't had the heart to break a tooth from the vampire, he was disgruntled, saying the strand of hair might do at a pinch but he was surprised, not to say somewhat disappointed, by the shoddy way in which I had fulfilled my instructions. One of his reasons for assigning this task to me was to test my suitability as a potential member of the Jehovah's Witnesses. Membership of the Jehovah's Witnesses naturally required rigid discipline and absolute submission to the will of Jehovah and his representatives on earth. Although I had passed his test only with extremely mediocre success, he would give me a chance.

With these words he opened the big black brass-handled trunk, and from it he took a simply cut grey flannel lady's suit and a dark-blue long-sleeved cotton blouse. He appraised my black leather jump suit and motorcycle boots with a disapproving glance and said that if I wanted to belong to the community of the chosen I would first of all have to change my wardrobe. I would have to get rid of my outfit forthwith, since it flagrantly contravened the clothing regulations of the Jehovah's Witnesses, and don the unassuming clothes left by his mother, a long-standing supporter of the Jehovah's Witnesses in and around Reading, who had sadly died of a stroke the previous April. He pressed the suit and the blouse into my hand, and after further rummaging in the big black trunk he unearthed a pair of light-brown lace-up shoes with crepe soles and solid medium heels, a pair of dark-brown woollen tights and a black cloche hat. He put the hat on my head, took a few steps back, looked at me and said that the colour and texture of my hair could hardly be said to coincide with the principles, aims and general moral precepts of the Jehovah's Witnesses. The cloche hat, which covered only a part of my head, could only be a provisional solution, sooner or later we would have to give some thought to the matter of changing my hairdo. A big square headscarf in a restrained colour might do the trick. Then Michael pointed to a little door which he said was the lavatory, telling me to change because we had to be ready to go to work at Piccadilly Underground station. When I didn't react, he pushed me towards the lavatory door, opened it and pushed me in.

All of a sudden I found myself in Michael's lavatory, the suit, the blouse and the woollen stockings over my arm, the shoes in my hand and the cloche hat on my head. I slowly sat down on the lavatory seat. Reverend Father, sometimes we do things that later make us shake our heads. In retrospect, the idea of agreeing to what Michael and fate had in store for me, actively participating in the proselytizing work of the Watch Tower Bible and Tract Society founded by the American Charles Taze Russell, struck me as absurd, but you must bear in mind that my previous erotic experiences had

169

sent me somewhat off the rails, that I had lost my bearings somewhat, some of the control of my life. The daily loss of blood had greatly enfeebled me, my resistance was exhausted, I had reached my limit, I felt sucked dry and unprotected and very much in need of someone to lean on. Whenever we find ourselves in those hopeless states, someone inevitably turns up who spots our situation in a flash and immediately exploits it for his own purposes.

So I sat on the lavatory seat wondering what to do. When Michael knocked on the door and said we had to go in five minutes, I stood up, took off my motorcycle jump suit and boots and slipped into the clothes of Michael's late mother. At least Michael would treat me well, at least he wouldn't be violent like Igor, I thought, while I pulled the brown stockings over my legs. He wouldn't lie and deceive me like Pablo, I said to myself as I buttoned up the cotton blouse. Ideologically speaking, Michael might have his peculiarities, but aside from that he struck me as an honest, affable man, a reticent man, largely free of destructive passions, a man who showed respect for women. I would give it a go. I opened the lavatory door and stood on the threshold wearing the grey flannel suit. Michael looked at me speechlessly for a minute, and then said quietly, with emotion in his voice, that it was astonishing how closely I resembled his departed mother wearing those clothes. Couldn't I put my hair up in a bun before we set off? he asked. I complied with his wish, which in my unbounded naivety I considered completely harmless, and armed with two packages of *The Watch Tower*, we set off for Piccadilly Tube station. Already waiting for us there was Gabriel Rothenberg, a converted Jew of German descent, whom Michael introduced to me as his comrade-in-arms and best friend. Gabriel, a tall, powerfully built young man with blond hair and a slight speech impediment, had, he told me, worked as a shop assistant in a Jewish delicatessen-cum-bookshop, and lived, not far from Michael, on the Tottenham Court Road where he lodged with a friendly landlady.

Michael handed about thirty copies of *The Watch Tower* to Gabriel who was going to take them on the Underground to Hyde Park Corner, to announce the message of the Second Coming and the Thousand-Year Kingdom. When Michael explained that Gabriel was by far the most rhetorically gifted of all the London Jehovah's Witnesses, and that the London Jehovah's Witnesses considered themselves lucky to have such a persuasive, rousing orator in their ranks, the young man brushed this aside with a modest smile and said that his talent, as in the case of the Attic rhetorician and statesman Demosthenes, was a typical example of over-compensation; if he hadn't had a slight speech impediment, if he didn't have a slight stammer, he would never have had the ambition to develop his eloquence. Our handicaps often prove to be our good fortune, he said as he left, the disadvantages with which a supposedly hostile fate has burdened us prove in many cases to be advantages.

As soon as the pleasant young man had disappeared, Michael assigned me a place in one of the Underground passages, after chasing away a blind mouth-organ player, and said he expected a restrained and dignified performance from me. I was only to speak when a question was asked of me, and I was to do nothing but mutely offer the magazine for sale. Before he took up his position at a corner nearby, he listed as a series of headings the most important doctrines of his religion. That would have to do for now, he said, I would have ample opportunity to acquire a more profound knowledge by means of a thorough study of the Bible and the pastor's seven volumes of *Scripture Studies*.

Regrettably, in the course of two hours I sold only three magazines, one to an old man who thought *The Watch Tower* was a journal dealing with the events of the First World War, and the second to a young street musician who was pulling her harp behind her on a little cart, who said there was far too little solidarity between us women who worked in the public arena, and she would buy a brochure from me, but she also requested my support if I should ever see her playing at her spot in Leicester Square. She stopped in front of me and chatted with me, prompting furious glances from Michael, who was watching me from where he stood. The young musician asked me whether I was familiar with the workings of harps, and when I mutely shook my head, she said the harp was a chordophone, whose strings ran vertically to the top of the soundboard. The strings strung between the soundboard and the neck were plucked with the fingertips of both hands. Even the ancient Egyptians had been acquainted with the arch harp, named after its shape, the corner harp and the frame. It was only with the introduction of the diatonic Tyrolean hook harp, however, that manual retuning had become relatively simple, thus increasing the number of notes available. The harp normally in use today was the forty-six to forty-eight string double-action harp, like the one she owned. The double-action harp was tuned to C flat major. With seven double pedals, each note in the C-flat major scale could be raised by a half or a whole tone, so that all the notes in the tempered tuning could be played. The range of the harp thus extended over almost seven octaves. She had inherited her harp from her foster mother, of whom she had been very fond. When she played, in her mind she was playing to her foster mother, who had adopted her, an orphan, although she had seven children of her own. What a woman, she said.

In order to demonstrate how her harp worked, the young woman began to play a simple English folk tune, whereupon Michael came running up, shouting that she was disturbing our business and telling her to skedaddle forthwith. At this the musician went on her way with her little cart and her harp, after whispering to me that I should come and visit her at her spot in Leicester Square that coming Saturday. She, along with her friend on the flute, would give a rendition of the Concerto for Flute and Harp by Wolfgang Amadeus Mozart, K299, or K297c, probably written in April 1778 for the Duc de Guines and his daughter, an accomplished flautist. Incidentally, the Duke had neglected to pay for the work for a long time. Of course I had to imagine the two violins, the viola and the bass, the two oboes and the two French horns. And in Leicester Square we would have a chance to talk about female solidarity undisturbed.

I sold the third *Watch Tower* to a stubbled man of about thirty, in a suit slightly too large for him and with his hair in a ponytail. Because of his hair and stubble I took him at first for a rather well-to-do tramp, and inwardly prepared myself for a brief discussion on a literary theme. After an introductory exchange, uneasily watched by Michael, it turned out that the man worked in advertising. He asked me to forgive his uninvited interference but he had seen *Watch Tower* sellers on a number of occasions on this particular corner, and he had always been amazed by their unbelievable sales strategies. I couldn't expect to target my prospective consumer group while wearing such an old-fashioned outfit. Obviously you had to advertise in clothing that corresponded to the unconscious desires of the potential buyer. Why didn't I sell my magazine in a nice chic catsuit? I was a pretty woman, after all. An orange catsuit would be ideal, orange was a very successful marketing colour, although market analyses had shown a fresh, optimistic pink to be a profit-maximizing hue. A suit like the one I was wearing didn't engender a desire to purchase, on the contrary, and shoes like mine nipped any consumer impulse in the bud. With a further apology he loosened my bun, and Michael ran over furiously again but was immediately drawn into a discussion with the advertising specialist. Hair such as mine, he said, was an invaluable advertising device and should clearly be exploited, it should certainly not be hidden. And the layout of *The Watch Tower* was also completely out of date, we should find ourselves a good graphic designer, there were enough of them around, after all. We could, for example, bring our material closer to a male audience as really cool comic strips, nothing obscene, of course, but mildly erotic in tone, that would get sales going. When Michael looked at him dumbfounded, he said that biblical truths in comic-strip form could also be printed on T-shirts, that would boost sales like mad, Adam and Eve under the tree of knowledge, or Mary Magdalen in the various stages of sinning, he wasn't too familiar with the plot, but that might be a possibility. It was hard to survive against the competition in every field, even where sects were concerned.

When Michael tried to intervene furiously and explain to the advertising specialist that the Jehovah's Witnesses were not a sect but a religion, the advertising specialist said he wasn't interested in such fine distinctions, he'd just thought he would help us with a few ideas for which other people would pay good money, didn't we understand that? We might also think about shooting a few short films, he continued, and project them on the white-tiled walls of the Underground passages. But we shouldn't use amateurs, there were enough unemployed actors ready to take on jobs like that for small amounts of money. And music, music was an extremely suggestive advertising strategy, why didn't we set our beliefs to music in a somewhat simplified form, get it recorded by some decent rock musicians in a respectable studio and play it through a proper sound system in the Underground passage? The rock musicians could play live as well, of course, that would be even better. We must forgive him, but we clearly had not the slightest notion of advertising, of the deliberate and non-coercive influence of human decision-making and opinion-forming in relation to economic and intellectual, political, cultural and also religious goals. But now he had to go, he had an important meeting. Anyway, he hoped he had given us some useful ideas which would make our work more lucrative. So saying, he handed us his card and strode off.

On the one hand Michael was attracted by the advertising expert's ideas, while on the other he was irritated by the fact that I seemed always to be drawn into conversation by people who hardly looked like potential converts and who just distracted me from the work at hand. He grabbed the packages of magazines and said that was enough for today, for my further instruction he suggested that we go to Hyde Park Corner and listen to Gabriel.

Gabriel was standing on an upended mineral-water box and talking to two interested listeners, a young girl in a nurse's uniform and an elderly lady with two legs in plaster, in a wheelchair pushed by the young woman. Next to him, surrounded by several hundred people, on a beer crate there stood a representative of the extreme right who, interrupted by enthusiastic applause, was calling for a revival of English alliterative poetry and the application of the fine old ghetto principle for the integration of foreign minorities.

Gabriel had trouble gaining attention and telling the lady in the wheelchair and her nurse about the vision of paradise on earth, which would become reality after the destruction of the forces of Satan in the bloody battle of Armageddon. At the mention of this future paradise I became attentive, because, as you know, I have always taken a great interest in ideas of paradise. All too soon, sadly, Gabriel had moved from the description of the yearned-for thousand-year Arcadian state to a condemnation of state and nation, just as the extreme right-winger began to glorify the nation state. In the middle of Gabriel's sharp and lucid critique of national service, the elderly lady asked her young nurse to push her wheelchair closer to the extreme right-winger, since his simultaneous exhortation to universal armament struck her as more interesting. Robbed of his audience, Gabriel got down from the mineral-water box and the three of us went to an inexpensive little vegetarian restaurant not far from Harrods.

I found the hearty friendship between Gabriel and Michael

attractive, they seemed to value each other not only as Jehovah's Witnesses but also as friends. Between lentil soup, stuffed cabbage rolls and millet yoghurt with bilberries, the two of them explained the tasks of a Jehovah's Witness more precisely, and revealed to me, among other things, that members were obliged to make a certain financial contribution. When I explained that the savings I had brought with me from Paris were slowly declining, and that apart from living and eating expenses I had hardly anything to spare, their faces darkened.

After a quick whispered confabulation, Michael said that if I wished I could live with him, and thus free up my living expenses for the association. Under normal circumstances I wouldn't have accepted this suggestion but the events of the most recent past had left me profoundly insecure, and I had a great need for friendship, for a sense of belonging, of being embraced by a community. We humans are full of contradictions, are we not? On the one hand we have a profound suspicion of community, and flee from it, while on the other hand we long for it and seek it out. Reverend Father, I fell into the trap of the religious community just as you have fallen into the trap of the religious community, as we all, sooner or later, fall into the trap of a religious community. What interested me was not the religious community's efforts, not the religious community's ideals, it was the religious community's home life.

Jonathan's abrupt demise had made my connection with the group of London tramps, whose stimulating intellectual climate had put me very much at ease, not only difficult but impossible. By the time the former professional boxer returned from the Scottish theatre festival, Jonathan's corpse would be found, and I, having disappeared, would be under great suspicion of having carried out the deed. So whenever I could I had to avoid the tramps with whom Jonathan had been on intimate terms during his months in London. This was very difficult since the paths of the London tramps and those of the Jehovah's Witnesses frequently crossed: both groups had a love of the London Underground network, both groups frequented the public streets and squares. I would have to be on my guard.

In retrospect, of course, the most rational thing would have been to leave London immediately, but just as we human beings are contradictory, we are also irrational, is that not so, Reverend Father? The longing for a religious community, that absurd emotion, kept me in London, and after the pleasant dinner in the vegetarian restaurant I accompanied Michael up the narrow, tall steps into the room with the barred window, planning to stay there indefinitely. In the absence of a second bed we shared the big mattress in the middle of the room, covered with a white sheet, and our relationship was just as pure as the white of that sheet.

Michael turned out to be extremely reserved, a quality that I valued after the relationship with Jonathan, which had sapped all my strength. When we lay side by side on the mattress after a day spent working for the Jehovah's Witnesses, he in his knee-length white linen shirt and I in one of his mother's two long, high-buttoned nightgowns with a pattern of pastel-coloured flowers, Michael laid a fraternal arm round my shoulder and said he was very happy that I had shown an understanding of one of the principles of the community, that one must stay unsullied by the world. Merely having the morally permissive advertising posters before one's eyes in the Underground and in the street disturbed him. And it was no good averting your eyes from an advertising poster, there were so many posters that the next one along immediately entered your field of vision. Everywhere you saw naked women's arms and legs, everywhere you saw women's eyes, mouths and hair.

And what was even worse, he said, distractedly stroking my upper arm which was covered by his mother's pastel flowers, as a Jehovah's Witness one naturally had to pay particular attention to those most urgently in need of the message of the

Second Coming, those hard-boiled sinners who hung around in the red-light districts, earning their livelihoods by practising unspeakable vices, or paying money for the same.

Shortly after he had joined the Jehovah's Witnesses, he said, the London office had sent him, in the company of two experienced Witnesses, over the Channel to the office in Amsterdam which was well-known as one of the most loathsome cities in Europe, a Sodom and Gomorrah criss-crossed by the gloomy waters of the *grachts*, distributing the Dutch edition of *The Watch Tower*, a kind of baptism by fire, so to speak. It had been terrible. Everywhere between the dark canals you could see instruments of bestiality on sale, appliances whose purpose he did not know but sometimes guessed at; everywhere there were semi-clad or naked white, yellow, brown women in shop windows, shamelessly offering themselves for sale. Whenever he thought of the initiation of the innocent young man that he had been back then, it made him shudder even today. He, who had inherited from his mother a propensity for headaches, had returned from Amsterdam with a severe migraine and had been unable to do any fieldwork for two weeks.

Not only that, he said, picking up the framed black and white photograph that always stood on the floorboards beside the mattress, and which showed his mother in a simple black dress next to a big man of solemn mien, not only that, but his mother, shown here on a trip to the United States with a high-ranking Jehovah's Witness from the Brooklyn Central Office, had suffered a stroke, but he was convinced that she, a sensitive woman repelled by everything coarsely natural, had been spiritually worn down long before by constant confrontation with a sinful world. This spiritual attrition had repeatedly manifested itself in the form of violent migraine attacks which could only be partially treated by prescriptions of ergotic alkaloids, and in his view, a view which, of course, had its roots not in medicine but purely in the emotions, had finally led to the fatal cerebral vascular embarrassment.

Reverend Father, thanks to Michael Minulescu my life had changed completely, had taken a turn that I would never have considered possible. We got up early, went to bed early, ate well, drank no alcohol and devoted ourselves enthusiastically to preaching the Second Coming which, although it had been originally expected in 1914 and had not happened, and although it had happened neither in 1918 nor in 1925 – both dates based on absolutely impeccable calculations – was due in the immediate future. Gabriel was not the only Jehovah's Witness I met. At the various compulsory meetings, the Bible classes, the gatherings for sermons and lectures, I met many modest but unwavering people from all social classes, who had put their life at the service of the Witnesses. Soon I was appointed, along with a pleasant unmarried librarian named Frances Flint, to make home visits to the unenlightened and bring a little light into their hitherto unilluminated lives. We got used to drinking tea on Regent Street with an open-minded retired Anglican minister who was always ready for a discussion. His cosy living room, furnished with massive dark Victorian furniture, became an oasis to which we could flee from a reality in which doors were often slammed in our faces, insults were hurled at us and English greyhounds or Irish setters were set at our throats.

And it wasn't just dull-witted fellow citizens who made our life difficult. Even worse was the hostility directed at us from the ranks of other religious communities. When two young male members of the strongly biblical Neo-Apostolic Community lay in wait for us one day at Parson Bond's house, pushed us down the steps and yelled at us as they ran away, telling us not to venture on to their proselytized patch again, an event which so infuriated the parson, who had rushed to help us, that his blood pressure rose alarmingly, and when we had only escaped a pursuing group of Grail Followers by lowering a railway crossing barrier between them and us, Frances and I had to separate and carry out our home visits in the company of a male Jehovah's Witness. And even that, as it turned out, was no guarantee of being unchallenged. One evening, when Gabriel and I returned from a long home visit to a Pakistani family in Brixton, both windows of his ground-floor rented room on the Tottenham Court Road had been smashed, and the words FUCK THE WITNESSES had been sprayed in black letters on the pale pink wall, which put considerable strains on the hitherto warm relations between Gabriel and his landlady. The next day a former member of the Ufologist sect, who had managed only with difficulty to break away from his fellow believers, told us that the perpetrators had been two particularly fanatical supporters of the cult of Ufology. I gradually began to wonder whether the fact that Michael had saved me from Jonathan the Undead was all that fortunate after all.'

I looked at the rain-damp profile of Magdalena who was sitting beside me. I wanted to tell her I wasn't surprised that she had got into such difficulties. In my opinion her problems were due to the simple fact that rather than taking the broad path, leading directly to salvation, of the one holy apostolic Catholic Church, she had opted for a crooked side alley, for one of countless sect alleys, all of which were cul-de-sacs. It was clear that she wouldn't find her way out of the jungle of compulsions and constraints, of conflicts and complications typical of us poor mortals, but that she would get deeper and deeper into them. The rain was still falling, drizzling gently on the dense canopy of leaves, which was beginning to succumb to its incessant accumulation, opening little gaps to let big drops through.

'So far things were still quiet at Piccadilly Underground station,' Magdalena continued. 'Sometimes a tramp whose face was familiar to me would sit down some distance away to beg. He looked at me with unusual frequency, and after lengthy reflection I recognized him as one of the three people who, under the direction of the former professional boxer, had discussed Peter Brook's stagings in the textile factory. Shortly after this I began to take note of the man, as I had read the following headline on the front page of the *Evening Standard* at a newsstand in the Tube: DEATH IN THE SHOWER: MYSTERIOUS MURDER AMONG THE HOMELESS. Could Jonathan's friend have become suspicious and begun to shadow me? I tried to ignore such unsettling thoughts, to pay the man no attention and concentrate on selling *The Watch Tower*. Occasionally the young harpist would turn up and direct my thoughts to other things, engaging me in conversations about women's solidarity and music composed for the harp, particularly the various settings of the Orpheus legend, such as those of Monteverdi, Gluck and Handel. At the moment she was trying to find six female harpists, or male harpists if necessary, in London's streets and Underground passages, she told me, to get together in Leicester Square to perform a simplified version of Richard Wagner's opera *Rheingold*, in which, as I doubtless knew, seven harps were used. Of course it was very difficult, if not actually impossible, to drum up this relatively large number of harpists, male and female, but she wouldn't give up so easily. She had already found one male harpist, a Croat by birth, and a former orchestral player from Zagreb, who was currently living under Waterloo Bridge and with whom she got on very well despite the fact that he was a man, since he too was an orphan. I, of course, as a non-orphan, would be unaware that nothing connects people so closely as the state of being an orphan, for how could non-orphans imagine being orphans?

Before the young woman moved on with her little cart and the double-action harp, she would always wish me luck with all my enterprises, particularly those of a female orientation. Now and again the blind harmonica player would turn up too, the one that Michael had chased away before my first engagement as a seller of *The Watch Tower* but whose presence he sullenly tolerated after I had intervened, appealing to his sense of social sympathy. I found the presence of the quiet, gentle young man, who had been born blind and lived in a home in Stepney Green, very pleasant.

After I had been selling magazines in Piccadilly Tube station for a number of weeks, a man laden with various utensils appeared in my section of the passage. He stopped opposite me, unfolded a little wooden chair, put up an easel and began to paint. Reverend Father, he had chosen me as the model for his paintings, just as Jonathan had chosen me as the model for his sculptures, although the circumstances this time were completely different. The man, who crossed the passage after three days of intense work on his painting, shook my hand and introduced himself, was none other than the respected sociologist and amateur painter Richard Thorneycroft who felt urged and compelled, by a profound empathy with those whom society had ill-treated, with society's outsiders, to descend into the passages of the Underground to capture such socially disadvantaged people on his canvas. It was reproductions of these paintings that lent his publications, which sold in dizzying numbers, a certain visual authenticity. Where the advertising specialist had found my clothes unsuitable, Richard – as he insisted I call him – found them authentic, even touching. Of course Michael tried to drive him away as well but was mollified when it was pointed out to him that the illustration of an active Jehovah's Witness in one of the sociologist's bestsellers would be good for publicity. Richard said that my face and my curly strawberry-blonde hair reminded him of the type of femme fatale that the Pre-Raphaelite English artists liked to paint. When Michael wasn't there, Richard asked me to loosen my bun, to stress the similarity with that type of woman more strongly. Sometimes he walked up to me, lifted my chin a little, arranged a strand of hair or told me to put the magazines in the other hand, always in a kind and respectful tone. Once he politely asked the blind mouth-organ player to sit next to me, and within two days he had produced a painting that he intended to use as a cover illustration for his new book about socially marginal groups, entitled *The Excluded*.

One day when he asked the harpist to lift her instrument from the little cart and let us have it for a moment, so that I could sit at it with my hair loose and finally he could tackle the picture that he had had in his mind for ages, the watercolour of a harp-playing red-haired angel in the Pre-Raphaelite manner, which he would call "The Angel of the Underground", she protested and said her harp didn't exist so that someone could sit pretending to play it, her harp was an excellent double-action harp inherited from her foster mother and not a toy, and anyway she had to go, because in half an hour, in an empty furniture warehouse not far from Leicester Square she was meeting up with the two male and the two female harpists that she had managed to drum up for the proposed performance of *Rheingold*.

The days passed like this, and I ignored the glances of the friend of the former professional boxer for as long as I could. But one day, when the former computer programmer and expert in English portrait painting appeared from the hangar in Docklands and sat down in the same place, I started to get seriously worried. Of course the attentive looks that he gave me and Richard might have been due to his fundamental interest in painting, but I felt his presence was rather curious, particularly as he didn't speak to me, just watched me from some distance away. One evening, my work finished, I walked the short distance from Piccadilly Underground station to Michael's room alone. The street was deserted, and, unsettled by my disagreeable experiences with the members of the various sects, I was frightened to hear footsteps behind me. When someone planted his hands on my mouth from behind, I was convinced that this must be a member of the Moonies wanting to intimidate me. But before the unknown man let me go and ran round the nearest corner, he hissed in my ear: What happened to Jonathan Alistair Abercrombie?

Reverend Father, you will understand that this event finally deprived me of my peace of mind. No longer was it the members of other religious communities who sent me into a state of fear and terror; increasingly Jonathan's friends, the tramps, were also making me feel threatened. I had the feeling that I wasn't safe anywhere any more, neither on the way to the home visits nor selling magazines in the Tube station. I grew increasingly distracted and nervous, which didn't exactly inspire confidence in my clients and meant that I sold even fewer copies of *The Watch Tower* than I had before. I was forever looking behind me, I jumped at the slightest noise, and at night I was tormented by nightmares in which tramps and sect members were hunting me in packs, chasing me into deep shafts of the Underground, up high television towers and along intricate systems of platforms, and finally cornering me against a fire wall, whereupon I woke up, and Michael took me in his friendly arms and comforted me.

At this time the humble room with the barred window at the top of the high, narrow steps was a place of refuge and recovery for me. Michael treated me with care and tenderness. We often spent the evening lying on the mattress in the middle of the room, discussing the conflict-ridden, aggression-filled, disharmonic situations with which our work with the public had confronted us throughout the day. Michael rested his sparsely covered head on the ruched front of one of the nightgowns that had previously been worn by his mother and now were worn by me, sighed contentedly and said how pleasant it was to be able to relax in a pure relationship with a woman, untroubled by any instinctual inclinations, and to be able to regain one's strength for the coming day. How many couples are there, he wondered, whose private relationship consists solely in the continuation of their struggle for survival in the outside world, whose nights are filled with excesses, with immoderation and extravagance of all kinds and who, because of their ungovernable passions, can find no rest? He was happy to have found a kindred soul in me, he said, putting his arm round my hip, covered by the pastel-coloured natural fabric of what had previously been his mother's nightgown, a twin, for whom terms such as modesty, a sense of shame and moral purity were not mere empty husks but a lived reality.

When Michael lay next to me and spoke with such conviction of the stainless character of our relationship, I had to agree, although his innocent caresses sometimes provoked faint physical reactions in me, of which I obviously gave no sign, since the slightest demonstration of any sensual arousal would have disconcerted him and thrown him off balance. He seemed such a sensitive, almost ethereal character that my robust nature sometimes felt unrefined in contrast with his fragility. I got used to those evenings of intimate conversation on the mattress, and if Michael came home later than usual because he had been going over the organization's books with Gabriel on the Tottenham Court Road, which naturally happened from time to time, I waited impatiently for the key to turn in the door.

Secure as I felt in my harmonious private life with Michael, I felt exposed and threatened when I went about the city on my own. When I walked past a gun shop on the way to the theocratic priests' academy, I decided to buy myself a little handgun to put my mind at rest. I entered the shop, and after thinking for quite a long time I opted for a handy-sized Smith and Wesson. The shop assistant, who was also the owner, wasn't particularly bothered that I didn't have a gun licence. When I had put slightly more than the asking price on the counter, he handed me the pistol and said that under no circumstances should I neglect to read the instructions. I put the Smith and Wesson in my handbag and felt considerably safer from then on as I went on my way. There didn't seem any need to tell Michael of my purchase. It wasn't long before I had an opportunity to draw the gun for the first time. One morning when I was walking through St James's Park, a habit that I had kept up since my time with Jonathan, and was threatened by a black man who jumped out from behind some azalea bushes clutching a Bowie knife, saying that I had sold my last copy of *The Watch Tower* on the territory of the Catholic fundamentalists, I pulled the lady's pistol out of the holster fastened to my belt and aimed it at the man, who immediately retreated behind the azalea bushes.

A few days later Gabriel and Michael asked me, over lunch in our little vegetarian restaurant, whether I wouldn't think of taking Gabriel's place on the mineral-water box at Hyde Park Corner and speaking about the coming thousand-year kingdom and the accompanying state of paradise on earth, since the organization's book-keeping was taking up more time than ususal. Reverend Father, as a Catholic priest who will have delivered his first sermon at some point, you will perhaps understand that I baulked at making such an appearance as an orator, particularly since I speak English with an Austrian accent. But because it was one of my favourite themes, the theme of paradise, I managed to overcome my shyness and agree to do it. In preparation I read something of the books of Charles Taze Russell, particularly his 1877 work *Three Worlds or the Plan of Redemption*.

When I turned up at Hyde Park Corner, the extreme right-winger was already standing on his beer crate delivering a speech, surrounded by a large number of listeners, about the revivification of the values contained in the Edda. I stood up on the mineral-water box and began to speak. When I realized I wasn't going to impress anyone by describing the paradise of the Jehovah's Witnesses, which didn't seem all that enticing to me, I changed my concept a little and began to bring in other ideas of paradise, although I didn't feel I was betraying the convictions of the religious community in any serious way. When I had first of all described the paradise of the Jehovah's Witnesses as something rather like the Elysium of the Greeks, also drawing on my memories of a wonderful summer I had spent in the Greek islands, I already had an audience of five standing in front of me. Then I went on to equip this paradise with all the attributes of the Land of Cockaigne, with roasted pigeons in the air, delicious fishes in the stream, and fruits dangling in front of the mouths of the inhabitants who lay lazily under the trees in the sun. This certainly appealed to people. Not only did a further nine join my audience of five, at least twenty turned in interest from the expositions of the extreme right-winger and moved towards me. At this, the extreme right-winger threw me a furious glance and began to rage loudly against the mixing of the Anglo-Saxon race with foreign elements, which had already done almost irreparable damage to the purity of English culture and language. I raised my voice too, and embarked upon the colourful description of a transcendent world which, strictly speaking, derived from the Islamic notion of paradise but which could be effortlessly transposed to that of the Jehovah's Witnesses. While I was going into great detail about the beautiful girls who would dance around the blessed in that idyllic realm, a further fifty onlookers broke away from the group around the extreme right-winger and began to listen to me attentively.

Reverend Father, when I became aware of the effect I was having on the audience, when the number hanging on my every word grew greater and greater, I was overcome by an almost indescribable feeling of elation. Inspired by the obvious sympathy of so many curious people, I soared to depictions of the greatest vividness and urgency.

Perhaps my euphoria was not unlike the exuberance that you feel when you look into the eyes of the faithful, turned excitedly towards you when you preach from your pulpit on Sundays and Catholic holidays, about the fall, fratricide and the flood. Unfortunately my enthusiasm and that of my audience came to an abrupt end when some skinheads from the inner circle surrounding the extreme right-winger approached my mineral-water box with unambiguously menacing gestures and

187

made as if to knock me off it. Given the worsening situation, I thought it advisable to leave the arena as soon as possible. While I was pushing my way through the crowd, I heard murmurs of disappointment. With the cry, Friends, I shall return! I left the field and disappeared among the azaleas of Hyde Park.

Having ended up including London's skinheads among my enemies, along with the tramps and the sect members, I began to consider leaving the metropolis. The same evening I informed Michael of my reflections on the matter. He clutched me and his mother's nightgown as a drowning man clutches a straw, and begged me to stay with him, he needed me, not only as a comrade-in-arms to promote his beliefs but also as a woman offering him new security in this world, from which his mother had departed the previous year. When I looked at the ruched front of the nightgown and saw that it was wet with his tears, I decided to postpone my departure. I told him of my decision, and, as a demonstration of his thanks to me, he covered me with kisses.

Reverend Father, I must confess that the fire and gratitude in these kisses had an effect on me which must have been counter to Michael's intentions. I could hardly conceal the excitement aroused in me by his kisses, entirely platonic in intent, which I could feel through the pastel-coloured nightgown.

During the weeks that followed, Michael continued to cover me with fraternal caresses from joy at my staying with him, and I didn't dare confess to him that these put me in the same sinful state that he so severely condemned in others. So I let them flood over me and tried to conceal the passion that they provoked, which was not very difficult, as Michael, in his innocence, was unaware of the fire that they unleashed. You, who, as a man of God, will be familiar with the way in which we sinners constantly swing between good and evil, who will be familiar with weak and feeble mankind's vacillation between virtue and vice, you will understand the problematic nature of the situation in which I found myself. What was I supposed to do? I couldn't encourage Michael to perform acts which starkly contradicted his views. To do so I would have risked toppling such a sensitive man into a deep existential crisis. But believe me, with every passing evening Michael's behaviour brought greater torment to a woman who was young and healthy, whose sensory apparatus was in excellent working order, and who reacted promptly to every kind of stimulus. I didn't know whether to wish that he would spend as long as possible sitting over the Jehovah's Witnesses' books or to hope he would come home as soon as possible.

One evening Richard Thorneycroft arrived at Piccadilly Tube station with a bottle of Veuve Cliquot, three champagne flutes and two free copies of his new book *The Excluded*. He handed one each to the blind mouth-organ player and myself, popped the cork of the champagne bottle against the white-tiled wall of the Underground passage and poured the three glasses full. We were to celebrate the publication of his new book, he said, to which the mouth-organ player and myself had contributed by agreeing to model for the cover illustration. Had Michael been standing in his corner, obviously I wouldn't have dared to drink alcohol. But because he had stayed at home with a migraine attack, I drank two glasses of champagne, went back to our room in an elated mood and lay down beside him on our mattress, whereupon he immediately wrapped his arm round me. Reverend Father, I know that my behaviour would be condemned both from the Catholic point of view and from the point of view of the Jehovah's Witnesses, but the effect of the champagne made me abandon my habitual restraint. Please understand me, it was not a deliberate attempt at seduction, it was more of an instinctive, spontaneous reaction to his protective gesture. I admit it, I forgot myself, and once more I crossed the solid boundaries fixed for my sex.

My mute but unambiguous display of sexual interest had its

consequences. Michael sat bolt upright and stared at me, as he had done on our first meeting when there had been other reasons for his surprise. Then he picked up the photograph of his mother and the solemn-looking man and held it in front of my eyes. On his fortieth birthday, he said, his mother had made him promise never to indulge in any physical activity with a woman, as this would reduce his energy which had to be placed undivided at the service of the Jehovah's Witnesses. Then he looked at me reproachfully and said I was more susceptible to temptation than he had thought. He suggested washing in cold water, that would bring me back to my senses. He had no intention of making our controlled relationship any less unique just because of a sudden and irrational eruption of appetite. Others might yield to such dubious impulses but people like ourselves, who, with our inner strength, had overcome our bestial nature and reached a higher spiritual plane, had risen above such stimuli. He spoke in such an insistent tone that I had no reply for him, indeed I was ashamed of my open display of desire, went to the little washbasin in the corner of the room and splashed myself with cold water. Then I returned to the mattress where Michael gave me a friendly welcome and soon fell asleep.'

Magdalena fell silent, and I allowed the scene she had described to pass before my inner eye once more. The atmosphere, including the little washbasin, made me think of the vicarage. Of course my sister and I slept in different rooms, but the pastel-coloured nightgown could have been Maria's. Darkness began to fall, and as my sister used to go to bed early, it was entirely possible that at that very moment she, too, was standing by the washbasin.

'The next day Gabriel and I made two home visits in the morning,' Magdalena continued, 'and at about four o'clock in the afternoon I took up my position in the Tube station with *The Watch Tower*. After the old man with an interest in the First World War had asked for a copy of the magazine containing a detailed description of the Battle of the Marne in 1914, the former fitter, now a Freud specialist, stepped out of the shadows of a corner of the Underground passage and tapped me provocatively on the chest with a pocket edition of *Civilization and Its Discontents.* He told me to have no illusions, Jonathan's friends knew only too well who had him on her conscience. I might have escaped the police, but I would not escape Jonathan's friends. Then he grabbed me by the collar of my dark-blue blouse, pulled my face close to his and sent a gust of halitosis into my face. There was no rush, he hissed, Jonathan's friends had time, and one day someone would find my corpse in the Thames, someone would find me with a knife in my back on a rubbish dump or strangled among the azaleas in Hyde Park.

Before another mode of death could occur to him, Richard came round the corner with his easel, his palette and a little chair, with the intention of starting a half-length portrait of me, to be entitled "Young Woman With Cloche Hat". When he saw me being threatened, he pushed the little folded chair into the tramp's back and the tramp ran for it. But at the same time two cloaked figures came charging down the Tube steps, tore my package of magazines from my hand, threw me to the floor and ran on, calling: Long live the Whitsun Movement! The young harpist, coming from the other direction, tried to trip them up with her little cart and harp, whereupon they knocked it over and ran round the corner. The harpist bent over me and helped me to my feet, but at the same moment three skinheads came towards me along the passage, brandishing rattling chains. Had the advertising specialist not turned up by chance, had he not rapidly grasped the seriousness of the situation and skilfully distracted the skinheads' attention from me by drawing them into a little conversation about the colour, form, material and emblematic significance of the current brands of bovver boot, I wouldn't have had time to draw my Smith and Wesson from my handbag, cautiously move backwards up the stairs and make my getaway. Utterly distraught, I ran towards Tottenham Court Road with a view to contacting Gabriel and Michael who were going over the books again. Arriving in front of the pale pink house, still disfigured by the black spray paint of the Ufologists, in my excitement I jumped on to a ledge a couple of feet up to tell them what had happened as quickly as possible through one of the broken windowpanes of the ground floor windows of Gabriel's rented room.

Reverend Father, what happened during the minutes that followed still lingers in my memory as a series of unconnected images, a scratchy silent film, a sequence of slow-motion movements. I looked through the big hole in the windowpane, into the room, expecting to see Gabriel and Michael sitting at the table, their heads deep in their ledgers. There was no one sitting at the table. My eye staggered around the room for a while like a disorientated bluebottle, slid over the flower-patterned wallpaper, an open fire and an old cupboard, and finally settled on a bed in one corner of the room. Reverend Father, I know that what follows will shock you as a Catholic priest, but to conclude this episode in the narrative, now heading straight for its climax yet again, I shall have to ask you to hear me out.

The bed was not at rest. The blanket was moving as the sea does in stormy weather, throwing up waves that swelled now in one place, now in another, and when I turned my eyes cautiously towards the top end of the bed, I saw two familiar heads, one thinning on top and one blond. The two heads could hardly be distinguished, they were jerkily twisting and turning. Then a man's back straightened up like a big winding snake, and although it was not covered, as it usually was, by the white linen shirt, I immediately recognized it as Michael's.

When I saw that naked back, the thin neck attached to it and the bald patch on the back of the head on top of that, my capacity for reflection, otherwise relatively well developed, abandoned me. The detail swam in front of my eyes, and when I could see clearly again I saw that the back was suddenly covered with blood, I saw it suddenly straightening again and then falling down on the second figure in the bed. I looked at my right hand, still holding the Smith and Wesson that I had used to cover myself as I retreated from Piccadilly Tube station. When I realized that it was a bullet from that Smith and Wesson that had pierced Michael's back, I leapt from the ledge, ran a short distance through the crowd in Tottenham Court Road, which was busy at that time of day, and turned into a narrow, deserted alley. I stopped for a moment, tried to think clearly and then ran in a zigzag through narrow alleyways and side streets back to our room. I threw my few belongings into a big Harrods carrier bag, ran back down the stairs, jumped on to the Puch 800 parked in front of the house, left London and headed southwards, towards the unusually red, unusually large rising full moon.

I cannot understand how I managed to find the approach to the motorway in my confused state, or even how I was capable of driving the motorcycle. What is certain is that I soon found myself in Canterbury and decided to spend the night in that venerable archbishopric. Only when I was lying in the bed of the simple little hotel was I able to think clearly again, and realized what I had done. In the affect, that intense, relatively brief reactive state of emotional arousal, drawing into itself all the psychic functions, the motor functions and parts of the vegetative nervous system, and in the course of which the power of judgment declines to the point of eliminating any critique, and the person's deliberate self-control has been lost, in such an extreme of affect, of emotion, in which actions happen more quickly than they otherwise might, in which one is often out of control, failing to think of the sense and possible consequences of what one is doing, I had severely injured Michael, if not actually killed him. The affect unleashed in my case had been rage, blind rage against someone who had talked constantly about virtue and who had repelled serious offers of love from a healthy, strong woman of child-bearing age by referring to the necessity of sexual abstinence, but, under the pretence of going over the books for nights at a stretch, had been having a homosexual affair. It was that betrayal, that unforgivable violation of the noble human value of honesty that had driven me to my action.

Despite all the extraordinary events of that remarkable day, I slept very well and was awoken the next morning by the ringing of the cathedral bells. I got dressed, went into the dining room, sat down at the breakfast table and opened the morning paper. Under the headline HOMOSEXUAL MURDER IN SECT CIRCLES on page three, there was a long report on what had happened. I had clearly fired not one but four bullets at Michael, one of which had entered his heart, one his liver and two his lung. Several eyewitnesses had seen a middle-aged woman in a grey suit and a black cloche hat climbing up on a ledge beneath the window of the apartment in question, firing shots and running away. Police were asking for any information about this woman. The victim's friend, who had been present during the shooting, was still in shock. By the time of going to press, they had only managed to get a few sentences out of him, about fanatical supporters of the Bahai faith.

Before I had finished the article I felt swelteringly hot: I was still wearing the suit and the cloche hat! I immediately paid the bill, dashed from the hotel, took off Michael's mother's clothes in the public toilet in the city park and put on my leather jump suit. Since I had been compelled to give all the money I had left to the Jehovah's Witnesses, I had practically no funds left. I went to the cathedral, entered the nave of the church that I had visited with Jonathan Alistair on our way to London – it was deserted at that relatively early hour of the morning – went to the niche with the delightful little statue of Mary and concealed it in a carrier bag. Then I climbed back on the sidecar bike and drove on to Dover where I managed to pass through passport control and customs unchecked, get on to the ferry with my sidecar bike and cross the Channel. The French border guards didn't cause me any trouble at Calais, either.'

Magdalena took a few deep breaths, stretched her long, slender neck and leaned her head against the tree trunk. Her hair and her face were damp from the rain which was still drizzling down, which the robinia's canopy of leaves could hardly contain, but by now her jump suit was also glistening with moisture and, as I could see if I twisted my eyes as far as I could towards the bottom left, little drops of water covered the triangle of skin above the zip where it opened for a couple of inches.

After the description of the incredible scene on which her gaze had fallen though the broken pane of glass, I had been unable to concentrate too well on the narrative flow. What Magdalena had described had shaken me, for it had shown that the sects which had split in supposed rebellion from the Mother Church were more deeply involved in sin and ignominy than I had suspected. How was it possible that people who claimed to be working in the name of God could participate in such unnatural acts? Could one sink so deep into a swamp of sin? How glad I was to be safe in the bosom of the one holy apostolic Catholic Church, in which such acts of deviance, such pathological degeneracy had no place.

In the meantime darkness had begun to fall and I was starting to flag a little. It was not only talking that sapped one's strength, as Magdalena claimed, listening took its toll as well. Magdalena stirred beside me, and I saw her silhouette moving to the sidecar machine and coming back with a dark mass over her arm, which, as she grew closer, I identified as a sleeping bag. She laid it on the ground beneath the tree trunk, and then something happened that I hadn't expected. Without a word, Magdalena began to untie the green nylon washing line with which I was bound to the tree. And when the rope was untied, she set about freeing me from the bonds with which my hands were tied to my back. There was a feeling of numbness in those hands, which now hung at my side. Magdalena took first my right, then my left hand between her palms and with a series of gentle movements she rubbed the skin for a long time. Gradually I could feel my fingers again. Magdalena let go of my hands and felt her way round my torso. She stroked the material of my dalmatic, a touch that prompted a curious sensation in me, like a thin layer of ice cracking with a delicate sound. She continued her caresses, and more and more fine cracks and fissures criss-crossed the ice until it finally shattered in tiny pieces and fell into the black water. Then she laid the sleeping bag beside me, took my fettered feet in her hands and guided them into the softly quilted opening. I slid in completely, and she slipped in beside me. When I tried to remove my gag, she reached for my hands and held them fast.

'Not yet,' she said. The rain had stopped, it was very quiet.

The next morning I was woken by the sun shining in my face. I opened my eyes and saw the strawberry-blonde back of Magdalena's head beside me. It was some time before the memory of the evening and the night before came back to me. My hands were free, I could have untied my feet and run off, although in all likelihood Magdalena would soon have caught up with me. I could have picked up the piece of green nylon washing line beside the sleeping bag and overpowered Magdalena, or at least tried to, even if she was physically stronger than I was. But I didn't so much as think of it. I enjoyed the warm proximity of my kidnapper, this quietly breathing man-killer, blinked into the sun and decided to wait for her to wake up. The birds sang, the countless raindrops that had fallen the previous day glittered in the grass and slowly evaporated in the morning rays of the early summer sun. Magdalena turned round, murmured something incomprehensible and buried her head in my shoulder. How could I have run from this woman after the night that had just passed?

She opened her eyes, smiled and kissed me on the cheek, most of which was covered by the gag. Then she slid from the sleeping bag, went to the sidecar bike, came back with bread, bacon and cherries, slipped back in beside me and began to eat. She didn't stop me when I pulled the gag from my mouth, so that the black Kashiyama body stocking lay round my neck like a towel, took a pair of cherries from her hand and put first one, then the second cherry into my mouth. The taste of the firm, sweet fruits on my tongue was wonderful. Magdalena turned towards me and put her right index finger to my mouth. There was no need to tell me to be quiet, at that moment I hadn't the slightest desire to speak. So we sat in the sleeping bag beneath the robinia and had our breakfast.

'You won't speak, Reverend Father,' said Magdalena after a while. 'Your time to speak has not yet come.'

I was ready to do anything this woman asked of me, as long as she kept me near her and continued the treatment with which she had delighted me during the night just past.

Magdalena picked up the jam jar that stood next to me.

'Oh,' she said, 'look what's happened.'

The jar was completely filled with water, and in the middle of it floated the praying mantis.

'She's dead. I should have thought of that. The rain has come in through the holes in the lid. The praying mantis has died.'

Magdalena unscrewed the lid and poured the rainwater, along with the praying mantis, in a high arc over the daisy-strewn meadow.

'We all return to the earth,' she said. 'It's a shame the male didn't turn up in time. It would have been interesting to see the elemental forces of Eros and Thanatos manifested in immediate succession.' Then she pressed herself up against my stole.

'But to return to my confession. I didn't know exactly where I wanted to go from Calais, I just knew that I had to put as great a distance as possible between myself and the island which had fallen so far short of my hopes that it might turn out to be a place of yearning, an island paradise. I decided from now on to avoid all islands, large and small, even the seashore from which they could be seen, and head eastwards, towards the centre of Europe. I travelled via Reims, where I visited the famous thirteenth-century cathedral in my nun's habit, talked to a Cistercian nun from the south of France about the motif of the labyrinth which often occurs in French cathedrals, and, after she had gone, removed a gilded chalice from a little side altar, its cup decorated with pretty leaf ornaments, and via Strasbourg, where I took a look at the magnificent cathedral, and, after an interesting, sadly truncated conversation with a secondary school teacher from Nancy about the famous Emperor's window in the north aisle, I took two delicate silver candlesticks and put them into spacious pockets that I had sewn into the lining of my habit.

Reverend Father, if you ask me why I committed the grave crime of theft from a church, not once but a number of times, I can give you no clear answer. First of all it was my sad financial situation that led me to act in this way, and to plan on selling these valuable objects to a fence. On the other hand I also felt curiously compelled to do so, like a kleptomaniac. As I remarked before, sometimes we do things that seem incomprehensible in retrospect.'

As I was free of my gag, I could have pointed out that these thefts were seriously sacrilegious but that God, in his infinite goodness and mercy, would forgive her if she repented accordingly. But I forbore from making any verbal intervention, since she had forbidden this with the gesture of putting her index finger to my mouth, and nothing was further from my mind than annoying her and thus perhaps ensuring that she would, in the night to come, refrain from the sweet and inexpressible actions that she had performed the previous night.

'As I have said, I first thought of selling off the statue, the chalice and the candlesticks to an interested party, but after crossing the Rhine, once I reached Offenburg, I suddenly realized that I was in an unfamiliar part of the world and had no opportunity of making contact with people involved in such shady dealings. After taking out my map at a motorway service station to get my bearings, I decided to make a short northward detour, convert the last money I possessed into chips at the casino in Baden-Baden, and try my luck at roulette.

After my arrival in the elegant old spa town, I took a room in a little pension on the hill near the Stiftskirche. At about ten o'clock in the evening I went to the casino, but the liveried man at the door refused to let me in as I was not suitably dressed. Although clothing regulations were considerably more relaxed than they had been some years previously, he explained, a woman in a leather jump suit and boots could not be granted entrance to the famous gaming room, decorated in the mid-nineteenth century by Parisian architects in the style of the French royal palaces, the most beautiful gaming room in the world, surely I could understand that. Slightly disgruntled I went back to the pension, took off the jump suit and put on the nun's habit including the white gown, firmly convinced that this solemn clothing would meet the high standards of the casino staff. I was sorely disappointed when the liveried gentleman at the door raised grave objections yet again. He was surprised, he said, that in the God-fearing state of Baden a nun, destined for a contemplative life, should feel the extremely worldly desire to visit a casino. He could not turn me away but he would consider it most inappropriate to see me sitting in the habit of my order at a roulette, baccarat or blackjack table. I was too proud to insist. Before I turned to leave, the gentleman scrutinized me and said that the similarity between myself and a lady in a leather jump suit whom he had had to turn away half an hour previously was very striking. Discouraged, I returned to the pension and was about to lie down on the bed when it occurred to me that I still had Michael's mother's flannel suit as well. So I changed once again and presented myself for a third time to the strict gentleman who at first ignored me, probably because of the inconspicuous colour of the suit, but then, with an arrogant wave of his right hand, ushered me in. I walked past him, and when I darted a backward glance I saw that the gentleman, who had clearly noticed yet another resemblance, was staring after me in bafflement. I quickly disappeared among the many players so he lost sight of me immediately. I bought chips and walked around the rooms of the casino for a while. Then I sat down at a roulette table between a fat woman in a low-cut pink satin dress and an elegant-looking old gentleman in a black suit. It was very busy, the players were crowded round the table, and I admired the croupiers who loftily took stock of the course of play, letting nothing escape them.

In one phase of my past life I had taken an interest in numerology, and now decided to let myself be guided by my modest knowledge of the field. First I bet on ten, the number of the totality in motion, the universality of creation, a number which struck me as profitable because of its eminent symbolic significance. When the ball came to rest on eighteen I placed my hopes on thirty-six, an extremely interesting number, that of cosmic solidarity, the movement of the elements and of cyclical evolutions. Twelve won, and I put two of my remaining five chips on nine, bearing in mind its significance as the number of plenitude, the symbol of the celestial spheres. It was no coincidence that it had a large part to play in the mythology and the shamanistic rites of the Turko-Mongolian peoples, and was regarded by the Freemasons as the number of immortality. Nine would bring me luck. When the fat lady in the pink satin dress had won a pile of chips with twenty-seven, I decided to put my last three chips on five, with good reason: was five not the number of union, the marriage number as the Pythagoreans called it, the number of the centre, harmony and balance? Did it not, for the Chinese, symbolize the merging of yin and yang, was it not, for the Maya, the symbol of perfection, the holy number? In ancient Mexico it was seen as the indissoluble connection of the light and the dark side of the universe, and among the Dogon and Bambara in Mali it was the chaos of the new beginning, of incomplete creation. Hildegard of Bingen even developed an entire theory of five as the symbol of man, and in Islam to this day they extend the five fingers of the right hand to ward off the evil eye, a gesture that gives the number magic powers. I would win with five, five would solve my financial problems once and for all. It landed on thirty.

In my grey flannel suit, dark-blue blouse and black cloche hat I sat in shock among the elegantly dressed patrons of the casino. I had no money left. Reverend Father, what I would now like to say to you will not surprise you as a priest: just when I had to acknowledge that I was ruined, when I had to admit to myself that my defeat was total, a miracle occurred. One of those infringements of the natural laws, the usual causalities, happened, and from the right a mountain of chips was pushed in front of my nose. I turned my head in surprise, and looked into the smiling face of the elegant old gentleman in the black suit. Thirty-three, he whispered, put everything on thirty-three! I bet on thirty-three and won. I won a lot.

When, an hour later, we were sitting in the spa restaurant over a light snack of oysters and a local white wine, Baron Otto told me he had felt moved to recommend thirty-three to me because he was born on the third of the third. In addition, Christ had been crucified at the age of thirty-three, and he had always had a very personal relationship with the crucifixion of Christ. Of course he could have bet on thirty-three himself, but he had only ever lost in the casino when he had made his own bets so he had made it his habit to look around the players, speaking to one who looked particularly blessed by good fortune, and asking him or her to bet on the number he had chosen.

Roulette was not just about the number but also about the hand and thus about the person who put the chips on that number. It had to be a particular hand and thus a particular person, a person born with a lucky hand, so to speak, he said, and raised his glass with a right hand covered with liver spots. He might say that his intuition was very strong, due to his having been born under the sign of Pisces, and that he usually recognized such people. He not only took pleasure in roulette itself but also in the game of intuitively choosing players blessed with such hands. If a player had a lucky hand, this did not mean, however, that he also had a lucky head, a brain that intuitively hit upon the right number. A combination of lucky hand and lucky head was something one came across very seldom. He, for example, was gifted with just such a lucky head but needed someone else's lucky hand to win, he said, and, with a withered hand, guided another oyster to his mouth which gleamed with dentures. The winnings themselves meant nothing to him, gracious good fortune had blessed him with wealth, his only concern was the game. He always gave the winnings to the person gifted with the lucky hand, who, this evening, was myself.

Reverend Father, I could hardly comprehend my luck, a happy incomprehension which, like every uncomprehending happiness, will fatally reveal itself to be a false emotion. Where was I staying? asked Baron Otto. Was I lodging in the Hotel Brenner? I answered that I was living in a modest pension on the hill near the Stiftskirche. The Baron, who I guessed was in his mid-seventies, leaned over the little round table with the white tablecloth, the sparkling white wine glass in his slightly trembling hand, and said he apologized for his indiscretion but for reasons of his own he would like to know more about the way I lived my life. I said I was an independent woman who travelled a great deal, whereupon he asked me if I would like to enter his service as a companion, it was very difficult to find a companion of any standard, only in the past year he had employed two companions and had been sadly obliged to fire them again after just a short time. Being a Pisces, he trusted his first intuitive impression, and his first impression of me had been predominantly positive. He would expect me to live and eat in his house, and he would pay me an appropriate salary.

Although Baron Otto struck me as a charming, cultivated, if slightly eccentric man, after my win at the gaming table, which he had secured for me and which had eliminated my financial worries for a long time to come, I was not especially interested in his suggestion, and refused. At this the Baron slumped a little in his seat, looked at me sadly and said it was a great shame that I wouldn't comply with his suggestion and live with him as his escort in Paradise. When I heard the word paradise, my ears pricked up. I asked the Baron what he meant by paradise, and he said that of course, as an outsider, I could not be expected to know that Paradise was the part of Baden-Baden where his villa was located.

Reverend Father, in all likelihood you will think me an extravagant person, but at that moment I decided to accept the Baron's offer. The possibility of moving into a paradise, even if this Paradise was merely a part of town that happened to bear the name, struck me as a favourable sign. The Baron was overjoyed, and asked me to explain my sudden change of heart. I briefly referred to my interest in all kinds of notions of paradise, and as a Pisces he showed a spontaneous understanding of my way of thinking, which might have seemed peculiar to anyone else.

The next day I drove the Puch sidecar bike through the wrought-iron gate that the gardener had opened for me and up the white-gravelled drive to the huge old villa which had been in the possession of the Baron's family for more than a century. The housekeeper, a native of Bohemia and daughter of a glass-blower, who had been in the service of the family for forty years, showed me to two large rooms in the east wing of the villa with a view of a tall plane tree. Then the Baron himself guided me around the house and the park with its ancient trees, surrounded by a high wall. He introduced me to the rest of the staff, with whom he led a reclusive life in the villa: the cook, from Basel, the Bohemian housekeeper, the gardener and the chauffeur, a man of about thirty for whom, because of his Austrian origins, I immediately felt a deep dislike. Then the Baron led me into the drawing room, offered me a sherry and informed me of some of the details of my future duties.

Among other things he inquired about my wardrobe, and when I truthfully told him that apart from my grey flannel suit I owned a leather jump suit with boots and a nun's habit, this seemed to raise his spirits for some inexplicable reason. Then he asked me, before his afternoon nap, a favourite custom of his, which he took every day between half past two and half past four, to read to him. The book that he pressed into my hand was a leather-bound, richly illustrated edition of the Indian work *The Kama Sutra*, with which I was vaguely familiar. I was a little surprised at the literary taste of my new employer, but then concentrated on the sensual text, reading to the best of my ability until he grew tired and dozed off on the sofa where he lay outstretched.

On the way to my rooms I met the Austrian chauffeur who was clearly going to his rooms in the west wing, and cast him a dark look. When it became clear to me over the days that followed that my duties consisted solely in taking meals with the Baron, accompanying him on extended walks in the park and reading to him, I rejoiced at the good fortune that had led this man across my path, a joy that was soon to turn into its opposite, as every joy sooner or later turns – must turn – into its opposite. In the generous leisure time allocated to me, I devoted myself to the intensive study of *The Divine Comedy*, which I had, thank God, been able to rescue from the textile factory during my hasty escape from Jonathan Alistair Abercrombie, and which I hoped, in the course of my life, to translate into German. What a pleasure it was to open the mildewed pages of the edition published by G.C. Sansoni in Florence in 1905 and read:

> *Nel mezzo del cammin di nostra vita*
> *mi ritrovai per una selva oscura*
> *che la diritta via era smarrita.*

When it was time, I closed the book again and went to the Baron's drawing room where he was impatiently waiting for me to indulge him with further chapters from the book by the Japanese author Ibara Saikaku, entitled *Yonosuke, the Lover of Three Thousand*.

Apart from Clemens the chauffeur, whom I disliked because he was Austrian, I found the staff to be pleasant. Sometimes I helped the gardener, who had, incidentally, worked for years as a part-time gardener in the Botanical Garden in Berlin and later in the park of Sanssouci Palace in Potsdam, to do the weeding, cut the boxtree hedges and prune the roses. It was summer, and after the changeable London weather I enjoyed spending time in the open. Sometimes the Bohemian housekeeper would join us, and if the cook from Basel had time, as she seldom did, the four of us sat together on the stone bench beneath the pergola twined around with dark-red roses. Once the cook asked me how I was enjoying my new job, and when I answered that I liked it very much, the Baron was an extremely generous and charming man, the housekeeper, gardener and cook fell silent all of a sudden and looked at me with faces that held something like pity. I couldn't understand their silence or their expressions, and quickly added that of course we didn't agree about some things, for example questions of literary taste, but that couldn't spoil our friendly relations. At that moment Clemens the chauffeur joined us, and I stood up and excused myself, saying I had promised the Baron to read him three further episodes from the unabridged version of *The Thousand and One Nights*.

One evening I was sitting over dinner with Baron Otto at the beautifully laid table in the dining room. When the cook from Basel had brought in a beef bouillon with home-made dumplings as a starter, the Baron said he was very happy with my work, he hadn't thought that a young woman like myself could have such understanding of a 76-year-old like himself. Then he stood up, walked the ten steps from his end of the table to mine, stood behind me and put something cold round my neck. He told me to stand up and look at myself in the mirror which hung between the two high windows on the wall. Reverend Father, what the Baron had given me was a gold necklace set with light-blue sapphires. When I blushingly objected that I couldn't accept such a gift, he was too kind; he said with a smile that it gave him joy to emphasize the natural beauty of a young woman. And it occurred to him, could I not do him a small favour and put on the leather jump suit and the boots I had mentioned next time I read to him from *Justine*? I must forgive him, but he was rather tired of always seeing me in the grey suit. At that moment the cook from Basel came in to take the soup away, and when she saw me standing by the mirror with the wonderful necklace round my throat, that curious expression of pity paradoxically reappeared in her eyes.

When I had spent part of the evening of that summer day in my rooms in the east wing engrossed in *The Divine Comedy*, or more precisely in the fifth canto of the *Inferno*, dealing with sinners of the flesh, I made the unforgivable mistake of writing to my family for the first time since leaving Austria. Reverend Father, perhaps the motive behind that letter was not entirely clear. But I ask you, should one hold it against a woman who has lived for months in great, or rather relative, poverty, who because of that poverty sometimes even saw herself forced into committing thefts, if she wants to tell her nearest and dearest that her situation has improved? Can one take it amiss if she wishes to express her joy that chance has brought her together with a millionaire aristocrat who spoils her, if she wants to share her joy with her relations? In my unbounded thoughtlessness and carelessness I mentioned, in my letter to my parents and my sisters, not only the Baron's family seat in so-called Paradise but also my miraculous win at the roulette table and the sapphire collar. When the heart is full, the tongue will speak, isn't that so, Reverend Father?

The next day I got dressed as the Baron had requested, causing Clemens the chauffeur, whom I met on my way from the east wing to the drawing room, to stop in his tracks and look me up and down with an expression of the most profound amazement. Before I continued my reading of *Justine*, the Baron, to my considerable surprise, put a riding crop in my hand and told me to hold the book in one hand and the crop in the other, that would look nice. I did as he asked. After dinner, which the cook from Basel served and then cleared again, giving me a sympathetic look as she did so, the Baron said he had something to show me. Passing the Bohemian housekeeper, who was coming up the stairs with a big jar of pickled gherkins and who gave me a worried look, we went down the steps into the cellar vaults of the house. We walked through the storage room, and then the Baron opened a little iron door and we entered a dark, high-ceilinged chamber. Baron Otto lit the seven candles of an old silver candelabra, and the flickering light of the seven candles illuminated a room which was unfurnished apart from a plank bed in one corner. He timidly asked me whether I could imagine tying him to that plank bed now and again while I read to him, and giving him a mild beating with the riding crop. Then he pointed to some mountings fixed to the wall, and said that if I preferred, of course, I could tie him to the wall, and then perhaps it would be easier to manoeuvre the whip. Before I could respond, the Baron picked up a number of differently shaped whips including a cat-o'-nine-tails, a number of leather strips and a dog's collar and lead from the floor, and said that all of these things were at my disposal, I could select the implements that seemed most suitable for my task.

I stood in the middle of the high-ceilinged, dark cellar vault and didn't know what to do. Of course what Baron Otto was demanding of me was extremely repellent. On the other hand, in his house I was leading a very comfortable life and I had no intention of giving it up at the moment. As often before, angels and devils fought out a battle within me, to use your jargon, and as often before, the divine messengers suffered a crushing defeat. When the Baron asked me, with a pleading, almost humble expression, to test the elasticity of the riding crop there and then, I fulfilled his wish, hesitantly at first, but after a few minutes somewhat more emphatically, since I could tell from his reaction that I was doing it properly. But after ten minutes I dropped the riding crop, ran up the cellar steps and out of the house, ran past the embarrassed-looking gardener and dropped on the bench under the pergola. When Clemens the chauffeur ambled along and made as if to sit next to me I didn't immediately have the strength to stand up and go back to my two rooms. For the first time, the fact that he was a compatriot didn't strike me as a disadvantage. After a lengthy observation about the mildness of the evening, the man with the dark curly hair asked me whether I felt lonely in the house, I sometimes looked so sad. I said absolutely not, he was wrong there, I felt excellent, and anyway I had to go now, it was late. I stood up and walked through the dew-moistened grass towards the house, and he called after me, asking whether I mightn't come from the east wing to the west wing some time and have some coffee with him, his mother had sent him an apricot strudel from Waidhofen an der Ybbs, I must know that

the apricots in and around Waidhofen an der Ybbs were among
the best in Austria. I was almost tempted to turn round and
accept his invitation, but then I walked into the house without
giving him an answer.

Reverend Father, it was clear that after one of my soaring
flights a decline had begun, had to begin. Over the weeks to
come I read to the Baron, dined with him in the evening and
then went with him to the cellar vault. Despite the horrific
turn that our relationship had taken, we treated each other with
politeness and courtesy, and even if the Baron asked me to do
things in the cellar vault which I would prefer not to describe
even to you, he did so with the utmost propriety, which one can
only describe as irreproachable. This civilized veneer to our
behaviour strangely contradicted the abysmal depths which we
were exploring at the same time. I must admit that there were
moments when I stood in front of the Baron as he hung like the
crucified Christ from the cellar wall, wearing the nun's habit
which he liked so much, and swung the cat-o'-nine-tails with
a certain pleasure. I wouldn't have thought that such actions,
expressly requested but cruel none the less, could have aroused
even a hint of pleasure in me. The moment the Baron and I
opened the iron door to the cellar, another weird subterranean
vault inhabited by quick-footed rats and mice and spiders, of
whose existence I had been ignorant, opened up within me, a
kind of medieval torture chamber with ancient blood sticking
to the walls. There was a tacit understanding between us which,
apart from the Baron's very obsequiously presented but always
precise instructions, had no need of words.

Although he wanted this treatment, although he yearned
for it and, because I did not deny it him, he idolized me
and showered me with presents, I was aware that I had
entered dangerous regions, and this awareness sometimes
led to feelings of guilt, so that I would break off what
I was doing, throw down the cat-o'-nine-tails and run up
the cellar steps into the open air, clasping the trunk of a

maple tree or leaning against one of the old oaks that gave the park its unmistakable character. The gardener, cook and housekeeper watched me silently, with knowing expressions, and only Clemens the chauffeur seemed not to suspect a thing, walking through the house whistling quietly and repeating his invitation to coffee.

At this time I made a habit of visiting the thermal baths. Although the Baron didn't like to see me leaving the walls of the family seat, from time to time he reluctantly allowed the chauffeur to take me, in the dark-brown Bentley with the soft leather seats, down from Paradise to the Friedrichsbad or the Caracalla hot springs where I immediately hurled myself into the thermal water. Doubtless there was a direct connection between what the Baron and I did in the cellar vault and the intense need to immerse myself in the warm liquid. Reverend Father, in the healing water rising from great depths in this volcanic region, I tried to wash myself of the guilt aroused in me by the roughness that the Baron gently but resolutely forced me to deliver. I would hold my hands, which had grasped the handle of the whip, and my feet, which I had placed in their motorcycle boots on the Baron's back, in the powerful stream of the underwater jets, hoping the water would absorb and wash away all the evil that attached to them. Sometimes my greatest wish was to sink beneath the water and never re-emerge. I think that you, as a man of the Church, for which baptism by water is a sacrament, will understand my attempts to use water to free myself from all wrong, and after one or two hours to emerge reborn from the big round basin, my desire for forgiveness and regeneration assuaged. When I climbed, damp-haired, into the Bentley and rejoined the chauffeur, he would always remark how refreshed I looked.

Reverend Father, when we have sunk to the very bottom, when we look at ourselves in the mirror and cannot believe that the innocent-looking person whose image is thrown back at us has actually done the terrible things that he has done, when we have reached that point, something beautiful opens up in another part of our life. Slowly, slowly, the terrible things subside to make way for something new and radiant. The more I was repelled by the repellent actions that connected the Baron and myself, the less repellent I found the society of Clemens the chauffeur. One evening, when I had helped the Baron up the cellar steps and into the drawing room, I felt the need to take a walk in the park. At the edge of the rose rondeau I almost bumped into the chauffeur who had been working on the Baron's Bentley in the garage and had forgotten the time. We sat down on the bench next to the rondeau, and the scent of the roses wafted over to us. Clemens lit a cigarette, and the flame of the match made the contours of his face look soft and mysterious. After a long silence he said that if I still wanted to try some of the apricot strudel that his mother had sent to him, I would have to visit him soon. This time I agreed.

When the Baron had fallen asleep after I had read a few pages from Boccaccio's *Decameron*, I gently stood up and went into the west wing. From a long way off the smell of freshly brewed coffee drifted through the passageways. The chauffeur's two rooms were spacious and light, with a view of the pergola and the gravel drive leading to the wrought-iron gate. On his little table were two cups, two saucers, two dessert plates, a bowl of sugar and a milk jug of flowery Gmunden porcelain, a sight which, as you can imagine, aroused ambivalent feelings in me. The apricot strudel tasted excellent, and my enjoyment of the Austrian baking made me feel a little more well-inclined towards the man from Waidhofen an der Ybbs. He sat, relaxed, on a rattan chair by the window, and his curly head suddenly made me think of the Apollo Belvedere.

Why had the chauffeur's attractive appearance not struck me before? He looked at me, then put a big spatula-shaped hand on my right knee and said he had the feeling something was troubling me, could he do anything? Again I shook my head violently and said no, no, I was fine, because of his great age the Baron was sometimes something of an effort, but apart from that everything was fine. Before I left, Clemens suggested that in the next few days we should have a little picnic in a remote corner of the park, we should make use of these beautiful days. I hesitantly said that the Baron took up a lot of my time, perhaps we could meet during his afternoon nap, between half past two and half past four? Clemens laughed and said, see you tomorrow, he would be by the drawing-room door with his picnic basket at half past two.

Reverend Father, although I was not tied to the Baron by any profound feeling of affection, nonetheless I felt the invitation to a picnic to be a violation of loyalty, a betrayal of him. Although Baron Otto was never lacking in consideration, since the beginning of our excursions into the cellar I had noticed a stronger sense of devotion on his part, which seemed to be turning into a kind of possessiveness. So I was far from sure whether he would approve of my new friendship with his chauffeur.

The following day, when I left the drawing room where the Baron was deep in his afternoon sleep, the chauffeur was indeed standing at the door. We took ourselves off to a corner of the park, a place not unlike the place where we are now, and Clemens spread the big blue blanket out on the grass. We ate what was left of the apricot strudel, which put me in a balanced state of mind and spirit, and drank a sharp white wine from the Wachau, which Clemens had been sent for his birthday by his former employer, and which made me forget the previous evening in the cellar vault. After a while Clemens raised his glass and said we should drink to his being thirty-three that day. The glasses clinked against one another delicately, and the autumn sun shone through me and, with its warmth, intensified the effect of the Wachau white wine, so that the cellar vault within me grew lighter and more spacious and I sank back on the blue blanket. I looked into the sun and closed my eyes, and little yellow lights floated in the red patch that I saw behind my closed lids. Then I felt a big soft mouth on mine.

During the weeks to come I led two completely different lives. One of them was spent in the cellar, obliging the Baron whose desires were growing ever more peremptory and eccentric. In my second, new life, I walked from the east wing to the west wing as often as I could, without awakening the Baron's latent suspicion. Thus a small part of the Paradise to which the Baron had lured me and which had then turned out to be the Inferno began to live up to its name, that part which included the chauffeur's two big high-windowed rooms, whose curtains were closed with a long pole. In the semi-darkness we lay on the floor, looked at one another and watched the shadows cast by the agitated leaves in the trees outside the window dancing on the natural white material of the curtains, solidly woven but looking transparent because of the sunlight that fell through them. Sometimes a shaft of light falling through the narrow chink between the two curtains would fall on a detail of our bodies, an elbow, a collarbone, making it glow, or we would roll into the big, bright rectangle that the sun had cast on the carpet and lie for a while blinking in its shimmer, arm on arm, leg on leg, so closely intertwined that no gaps remained. Sometimes we would see the shadow of the gardener, the Bohemian housekeeper or the cook from Basel appearing on the curtain, stopping and then slowly moving on its way. They knew. Just as my hands were healed beneath the jet of water, so too they healed when they slipped through the chauffeur's thick hair as if through soft undergrowth, clenched into fists and held tight to his curls. And my feet grew healthy again when he took them in his hands, pressed the soles to his warm belly and stroked my instep until I lost all sense of time. Paradise is in the middle of Hell, Reverend Father, it is the centre, and before we can get there, we must cross Hell itself.

213

There were days when I hid my edition of *The Divine Comedy* under my nun's habit and went to the drawing room to see Baron Otto who was delighted with my outfit, opened Sacher-Masoch's *Venus In Furs*, read from it and, when he had gone to sleep, went on to the chauffeur in the west wing to read to him from the *Paradiso*. We lay on the soft material of the nun's habit, and Clemens understood not a word that I uttered:

> *E come in fiamma favilla si vede,*
> *e come in voce voce si discerne,*
> *quando una è ferma a l'altra va e riede,*
> *vid'io in essa luce altre lucerne*
> *moversi in giro piú e men correnti,*
> *al modo, credo, di lor viste eterne.*

But he listened, kissed me on the temple, took the book from my hands and tried stumblingly to read for himself.

> *Non fur piú tosto dentro a me venute*
> *queste parole brevi, ch'io compresi*
> *me sormontar di sopra a mia virtute;*
> *e di novella vista mi raccesi,*
> *tale che nulla luce è tanto mera*
> *che gli occhi miei non si fosser difesi.*

We read no more that day.

Three weeks it was, Reverend Father, three weeks in the two rooms with the natural white curtains. The wider the cramped cellar within me grew during this period, the more blinding the brightness which, emanating from an unknown source of light, flooded through the cold space to illuminate its last corner so that all the mice, rats and spiders sought escape, the more the old walls began to collapse beneath the chauffeur's caresses, the darker grew the real cellar vault in which the Baron locked us every evening, the more searing the orders that he gave to me. As if asleep I did everything he asked of me, it was I and not I who beat him, and the woman who later untied him and offered him her arm to lead him up the stairs was different from the woman with the pale face and the thin-lipped mouth who stayed in the cellar clutching the riding crop.

When, at the end of the three weeks behind drawn curtains, I bent over the chauffeur, who was lying on his back with his eyes closed, his beautiful neck open to my gaze, I was suddenly struck by his jugular vein, in which shimmering blue blood was regularly pulsing. And all of a sudden I was overwhelmed by a violent desire. I wanted to bite his strong, tanned neck with its highly visible Adam's apple. I wanted to yield to this impulse and bury my head in his neck, but a curious reserve held me back, something like the beginning of an unpleasant memory. At that moment the chauffeur opened his grey-green eyes and pulled me to him. He was tired, he said with a smile, I wouldn't leave him alone, sometimes he had the feeling I was sucking all his strength from him.

During the days that followed, the need to sink my teeth into his throat became almost irresistible, and only by mustering all my willpower could I keep from doing it. My apprehensiveness about this craving grew stronger and stronger, until finally it turned into a suspicion, particularly since, when glancing occasionally in the mirror between the high windows, I noticed that my upper canines looked unusually strong. The next time Clemens drove me to the Friedrichsbad, I asked him to drop me in front of the city library, they might have German translations of *The Divine Comedy* and then I could read him the Italian passages, which he liked so much without understanding them, in our mother tongue. I entered the library, pulled out the catalogue drawer for authors Scha to Sty, flicked through the cards, fingers flying, and found the reference to Bram Stoker's *Dracula*. I found the book, took it from the shelf, and when I had shown the assistants my identity card and filled in a form, they allowed me to take it home.

Reverend Father, my inexplicable concern proved to be all too accurate a premonition. In the library of the British Museum in Great Russell Street I had skimmed the pages of the book so quickly that something important had escaped me: a person on whose blood a vampire has fed becomes himself a vampire. Michael Minulescu, who, from the paternal side of his family, had known something about the undead, had clearly been unaware of this detail. Or could his fear of infection have been the real reason for his reticence towards my approaches? I will never know.

As a Catholic priest you will not, of course, know the emotion that I first encountered after I bumped into Clemens in the park on the eve of his thirty-third birthday, of course you're not allowed to know that emotion. But since you have empathic gifts, as I noticed long ago, you will understand how terrible it was for me to discover that I was a vampire. After all my odysseys I had met someone of whom I couldn't have enough – and it had lasted for three weeks now, despite the depressing fact that he was an Austrian – and I felt as if I was at the beginning of a journey that made hopes seem justifiable, not, for once, finding myself in the usual one-way street, the usual cul-de-sac. He was a man who didn't say much, didn't ask any questions, who was neither melancholic nor jealous, neither faithless nor a parasite, and not ideologically contaminated, a man who, for the first time in my life, had just what I needed. And I would have to give up this man, I would have to give up those astonishing acts carried out in the changing semi-darkness of the two rooms if I didn't want to turn him into one of the undead as well, a living corpse, forced to wander about restlessly at night in search of human blood, never finding rest. Reverend Father, for the first time in my life I thought less of myself than of someone else. I didn't feel sorry for myself, for having been turned into a monster by Jonathan Alistair Abercrombie's welcome caresses, I was concerned not to inflict the same fate on Clemens the chauffeur. That must be what you praise from your pulpit as Christian brotherly love, mustn't it?

When I had spent a long time thinking how I could tell the chauffeur that our relationship, blossoming as fragrantly as the roses in the rose rondeau, was at an end even before it had really begun, how I could explain why my path suddenly took me not from the east wing to the west wing but only into the drawing room, and when I had come to no conclusion, the problem resolved itself by our being betrayed.

One Thursday morning Baron Otto summoned me to the drawing room, which surprised me, since he didn't usually lay claims on me at that time of day. When I walked into the room, he was not lying on the sofa as usual but standing upright with his back to me, by the window. As soon as he heard me he turned round with an expression that I had never seen on his face before, not even during the most severe punishments in the cellar vault. His face reflected anger mingled with pain and disappointment. He had, he began in a controlled voice, he had taken me into his house and treated me like a daughter, showered me with presents – the gold necklace specially commissioned from a goldsmith in Freiburg im Breisgau, with sapphires to match the colour of my eyes, the carved rococo ivory bracelet from Nuremberg, which had cost him a fortune, the diamond earrings for which he had even taken the trouble of travelling to Antwerp, nearly getting involved in shady business with the Mafia, to mention only three, he had fed me on dishes of exceptional quality and pleasant appearance, put suitable accommodation at my disposal and paid a considerable salary for tasks which, it is true, had required special qualities such as human empathy and manual dexterity, but which had not taken up a great deal of my time, quite apart from the fact that at the beginning of

217

our acquaintance he had helped me win a considerable sum at roulette. Apart from this, he had never failed to show me the respect that was my due, and never molested me in any way, whether through touches or words. For giving a woman, without references and solely on the basis of faith and trust, a post which, in his view, could be considered senior, one might have been permitted to expect in return – apart from competence and a certain command of the job at hand, which, he must say, I had not lacked – a minimum of integrity and loyalty, or did I not share his opinion?

When I meekly began to answer, he interrupted me, saying that even if I had lacked the requisite trustworthiness in his household, others had proved theirs, telling him that I had not kept myself to resting from my tasks in the east wing, or preparing for them, but that in a thoughtless show of independence, in an ill-considered lust for adventure, I had gone far beyond my fixed boundaries into the west wing, to the chambers of his chauffeur, of whom such a betrayal, given both his Austrian origins and his status as a Bentley expert, was also unimaginable, that I had indulged in activities which were certainly not compatible with a post in his house.

So saying, he drew some black-and-white photographs from the pocket of his tweed jacket and held them icily to my face. There was not the slightest point in denying it, he said with a tremble in his voice, the true vassal had found ways and means to confront him with my damnable activities without himself having to go to such humiliating lengths as to spy on me. I took the photographs from his hand. Someone – and we might assume that that someone was the gardener or the Bohemian housekeeper, because although the cook from Basel was capable of conjuring up the most refined haute cuisine recipes and having them on the table in an astonishingly short time, I did not imagine that she would have known what to do with the simplest camera – someone had pointed a merciless photographic eye at us through the little chink in the curtains and pressed the shutter release while the chauffeur and I were in positions normally described as compromising.

Again I tried to voice a half-hearted apology, and again the Baron interrupted me. He did not expect an answer from me, he said, any answer would be a mockery, the photographs spoke for themselves. In view of the fact that it would be difficult to find a substitute for me, with the current lamentable lack of trained staff, he would keep me at home. However, he would have to cut my salary and stop giving me presents, and he also saw himself obliged to have his meals no longer with me but with the Bohemian housekeeper. Where the chauffeur was concerned, he was sad to lose an excellent driver and Bentley specialist, who had been working for him for four years now and to whom he had been about to offer both a pay rise and the familiar mode of address, but it was obvious that such a breach of trust could be punished only by immediate dismissal, particularly since in his case it would also be rather easier to find a replacement.

After this conversation I retreated dejectedly to my room and tried to find comfort in the *Divina Commedia*. And it actually gave me heart to think that Dante had lost his Beatrice on earth but found her again on his mystical pilgrimage. I too would lose Clemens, and paradoxically the betrayal of the staff made the separation easier for me, because I no longer had to put it into effect myself, a task which would have taken me to the limit of my psychological capacities; it was imposed upon us from without. The little paradise that we had created for ourselves in the middle of the Inferno was lost, but when I had read some more verses from Dante's *Paradiso*, the possibility of winning him back some time, somehow, no longer seemed completely absurd.

I put Dante on my bed and sank into a kind of half-sleep, in which the face of the chauffeur appeared, his expression at first friendly and loving, but soon becoming more strict, more rigid. Then he was suddenly the one menacingly swinging the cat-o'-nine-tails, and with a faint cry I awoke. At that moment there was a knock at the window. It was Clemens, who wanted to talk to me. I opened the window and had time to see the Bohemian housekeeper disappearing round the corner and looking back at us suspiciously. Clemens leaned over the windowsill into my arms, and said the Baron had just fired him and had so profoundly humiliated his chauffeur's sense of honour that he would leave the house that same day, but not without me. He realized that three weeks was not a long time, but it had been enough for him to make his choice. And he was sure that I, too, would think it a good idea to go with him to Waidhofen an der Ybbs and marry in the late-Gothic church there. He could start work again at the car workshop of his former employer, and feed us in an honest and respectable way. His father had died some years ago, but his mother was still alive and would be happy if he married, for years she had been voicing the wish that he would finally start a family. We would live in his mother's one-family house, he was a bit of a handyman and intended to renovate the loft. From me he expected the preparation of three meals per day, the upkeep of clothes and laundry, the cleaning of the renovated loft, a certain amount of knowledge about the growing of vegetables, plants and flowers, and obedience to the orders of his mother, as this would make the coexistence of two generations in a one-family house considerably easier. His mother was a very good-hearted woman, but since her marriage, which had not always been harmonious but which had nonetheless lasted for decades, to his late father, an equally good-hearted but rather weak man, she was accustomed to the absolute submission of others to her will, and in this respect one could expect no fundamental change in a woman of her age.

Then his expression softened, and he added that of course he also hoped for children, and had no doubt that as a healthy strong woman of child-bearing age I would give him the four sons and two daughters he had always dreamed of. The upbringing of these children as decent Lower Austrians he would leave to me, as he would be fully occupied with his work in the car workshop and with the tasks that needed to be done in and around the one-family house. After this speech, the longest he had delivered since the beginning of our acquaintance, he fell silent and looked at me expectantly. Before I could begin to answer, I asked him to climb through the window and sit down for a moment in the comfortable armchair in my room. He swung one leg over the windowsill, and just as he was pulling the second after it, the gardener came along the gravel drive, looked in astonishment in our direction and disappeared into the tool shed.

When I had gently pushed the chauffeur into the lime-green Art Deco chair and sat on the arm, I said I was honoured by his offer, it was the first proposal of marriage I had ever had in my life. During the three weeks spent largely on the floor of his two rooms, it would probably not have escaped him that the intensity of my feelings towards him far exceeded the norm. The image of the future that he had just described in such vivid colours struck me – a few small and fundamentally trivial details aside – as being entirely worthy of translation into reality.

Then I gave a deep breath, reached gently into his thick curly hair and put all the resolution and gravity I could into the tone of my voice. But we must not, I said, think only of our own happiness, such an attitude would be extremely selfish and egoistical. He was still young and had his life in front of him, but the Baron was old and frail and needed me. He had been deeply hurt by my relationship with him, Clemens, which had perhaps begun too impulsively, and my conscience would not allow me to leave him. He, Clemens, knew just as well as I did that the Bohemian housekeeper, the cook from Basel and the gardener thought of nothing but his money; I considered these three superficially charming but basically amoral staff capable of the worst in this regard. What if the Bohemian housekeeper locked him in the cellar and let him starve to death? What if the cook poisoned him? What if the gardener dropped the sawn-off branch of an oak tree on his head? The Baron was incapable of resisting this dubious trio on his own, he needed support. I could not refuse him that support, even if he had caused me great pain by firing him, Clemens. I knew that I was asking an impossible amount from him, Clemens, in expecting him to show an understanding of my thought processes. He could be sure that I would suffer just as much as he would from the separation imposed upon us by an adverse destiny. But we had to prove ourselves to be mature and responsible human beings, and do what reason dictated. One never knew, perhaps destiny would bring us together at some later date, we need not rule that out, I myself had seen destinies fulfilled in the most astonishing manner. But now he must climb back out of my window because the Baron would be waiting for me to read to him in a quarter of an hour.

What should I have done? Every word I said to Clemens the chauffeur cut into my heart, and the increasingly disconsolate expression with which he listened to my explanations and looked up at me, sitting on the lime-green arm of the armchair, pained my soul. But I couldn't reveal to him that he was in fatal danger, that he had spent the last three weeks not in the arms of a normal young woman but in those of a vampire who had the power to transform him, too, into just such a revenant, just such a parasite.

I had deeply upset him. With his upper lip trembling, and in a halting voice, he said he had no choice but to respect my decision, but during my rather strange and not entirely logical exposition his brain had grown more and more confused, and he no longer understood a thing.

He rose to his feet and said he would return alone to Waidhofen an der Ybbs and try to find the girl to whom he had proposed ten years ago on a bench in the square there, because he was neither able nor willing to abandon the plans for the future that he had just roughly outlined. I wished him luck, and when he had held me in his arms one last time, he climbed out of the window and vanished from my life.

I lay down on the bed and unleashed the tears that had been building up during this farewell. Then I pulled myself together, donned the nun's habit, went into the drawing room and read to the Baron from *Fanny Hill, or the Memoirs of a Lady of Pleasure*. While I was reading I would sometimes cast a glance at the rich old man, who lay on the sofa listening attentively. Reverend Father, that afternoon I began to hate him. Not content with drawing me into the vicious circle of his depravity and inciting me to perform unnatural acts in a dark cellar, now he had also barred for ever my way into the two light, big rooms with the natural white curtains in the west wing of the house. With every stolen glance that I darted towards him, I was more repelled by this man who was supposedly a patron but was in reality an enemy, and who had prevented my happiness with the chauffeur when it had been immediately within reach. My feelings of grief at Clemens' departure were replaced by vague notions of revenge, which in turn were interrupted, if not abandoned, one day by the unexpected arrival of my elder sisters.

One afternoon, when I was walking in the park and enjoying the glowing yellow, the rich red and warm brown of the autumnal leaves, the elder of my two elder sisters suddenly emerged from behind the trunk of an oak tree. I couldn't believe my eyes at first, closed them for a moment and opened them again, convinced that the ghostly apparition would have disappeared. But my elder sister was still standing there, and she smiled and immediately began talking. She was very happy to see me at last, because it had been far from easy to get close to me, a man in a pair of blue working trousers and a white vest had turned her away at the wrought-iron gate and, when she asked if she could speak to Magdalena Leitner, had answered that she must be mistaken, no woman of that name had ever lived in this house. When she had pushed the envelope that I had sent her through the bars and pressed it into the hand of the man, who must have been the gardener, he had quickly glanced at the sender's name and address and said there must be a mistake, and apologizing that he had to get back to raking up the leaves and piling them up, had abruptly turned away. But she hadn't been discouraged by the man's resistance.

At that moment the younger of my two elder sisters emerged from behind the smooth grey trunk of a beech tree, and continued the elder sister's story. They had walked along the wall surrounding the property, and when they had failed to find an open side gate they had climbed over the wall, which had been very difficult. The elder sister had stood with her back to the wall and linked her fingers, whereupon she had climbed up on those linked fingers and, summoning all her physical strength, had pulled herself up on to the wall. Then she had stretched her arm towards her sister and helped her to clamber up the wall in her turn. Then they had jumped from the wall on to the thick lawn and cautiously entered the park, where fortunately they had soon seen me.

After this opening, the younger of my two sisters came up to me and made as if to embrace me, whereupon I took a few steps backwards and, as nicely as possible, asked the reason for their surprising arrival.

My letter, the elder of my two sisters explained, had greatly cheered both them, my sisters, and my parents and my four nieces and three nephews, because it had revealed that I was living in good conditions, quite unlike their own. They wanted to congratulate me on my favourable new financial situation, and on the fact that fate had lately treated me better than it had them, my parents and my three nephews and four nieces. I knew that the price of groceries in Austria was constantly on the rise, that it cost huge sums of money to bring up seven children. And on top of that, the younger of my two sisters said, on top of that she planned to marry a man who was very nice but completely impoverished after a number of misfortunes. And finally, one should also bear in mind that our parents weren't getting any younger, and it was the duty of the children to grant them a relatively carefree old age. During these observations my sisters had been coming closer and closer. In view of the unmistakable fact that the wheel of fortune had gone on turning, continued the younger of my two elder sisters, who had received a higher education which was, if not entirely watertight then at least moderately useful during her novitiate with the Barefoot Carmelites, and that I was now at the top of the wheel, while the rest of the family was in decline, they thought it only fair that I should support them in the difficult situation that was currently afflicting Austria, and consequently my whole family.

Reverend Father, after I had taken the greatest efforts to escape the demands of my family, after I had foiled their opaque plans for me at the last minute and thwarted their intentions of turning me into a madwoman, an aunt or a Carmelite, after I had managed, making considerable sacrifices, to preserve my independence, my family had finally caught up with me. I immediately understood the gravity of the situation.

You, as a member of a community of interests which considers the natural bonds, the so-called blood ties, to be unbreakable, you will obviously protest when I say that the family is the most dangerous place that it is possible to be, that you are nowhere more exposed and threatened than in the so-called circle of your loved ones, and that, if you value your life, you should – you must – escape that place of disaster, that realm of doom.

As you will have noticed, my independent lifestyle has often placed me in situations which were, without a doubt, risky, with people who were categorically unstable. Such situations, such people, are harmless in comparison with the situations, the people with whom one comes into contact every day as the member of an average family. The supposedly secure refuge is in reality a snake pit, a place of execution, a Golgotha where people, under the pretence of mutual assistance, are engaged in merciless battle where, while feigning unswerving affection, they inflict fatal injuries upon one another. Nowhere are lack of freedom, restriction and compulsion greater than in the so-called bosom of the family, nowhere do people hate each other with greater vehemence, nowhere do they lie to one another, betray one another more barefacedly, nowhere is rivalry more bitter, envy more nagging, the striving for dominance more stubborn than beneath the surface of harmonious family relationships. This institution, applauded most vigorously by the overwhelming majority of politicians, ministers and teachers, psychologists, psychiatrists, psychotherapists and psychoanalysts, in the face of all the evidence to the contrary, as the nucleus of the state, this institution seldom produces independent-minded, autonomous, upright people, more generally crouching, crippled, helpless individuals.

You as an Austrian priest, for whom the preservation of the Austrian family tie is, of course, and must be a major concern, will violently contradict me, must violently contradict me when I say that of all family destruction machines the Austrian family destruction machine is one of the most efficient in the Western world, since it is aimed particularly at the most sensitive, intelligent and talented members of the family, and generally doesn't take long to destroy their inherent sensitivity, intelligence and talent. It is no coincidence that the family, in particular the Austrian family, is the most frequent scene of acts of violence. I, who have dared to visit the most rundown parts of cities at night in the course of my travels, who have climbed into the cabs of unknown long-distance lorry drivers on remote dust roads in eastern Anatolia, assure you that it is not in the places most widely considered menacing that the most terrible crimes are committed, but that the nuclear family, and the Austrian nuclear family in particular, is the most appropriate setting, the ideal background for the most terrible crimes.

The classical Austrian family tragedy normally runs more or less as follows: one Saturday evening in May the hitherto unimpeachable, quiet, hard-working non-smoker and tee-totaller Gustav A., who has been working for fifteen years as a gas fitter in the small Upper Styrian town of T., takes a pipe wrench and smashes in not only the skulls of his 32-year-old wife Ilse, his ten-year-old son Thomas and his little five-year-old daughter Daniela but also that of his three-year-old dog Rex, and then, without a hint of emotional distress, turns himself in at the local police station. Sometimes there are variations, for example the case of the pretty, much-loved 27-year-old wife of the well-known ear, nose and throat specialist Gernot S., from H., throwing first her younger daughter Sabine and then her elder daughter Christine out of the bedroom window of their spacious doctor's apartment on the seventh storey of the only high-rise in the regional capital and jumping after them, or the no less typical occurrence of 37-year-old unmarried wine-grower Johann C., from the village of W. in South Burgenland, a level-headed, cheerful man of unstained reputation, strangling his parents and the eighty-year-old great-aunt who lived under the same roof, with a Riesling vine.

Allow me to return from this little excursion into the realm of the family, particularly the realm of the Austrian family, and continue with my confession, and listen to the answer I gave my two elder sisters in response to their request. It is true, I said, that Baron Otto, who has so generously taken me into his employ, has occasionally allowed a little jewel to come my way, nothing valuable, a little jade pendant on a thin nickel-silver chain, a simple slender gold ring with a tiny heart-shaped rose quartz, oh, and the pretty dark-red glass drop earrings that he brought me from the flea market by the Old Station. When the elder of my two sisters impatiently interrupted me and asked me about the sapphire necklace that I had mentioned in my letter, I had the presence of mind to reply that this had, of course, been merely a copy that Otto had been so kind as to give me; the original, a very valuable old piece from the East Prussian branch of the family, was in the safe. After a short, rather helpless silence the younger of my sisters said I could at least give my family a share of the big win I had had at roulette, which I mentioned in my letter, to which I replied that I would be only too happy but first of all the win was not as high as they probably believed, and secondly I had already invested it all, down to the last pfennig, in a limited company with extensive properties in Argentina.

After a further pause, the elder of my sisters said she hadn't come all the way from Lake Ossiach to Baden-Baden for nothing, surely I could at least pay their travel expenses. I asked her to be patient for a moment, I would be back in a second, went into my rooms, took the stolen chalice and the two silver candlesticks out of the cupboard and returned to my sisters. I surprised the younger one with the gilded chalice, and said the Baron had given it to me as a present, it came from his private chapel, as did the two candlesticks. So saying, I pressed one silver candlestick into my elder sister's right hand, and the other into her left hand. They seemed pleased with this, and when I told them they must excuse me, the Baron was waiting for me to join him for tea, they clearly had no objection to this impromptu farewell. I helped them climb over the wall with the stolen goods, and before they jumped over to the other side I sent hearty greetings to my parents and my seven nieces and nephews.

Reverend Father, when my two elder sisters had disappeared, I sank into one of the wickerwork chairs beneath a weeping willow and fell into a frenzy of self-recrimination. What kind of a person was I? What kind of a woman was I, who had no hesitation in violating the Ten Commandments that said thou shouldst not bear false witness against thy neighbour, who lied in her sisters' faces, just so as she could avoid helping her family, which might well have been in distress, and who, by refusing to share with her loved ones the fortune brought her way by a happy accident and instead greedily keeping it for herself, was also committing the deadly sin of *avaritia*? Like a pig in filth I wallowed in my badness. After I had rebuked myself like this for a while, I went slowly back to the house, and when I passed the two drawing-room windows I saw something that I probably wouldn't have seen if I hadn't been gifted, by the genes on my father's side of the family, with unusually keen eyesight, because the view through the delicate white net curtains was a little restricted.

You won't believe it, but there in the drawing room stood the Bohemian housekeeper, and standing behind her the Baron was fiddling with the clasp of a chain with a pendant in the shape of a flower, whose petals could be identified, even through the net curtains, as emeralds, rubies and diamonds. I returned to my room and threw myself on the bed. My suspicion was confirmed, it had indeed been the Bohemian housekeeper who had photographed myself and the chauffeur. I forgave the Baron for not giving me any more presents, although it was painful to me; I could bear the fact that he had cut my salary, and I could even have tolerated him dining with the Bohemian housekeeper. But that she was now the one standing in my place at the mirror in the drawing room, allowing the Baron to drape her with jewellery that should have been mine, that was too much for me. If I had betrayed the Baron, as he claimed, by embarking on a relationship with the chauffeur, this betrayal on his part was at least equally shameful. The vague thoughts of revenge that had run through my head when I read to him from the *Hundred and Twenty Days of Sodom* and glanced at him discreetly from time to time became more concrete as I lay in bed and waited for the evening when we would, as usual, go down the stairs into the cellar vault.

The simplest thing would have been to bite him in the neck, an act that would not have surprised him particularly, being completely harmless in comparison with our other behaviour. What kept me from doing so was not the concern that he might infect the Bohemian housekeeper, and it didn't matter to me that I might also put the gardener in danger. But I didn't want the cook from Basel to be turned into a vampire. That woman, an extremely talented cook with a sense of taste attuned to the finest nuances, deserved better.

When I rose from my bed and went to the Baron wearing my leather jump suit, my plan was settled. The bizarre amusements that the Baron allowed me to arrange for him were many and various. Among other things, he took pleasure in my tying him to the wall fittings with four silk scarves, and tying a fifth round his throat so long and so tight that he could hardly breathe. That evening I suggested this pastime to him, and he thought the idea was marvellous. So I bound him with four brightly coloured scarves from an Indian boutique in Baden-Baden's pedestrian precinct. Then I tied the fifth, a very pretty orange batik scarf of Shantung silk with a tasteful pattern of blue semi-circles, round his thin, withered throat, and pulled it tighter than usual. The Baron, who hung from the iron fittings like the Christ on the cross so cherished by you and your congregation, and who, in the context of this particular pleasure, was unaccustomed to such vehemence on my part, looked at me in astonishment and immediately understood what I had in mind. He only managed to utter the first words of a sentence in which he wanted to dissuade me from my plan, the second half of which, however, because of the progressive strangulation of his organs of speech, emerged as an inarticulate groaning.

It was not difficult to throttle the Baron, as his constitution, because of his age and the physical sanctions to which he had willingly submitted himself for years, was not of the most robust. When I garrotted him, at the same time I was killing all the people in my life who, by persuasion or by the use of force, had drawn me into acts that I basically didn't want to perform. Of the seven men I have murdered he was the one that I killed most resolutely, most cold-bloodedly. I looked at him. He hung lifeless on the wall, his head lolling to the side and his eyes open. He would not rise again, unlike the Christ so cherished by you and your congregation.

I untied him and removed the orange scarf. Then I climbed on a chair and threw one of the leather straps over an iron hook in the ceiling. I took the light body in my arms, climbed up on the chair, fastened one end of the strap round the thin neck and pulled on the other until the Baron appeared to be standing on the chair. Then I knotted the strap, got down from the chair and knocked it over. It would look like suicide. I cast another glance at the gently rocking Baron, turned round and closed the iron cellar door behind me for ever.'

Magdalena fell silent, then she reached into the little basket beside her and ate two cherries. I looked at her slender hands. The portrayal of the sixth of the murders she had committed had left me more exhausted than the description of the earlier horrors. I could hardly believe that the hands whose caresses had, the previous night, roused me to a state comparable only to the mystical ecstasy experienced by some Catholic saints, those same hands that had devoted themselves with unparalleled tenderness to my body, first beneath the sleeping bag and later beneath my priest's habit, had mustered the strength to strangle a man. And the frank description of the – in my view – extremely pathological excesses in the cellar vault had horrified me. How could a woman who, as I knew since the previous night, possessed such female warmth, descend to such acts of perversity? Women – and Magdalena in particular – really were extremely mysterious and unfathomable creatures.

But despite the revulsion that her story had temporarily provoked in me, I was only waiting for night to fall. Again I could have delivered a professional judgment of her story, pointed out to her that she had entered the path of evil when

231

she had entered the cellar vault, but that her soul, because of the ineffable love and goodness of God, was not lost for ever, and again I preferred to remain silent.

Magdalena handed me a few cherries.

'I'm afraid I'm going to have to go back to the village,' she said. 'As we will soon be leaving this lovely place and driving on, we must be sure that no one recognizes us. In the filling station I saw some cans of car body paint on a shelf. I'm going to find a suitable colour, and then we can repaint the Puch 800 together.'

Magdalena slid from the sleeping bag, went to the motor-cycle and returned with her nun's habit. She slipped from the jump suit which covered her like a second skin, and whose thin leather, as my hands had felt the previous night, was very soft and malleable. This time I felt strong enough to allow the confusing sight of her stainless white body to have more of an effect on me, but before I was able to concentrate on it she had already donned the black item of clothing that had previously gagged me. She put her hands on her waist and walked up and down in front of me, swinging her hips. From a distance I had, it is true, seen women holiday-makers in bathing costumes on the shores of Lake Ossiach, and on one occasion I had accidentally surprised my sister dressing in the bathroom, wearing a corset which was rather large and pink, and which, although it bore a remote similarity to the feather-light item of underclothing called a body stocking, was as different from it as could be imagined.

'Do you like it?' asked Magdalena. 'An expensive number. The neck is Brussels lace.'

And she walked up to me where I was still sitting in the sleeping bag, and bent towards me.

'Feel,' she said, and it wasn't an invitation but an order.

When I suddenly saw her cleavage, which was considerably deeper than the cleavage of her jump suit, right before my eyes, when these dangerous curves and swellings were within my reach, I felt dizzy again, and when I rather hesitantly stretched out my right hand, she had already stood up and was in the process of putting on her habit.

'You stay here, Reverend Father,' she said. Then she looked at me and smiled. 'I won't tie you up again. I don't think that's going to be necessary. Goodbye.'

And she tugged the folds of her habit into place, and disappeared again behind the dense foliage of the juniper bush.

Magdalena's assessment of the situation was correct. Twenty-four hours ago I had been feverishly wondering how I could free myself from the power of my abductor, but in the meantime our relationship had changed so drastically that I was already yearning for her return. I realized that it was a scandal, and not only from the point of view of Catholic doctrine, for a consecrated Catholic priest, a man respected and popular both in his parish and beyond its borders, to be on the point of entering a frankly erotic relationship with a woman leading an extremely indecent life in comparison to the overwhelming majority of her sex, who had abducted him at gunpoint, but that it also, from the perspective of so-called common sense, revealed a rashness bordering on insanity, which could lead to my excommunication. But I simply swept such considerations aside. The idea that I would soon be standing in the pulpit of my church again, practising my office, was not very enticing at present, presuming as it did that Magdalena would be vanishing from my life. I put another cherry in my mouth and decided, for the first time in my life, to embark recklessly on something new. Even Magdalena's claim to have been bitten by a vampire, and now to be one herself, could not hold me back from my life's first love affair. A Catholic priest believes in the dogmas of the Church and not in rumours put about by ignorant, superstitious Romanian peasants and translated by some dubious Irish novelist into an overblown piece of hack work. I suspected Magdalena of embroidering her confessions from time to time, weaving in events that had happened rather differently in reality. Not that I attributed the tiniest degree of malice to her on this account, it was more as if the wings of her imagination sometimes took her to spheres only very loosely connected to tangible reality. I briefly considered going for a short walk, but then I decided to stay in my sleeping bag, its folds still permeated by the scent of Magdalena, and dream of her return. I lay down, closed my eyes and began to imagine the coming night. Soon I was so immersed in my visions of longing that I lost all sense of time. When Magdalena's voice finally interrupted my fantasies about the immediate future, it was as though she had just left. I opened my eyes, and she was standing in front of me with a green plastic bag.

'The selection was very limited,' she said. 'Bright red struck me as most appropriate.' She took two tins from the bag and put them on the ground. Then she drew two brushes and a few sheets of sandpaper from it, and finally a numberplate.

'There was a motorcycle parked in front of the filling station, a good opportunity to get a new numberplate. While the attendant was busy serving somebody in the shop, I quickly took it off.' She took the Swiss Army knife out of one of the many folds in her habit. 'There's a little screwdriver attachment on my Swiss Army knife. Very practical, these Swiss Army knives.' She put the knife back, took a newspaper from the plastic bag and opened it.

'We must find out, Reverend Father. I'm excited to find out whether anyone knows anything more about where we are. Look, information is requested about a black Puch 800 with Felber sidecar, registration K180.488. One of your faithful seems to have had good eyes. Excellent idea, taking off the numberplate. By the way, the cardinal's offered a ransom. He's called for donations, and the Austrian Catholics have proved to be very generous. They've donated more money than they've ever given to the Church charities. What do you say about that? The East Tyroleans have been donating particularly heavily. Sunday service in St Stephen's Cathedral also seems to have been a great success. They say there were huge numbers of people. The forecourt of St Stephen's Cathedral was thronged with the faithful. At the cardinal's express instructions, they rang the Pummerin bell for half an hour. Big white flags with your portrait were draped from the outside wall of the cathedral. Speaking choirs in front of the church intoned the sentence "The only good abductor is a dead abductor". The cardinal spoke from the Pilgrim Pulpit. He expressly spoke out against the death penalty, but he said that this particular case, in which taboos had been broken which simply must not be broken, naturally required an atonement in proportion with the unforgivable transgression of taboos. And if the Austrian faithful, and the East Tyroleans in particular, stuck together in this difficult hour, they would find the man who had abducted you, of that he was sure, God was just. Then he asked the people to remain silent for a minute, think about the abducted priest and thus show their solidarity with the victim of the brutal abduction.'

Magdalena giggled.

'If the cardinal knew how we spent last night, he'd be very surprised, the cardinal, wouldn't he?' Then she went on, 'At the moment we don't seem to be in danger. But the filling station attendant looked at me very strangely this time. And when I left the filling station, he looked after me for a long time, I did notice that. Perhaps I should have told him a story, given him a plausible explanation for buying two tins of car body paint and two brushes. Why would a Carmelite nun buy two tins of bright-red car body paint and two brushes? I've probably made a mistake in not having an explanation to give the filling station attendant. Be that as it may, get up, Reverend Father, and let's paint the bike and sidecar.'

I stood up and she pressed a tin of paint, a brush and some sandpaper into my hand and pushed me towards the motorbike. Quickly, so quickly that I only cast a short glance at the black lace, which sent a shiver down my spine that can only be compared with the sensation experienced by Saint Teresa at the visionary sight of Christ, she removed the nun's habit and put on the jump suit, and turned towards the bike. She took the numberplates off and started to rub down the front mudguard with sandpaper, while I concentrated on the sidecar. We worked on quietly like that. Above us, on a gently springing branch of the spruce tree beneath which the bike was parked, the bullfinch twittered.

'Where had I got to?' said Magdalena after a while. 'Oh yes, leaving the cellar vault in Baron Otto's villa for the last time. I climbed the steps, strode quickly to my rooms and packed my things. It must have been about midnight. It was quiet in the house, the Bohemian housekeeper, the gardener and the cook from Basel were asleep at that time of night. I got the Puch sidecar bike from the garage, pushed it down the white gravel drive to the wrought-iron gate, opened the gate, behind which there shone a big, white full moon, and kick-started the bike. It was night-time, and I didn't know where to drive to. On the off chance, I drove along the Sophienstrasse into the centre of Baden-Baden, and when I turned off to the right for the Old Station, some distance away I saw the casino where the Baron had passed the mountain of chips to me and thus, without knowing it, hastened his end. The city slept, and I drove past the Old Station, then on to the New Station and finally to the autobahn for Karlsruhe. Before Karlsruhe I turned off towards the east for Stuttgart, and when I realized I was getting tired I parked at a picnic area, got into the sidecar, made myself as comfortable as possible and went to sleep.

I woke up in the bright light of morning, and the long-distance lorries were thundering past. I got out my map and decided to head for the heart of central Europe, for Prague, a city comfortably remote from larger and smaller islands which resembled paradise from a distance but which were disappointing close up. In Stuttgart I had a snack in a pub, then missed the exit for Nuremberg and, without really wanting to, continued in a south-easterly direction towards Ulm. I intended to turn off towards Regensburg in Ulm and go on to Prague, but again I went in the wrong direction, to Munich. I consoled myself with the idea that it would still be possible to reach Prague from Munich, but began to wonder whether a mysterious power was drawing me back to Austria, that country where the cultivated cultured classes, particularly the psychologists, psychiatrists, psychoanalysts and psychotherapists, as well as my parents, my two elder sisters and my seven nieces and nephews were lying in wait for me, and where people either looked through me or looked at me as something abnormal, a curiosity, a monstrosity. What was it that drew my Puch 800, as if bewitched, towards Munich and on to the Austrian border? The puzzling pull towards the south-east began to preoccupy me so much that about twelve miles past Augsburg I drove too far to the left and almost crashed into a Toyota with an Ingolstadt registration, which was just overtaking me. Just before Munich I had delved so far into my semi-conscious mind that, after a number of other dangerous situations, I had to admit it was Austrian baking that exerted this magnetic attraction on me, and not just any kind, but an apricot strudel made with apricots from the region of Waidhofen an der Ybbs, like the one offered me by the spatula-shaped hand of Clemens the chauffeur, on a dessert plate of flower-patterned Gmunden porcelain.

This realization so overwhelmed and confused me that I soon found myself back in the centre of Munich, which I actually wanted to avoid. It was early evening, and since I was in Munich, I parked my motorbike in a side alley and set off for a café where I intended to have a drink and perhaps eat a little snack. About ten yards away, on a not particularly inviting façade, I saw, in bright green neon writing, the words Hansi's Café. The capital H in Hansi was flickering. I had no wish to spend a long time looking, and entered the rather shady establishment. When I had sat down in a corner and ordered a glass of beer and a warm *Leberkäs* from the sulky bleached-blonde waitress, I went on thinking about the meaning of this longing for a piece of apricot strudel handed to me by Clemens the chauffeur, and reached the conclusion that it must be a state of mind known popularly as love. This recognition, late in the day and crystal clear, was so shocking to me that I immediately ordered another glass of beer, which I quickly finished.

I stared into the tall, empty glass. In all likelihood the chauffeur had been in Waidhofen an der Ybbs for ages, and his proposal of marriage to the girl he had asked to be his wife ten years before, and whom he was sure to have found, would already have been delivered. This idea depressed me so much that I asked for a third glass to cheer me up a bit. Paradoxically, it only made me more despondent. To distract me from the alarming fact that for the first time in my life I was experiencing that state of mind popularly known as love, something I would never have thought possible, I looked around. Three other people were now sitting in the café, a middle-aged couple holding hands and a dark-haired man of rather muscular build, as far as I could tell from that distance. Now a kind of MC in a light-grey jacket came on to the little podium to the rear of the café, occupied by a VCR and a television screen, picked up a microphone and said it was karaoke time. At the same time the sulky waitress handed a list to everyone in the café. The MC cheerily encouraged everyone to be brave and be a star for once in their lives. He seemed disappointed that neither the middle-aged couple nor the dark-haired man wanted to try their hand at being a singer. I cast a fleeting glance at the list of music videos available, and saw that Rod Stewart's "The First Cut Is the Deepest" was among them.

Reverend Father, don't ask me what prompted me to get up on the podium, it was probably the pain of realizing, all the more intense for being delayed, the understanding, belated but all the clearer for that, that that state of mind popularly known as love had been briefly won and lost again, mixed with a fleeting memory, hinted at in the title of the song, of the vampire Jonathan Alistair Abercrombie, who had made that state of mind popularly known as love impossible from the start. Anyway, to the delight of the MC I picked up the microphone and sang the song, and I put all the feeling, all the ardour I could muster into my performance. Even the MC seemed to be moved, because when the song was finished he was silent for a while, before he cleared his throat and said it was a shame that aside from the waitress and himself, only three people had been lucky enough to hear a voice whose like one seldom had the chance to hear, a voice that had touched him, personally, right in the heart. The couple and the dark-haired man applauded loudly, and I took a bow and sat back down at my table, whereupon the waitress came over with another glass, saying that this time the beer was on the man at the bar, clearly meaning the dark-haired man. I glanced in his direction, and he nodded his head in greeting. When I smiled back to thank him, he came over to me holding a glass of wine, and asked politely whether he might join me for a while. As he seemed perfectly pleasant, I pushed my chair aside a little as an invitation to sit down.

He put his glass on the table, took a seat, laid his forearms on the Formica table top and said he couldn't tell me how moved he had been by my rendition. It wasn't so much to do with the meaning of the lyrics, although that too had stirred his emotions, and even the tune hadn't been the reason for the curiously emotional response that my singing had awoken in him, entirely pleasant though it had been. It had been my timbre, my special vocal colour, that had awoken painful memories in him, memories that he had thought were long gone, memories of the early days with his second wife Erika who had sung for years in Wetterstein Mixed-Voice Choir, and indeed still did so. My timbre could be mistaken for that of his second wife Erika, and he hoped he wouldn't appear presumptuous if he now asked me for a second opportunity to sample my talents. Then he held out his right hand over the Formica table and introduced himself as Karl Danzinger, swimming instructor at the largest public swimming pool in Garmisch-Partenkirchen. Reverend Father, I wasn't exactly over the moon about the comparison of my voice, which is not particularly outstanding but is still fairly unique, with that of his second wife Erika. Who wants to be compared with someone's second wife Erika? But his handshake did appeal to me. His hand was dry and warm, with a delicate, flipper-like shape and skin of an elastic consistency, at once firmly solid and yieldingly soft; in short, a hand that I wasn't disinclined to get to know better, although possibly it was not very sensible to trust my physical sensations quite so recklessly after four glasses of beer.

Anyway, we fell into conversation, and I told him, in my unbounded thoughtlessness and carelessness, that I was an independent woman who travelled a great deal, and at the moment I planned to travel to Prague, a plan that would not be as easy to fulfil as it seemed, as I had been drawn for some time, mysteriously and against my will, away from Prague and towards the Austrian border. To this he replied it might be silly to try and force a particular direction, I would be better off yielding to that unknown compulsion. Then he glanced at his digital watch, and said my presence had made him completely lose track of time, he hoped he hadn't missed the last train to Garmisch-Partenkirchen. How was I travelling? he added. When I told him the truth, in a black Puch sidecar bike parked a few paces away, he was excited. That was a Styrian make, he said, a real rarity, a collector's item, and could I maybe show him the machine?

He paid the bill and we left the café and walked to the Puch 800. He walked round it curiously a number of times, examining it very carefully, and in the end he asked what I thought of the idea of driving him to Garmisch-Partenkirchen in the sidecar, and being a guest in his own house for a few days. As I doubtless knew, the countryside around Garmisch-Partenkirchen was very charming, and he would consider himself lucky to be able to show me some of the delights of the landscape. The location of Garmisch-Partenkirchen on the northern foothills of the Wetterstein mountains made it an ideal starting point for mountain tours, and as he also, apart from his main job as a swimming instructor, sometimes worked as a mountain guide, the opportunity presented itself to use the unusually mild autumn weather for a few gentle hikes. Then he smiled and added that in this way I wouldn't be resisting the pull drawing me south-east rather than north-east. As he had already indicated, he himself did not think much of responding stubbornly and incomprehendingly to something that was clearly a directive of fate.

Having said this, Karl Danzinger swung himself into the sidecar. His life, which had not always been easy, he continued, had taught him that there was no point in resisting forces that were stronger than man, that it was much more a matter, not exactly of yielding completely to those forces but of cautiously adapting to them. So saying, Karl Danzinger took the motorcycle goggles and the leather helmet left me by my great-uncle (who had, curiously, had the same Christian name) which I always kept with me but seldom wore, out from beneath him, having sat on them accidentally. While he was trying to convince me that my stubborn insistence on continuing on to Prague would in all likelihood have a disastrous effect on my subsequent fate, and that it could hardly be a coincidence that he lived right on the road that my motorbike wanted to take, he put on the goggles and the helmet. He fastened the helmet under his chin, straightened the goggles and said that coincidences as such didn't exist as far as he was concerned, all that existed were phenomena which looked like coincidences but which, if you examined them carefully, were anything but coincidence.

Reverend Father, in my fragile state of mind, caused by the recognition, as belated as it was powerful, of the irrevocable loss of the sole and solitary instance of the state of mind popularly known as love in my life, I didn't have the strength to resist Karl Danzinger's impetuous temperament. While he went on to differentiate between absolute chance, which was neither essentially necessary nor clearly determined by cause and effect, and relative chance, the unintentional, unpredicted, indefinable, unplanned, unregulated encounter or occurrence of things and events that might individually be causally determined but which, overall, didn't need to happen in that way and could equally well have happened otherwise and at a different time, I silently climbed on to the motorcycle and set off for Garmisch-Partenkirchen, towards a temporary idyll which, like all idylls, would prove to be extremely fragile.

Karl Danzinger lived in a tidy detached house on the edge of the forest. We arrived there late in the evening and parked the Puch 800 in the front garden, with its well-tended lawn. My host showed me to a friendly room with larch furniture on the first floor, and asked me down to the living room for a glass of *zirbengeist*, a schnapps made from spruce cones, before I went to bed, and to sing something for him. I hung my grey flannel suit and nun's habit in the ornamentally carved wooden wardrobe, stepped out on to the solid wooden balcony, likewise adorned with skilful carvings, and looked out over the lights of the town and inhaled the fragrant mountain air.

In my naive and completely unfounded optimism, which has on more than one occasion led me into complicated situations which I escaped only with the greatest difficulty, in that absolutely unfounded optimistic naivety that has repeatedly taken me to the brink of disaster, I looked out over the silent nocturnal landscape and thought, maybe Karl Danzinger was right, maybe the best thing was indeed to abandon oneself to the natural movement of life and not to swim against the current, which was too strong for me to defeat with my normal but not inordinately powerful forearms, my long if not especially strong legs.

Some distance away an owl hooted. Just when my pain at losing the chauffeur had been at its greatest, an obviously favourable turn of fate had led a stranger to me, someone who wanted to care for me. After all the vicissitudes in my unsettled life I was grateful to my benefactor for his hospitality, for the chance he had given me to spend a few days resting in healthy mountain air.

I went down the wooden stairs, the effect of the banisters also softened by pretty carving, and into the living room, where Karl Danzinger was already waiting impatiently for me with a bottle of *ʒirbengeist*. We chatted for a while, and after drinking three little glasses of *ʒirbengeist* I let him persuade me into performing a rendition of the Beatles song "Let It Be". He listened to me reverently and gently, and, with his delicate, flipper-like hands, in stark contrast to his muscular arms, touched my elbows, provoking a sensation like a tiny electric shock that shot into my fingertips. Again I attempted the most lyrical interpretation possible, and thus generated a tremendous atmosphere, unfortunately ruined by the unpleasant shrilling of the telephone right next to me. It seemed to be something important, and when Karl Danzinger still hadn't hung up half an hour later, I stood up, quietly climbed the larchwood stairs and lay down on the pleasantly notched larchwood bed. I slept exceedingly well, and, when I awoke the next morning, I attributed this to the healing climate of the spa. The sun was shining into the room, and as far as I could tell from my position lying in bed, the sky was cloudless. There was a knock at the door, and Karl Danzinger came into the room with a little round tray with my breakfast on it. He put it in front of me and sat down on the edge of the bed. I must forgive him, he said, last night's troublemaker had been his first wife Susanne.

The marriage to his first wife Susanne, he explained, that marriage which had started out well but which had been made increasingly unhappy by the alcoholism of his wife, a trained pharmacist, which had become more glaringly apparent by the day, had ended in divorce a good ten years ago, after a tedious legal process that was extremely painful for both of them. Although he himself had no wish whatsoever to remain in contact with his first wife, she had telephoned him regularly since the divorce. These telephone conversations, most of which were considerably longer than the average, dealt either with problems relating to her alcoholism, which had not improved in the slightest since their separation but had instead deteriorated continuously, or problems arising from the unusually stormy childhood and adolescence of their son Martin. Their conversation the previous evening, for example, had been about the cost of repainting the outside wall of the public baths, his workplace, on which their son Martin, who was now fifteen, had sprayed the words FATHER, WHERE ARE YOU? in black paint, a somewhat ill-considered act in the middle of which he had been surprised by a security guard. Susanne had, incidentally, been calling from the private clinic where she went periodically in an attempt to conquer her drink problems; he put up part of the expenses for this.

While I drank the delicious coffee and ate the croissants that Karl Danzinger had helpfully buttered, I gradually began to understand why he had briefly referred to the difficulty of his life the previous day. After going into greater detail about Susanne's drinking habits, he said he would have to go to work at the baths, left me a key ring and told me to feel at home. At the door to the room he turned round and said he'd be glad of a hot meal when he came back at about five o'clock in the evening, but he didn't want to put any pressure on me. However, if I did feel disposed to prepare a meal, I would find the requisite ingredients in the fridge.

With this remark he left the detached house. His request

for a meal struck me as somewhat surprising, although it had been voiced politely. But when I had considered the fact that this hard-tested man had been through years of martyrdom in a marriage to a severe alcoholic, which still unpleasantly influenced his present, that he was also the father of an adolescent son who was clearly difficult, and who used illegal acts to try and tell him he thought he was a bad father, I decided to do him that small favour and cook him dinner. There was plenty of time before evening, so I buried myself in the thick feather bed again, and slept for another few hours. When I was fully rested I got up and opened the balcony door. The view that presented itself was breathtaking: before me was the extremely pretty little town with its red and grey roofs and the church with the typical Bavarian onion tower; behind it stretched bright green meadows, with little haystacks and dark-green woods scattered behind it; and right at the back there rose abruptly the powerful massif of the Wetterstein mountains.

This time my happiness was safe, I thought, here I would recover from the strains, the unpleasantnesses of the past, most of them the consequence of the unusual character of the men I had met, here I would finally find calm and peace, and this rediscovered calm, this rediscovered inner peace might even transfer themselves to a man who also seemed to have been through some difficult years. I decided to go for a walk through the town, to get my bearings and have a look at the public baths where Karl Danzinger worked.

When I had strolled through the town, it struck me that people were looking at me with a certain displeasure, a kind of unease, which faintly reminded me of the glances of my compatriots. I looked down at myself but couldn't see anything unusual there, unless my black leather jump suit and boots had alarmed the inhabitants. After brief but intense reflection, I wondered whether the suspicious glances of the locals were in any way influenced by the geographical and religious landscape, whether the similar outlooks of Austrians and south

Bavarians lay in their both inhabiting Catholic landscapes in the foothills of the Alps. Before I could pursue this interesting thought any further, I found myself in front of the baths and saw Karl Danzinger excitedly knocking on the huge pane of glass that provided a view of the indoor pool, clearly trying to signal to me.

I walked into the foyer and he hurried towards me in his swimming trunks. He was very happy that I was visiting him, he said somewhat breathlessly, but he was busy taking care not only of the swimmers but also of the elder of his two daughters from his second marriage to Erika, about whom he had already told me. This daughter was a girl with a very sweet character, but since birth she had suffered from curvature of the spine, which was why he gave her special swimming classes whenever his wife allowed him to do this. Before he turned away to devote himself to his duties as a swimming instructor and to his daughter, he asked if I had already begun cooking dinner, he was really looking forward to it.

So I went back to his home, an appealing house made partly of stone, partly of dark wood, behind a green painted wooden fence, and began to prepare the meal. As I couldn't find much that was usable in the fridge, I opted in favour of a simple recipe that would sit harmoniously with the mountain landscape: Tyrolean dumplings in a beef soup. Just as one dumpling after the other was rising to the surface of the water, Karl Danzinger returned from the baths and sat down at the kitchen table. He clearly enjoyed the dumplings, but at the end of the meal he remarked that they'd been a bit too salty, and I hadn't used quite enough flour, which was why they had been a little too soft. Susanne, although she had been an alcoholic, had been a wonderful cook, her Tyrolean dumplings had been incomparable. Part of her secret had probably been the smoked meat that she had only ever bought from a farmer who lived high on the mountain, not far below the Zugspitze, and which came from free-range pigs.

He would ask Susanne for the recipe so that I knew for the next time.

I choked back the minor disappointment that this criticism caused me, and thought that Karl, as I already thought of him, deserved sympathy, given that he had a daughter afflicted with curvature of the spine. The rest of the evening was very pleasant, not least because of the *ʒirbengeist* which flowed in abundance, and towards midnight we climbed the larchwood stairs and shared the larchwood bed. The swimming instructor's gentle, flipper-like hands ran over my skin with incredible deftness. I hadn't been mistaken. Shortly before I fell into an exhausted sleep, I thought I heard the quietly breathed words "Norma Jean . . ." coming from Karl's mouth, but before I could register my surprise I was already asleep.

The next day was Karl's day off, and after he had, to my delight, allowed his gentle hands to glide across the landscape of my body far into the morning, as a pianist glides his fingers over the ivory keyboard, he suggested a little outing into the mountains, an idea that I welcomed. Our departure was delayed, although not by much, by another telephone conversation. While we were driving up a narrow mountain road in Karl's Land Rover he asked me to forgive the short delay caused by the phone call, this time it had been his second wife Erika, and again it had concerned a tiresome financial matter. As I knew, for years Erika, one of the few true sopranos – most supposed sopranos were actually mezzo-sopranos – had been an indispensable part of Wetterstein Mixed-Voice Choir which, some six years before, had indirectly and fatally led to the dissolution of that hitherto harmonious marriage. Shortly after becoming a member, Erika had become increasingly attracted to another choir member, a baritone about seven years younger than herself, from the other side of the border, from Seefeld in Tyrol. I must understand, Karl said, skilfully driving round a little pothole, that membership of a choir holds dangers for long-term relationships. Wetterstein Mixed-Voice Choir had often travelled on concert tours of shorter or longer duration. It was fundamentally understandable that the strongly emotional activity of singing should sometimes spark the eruption of feelings of which people might not be aware in sober surroundings, for example if they were working together in a factory or a laboratory.

A performance of Verdi's *Requiem* had done it for Erika. Karl briefly turned his face towards me, not entirely a safe thing to do on such a twisting road. I must know, in fact, that Erika had never gone behind his back, she had told him from the beginning of the blossoming of her affection for the baritone seven years younger than herself, she had given him complete descriptions of the torments that unexpected emotion had caused her. Erika could be accused of many things, he said, taking a not very clear bend a little too impetuously for my liking, Erika, like everyone, had had her failings, but she had always been honest with him. Anyway, the choir had gone to Kempten in the Allgäu, to perform Verdi's *Requiem* in the St Lorenz Church. When Erika returned from this two-day journey, he had immediately noticed a change in her. And she had admitted to him straight away that the summer storm, whose lightning flashes illuminated the semi-darkness of the nave and thus the young man's face, and the power of the music had revealed to her that she loved him.

When Karl had parked the Land Rover by the side of the road and we had walked a short way up the well-marked hiking path, he tried to explain the pain caused him by the loss of his second wife's love and her affection for the young man from the other side of the Wetterstein mountains. We spent the first half of the rest in a pretty glade which we reached after about an hour and a half of brisk hiking, in the course of which Karl managed to arouse my sympathy, eating bacon sandwiches and drinking a few glasses of *zirbengeist*, and Karl also made use of this time to give me a detailed description of their first period of separation, which his second wife Erika had spent soon after that fateful performance of the *Requiem*, in Kempten in the Allgäu, with a view to starting a new life with the baritone.

During the second half of our break, Karl fell silent and, to my delight, allowed his hands to speak, helping me to come to terms rather more easily with the somewhat irritating fact that on the way back to the Land Rover he talked constantly about his failed marriage to Erika and the divorce, which had clearly not been quite as painful as his divorce from Susanne but which had left deep traces nevertheless. We climbed into the Land Rover, and while he drove downhill at breakneck speed, probably because of the consumption of the *zirbengeist*, Karl complained that Erika refused him the right, expressly established in the divorce documents, to see the two daughters from their marriage – the elder of whom, as he had told me, suffered from curvature of the spine, while the younger one was healthy, apart from a not particularly disturbing but noticeable congenital squint – every other week, on the grounds that it would only confuse the daughters to have two fathers, a natural father and a stepfather, and it would be considerably better for their psychological development to sever contact completely with him, Karl, their natural father.

Back at his house we sat down in the living room where Karl wanted to speak in rather more general terms about the problems of children from broken marriages, but stopped when he noticed that I was no longer listening to him as attentively as I had at the beginning of our little outing. I was actually rather tired, a tiredness that vanished when we retired to the room with the larchwood bed. Before we went to sleep Karl asked me whether I knew Verdi's *Requiem* at all well, and whether I could perhaps sing him something from it. Although I am not otherwise especially familiar with the work of Verdi, I did know the *Dies Irae* from the *Requiem*. In order to grant Karl this pleasure, since he had just given me such pleasure with the purposeful application of his flipper-like hands, I sat up in bed and began to intone that impressive passage from the Mass for the dead. When I had finished, Karl fell silent, and said after a few minutes that my rendition had impressed him beyond measure, although this time he was struck by the fact that although my vocal colour was similar to Erika's, in his view I wasn't a real soprano, but at best a mezzo-soprano, if not a contralto at the top of the range. But that had not diminished his pleasure, or at least not very much.

At about three o'clock in the morning I started awake when Karl, clearly in response to a dream, leapt up in bed calling, in English, "Don't go, Norma Jean, I need you and the twins!" Then he lay down again, and after murmuring something that I didn't understand he went back to sleep. I bent over the man whose past seemed to follow him even into his dreams – for we could assume that Norma Jean, whom he had mentioned twice, had also been an important chapter – and pitied him. But the pity I felt mingled against my will with a desire that was familiar to me when I saw his muscular throat that lay so unprotected in front of me. I had to suppress my desire to sink my teeth into his firm flesh, an impulse that frightened me, even if it wasn't as compelling as it had been with Clemens the chauffeur.

When Karl brought me breakfast the next day I told him what he had said in his sleep. He sighed, and said that had been another unhappy tale, but at the moment he had no time to tell me about it since he had to go to the baths. He suggested that I come and swim a little, he could get me free tickets. Then there might be an opportunity to talk about that section of his life. After that he left me. I slept a little more and then went to the public baths, where Karl handed me a block of ten free tickets. I stepped into the water and swam a few lengths. As when I had been walking through Garmisch-Partenkirchen the previous day, it struck me that the other swimmers were glancing at me curiously, as if there was something disconcerting about me. At first I couldn't imagine what it could be, but then I realized it was probably my black Kashiyama body stocking, which I had put on instead of the traditional bathing costume and which was in fact a little tight and revealed a few square inches of flesh through the lace here and there, that was drawing their eyes to me.

Soon Karl jumped into the water and swam beside me for a while, to tell me more about Norma Jean, his third and so far his last wife, a Californian high-diver whom he had met at an international high-diving championship in the outside pool, complete with diving board, at these very same public baths. I couldn't imagine, he said, swimming on his back for a while, how elegant Norma Jean's diving had been. She hadn't won the competition but she had won a respectable silver. After the competition he had gone up to her and told her, in his reasonably fluent English, that he hadn't thought the jury's verdict quite right, her forward dive from standing had been immaculate, and her back flip had taken his breath away. The reverse double somersault had perhaps not been one hundred per cent successful, but in his view it was she who had deserved the victor's medal rather than that ugly Czech girl, the merits of whose run-up and twist were at best arguable.

Yes, that's how it had all started with Norma Jean, he said, leaving me briefly to put a plaster on the knee of a little boy who had slipped on the damp tiles. Then he came back and said Norma Jean had been very attractive, with a typically Californian kind of attractiveness, strong white teeth, healthily tanned skin, radiant smile, sun-bleached blonde hair, and after her performance, sensational to him if not to the jury, he had immediately fallen violently in love with her, and the feeling had been mutual. Norma Jean had flown back to the States later than planned, after a few magical days and nights spent in his detached house, recently abandoned by Erika, and had then called him almost every day from her home town and birthplace, Eureka. Finally she had returned with three suitcases, and a few weeks later they had married in Garmisch-Partenkirchen register office, a fact that had enraged both Susanne and Erika, he was not sure why, perhaps because Norma Jean had been a foreigner.

Karl did the crawl for a few yards, and then said that the twins had been born fifteen months after their marriage, dizygotic twins, a boy and a girl, who must be four years old by now. The problem, he said, briefly ducking his head under the water, the problem had been that Norma Jean, with her California mentality, her typical West Coast mentality, had never been able to get used to the landlocked state of Bavaria. She had been used to the Pacific, surfing, high waves, and the nearby Eibensee had not, even though it was a natural lake rather than a swimming pool, been enough for her in the long run. Karl took a brief pause, which I used to point out that the elderly man in the black swimming trunks with the tight-fitting red bathing cap on the other side of the pool had clearly swallowed too much water, couldn't he see that the man was coughing a lot and turning a strange colour? He, Karl, should go to his aid, I had freshened myself enough, and would return to his house.

In the early evening Karl came back from the public baths and immediately devoured the dinner I had prepared, steamed calf's sweetbread with vegetables and apple sauce. To my relief he enjoyed it, with the reservation that although steamed calf's sweetbread was an excellent dish, he personally preferred baked calf's sweetbread. Had I perhaps forgotten to simmer the sweetbread in salt water? he asked. It seemed to him that the taste of this sweetbread was rather different from the sweetbread that Susanne had sometimes cooked for him. When I assured him that I had indeed simmered the sweetbread in salt water, he said that maybe I hadn't quite brought the water to the boil, or else I hadn't used quite enough salt. Susanne had always stressed that the correct preparation of calf's sweetbread was a very delicate matter. I was pleased that

Karl thought the apple sauce a success, by and large, although he thought it was a shame that I had only used cloves and no cinnamon sticks. When I said I'd added a pinch of ground cinnamon, as I hadn't found any cinnamon sticks, he said a cook must always ensure that all the ingredients she needs are in the house, I should have walked down to the nearest grocery, twenty minutes' walk away.

And so the days passed. Karl worked as a swimming instructor, I cooked for him, sometimes sang for him and swam regularly, and on his day off we went into the mountains. It was a peaceful, healthy life, often disturbed by eruptions of Karl's past into our present, but it seemed to do me good, as evidenced by my fresh complexion, my slight increase in weight and my strong physical constitution overall.

One day, when Karl suggested that, since I wasn't using my motorcycle, maybe I could fill the sidecar with soil and plant flowers in it, that would look very nice, I was very sceptical at first but agreed when he put his arm round me and added with a smile that his Land Rover was enough for both of us, and surely I had no intention of leaving him as his three wives had left him? So one sunny morning I filled the sidecar with compost and planted a few pink hortensias. He was right, it did look pretty.

The only thing that worried me during that first tranquil period with Karl Danzinger was the hunger I felt for his neck each evening. Since he talked in his sleep every night, and woke me up every night by doing so, I had too much time to look at his sinewy neck in the darkness of the room, which was really a semi-darkness, lit by the stars that shone through the clear air and through the curtainless windows. I did feel a certain affection for Karl, but that feeling was a long way from the intense state of mind popularly known as love that I had felt for the chauffeur. This time, on a number of occasions I came very close to giving myself the pleasure of a powerful bite. An incident freed me from the worry that my urge might become overwhelming and make me turn the fundamentally good-as-gold Karl into one of the undead. One day when I was in the public baths, in the water near the starting blocks so that I could hear Karl better as he sat on the edge of the pool telling me about his separation from Norma Jean, who had decided, because of her problems in adapting, after three years in Garmisch-Partenkirchen, to return to Eureka with the twins, a decision that had plunged him into an abyss of despair, a thirteen-year-old, well developed for his age, jumped on my head from starting block number one.

Reverend Father, I don't know whether in the course of my confession I've already referred to the fact that I've had a heart problem since an attack of endocarditis failed to heal completely when I was eighteen, and this in turn is the cause of what is known as a left ventricular insufficiency, or inadequate pumping in the left ventricle, and that this insufficiency makes my heart very susceptible to all kinds of strain. The little shock caused by the violent landing of the thirteen-year-old on my head inevitably caused shortness of breath, so that I fainted. The doctor, whom Karl had called immediately, injected a drug into my heart, whereupon I revived fairly quickly.

That moment marked the end of my desire to bite a man's neck. I assume that the penetration of the needle must have had an effect comparable to that of a stake being driven into a vampire's heart. You can imagine how pleased I was no longer to be a danger to men with whom I was close.'

I looked at Magdalena, who was sitting in the grass beside the bike and had started painting the petrol tank red. She seemed slightly hot, perhaps from the combined effort of telling her story and painting, and this increase in her body temperature made her even more attractive than usual. Her cheeks were flushed, and she licked little drops of water from her swelling upper lip.

I hadn't really believed the vampire story but I wasn't entirely sure whether it was really a figment of Magdalena's imagination. What if she had been telling the truth? What a tragic irony of fate it was that she had sent the man of her life away with an excuse, to save him from becoming one of the living dead, and then not much later she was freed, by a curious concatenation of circumstances, from her terrible vampiric nature, too late to enjoy happiness with the chauffeur! In the case of this woman who had not been exactly spoiled by love, I considered it entirely possible that the weak heart she had mentioned was not the result of endocarditis but the lamentable yet not unreasonable consequence of having a heart broken time and again by careless, egoistic men.

But while I was feeling sorry for the woman, who had had to cope with terrible things, I realized that if the chauffeur had married his childhood sweetheart, then it could only be to the benefit of me and my newly unfolding relationship with Magdalena. The chauffeur was lost to her but perhaps in the course of the following night, which I so longed for, her time with me might far surpass the time she had spent with him. But I was careful not to utter a word about my hopes, as I was certainly not about to break the vow of silence she had imposed upon me before her confession came to an end.

'That remarkable and doubtless positive event, which meant the end of my time as a vampire,' Magdalena continued, after she had poked the pink tip of her tongue enchantingly between her lips as she tried to apply the paint evenly, 'that injection that the doctor gave me also represented a curious turning point in my relationship with Karl. Anyway, it was around this time, at first almost unnoticeably, that the inexorable decline began. The idyll with the hortensias in the sidecar was beginning to show a series of fine cracks.

Our first difference of opinion arose out of Karl's request that I join Wetterstein Mixed-Voice Choir. He thought I had a voice of which the public should not be deprived, in which the world at large should be allowed to share. And there was also a reasonable hope that with constant practice and training my mezzo-soprano might turn into a soprano, a goal for which, he thought, every woman should strive. Reverend Father, and I remember mentioning this before in the course of my confession, every appeal to my so-called duties as a so-called member of society inevitably produces the greatest resistance on my part. Yet again, my first impulse was to reject Karl's notion. But as I didn't want to risk him depriving me of unlimited access to his gentle hands, I said I was prepared to attend a choir rehearsal.

One Tuesday evening I went to the hall of the local girls' school where the rehearsals were held. I was wearing my leather jump suit, having recently given the grey suit to the Red Cross in Garmisch-Partenkirchen since it reminded me too much of Michael Minulescu and his betrayal. My jump suit visibly disconcerted the highly respected old ladies in the choir, who had placed their by now very tremulous voices at the disposal of the choir for decades. I had to put on a long black gown like everyone else, the oldest of the awe-inspiring, almost terrifying older choir ladies said strictly, no exceptions would be tolerated. My timid remark that I would be prepared to stand in the back row, in the back row my jump suit, which was black like the gowns, would not stand out, was dismissed out of hand. The oldest of the choir ladies put the score of the *St John Passion* in my hand, and I tried to sing along as well as I could. Beside me stood a small woman with piercing eyes and hooked nose, who trod hard on my toes during a fugue and hissed in my ear that I would soon be sorry for parking myself in the detached house where she had lived for years, which led me to conclude that this was Karl's second wife Erika. Clearly people in Garmisch-Partenkirchen already knew all about Karl Danzinger's new acquaintance.

During the break I was approached by a woman who introduced herself as an employee at an alcohol withdrawal clinic and said I should think very hard about whether I wanted to go on living with Karl Danzinger, his first wife Susanne had been both physically and psychologically destroyed by her outwardly very charming but in reality very dangerous husband. Finally, the local registrar, who was also a choir member of many years' standing, came up to me and asked me if I knew that Karl Danzinger was still married to a Californian high-diver. I found this all so disagreeable that I left the girls' school hall before the end of break time and went back to the detached house where Karl accused me of trying to escape my social obligations and failing to fit in with the small-town community, just as Norma Jean had done.

Since he had mentioned Norma Jean, I asked him whether it was in fact true that he was still married to her, whereupon he flew into a rage and asked what schemer had whispered that in my ear, but didn't supply a direct answer to the question. Then he said the pork goulash that I'd cooked and heated up for him had been inedible, I should have used loin rather than shoulder, and apart from that I'd used hot rather than sweet paprika, and his mouth was still on fire. He picked up his coat and said he was going to see Susanne, who had just been allowed out of the clinic. He had mentioned the topic of my pork goulash in the telephone conversation he had had with her a quarter of an hour before, about his son Martin's spelling, whereupon Susanne had kindly invited him to go and eat something at her house, she had a lamb ragout on the stove.

Although Karl was in conciliatory mood again two days later, when, after a nightmare in which his son Martin had threatened him with a machine-gun, I had listened sympathetically between the hours of three and five in the morning while he told me about his son's dyslexia, caused by the separation of his parents, as well as Norma Jean's constant demands for money, by phone and mail, our relationship was no longer the same after my refusal to join Wetterstein Mixed-Voice Choir. We spent just as much time in the larchwood bed, but Karl's manipulation of my body, which required a great deal of concentration, was interrupted with increasing regularity by phone calls from Susanne, Erika or Norma Jean.

More serious than his increasingly critical assessment of my voice and my cookery, however, was the observation that he made one evening in the larchwood bed. Norma Jean's physical control, he said, had bordered on the miraculous because of the years she had spent training as a high-diver, and it was not only in the water that she had been like a beautiful marine animal, like some mysterious octopus. You could twist and turn and bend her like a rubber toy, he said. He was glad that I swam regularly in his baths but obviously this wasn't enough to keep me in athletic shape, or in a shape anywhere near the admittedly extraordinary shape of Norma Jean. He advised me to supplement my regular swimming with an evening class in apparatus gymnastics. Apart from high-diving, apparatus gymnastics was an ideal way of keeping a woman's body elastic.

Reverend Father, I didn't like this remark. Hitherto, Karl had restricted himself to disparaging the quality of my voice and the meals I cooked for him, and because of my innate good nature I had put up with his complaints. But the fact that his criticism was beginning to impinge on an area about which I feel very sensitive hurt and enraged me. I controlled myself, however, and swallowed my annoyance. Karl's suggestion, although it was an insult to my femininity, was perhaps worth taking up. After all, it was in my own interest to stay in good physical condition. I clenched my teeth, registered for the evening class in apparatus gymnastics, which had just started, and the following Wednesday I went to the gymnasium of the girls' school where it was held. I hadn't thought about getting a special gymnastics leotard and turned up in my black body stocking, which struck me as elastic enough for apparatus gymnastics.

The housewives of Garmisch-Partenkirchen, who largely made up the classes, clearly thought this item of clothing was not entirely suitable, conveying this to me with their furious expressions. I tried to be friendly and concentrate on the exercises, but the housewives did not appear very comradely. It was customary for an experienced gymnast to stand beside the apparatus to help the less experienced ones. I relied on this support, but when I had taken a few frightened steps on the unfamiliar beam, lost my balance and, as I fell, tried to grab the hand of the chemist's wife who was standing ready beside it, she simply turned away as if she hadn't seen anything and I landed heavily on the floor, bruising my left thigh in the process. And when my arms proved too weak for a flank vault on the horse, the notary's girlfriend pulled away her helpfully outstretched hand at the last minute, leaving me with a slightly pulled muscle in my left shoulder. I refused to be discouraged, picked up a leather ball from the floor, smiled at the wife of the owner of the biggest sports shop in Garmisch-Partenkirchen and asked her if she wanted to play with me. I was very glad when she agreed, as her approval suggested to me that the apparatus gymnasts were by no means as ill-disposed to me as I had begun to assume. But when the sports shop owner's wife hurled the ball as hard as she could at my eye, leaving it temporarily closed, I once more began to harbour doubts about the goodwill of the housewives and sat down somewhat dejectedly on the wooden bench at the end of the gymnasium, staying there until the end of the class.

When I returned despondently to Karl's house, he led me to the sofa, obligingly put an ice pack on my eye and told me not to give up, not everyone had the natural assurance of movement with which Norma Jean had distinguished herself, and it would certainly be a lot better the second time. When we were lying in the larchwood bed that evening, he said he would dispense with the caresses as I needed to be looked after, with my pulled muscle, which, however insignificant, would surely still be giving me twinges. Apart from that, he might accidentally brush the bruise on my thigh, and he could not bear to give me the slightest pain.

The next day I stayed at home to recover from my injuries. At about five o'clock in the afternoon the telephone rang. It was Erika, wanting to speak to her ex-husband. I said he was coming back from the baths a little later than usual, and could I pass on a message. At this she burst into tears and said she cursed the day she had met her current husband, and when I asked whether she meant the day of the performance of Verdi's *Requiem* in Kempten in the Allgäu, she at first seemed a little surprised at my knowledge of her life story but immediately went on to describe her difficulties with the baritone.

It was hard to imagine, she said, but sensitive, impulsive, talented singer that he was, he had fallen in love with her thirteen-year-old daughter. I asked her if she meant the one with curvature of the spine, a question that surprised Erika once more, and to which she replied yes, exactly, that one, she had no idea what to do, and she wanted to talk to Karl about it but Karl wasn't there. I told her she could make do with me; of course I didn't know her at all, but throughout my eventful life I had acquired a certain knowledge of human nature and could perhaps give her advice of some kind. So we continued talking about Erika's problem until Karl came home and I told her her ex-husband had arrived, I would pass him the phone. She said she first wanted to thank me for my understanding, and apologized for deliberately treading on my toes at the choir rehearsal. I replied that it wasn't serious, I had my motorcycle boots on anyway, and passed the receiver to Karl who was already standing impatiently beside me.

The next day Erika rang at about half past two, and when I asked her if she didn't know that Karl was always at the baths at that time, she said yes, she did know, but yesterday's woman-to-woman chat had done her so much good that she needed to talk to me again. She was thoroughly confused, because three hours before, her present husband had walked up to her with her daughter and told her that they, he and her daughter, could no longer conceal their admittedly unusual love from a hypocritical society and had resolved to go to the pedestrian precinct of Garmisch-Partenkirchen and stroll up and down together in an attempt to break through their social ostracism.

Imagine, Erika cried on the telephone, in the pedestrian precinct! She had been born in Garmisch-Partenkirchen, the consequences of such a scandal could not be overlooked; her father, a respected citizen and Catholic, had been so horrified by her divorce that he now wore a pacemaker. I tried to calm the distraught woman as well as I could, and finally she said she felt better already, that this was thanks to me, and she would stop bothering me and help her second daughter with her homework.

Although my injuries hardly hurt any more I didn't get the opportunity to feel Karl's gentle hands anyway because we were too busy discussing Erika's grave problem, in the hope of finding a solution for her. I could understand someone feeling responsible for a former marriage partner even after separation, and I was also starting to deal with Erika's difficulties more and more myself, particularly since she was making a habit of calling me every day at about midday to tell me about developments in her family situation. I gave her the best advice I could, drawing on the fund of experiences that I had gathered in the course of my nomadic life. In return, Erika taught me some little tunes that meant a lot to Karl, but this only happened two or three times, as she was generally not in a singing voice, understandably enough.

I tried to revitalize my relationship with Karl, which had been ailing since my refusal to join the choir, and even continued the apparatus gymnastics class which, given the way the class had gone so far, was no small sacrifice on my part. The second and third class were hardly more encouraging than the first. Among other things, the wife and sister-in-law of a respected hotelier quite deliberately tripped me up with a skipping rope, making me bash my nose, and the attempt at a free circle on the asymmetric bars ended unhappily when the daughter of the ski-lift owner pretended to show me how to hold on to the bar but swiftly dislodged my left hand when I was in the middle of the exercise. The resulting fall led to a bruising of the coccyx, after which Karl, saying I needed complete rest, withdrew his flipper-like hands for four days. Even if he hadn't withdrawn them, there would hardly have been time for the treatment that Karl usually bestowed on me as he was forever holding transatlantic conversations with Norma Jean because the dizygotic twins, who had been very small at the time of the divorce, seemed to have been coping badly with the separation from their father, which they demonstrated by wetting the bed every night.

The only thing that we both really enjoyed was our hikes in the open air, although we had to keep to slightly lower altitudes since snow had already fallen in the rocky regions. In the mountains we were far from Erika and Susanne and their problems, which impinged on us more and more, and our greater distance from the telephone made even Norma Jean seem further away than ever. When we were sitting one day on the rock known as the Maiden's Leap, high above Garmisch-Partenkirchen, which had become our favourite place, Karl put his arm round my shoulders and said that although he had five children, all of them were alienated because of his separation from their mothers, a fact that often depressed him, as I might have noticed. Could I imagine, he asked, looking at me seriously, was it unthinkable that I should be the mother of his sixth child?

Reverend Father, I remember that autumn day well. Cirrus clouds drifted high above us, and from the valley rose the faint echo of the Sunday bells of St Martin. As the bottle of *zirbengeist* had passed back and forth between us a number of times, and had put me in a suitably life-affirming frame of mind, I was close to giving a positive answer to this sorely afflicted man. For a moment it even crossed my mind that if we cleared out the hortensias and compost we could use the Felber sidecar as a cradle for the child. This child would grow up in a healthy environment, in a detached house with a garden, in secure circumstances the like of which none of the men in my past, with the exception of the Baron, could have given me, quite apart from the fact that aside from Clemens no one had ever approached me with such a question, and his desire for children had struck me as worryingly immoderate.

I don't know, Reverend Father, why I gave Karl an evasive answer. Perhaps it was the keen eyesight inherited from my father's side of the family that made me spot the impossibility of my realizing such a wish. In any case, during the days and nights following that outing, my hesitation proved to have been an instinctively correct reaction.

One evening in the larchwood bed, Karl presented me with the *fait accompli* that his first wife Susanne and his son Martin would shortly be moving into the detached house with us. When I looked at him in horror, he said I shouldn't look at him in horror like that, he was the last person who would approve of such an arrangement. But in the wake of the divorce process, ten years ago now, in his youthful rashness and inexperience, he had agreed to a clause included by the opposing lawyer in the divorce decision, according to which he was obliged to care for his former wife should she ever, for either physical or psychological reasons, be unfit for work. Susanne, who because of her constantly deteriorating alcoholism had not been capable of practising the profession of pharmacist for which she had been trained, had now called this clause into effect, and he had no choice but to take in both her and their son, a minor, as he was not in a position to provide the two of them with an apartment of their own. After all, he also had to pay for the upkeep of his two daughters from his marriage to Erika and for the Californian twins, and in any case he had been on the brink of financial ruin for a long time, and without his sideline as a mountain guide and the small sums that his parents sometimes sent him, he would have had to sell his house long ago.

After this revelation I was silent for a while, and then said that in these altered circumstances I couldn't really imagine our acquaintance continuing, and I would probably set off on the road again and resume my independent way of life, despite the fact that some aspects of the settled life very much appealed to me.

Karl's reaction to this information was exactly the same as Michael Minulescu's, except that this time I wasn't wearing a pastel-coloured nightgown for Karl to clutch. He sobbed that I couldn't leave him alone in this situation, without me he wouldn't be able to bear Susanne the alcoholic and her difficult son and would become an alcoholic himself, towards the end of his relationship with Susanne he had come worryingly close to that state. And apart from that he had grown so used to my voice, even if I wasn't a pure soprano, and my cookery, even if the coordination of the various nuances of flavour sometimes left a good deal to be desired. He knew that he hadn't given the landscape of my body quite the attention it deserved, but he promised to improve in that respect.

What can I say, Reverend Father? The sympathy, the understanding that I had unfortunately felt for this man from the first triumphed over my reservations about him. A short time later the ghastly consequences of that understanding, that sympathy, became apparent, and since then I no longer stand up for sympathy and understanding but for ruthlessness and heartlessness. Once you begin to show sympathy and understanding, the end is nigh. Sympathetic and understanding people, with their sympathy and understanding, set the most terrible things in motion. Instead of being merciless and pitiless and thus helping the weak, who are constantly appealing to their understanding, their pity, to achieve greater strength and independence, they make the weak even weaker; with their sympathy, their understanding, they drive them into decline. You must guard against helpers; as soon as a helper approaches with a view to helping, it is advisable to take to your heels immediately, as the slightest bit of help from a helper leaves you that bit more in need of help, while the helpers grow stronger and stronger, an indisputable fact well known to the majority of helpers, and the logical reason why they are so keen on helping. The so-called helpers, the so-called good people are the ones who make the others really weak, really bad, that's just how it is.'

Magdalena had got herself so worked up that she looked irresistible. Her eyes darkened dangerously and flashed, and she lifted her right hand, the one with the brush in it, reproachfully into the air. I saw with delight that the sun was going down, and that it would not be long before nightfall.

'A few weeks later Susanne and Martin moved into the house. Susanne lived in the Scots pinewood room on the first floor, and Martin in the sprucewood room between the Scots pinewood room and my larchwood room. Martin was not particularly sociable. When he was at home he usually locked himself in his room, and during meals, which were now, at Karl's request, no longer prepared by me but by Susanne, he remained totally silent. As long as Susanne was cooking, the symptoms of her alcoholism were barely noticeable, except that she used an unusual amount of alcohol in the preparation of the recipes. When she cooked she was a different person, and she cooked well. But the rest of the time she drank, and she drank to excess.

When I came back from my gymnastics class one evening she was lying at the foot of the stairs, and when I asked her what had happened, I heard her mumble that she had fallen down them. She had only a scratch on her right knee, but as my own mobility was somewhat restricted because the dentist's wife had pushed me off the trampoline under the guise of helping me and I had sprained my ankle in my impact with the floor, it wasn't so easy to drag Susanne up the stairs and into the Scots pinewood room. Apart from the minor injuries that she sustained in trivial accidents in and around the house in a state of complete intoxication, our life together was relatively trouble-free. She couldn't bear Erika and Norma Jean, but she liked me. Her dislike of Erika was based on the fact that she seemed to have dealt the death blow to a marriage already largely shattered by Susanne's alcoholism.

The abysmal depths of this animosity became apparent one day when Erika paid me a visit, without knowing that Susanne was living in the house again. Erika had phoned me and said she was in the area, could she call in, it would be nice to meet me personally after all our telephone conversations, our brief meeting at the choir rehearsal didn't really count. I agreed out of politeness, and five minutes later Erika was standing behind the green painted wooden fence with two pieces of cheesecake. Over coffee and cakes we first talked animatedly about the fact that Erika's second husband and her elder daughter had left her and wanted to go to Seefeld in the Tyrol, so animatedly that Erika's beautiful voice must have carried through to the Scots pinewood room on the first floor and woken Susanne out of her alcoholic stupor. At any rate she was suddenly standing, hair dishevelled, at the top of the stairs.

I can't remember the subsequent exchange word for word, but Susanne, far from willing to draw a line under the past, first accused Erika of marriage wrecking, then of maliciously attempting to destroy her life's happiness, a happiness which, for all that she, Erika, had tried to do – and here she raised her head and smiled triumphantly – was indestructible, as proven by the fact that Karl had taken her and her son back into the house that the two of them had built with the labours of their own hands. At this Erika rose to her feet, walked a few steps towards the larchwood stairs and cried scornfully that Karl could only have taken such a step because he didn't want to pay for her visits to the clinic any more, and she, Susanne, had been the laughing stock of the whole of Garmisch-Partenkirchen for years, and as for her good-for-nothing son, that criminal graffiti artist, it was already clear that he would end up in a shelter for the homeless.

Thereupon Susanne came three steps down the stairs and shouted that she, Erika, had her, Susanne, and her son on her conscience. For years she, Erika, had lain in wait for Karl on every street corner of Garmisch-Partenkirchen, thrown herself round his neck at every opportunity, and even the most faithful husband – and Karl had, at least when married to her, been among the most faithful – could not resist a woman for ever if she had taken it into her head to destroy a marriage out of pure malice. Yes, it had been pure malice, she said, drowning out Erika who was about to begin a speech in her own defence, pure malice, because she, Erika, unlike her, Susanne, had never loved Karl, everyone in the town knew that from the very first she had had her eyes only on the house built by the labours of Karl and herself, the house and Karl's swimming instructor's salary, love had never come into it.

With a menacing look on her face, Erika climbed four stairs two at a time, pressed her hands to her hips and said quietly but emphatically that it was monstrous to say that she had never loved Karl, she had loved him very much, she had loved him to the point of madness, and only out of love had she decided to liberate Karl from the stranglehold of a hysteric, a drinker who had converted most of his hard-earned swimming instructor's salary into *ʒirbengeist*, and who had almost managed to transfer her self-destructive urges to Karl, that good, good man.

Clutching the banisters, Susanne came down three more steps, clenched her free hand into a fist and cried, *liberate*, don't make me laugh; in her greed, she, Erika, had taken every last pfennig out of Karl's pocket, it served her right if she'd been landed with a cross-eyed daughter and another with curvature of the spine, although the curvature of the spine obviously didn't stop that daughter appearing hand in hand in the pedestrian precinct with that little whippersnapper that she, Erika, had taken as her second husband, the birds were singing it from the treetops, the fact that the daughter with curvature of the spine was having an affair with her mother's husband.

When Erika had resolutely climbed another five steps towards Susanne and there were only three steps between them, she said that was quite enough, she wouldn't listen to another word of her, Susanne's, contemptible slanders any more. Finally — and here she turned briefly towards me — finally she had a witness who would be able to testify to a court about her husband's first wife's vicious tongue. She, Susanne, could consider herself lucky that she, Erika, would not attack a pitiful alcoholic, otherwise she would have scratched her dilapidated alcoholic face to pieces that very minute, although from the aesthetic point of view it wouldn't have made all that much difference.

At this, with a cry of rage Susanne came down the remaining three steps, hurled herself at Erika and began pulling her hair. I stood up and was about to step in when the phone rang, and when I picked up the receiver the two fishwives interrupted their quarrelling, assuming that the caller was Karl. But it wasn't Karl, it was Norma Jean from Eureka, who asked me to tell Karl she had finally found a therapist who she thought might be able to cure the twins of their bedwetting, but he wasn't cheap. When I answered Susanne's and Erika's impatient questions truthfully, saying that I was talking to Norma Jean from Eureka and not to Karl, Erika ran down the stairs, wrenched the receiver from my hand and started berating the Californian. What did she think she was doing, bothering Karl, years later and far away, with her two brats who had been so ugly, even as children, that the people of Garmisch-Partenkirchen, when their eyes chanced to fall on the twin perambulator, had crossed themselves in terror?

Susanne, who had by now staggered down the bottom half of the stairs and across the rustic carpet to the telephone and stood next to Erika, nodding violently, now grabbed the receiver and said that although she didn't see eye to eye on everything with Erika, on this point she agreed with her absolutely. She, Norma Jean, should finally leave Karl, whom she had bewitched with her high-dives, in peace and find herself a Calfornian stupid enough to saddle himself with her, Norma Jean, and her two horrors. Where she, Susanne, and Erika were concerned, she, Norma Jean, should not dare ever to return to Garmisch-Partenkirchen. She, Susanne, and Erika would use all their influence on Karl, all their standing in Garmisch-Partenkirchen, to drive them all away, Norma Jean and her spawn, without further ado.

Before I could tell Norma Jean when Karl could be reached by telephone at home, Susanne put down the receiver. Far from continuing their dispute, the two ladies sat down at the coffee table and Susanne ate my remaining piece of cheesecake, turned towards Erika and said the cake was delicious and had she baked it herself. Referring to her busy professional and musical activities, Erika said she hadn't, adding that Karl had always praised her, Susanne's, cookery very highly, in that respect she must really have spoiled him, quite unlike his third wife Norma Jean who, as Karl had once confessed to her, hadn't known how to cook so much as a soft-boiled egg. Yes, she had heard that, Susanne agreed, and took a drink of coffee from my cup, Karl had spent huge sums of money in restaurants for the simple reason that Norma Jean's meals had been inedible. While the two of them continued their lively conversation about Norma Jean's characteristics, I stood up, climbed the stairs to the larchwood room, took the statue of Mary from Canterbury out of the wardrobe where I had put it, knelt before it, and wept.'

Magdalena fell silent. By now both bike and sidecar had received their first coating of red paint. I stood up, took a step back and looked at our work, but it was already too dark for careful examination, and in the late evening light the bright red looked more like burgundy. Magdalena rose to her feet as well, blew a curl from her face and wiped her brow with her forearm.

'Not bad, Reverend Father, not bad at all, the work we've done together,' she said. 'We'll apply the second coat tomorrow. And you've earned yourself a dinner.' Then she added, with a delicate smile, 'And maybe a pleasant night's rest, as well.'

This lightly uttered sentence catapulted me into a heaven of anticipation. This woman who aroused the most cherished hopes in me, could she be the same as the one who had, in a rustically decorated bedroom, knelt down before a stolen statue of Mary and wept?

From the pannier Magdalena took bacon, bread and mineral water, and we sat down on the sleeping bag beneath the robinia and ate in silence. Her description of the little scene in the larchwood room had proved to me that she was not such a hardened sinner as her actions might have suggested, and this came as a great relief to me. I could understand her inability to come to terms with Karl Danzinger's turbulent past, and I found it astonishing that she showed so much patience and sympathy to strangers, that she had a ready ear for all the gropings and strayings and alarums and excursions that inevitably form part of the worldly life. In the dark beside me she cut the East Tyrolean bacon into thin slices with the Swiss Army knife, put them on a piece of bread and handed them to me. I held the bread in my right hand and put my left hand round her shoulder. I could feel her warm skin beneath the thin and tightly fitting leather. She kissed me quickly on the chin and went on with her story.

'I wept for a long time. I wept frustrated, hysterical tears. Suddenly I felt completely out of place in that town, in that house, with those people who drew me more and more relentlessly into their life stories and whom I was unable to resist as well as I should have. When Erika had gone, and Susanne had opened another bottle in the Scots pine room, I sat down on the sofa to reflect on my situation, but immediately Karl came into the living room and asked about dinner. Reverend Father, at that moment I realized that my understanding and sympathy had been used up. Nevertheless, at that moment if anyone had told me I would kill Karl the following Sunday I would have told them they were mad.'

Magdalena put the bacon and bread on the grass, took a drink of mineral water and handed me the bottle. Then she yawned and stretched out next to me on the sleeping bag. By now it was so dark that I could only see her face as a black oval outline. I rested the back of my head against the robinia trunk and enjoyed the silence, the darkness and Magdalena's closeness. The water in the little stream trickled quietly, and a cricket chirped. More and more stars appeared in the sky. Suddenly I felt a hand tugging at the sleeve of my dalmatic. When I didn't react immediately, the hand tugged harder and I understood that it was trying to tell me to assume a reclining position as well. I must have yielded to the hand's wishes, although I can't remember exactly what happened next, or, more precisely, the memory I have of what followed is not mental but entirely sensual. My sensory nerves, my sensory cells were working in overdrive to turn into nervous arousal the many and various stimuli that Magdalena was ceaselessly administering, and only the sense of sight seems to have been more or less disconnected, since I soon closed my eyes. Where the impressions of my sense of hearing are concerned, I can remember purring, murmuring, gurgling, whispering, humming notes from Magdalena's mouth, a sweet music growing louder and softer, a rising and falling mellifluous melody, plaintive crescendi and sighing decrescendi. At the same time my olfactory organs perceived smells that were fruity and flowery, and a delicate hint of musk, of vanilla penetrated my olfactory tissue when Magdalena pressed herself to me. The taste receptors in my oral cavity categorized the taste of her mouth as at once sweet and bitter, and the tastebuds at the side of my tongue registered the taste of her skin as predominantly salty.

But what almost rendered me unconscious was the intensity with which my touch receptors received all the touch stimuli that Magdalena conveyed to me. Unlike the previous night, when I had felt Magdalena's caresses through stole, dalmatic and alb, this time she freed me slowly, slowly from one layer of clothing after the other, until nothing remained between her fingers and my skin. It was as though a hundred hands were caressing my epidermis, and my fingertips felt their way over soft, warm, yielding surfaces, over hills, plains and valleys and through soft little woods until they could no longer distinguish my skin from Magdalena's. For her body, likewise, was no longer covered by the second skin of her leathers, and I can't remember whether it was my hands or hers that opened the long zip fastener, just as it has slipped my mind why the body stocking was suddenly between us, a delicate little ball. We lay there like that on the sleeping bag beneath the robinia, in a warm early summer night.

It was the Fall that followed the eating of the cherries, and while we sinned and sinned, it vaguely crossed my mind that with this *felix culpa*, this happy sin, I was not being driven from a Garden of Eden but led into a little garden of paradise. At some point I fell asleep on Magdalena's breast.

The next morning I was awoken by a faint touch on my forearm. I opened my eyes and saw that a little blue butterfly had settled on my right arm, which had rested on Magdalena's waist. I looked at it until it rose and settled again on Magdalena's cheek. She gave a quiet sigh and touched her face with her hand, making the butterfly fly away. Then she opened her eyes. I looked at her and reflected that we would apply the second coat of paint today, and soon we would drive away together, away from East Tyrol, away from Austria, into a warmer country. A successor would be found for my parish.

'Good morning,' said Magdalena. She stretched, lay down and stroked my chin and blinked into the sun. In the morning she seemed to be awake in a flash. 'Good morning, Reverend Father. Don't speak before I have reached the end of the seventh story. And I shall tell it right now.' She sat up and gently laid my head in her lap.

'The following Sunday Karl and I took a trip in the Land Rover to the Maiden's Leap that we liked to visit. It was a sunny late-autumn day, and the wind that was blowing was just as cool as the atmosphere between us had been for some days. This was down to the fact that Karl had asked me, in the larchwood bed, how we spent our time at the apparatus gymnastics class. Had my body not been covered with bruises he wouldn't have believed my assurances that I was still visiting the classes every Wednesday, because my agility left much to be desired and could still not be compared with Norma Jean's supple litheness. And on top of that I had slept badly because a bluish full moon had filled the larchwood room with a ghostly light.

Karl parked the Land Rover near Maiden's Leap, and sitting on a blanket that I had spread out in the grass, we ate sandwiches that I had prepared. My mood did not lift when Karl parted two slices of bread and asked where the gherkin was, didn't I know that he only liked liver pâté with gherkins, and why I hadn't left the sandwich-making to Susanne, Susanne had known his tastes for far more than a decade. To avoid shouting at Karl I sang a song, an Alpine folk song based on the love song of an abandoned girl, and one which, it seemed to me, chimed nicely with the locality of Maiden's Leap. Even before the first verse was over, Karl brusquely interrupted my singing and said I was completely out of practice, my mezzo-soprano was declining more and more into a contralto instead of rising to the clear soprano heights, just like a body a voice had to be trained but like a coward I had refused to join the Wetterstein Mixed-Voice Choir.

Reverend Father, Karl wouldn't stop talking, and I felt something dangerous and uncontrollable rising within me, a kind of heat that came from the middle of my body. Lest I do anything rash I stood up, did a few knee bends, and walked along the abyss, its edge covered with hard tufts of grass. All of a sudden Karl was standing next to me. He put one hand on my shoulder and with the other he pointed towards a patch of water far away, a green shimmer. That was the Eibensee, he said, the lake in which he had often raced against Norma Jean. He was a good swimmer, but Norma Jean had always beaten him by several lengths. It had been a pleasure every time to see her slim body cutting the transparent water like a fish.

Reverend Father, I swear to you, I didn't push Karl into the depths deliberately. It must have been an unconditioned reflex, the involuntary and automatic response on the part of the organism to an external or internal stimulus. With Norma Jean's name on his lips, Karl staggered over the hard tufts of grass at the edge of the Maiden's Leap. Unlike the Frisian, he didn't end up hanging from a tree trunk.

I drove back to the house in the Land Rover, walked into the front garden and, beneath the blurred gaze of Susanne leaning crookedly against the green painted wooden fence, I removed first the hortensias and then the garden soil from the sidecar. Then I went into the larchwood room and packed my few belongings into the grey hiking rucksack that I had bought in Garmisch-Partenkirchen. When I drove off, Susanne bent clumsily over the wooden fence and waved after me with an unsteady hand.'

Magdalena fell silent and pensively stroked my stomach. At that moment we heard a cracking noise in the undergrowth, and I grabbed Magdalena's hand in terror. It had happened, it ran through my head, here were the heavily armed members of the anti-terrorist unit that had flown in from Vienna. While Magdalena had been describing the fatal end of the seventh episode, they had surrounded the clearing and aimed their machine guns at us. Soon Magdalena would be urgently advised, by a piercing voice amplified by a megaphone, to give herself up.

The hazel bushes parted, the yellow pollen spraying in all directions, but what emerged were not the Austrian anti-terrorist fighters but two East Tyrolean gendarmes dressed in discreet grey uniforms, clearly disconcerted at the sight of the abductor sitting naked under a tree, the equally naked priest whom she had abducted lying in her lap. And behind the two guardians of the law there appeared, to my surprise, the face of my sister Maria. That face, familiar to me down to its tiniest details, reflected in rapid sequence the most contradictory emotions, finally settling on an expression of profound disbelief. Then the small, narrow mouth in that face opened, and from it escaped a single word.

'Christian!'

What came next happened extremely quickly. Before the gendarmes, too stunned to react promptly, could draw their pistols from their holsters, Magdalena pushed me away from herself, leapt to her feet, quickly pulled on the nun's habit that was lying in the grass, swung on to the saddle and drove off, past the juniper bush and on up the bumpy forest path. The bullets fired, with some hesitation, by the two baffled East Tyrolean gendarmes just sent some clumps of earth and a few stones flying on the stretch of forest path which Magdalena had already left far behind.

I turned my head and saw my sister Maria coming up to me. All at once I understood what I had lost. I jumped to my feet, ran over to the forest path and looked towards the point where the bike had disappeared. Not so much as a tip of the nun's habit, not so much as a tiny cloud of dust were to be seen.

'Magdalena!' I cried.

But my sister was already standing next to me, she led me attentively back to the robinia and, one by one, she helped me into the items of my priestly garb which lay scattered on the ground. Then she put her arm round me and guided me slowly to the white police Golf some distance away. One last time I looked over to the point on the horizon where the forest path disappeared behind a hill.

Magdalena. She'd get by. And I would respect the confidence of the confessional. I would not betray her.